Planet of the Orange-red Sun

Series Volume 3

Age of the Towers

Planet of the Orange-red Sun Series

Volume 3
Age of the Towers

by Vic Broquard

For Morgan and L. Ron Hubbard

Table of Contents

Part I The Crystal Networks

Part II Mass Destruction

Part III The Blackwater Ultimatum

Part I The Crystal Networks

Chapter 1 Enforcement Versus Curiosity

"Padre, how can you let them take a quarter of our flock?" Luisa protested angrily to her father, Carlos Mundo. The eighteen year old teen, her hands defiantly on her hips and feet spread apart, glared at her father. Her long black hair had come slightly undone from her bluebird clasp back of her head, adding to her defiant image. She wore woolen leggins beneath her tartan wool skirt and thick matching plaid shirt. Her tall black leather boots contrasted sharply with the skirt but matched her black belt that held a small dagger. She had thick black eyebrows that added to her domineering face, with its pointed nose and high cheekbones. Her twin brother, Diego, had shoulder length black hair, wore a matching plaid shirt, thick pants, and identical black tall boots. He carried a similar dagger around his waist. Diego merely had his muscular arms crossed over his chest, again in defiance. Both twins had yellow eyes with brown speckles.

Forty-five year old Carlos was dressed similar to Diego, but he had a black beard and moustache. Weary facial lines suggested he was far older than his years and in many ways he was. Hacienda Lago del Fino was a small sheep ranch some fifty miles northeast of Valen, whose tower controlled all of Trujillo. Located here in the Westerlings foothills of the great Goza Mountains, the land was extremely rocky with many isolated, grass covered valleys and lakes. His manor house was built centuries ago at the edge of Lago del Fino. His grasslands fanned out for nearly ten miles across this entire bowl, though there were many rock outcrops dotting the landscape. Both remote and picturesque, Lago del Fino had been in the Mundo family for over a century now, ever since the Great Weather Change occurred back around 1000. The current date was mid-August 1131.

"Hija, you know why just as well as I do," the patriarch replied somewhat sternly. He was annoyed, yes, perhaps even angry, but what could he do? Nothing. "It is the law, you know. The Valen Tower always takes a quarter of our flock each year.

That is the price we must pay for their protection. I have no choice but to pay."

Across Tierra, the eleven *Círculo de la Torres* now had absolute control over the entire continent, via the Brom Compact. Each tower allowed the many local *Jefe* and Lords to control their own lands, but extracted a yearly tithe from each ruler. In turn, these provincial rulers took this opportunity to tack on a little extra for their own support. At least the tithe was based upon what the individual could pay. In the case of the extended Mundo family, it was sheep. Others in the breadbasket paid in wheat, grains, dairy products, and so on. Within the larger cities, local merchants paid in wares they produced such as cloth bolts and copper products. Some opted to pay their tithe in silver and copper coins, but those were mostly city dwellers. The idea behind this was to provide for the total physical needs of their ruling tower and their inhabitants, leaving these incredibly powerful men and women free to work their incredible magic using their psi skills.

The soldiers from Valen had come early this morning to extract the yearly tithe from Carlos. The twins had to separate out the quarter for the men. Now that the soldiers had left, they took their ire out on their father. Both finally calmed down. Of course there was little they could do about the tithe other than pay it. However, they had already worked their own devious way around this substantial loss. It had worked successfully for the last three years now. They had their two older brothers take a quarter of the flock, march them into a secret corner of the valley, and hold them there until the picking was finished and the soldiers left. This remote corner was not visible from the manor house or from the surrounding grasslands. Only when one approached its narrow, rocky entrance between two large mounds could one see the small hidden grasslands inside. Goyo and Enrique, twenty-five and twenty-three respectively, had loved the twin's idea and implemented it. None ever told their father about it.

Why? The soldiers brought along an Ama whose *mentales* gift was the ability to detect a lie. Carlos swore the herd as gathered was his entire herd and the quarter cut from them. Later on when the first snow came, the older brothers quietly brought the hidden sheep back down to the others in the winter enclosure. Their father was none the wiser, at least for the last three years now. This way, the siblings retained approximately sixty more sheep each year out of the herd size of around a thousand, about a twenty percent reduction in the annual tithe. Yes, they were clever. Not even their older sister, Juana knew of their conspiracy, though she wondered about the seemingly extra wool that was produced each year. She was twenty-one. Although Juana was now married and had a one year old little boy, she was the chief woman around the hacienda, aided by Goyo and Enrique's wives. Their mother, Dorita Minga e Mundo, Carlos' second wife, had died in childbirth when the twins were barely six years old. Their three older siblings came from his first wife who also died young during childbirth of her fourth child.

Dorita was something of a big mystery to the twins. She definitely came from the Sisterhood. Luisa still kept her mother's double horse head earrings worn by all women who joined the Sisterhood. Juana told them she had met Carlos and the two had taken to each other. Dorita took Carlos as her free-mate and chose to dwell here at the Lago del Fino for several years before she died. The twins inherited their *mentales* gifts from her. None of the others in Carlos' extended family had it. Quite why Dorita had joined the Sisterhood no one knew, save perhaps Carlos, who never spoke of it. That didn't stop the twins from trying to find out more about their mother. From the little their older siblings told them, they gathered she had been severely mistreated by men. What that meant, neither knew and probably would never know.

Carlos then reported, "The Ama also said you both are to report to the Valen Tower during the first week of September for your testing. She said she would return around then and take you there." He caught them both by surprise, turning some of their outrage back at them.

"What if we don't want to go? Padre, we don't want to be tested," Luisa protested even more strongly.

"Right, we won't go, Padre," Diego backed her up.

"You both know darn well you don't have any choice in the matter. It is the law of the land. Anyone who has this *mentales* thing has to get tested when they turn eighteen. Your eyes tell everyone you have it, just like your mother. Look, I'm told if you are suitable, you will be given some stone, which will help you with your powers. Lord knows, we can use more of that around here. Besides, it's only a year you have to serve them and that is a whole lot better than your older brothers. When they turned eighteen, they had to report to Valen to be trained as soldiers, should a war come our way. At least neither had any real soldier potential and was dismissed after a year. It could have been far worse. Shepherds have no need of soldiering skills. Never have, never will. Now go get cleaned up, Juana has our supper nearly ready."

Both twins stumped out of the room. *But I don't want to go. Why us?* Luisa sent her brother as they walked up the stairs to their rooms.

Neither do I. I want to stay here and work the farm. Guess we don't have any real choice. At least they will give us our own crystal. It is supposed to help us, he replied.

"But we don't have any real choices here, sis," he said as they paused at their two bedroom doors. "Look, we know Goyo will inherit Lago del Fino, but he'll keep Enrique and his family here helping him work the spread, along with Juana and hers when she marries. But us? You know as well as I that our *mentales* gifts have removed all choice from our lives, just as it must have done for mom. Otherwise, Goyo probably would keep us here too, and just as padre did for our older siblings, he'd arrange marriages for us in such a way he and the farm would benefit. No choice there either. So sis, we have to get this testing thing done or get arrested and in the end still endure it. After that, we both know the tower people will tell us whom we are to marry and produce more *mentales* gifted children. We simply don't have any choices left to us."

"What kind of a life is this anyway?" Luisa said sullenly quite depressed. Both had more or less been putting all this out of their minds, but now they could not pretend it didn't exist any longer.

"Look, sis, at least neither of us got sick like so many *mentales* gifted children do," he tried to comfort her a little.

"Maybe we should have and just died! Brood lamb,

that's all I am. Maybe I can die instead of giving birth to another one of us!" she retorted and ducked into her room, shutting her door. After a little round of crying, she cleaned up for supper.

Ama Margaretta arrived on the fifth of September along with a small group providing protection. Several had lesser gifts and all were well equipped for fighting. Valen Tower specialized in the many forms of psi attacks. She was in her forties, stern and unforgiving. "*Jefe* Carlos, present the two for my inspection now," Ama Margaretta stated dryly as she stepped into the hacienda. After leading her into the spacious dining room, Goyo ushered the twins into her presence.

Carlos introduced them, "This is Luisa and Diego. I swear they are eighteen, Ama. You realize if I lose them from my ranch, I will be extremely shorthanded and will not be able to produce as large a flock as we have been." The twins sensed this was his last, best hope for getting the twins back here on the ranch. He certainly dare not threaten tower folk openly, that was tantamount to suicide. The Ama probably could slay him on the spot! Still, Carlos had eighteen years to come to grips with the fact this day would come — the day when his twins would be taken from him, likely forever. It didn't lessen his sense of loss. Perhaps, Luisa thought, that was why he usually didn't show them the same amount of affection he did to the older three.

Ama Margaretta walked up to Diego, but didn't say a word. She merely used her fingers to open his eyes wider and stared at them. Then, she did the same to Luisa, who couldn't help retort, "Have they turned purple yet?"

"Silence, child! Speak when you are spoken to," she barked. In a calmer tone, she said dryly, "*Jefe*, by law, they are to be taken to the Valen Tower to be tested. If found worthy, they will be given their germanium crystals and trained. Beyond that, I cannot say. Children, you have two minutes to pack what you desire to bring with you in one saddlebag. Clothing and such will be provided for you when we reach the tower. Move! I haven't got all day."

They dashed out of the room. "One bag! Is she nuts?" Luisa cried out in protest.

"We aren't children!" Diego complained. "She's a bitch, that's for sure! Hurry up, sis. If she tries something, I'll protect you." While stuffing a few things into his bag, he tried to pry into Ama Margaretta's mind, but was very surprised to find he was unable to touch even her surface thoughts. In return, she sent him a painful blast of psi energies that gave him a sudden, intense headache. Fortunately, it passed momentarily. He cursed her thrice before finishing his packing. Diego had little to pack, possessions he could call his own were very few. Lovingly, he packed his sheering knife into his bag, the sole gift from his father when he turned twelve and was finally allowed to help with the massive spring sheering. It was made from alien steel, extremely sharp and strong with a beautifully carved handle, his prized possession.

Luisa unwrapped her mother's double horsehead earrings from the fine silk handkerchief in which she always kept them. Mom, she thought with a longing sigh. She wrapped them carefully and stuffed them into her pocket. Her prized possession was a small arpa, a foot tall and wide, made from a dense oak, beautifully carved and polished with gut strings. The harp was the sole gift from her father that she ever had, save clothes, and he'd given it to her when she was twelve. Briefly, memories of her playing and singing around the living room during the long winters washed over her. She wrapped it in a silk shawl and it filled her bag. Looking around her room, there was little else to pack, since the rest was merely apparel. They lived a frugal life, but a happy one up to this point in time when her world was crumbling around her. She wiped tears from her cheek, wondering if she'd ever see her own bedroom again. For a moment, she wondered if her mother ever played.

After hugging their father and suppressing tears all around, they were ushered outside where two horses were waiting them. Diego noticed there were several well-loaded packhorses. A heavy and oiled cloak was also fastened to each horse, protection from the cold rains, which often came now that winter was close at hand. Like robots, they were told to mount and they complied. They rode off in silence, both twins taking last looks at their extended family waving to them from the porch of their childhood home, their hacienda. Then they rode across the grassland valley and up to the rim and off towards the great city of Valen and the cursed tower and their unknown fates.

Some twenty miles later, they halted. Already the cold rains had started and the group made camp at the side of a large rock outcrop, where a few pines grew and the grass was lush for the horses. Diego suspected they were about five miles from the village of Lita and wondered why they hadn't gone there for the night. The twins merely watched as the group hastily made camp. No one said a word to them until the camp cook bad them join the others for a hot meal of stewed rabbit, bread, and mixed veggies. Shortly after that, a bedroll was handed to each and they emulated the others, crawling into one of the two tents for the night. Ama Margaretta still had not spoken to them, leaving them in complete mystery.

The next day was more of the same until late afternoon, when they crested another ridge and saw the huge city of Valen with its dramatic tower-castle ahead of them. Neither had ever been this far from their ranch, let alone see such a giant city, boasting a population of nearly thirty thousand and still growing. Neither knew most of the growth was to support the ever enlarging tower dwellers. The main tower was surrounded by a huge castle whose outer walls rose some thirty feet topped with barbicans. Roughly square and a quarter mile on each side, the walls enclosed two three-story, huge manor houses that joined with the tower. Never had the twins ever seen so many chimneys thrusting skyway, grey curls drifting towards the distant mountains.

The party skirted the northern edge of the city and made for the main western entrance causeway, a thirty-foot wide stone paved formal entrance to the city, raised a foot above the spongy ground. A small marsh lay at the western edge; hence, growth had been to the north and south. A giant slice of the mountainside to the east of the city got their attention. Here stone was being quarried for the vast ongoing constructions, though the twins saw no one there at work. The city streets were swarming with people and a multitude of shops lined this main thoroughfare along with several guard stations. As they approached each one, a guard in a green uniform stepped before them, but quickly yielded as soon as he spotted Ama Margaretta who now had donned a crimson cloak.

The enormous gatehouse appeared at the end of the long causeway, the sole entrance to the Valen *Círculo de la Torres*. Diego saw it was designed to provide a powerful defense to the complex beyond. It was heavily guarded, but again, they were not stopped and the twins entered, gaining their first glimpse at their new home. Stonework construction was ongoing nearly everywhere. The two huge manor complexes were still being built. To their right lay an enormous stable and corral. Over a hundred horses could be seen milling around inside. A single story building housed those who tended them. To the left was a spacious courtyard and formal gardens complete with a small water pool in its center. They saw a number of men and women wearing traditional clothing going about their chores, but also they spotted a number of others who also wore similar crimson cloaks. They rightly concluded that here the *mentales* gifted wore the cloaks.

They were led to the stables and told to bring their saddlebags with them. Still looking in all directions in awe, the twins dutifully followed Ama Margaretta into one of the smaller doors of the manor house closest to the stable. A sign over the entrance read: South Dorm. Inside, the floor was carpeted, and they were ushered into a side room and told, "Sit. Someone will be with you directly. Sit," the stern voice commanded. The twins did as asked, content to examine the room. Elegance was the byword for this room, though they would soon discover the rest of the complex was equally similar. Tapestries hung on the stone walls. The mahogany table was highly polished; the matching chairs had soft cushions. The back of each chair had an intricate carving of a horse's head, superbly done. A faint odor of polish could be detected in the air.

A side door opened and two more entered, both wearing crimson robes, a man and a woman. Both appeared to be in their thirties, Luisa guessed, comparing them to her siblings. Both had typical Westerlings black hair, though the

Vic Broquard

woman's was quite long and wavy, held in the back with a bluebird clasp. Each had a glowing stone on a thong around their necks. In contrast to the stern countenance of Ama Margaretta, their faces seemed more pleasant.

"Hello. I am Ama Lucinda. Amo Arsenio. We are going to test you first and then we'll get you settled in. I'm sure you'd like a nice hot bath after your journey."

"We don't want to be tested!" Luisa took this last opportunity to protest. Instead of the expected gruff reaction, Ama Lucinda smiled.

"Don't worry, Luisa, it doesn't hurt and only takes a moment. Now just sit there and try to keep your mind free of thoughts," she replied softly. As Luisa watched, the crystal around her neck seemed to glow more brightly and she felt a soft, rather intimate touch in her mind, not unpleasant. Similarly, Diego felt the touch of Amo Arsenio in his mind. While he wanted nothing more than to kick the man out, he knew not how to do so.

"There, that was not so bad was it?" Ama Lucinda said after a minute or so. She continued to smile, disarming Luisa all the more. How could she be angry with such a pleasant woman?

"So is that all? Can we go home now?" Luisa asked, though the strong protest she wanted to place in her voice somehow failed to form.

Lucinda gave a short chuckle. "Oh, hardly. You will need to get your own crystals, learn how to use them, and learn to master your precious *mentales* gifts. Then, we'll see, dear. Now, each of you will be assigned a mentor to accompany you for the time being. One can easily get lost in our huge complex here. First, a bath is in order. Then, you will find we have clothing prepared for you. Each will also have a formal crimson robe to wear, identifying you as a tower member. In the morning, we'll get down to business."

At that moment, the side door opened and two teens entered, both were only a year older than the twins. Luisa didn't see either adult call out or signal for them and presumed they had summoned the two by telepathy. "This is Macarena and this is Bernardo. They will accompany you

10

everywhere for the time being. We can't have you getting lost in here."

After quick introductions, Macarena tugged on Luisa's hand. "Come on, I have the bath ready. She's right, you know, this place is positively huge! Come on, I'll show you. I bet you've never had such a luxurious quarters before. I know I never did. I was a maid and bartender at my dad's inn before. Positively crude it was, compared to this! Come on."

Bernardo led Diego off through a different door. "That's the girls section. This way to the men's quarters. So I heard you were a shepherd. I was too before I came here. This place is enormous and almost beyond description. You are going to love it here." Diego followed him, feeling a little more relaxed since he was apparently a shepherd too, though he didn't trust the lad.

"Our rooms are on the second floor. Most of the first floor is kitchen, dining room, living room, and meeting rooms. All we women live on the north side of the second floor, the guys live on the south side," Macarena gaily chatted away. "You are going to love it here. I sure do. We live like queens, if you ask me. Here we are, this is our room. We share a room and a bed; I hope that's okay with you. It's been a bit lonely without a roommate. Manola got moved to another room a month ago. Isn't this something else?"

Luisa could not believe her eyes. The carpet was even plusher in here, crimson. Their bed was quite large and had silk sheets and well-made quilts covering it. Each girl had her own walk-in tall closet cabinet. There was even a private commode hiding the chamber pot. A small desk, a full-length mirror, and two chairs completed the arrangements. "Dump your bag on the bed and follow me. I'll show you to the ladies bathroom. I've got it ready for you. Ama Lucinda let me know when you were coming so I could get it heated up nicely for you. Come on."

The bathroom held a dozen elegant tubs carved from stone. Just how the water was heated was a mystery to Luisa, but she eagerly took off her clothes and climbed in. "We've got lots of choices for scents. I like lavender personally, but I thought I'd let you choose yours." Luisa decided to forgo that for now. The water temperature was ideal and she soaked for a bit and then washed. Macarena chatted away. "We leave dirty clothes in the box just inside our door. The cleaning staff come by each night at suppertime and remove them. After washing them, they place them back beside the box, usually by the next day."

"Where do they get all the staff?" Luisa asked curiously.

"Oh, most are those poor folk who only have a little *mentales* or none at all. Since you are here with me, you don't have to worry about that. The testing sorts out those poor ones who don't have much of a gift, you see. Obviously, you and your brother have a powerful gift, you see." She didn't, but it felt good to hear she wasn't going to be in that poor folk category.

When she finished, Macarena had a new outfit waiting for her. Never before had she had silk panties or a silk blouse and Luisa was amazed at how soft and delicate they felt on her warm body. She slipped on a warm tartan wool skirt and donned the tartan woolen socks, which came up to her knees. A pair of soft leather slippers rounded out her new look. At last, Macarena helped her slip the crimson, silk robe over her, adding a bit of extra warmth to their outfits. "Come on, when we get back to our room, I'll do your hair. My, yours is so lush and long."

"My sister kept it cut so it falls to the small of my back, but my bangs are getting a little long," Luisa admitted.

"I wish mine would hurry up and grow more. I had to keep mine short while tending the bar for my dad. Ever since I came here last year, I've been letting it grow." Hers was also black and somewhat curly but only fell to her just below shoulders. Like Luisa, she wore a bluebird clasp on the back of her head holding some of it in place.

"So what's supposed to happen to me now?" Luisa asked while Macarena began brushing out her hair.

"Oh the really hard part starts tomorrow after they give you your own crystal. It really does magnify our gifts enormously. Then, they train you in the forms of mental combat. Here at Valen Tower, everyone gets this gift perfected. It's said there are no finer *mentales* attackers than us at Valen

Tower. That's going to be the hardest part, learning to defend yourself from other attackers, but it only took me two weeks to get it all down. Now I know I can both defend myself from another one's attack as well as dish it back out, though of course, I don't ever expect I'll need to do so. Not anymore, that is. I always was hustled by the gross men that came to dad's bar. Well, not anymore. I'm never going back to that mess, not ever! Well, I was able to take care of myself pretty well from the fawning men, but not like I can now," she admitted.

Once Luisa's hair was done, Macarena said, "Come on, I'll show you around more and then take you to my favorite place. There's just enough time before supper hour." Her favorite place was a bench sitting beside the small pond in the middle of the gardens. Although it was fall and chilly, somehow the garden still had flowers blooming. Luisa suspected someone was using their gifts on the gardens, but she didn't have a clue how.

Dinner was held in their Great Hall and nearly everyone was present. The unmarried women were on one side, the men sat opposite them, while the married folks occupied the middle tables. Perpendicular to the many tables was another line of tables where the top leaders dined. "There's Venerado Amo Augusto Valen himself!" Macarena excitedly pointed to the older man sitting in the central position of that table. "He runs this whole place. Beside him are the three Capos. Those are the leaders of the three active *Círculo de mentes* beside him. At least one circle is working all the time. There's talk of adding a fourth *Círculo de mentes*. I hope I'm selected for it. Those who work the circles wield the greatest power and command the highest respect of everyone, you see." Luisa didn't but accepted her opinion.

She looked around and found Diego. He too wore a crimson robe over his new clothes. He was busily chatting with several other young men and she relaxed a little. Perhaps this was not going to be utter torture after all. Later, she relished slipping in between the silk sheets with Macarena. It was an entirely new experience for her, one of total luxury.

The next morning after breakfast Amo Arsenio and Ama Lucinda presented them with a germanium crystal, each about two inches around. After attuning them to the twins, they worked a short while with them, showing them how to use the crystals and to protect themselves by slipping the crystals into a small pod silk pouch. "Do not allow another *mentales* gifted to touch your crystal without them being in full rapport with you," Ama Lucinda cautioned. "Here's why." She touched each twin's crystal, sending a strong psychic shock into each of their minds.

After their curses and complaints died down, she added, "Now you appreciate what I just told you. Okay, time to train you to shield your thoughts and to block out others. Honestly, both of you have been broadcasting your thoughts loudly ever since you got here." A few days later and they had the two skills down pat, for which all the other telepaths around them were quite grateful.

Then came the hard and painful training, learning to defend and attack using their mental psi energies. As with all *mentales* actions, each required the usage of their finite reservoir of psi-energies, some required more than others. Amo Arsenio began, "My personal favorite attack form is the Psi-Shock. You send out a huge wall of uncontrolled psi-energies that hits everyone within the expanding cone from me, head blind and *mentales* alike. It is costly to use and you will probably only be able to get off four of these in one day without using your crystals. If successful, the head blind collapse unconscious for a time, while others will believe you have mortally wounded them and often retreat from combat, yielding the field to you. With this form, you just let loose a volley of psi-energy without much thought about it. I like it because I can impact a number of opponents with one shot."

"If you have a single combatant who is very dangerous, then use the Neuron Crush. While not as costly to use, you focus your psi-energies onto the opponent's neurons. If successful, your opponent suffers actual wounds, often bleeding from their eyes, nose, and ears. Nasty. Used several times in succession on a person, it can kill."

"Another tactic is called the Ego Assault. Costing about half as much as the crush, it does require you to send out thoughts designed to attack the person's own ideas of their self-importance. If you win through and send out the right thoughts, the victim stands around in a daze for a considerable time. Of course, with this form of attack, it is best used when you have some knowledge of your opponent. Otherwise, you don't know what the person might be sensitive to, you see."

"About as costly as the assault is the Subconscious Uprising. With this attack, you attempt to arouse your opponent's subconscious fears and dreads. If you are successful, you drive him temporarily mad. Finally, the cheapest cost is the Mind Stab. With this attack, you send out a single dagger-like bolt of psi-energy. If it is successful, you disable a bit of his *mentales* gifts until they have rested fully. Personally, I seldom use this form because I am more interested in winning the battle. If there are many opponents, I opt usually for a Psi-Shock first. If I face particularly powerful *mentales* opponents, then I opt for the crush or uprising because, if successful, they are out of the combat. Only if I have prior knowledge of my opponent do I take a gamble with the Ego Assault."

Luisa looked a little uncomfortable. "These sound awful. How do we defend ourselves from them? How do we know which one will be used to attack us?"

Ama Lucinda took over at this point. "The second question is easy because you don't know which one they will use. Thus, you put up what you think will serve you the best against what you guess you might be hit with, hoping for the best. Your first question is more difficult to answer. There are also five defense forms to protect yourself, Luisa. Some are simple and cost you nothing at all to put up. Of course, the protection isn't as good that way. There are others that are a bit costly to use, but provide better protection. The worst aspect of defending is some forms of defense are good against certain types of attack but really poor against other forms of attack. Choose the wrong defense and you could be helping your attacker. If you choose the right one, then you are both hindering his attack as well as defending against it."

"Now the cheapest one, which costs you nothing at all to use, is called the Blank Mind. It costs nothing because all you do is put all of your thoughts out of your mind. That's why it's called the Blank Mind. It is particularly effective against only the Subconscious Uprising attack because you have no thoughts in your mind. With other attacks, it helps the attacker somewhat, as there are no other thoughts for those attacks to have to first penetrate. With the Mind Cloud, you throw up a host of random thoughts, which makes your mind seem totally confused to your attacker. It is a good defense except against the Uprising and the Neuron Crush. You could probably put up dozens and dozens of these each day. Quite inexpensive to use."

"The Thought Chant is a more expensive defensive mode and requires you to chant the same thought over and over. It is effective against everything except the Uprising. Then, there is the Mental Fortress, which costs even more to put up, but this one is effective against all forms. Of course, the ultimate defense is the Steel Will and it is the most costly of the defenses to raise. My guess is you could throw up five of these each day. It gives you the absolute best protection against all these attacks. It is the one I usually use, since I don't want a man messing with my subconscious."

Alice flashed them quick smile before continuing, "Now, to the training. Be prepared to feel some pain until you get these mastered."

The twins had massive headaches for the next couple of weeks before they had the ten skills fully mastered. When they finally passed them, Diego was extremely pleased. "Now we can really defend ourselves and attack our enemies, sis!" He was very enthusiastic about their accomplishments.

Luisa, on the other hand, was not. "But we don't have any enemies, Diego." She sensed they were starting to drift apart from the closeness they shared while growing up. He excited about learning these skills, she was not. Would they now be allowed to go home? Something told her no. Perhaps, it was the enthusiasm Macarena displayed when Luisa told her they finally had passed. "Great Luisa! Now you can become a part of something really important!" She wouldn't elaborate further, citing the rules. "You'll find out tomorrow, I'm sure."

They did. After breakfast, Amo Arsenio and Ama Lucinda took the twins aside. "First, we know you both were born with a number of special gifts or powers. We are going to show you just how much your crystals amplify them. After that, we will initiate you into the work we are all doing in the tower, the *Círculo de mentes*. On your own, you can experiment with your other inherent gifts."

Ama Lucinda took Luisa aside and chose to work on Luisa's native ability to give an object a solid push. "Well, I always have used this a lot while watching the sheep. If a wolf or other predator gets too close, I shove them away," she explained. First, she was asked to apply her push against a wagon in the courtyard and then to do it again activating her crystal to amplify its effect. It rolled slightly when she didn't use her crystal. The second time, it rolled halfway across the large courtyard. Luisa was impressed.

Diego was even more enthralled. Amo Arsenio had him use his psi-punch on an old barrel. Without his crystal, Diego gave it a good sock and cracked a few of the old slats. With his crystal amplifying his punch, the barrel shattered into many small pieces. "Wow! Now that *is* useful!" he exclaimed, very much excited over the power of his crystal. He felt more powerful than he ever had before.

Don't let it go to your head, Diego, Luisa sent him. He ignored her.

"Walk with us to the other manor house, please," Amo Arsenio requested, explaining as he walked. "You see, some four decades ago, Felix and Lilly Brom discovered these crystals, but they also discovered something far, far greater and you are about to see this for yourselves. They found two things actually. First, they invented the means by which a large number of us can join together, the *Círculo de mentes* it's called. Say ten join together, that's the usual number we are now using. Nine focus their entire psi-energies to the tenth, who is highly trained and is now called the Capo or leader. The Capo then wields the combined power of ten. In terms of your push and punch, Luisa, Diego, the Capo's effect would be more than ten times greater than yours."

"Wow! Super!" Diego exclaimed. Amo Arsenio had purposely paused anticipating his reaction.

Luisa was unimpressed, though. "But we only need a

17

slight push to get the wolves away from our sheep, Diego. No need to kill the wolves."

Amo Arsenio cast a knowing glance at Ama Lucinda, but ignored her comment. "The second thing they discovered is some of these germanium crystals can be united together into what we now call a Network. Here's the main entrance to the Work Manor House. If you will note the crystals embedded in the archway." He pointed to a dozen glowing germanium crystals set within the stone arch itself. "These have all been attuned to the same frequency and psi-power. They will deny entry to anyone who is not wearing a germanium crystal around their neck. Take yours off and try it."

Diego quickly handed his to Luisa, making sure it was in its pod-silk pouch, and stepped boldly towards the door. When he came about a foot from it, he felt a solid push backwards. Try as he might, he could not actually reach the door. "Way cool!" he exclaimed after he put his crystal back on and tried it once more, this time feeling not the slightest resistance.

"We use it to keep non-trained personnel out of our working rooms. Now I must caution you both further. Only the members of a *Círculo de mentes* are allowed entrance into the actual five story tower. A set of stones prohibit others from entering. Likewise, inside the working manor house, there are some rooms that are protected from all forms of scrying. Eavesdropping is not allowed in certain locations. Similarly, no scrying of any kind is allowed anywhere within the actual tower proper. Plus, there are a number of other crystals, which prevent other things from happening within the tower. It is the most secure location in the entire complex and rightly so, as you both will soon see."

Once inside, Amo Arsenio led them to one large workshop, where six men and women were busily working on a strange metal contraption. "Here some of our people are working on making a flying air car, roughly based on those the aliens call shuttle craft. We know the aliens use them to fly all around, cutting travel time from days to minutes. For the last six years, all the towers have been working on their own models. Amo Domingo, why don't you show our two new

18

recruits how it is working so far."

A young boy perhaps two years older than Diego proudly stepped forward. "It is still under development. Diego, hop in. We can only carry one passenger at the moment." He and two others climbed in and as Diego watched, the three joined into rapport with each other and then Domingo took control of their combined power. Slowly, the metal box lifted off of the floor a few feet and moved around the spacious room before settling back down.

Amo Arsenio explained, "Right now, it takes the combined power of three to power the craft and they can only carry the weight of one passenger. I admit, it's not too efficient yet, but progress is being made. One day down the line, we will have our own shuttle craft that can fly across all Trujillo in a matter of minutes, not weeks on horseback. It will revolutionize transport of goods and even people."

"Way cool!" Diego exclaimed.

"I can see this would be quite useful," Luisa admitted, "once it can carry enough to make it worthwhile." She definitely had to concede this one.

"Currently, we have six of these research projects ongoing here in the workshop. Now if you will each put these medallions around your necks, we will show you a *Círculo de mentes* at work," Ama Lucinda suggested, noting this greatly interested both twins just as she hoped it would.

They went down a corridor and passed through another archway that led into the first floor of the actual tower. She pointed out the crystals in the archway that prevented non-circle members from entering, but these special visitor passes allowed the twins access. They climbed up to the top floor and entered a room with no windows. The room was illuminated by the soft blue glow of a great many germanium crystals. Some were embedded in the walls, preventing scrying and unauthorized access. Some provided a little light. A large ring of a dozen larger germanium crystals sat on the floor and were glowing brightly. Ten men and women sat around them in a circle. An eleventh woman sat back from the circle.

"She's their Regulator, watching each member's physical body for them, easing cramps, calming nerves, whatever is needed. The man with the hat is their Capo and the others are funneling their combined psi-energies into the ring of large ones that are attuned to the Capo. He in turn is drawing on the tremendously amplified energies to carry out his work. Now if you will step outside on the veranda, I can show you what they are doing," Ama Lucinda explained.

The veranda was a tiny ledge with a tall railing that curved around this fifth floor, over a hundred feet above ground. She pointed to the rock quarry the twins had seen when the first came into Valen. She pointed to a small cloud of dust rising. "There, the Capo is carving out stone blocks from the bedrock. Each stone is precisely cut. If you watch, he has this block about finished. Ah, yes. Notice the dust has settled. Now watch."

The twin's eyes stared at the stone block that slowly rose from the quarry bed until it was high in the air. Then, it slowly moved towards them. From this vantage point, they could see both manor houses were still under construction. A fourth floor was slowly being built, stone by stone. The enormous, perfectly cut block floated over the northern manor house and lowered into position perfectly, fitting so snugly that one could not even slide a thin piece of paper into its joints with the block below or beside it. "Yes, we are slowly building our two manor houses. This entire complex, except for the original tower, has been built using various *Círculo de mentes* over the years. No stone mason is needed, save to work up the architectural plans in the first place. Impressive, yes?"

Both twins were very much impressed with this. At last, Luisa began to change her viewpoint. Perhaps the tower did have something of great value to offer. Sensing the change in her attitude, Ama Lucinda made her pitch. "Luisa, Diego, you both have great potential. We are in the process of manning up another complete pair of *Círculo de mentes*. We would like you to join them. While neither will be full, your additions would allow them to begin operations. You will be well paid and lack for nothing. Circle members are the highest paid personnel, are held in the highest respect, and get only the very best amenities the tower has to offer. What do you say?"

"Count me in!" Diego exclaimed without any hesitation.

"I am all for it."

"I suppose so too, as long as our work is really beneficial," Luisa agreed. "How long do we have to work in the circles?"

"At least a year. After that, you can leave at any time, but honestly, Luisa, very few ever leave. Just between us, while circle members work very hard, no denying that, there is no more powerful position than theirs, especially for women."

Chapter 2 Alien Moves

Retro-thrusters firing, the sleek battle cruiser slowly settled down towards the spaceport on Ashford-5. Fifty year old Lech Kuba, his arm around his wife, Karolina, stood at the viewport gazing at the strange orange-red sun of this backwater planet. Like all those from Rigel-3, he was quite tall, quite thin by Tierra standards, with grey skin and coal black hair and eyes. All his life he'd worked for the Imperium. Thus, he knew the ways of the massive bureaucracy and played them like a master musician, working his way up in the Intelligence Division. Why the ID? Simple, he was intensely curious about just what was going on. It didn't matter whether it was the latest court intrigue or a subversive plot. Lech loved a mystery, and only in the ID could he have the necessary tools to lay such bare. Of course, once the mystery became known he then lost all interest; it was no longer a mystery.

Ten years ago shortly after his promotion to Deputy Sector ID Minister, he'd gained access to far more intelligence. The newly opened Rim Sector 15 zone caught his interest, as he trolled through the vast files of reports on his computer using his newly activated clearance code. Recently opened, this sector was a critical transfer area for the huge merchant fleets, made possible by the discovery of a local source of fuel. Nothing like having the source of fuel right there at the spaceport. He culled through over a century of reports from the Sector ID Minister Ania Anka, a most powerful minister.

It seems that initial contact had made some grave errors in judgment and she had to step in to rectify the mess. Even more curiously, she invoked the Imperial Directive #5, effectively closing that world to all trade and interaction with the Imperium. "Primitive culture is to be protected." That was her official entry. Considering the vast number of stars in the galaxy and the sheer number of inhabitable planets, statistically he expected to encounter a fair number on which primitive peoples dwelled. That directive in and of itself was not all that significant and he probably would had let it go at that had he not then discovered a large number of Ania's personal files which could not be opened. *Ah, a mystery,* he thought. *Why should I not be allowed access to these? I have the clearance for it now.*

Try as he might, he simply could not gain access to them. No one at HQ had her password. With the latest 4096-bit encryption, without that password, the Imperium Central Computer Banks would need at least a century to crack it for him. Now had there only been one such file, he would have shrugged and left it at that: someone's personal file or journal. However, Ania had many dozen such files! "Why should she have so darn many secret files, eh? Something must be going on," he explained to his wife.

Karolina, a Galactic Meteorologist, also loved a good mystery, only hers lay in predicting the weather on any given planet. Highly trained and very knowledgeable, Karolina was considered a leading expert on Planetary Weather Forecasting. Her innate curiosity meshed with his, yielding a good marriage, based on mutual interests. She also was a gorgeous woman, who always wore striking makeup. She used a bright blue eye shadow and brilliant red lipstick, the kind that always gave the appearance of being super moist and yet did not rub off onto every cup that touched her lips. She had no time to waste on such messes. Her nails were always kept perfectly manicured, always extending an inch from her fingertips, always a matching red. Lech's interest pricked whenever he heard the familiar click-click of her nails on her computer keyboard. Of course, she was keenly aware of this effect too, using it to her advantage on more than one occasion. She replied, "Well, she is obviously hiding something. Now I wonder what it could be? Ashford-5 is a closed world, Directive #5, right? Curious, dear."

"Yes, I must find out what is going on there. What does she have to say that is so highly classified, I wonder?" he replied. Although he spent weeks trying to find out, he got absolutely nowhere. However, like any good Field Agent, he set to work on unraveling it from another angle. Always one could count on there being some critical information in the many other reports. One only had to filter it out and the picture would clear. He spent nearly a year at it.

He was a master at using the Google-Central, an intelligence sifting program which could search a multitude of documents, finding and coordinating various threads. Lech had not risen to his high position without having become a master of this computer software, essential to galactic espionage. He entered key words and the program sifted through hundreds of documents, presenting a coordinated picture, discarding all the irrelevant passages. Thus, he finally gained some insight on Ashford-5.

An exploratory mining crew discovered deposits of psi-crystals on the planet. A refinery was setup, but a serious accident resulted in a devastating explosion caused by a failure to apply the Imperial Directive #5, which Ania had rigidly enforced upon her arrival. Without Google-Central, the ball would have stopped here. However, the program attached related threads from other sources elsewhere. A major secret research project on Calgan-4 began shortly after that, importing a substantial quantity of psi-crystals from Ashford-5, along with pulverizing equipment. Over a hundred test subjects were given doses of the psi-dust and changes and developments of their pituitary glands were well documented in the medical journal reports that subsequently were published from the study. The computer program then joined enlarged pituitary glands with other studies done long ago in the area of psionics and telepathy.

Lech put two and two together. Ania must have discovered somehow the interference on Ashford-5 had led to the primitive's pituitary glands enlarging and to subsequent development of at least telepathy among the primitives. How curious, he thought. Yet, he could find no direct mention of this effect in any of Ania's open reports. Throughout the gigantic Imperium, telepathy was exceedingly rare and high valued, for obvious reasons, especially in the Intelligence Division.

When they received word he was to be stationed on Ashford-5, Karolina had asked a leading question which Lech later followed up. "How's the weather there?"

Again, he found many reports of anomalies. When he

relayed this to Karolina, she then took it on herself to discover what these were. Upon arrival, she found over a century of weather observations from the geo-synch satellites was available and she took full advantage of them. Into her weather prediction program, she painstakingly inputted the entire known weather data from Ashford-5, some 1.5T, that is, one and a half terabytes, or roughly one and a half trillion characters of data. She then set the search parameters for patterns that did not fit known weather patterns.

Known patterns were vitally important. Many worlds had tornados and hurricanes. Occurrences of these simply had to be predictable and their paths known. Only a fool would fly his commercial ship or shuttle craft into a tornado or hurricane. That science was now extremely well known and in widespread use throughout the vast Imperium. Thus, even on closed Ashford-5, the meteorologists fully documented the weather patterns, though they did not provide any of this information to the primitives there. That would be in violation of Directive #5. After all, who cared whether or not a primitive lost his or her life in a severe storm?

A month later, Karolina watched dozens of anomalies on her display screen, a wall mounted, flat screen five feet wide and three tall. "Looks pretty, dear, what is it?" asked Lech.

"Anomalous weather tracks, love. The red line is where by all scientific predictions the storm should follow. As you can see, the storms veer off the predicted path. I've got well over a hundred major storms that do not follow their predicted paths," she pointed out, quite used to his not grasping her field.

"So that means your prediction programs are in need of improvement?" he suggested.

She puckered her red lips. "Absolutely not! The prediction programs are now rock solid and work one hundred percent on all known worlds, including the gas giant planets. No, you are looking at unexplained anomalies, which by all scientific means should not exist and should not exist. Look, dear, one planet in the universe simply cannot have weather patterns following some other universal laws. Gases and atmospheres behave in known, predictable ways across the galaxy. You cannot have one set of laws for one planet and a wholly different set for another. You are looking at *the* single planet in the known universe that has anomalous weather patterns. Now that is indeed extremely curious, don't you think? We should launch an extensive study of this Ashford-5 and I aim to do so."

Now both were intrigued with this strange planet with its unusual orange-red sun. So much so, that in 1029 when they learned of the death of Ania Anka, the Sector ID Minister, he put in for her vacant position. Ania had lived one hundred sixty-nine years, aided by several rejuvenation treatments. His good work was rewarded and he was promoted to Sector ID Minister to be stationed in Rim Sector 15 with his choice of planets or stations. He naturally chose to continue at the Imperium base location there on Ashford-5, stating it would cause the least disruption.

June 15th, 1030, their battle cruiser was now on its final landing approach, settling down at the huge spaceport and base at Plateau Grado. The two stood arm in arm watching the descent, commenting on the orange-red sun, so unlike that of their blue-white Rigel-3 sun.

"The air is so thin and cold," Karolina commented as they walked down the stairs onto the concrete pavement of the base. Ahead they saw the thirty story Admin building and their new dormitory building, some twenty stories tall connecting to the south side of the Admin building. These were on the north side of the station. Far off to the south, they saw the huge fuel depot and the main landing zone with some fifteen ships on the ground, either unloading or refueling. Another ship roared down to a landing, drowning out further conversation, but a tall man came running up to them, motioning for them to follow him.

Once inside the Admin building, the outdoor noise was suppressed. "Welcome, ID Minister. I am your Geology Minister Bolek, I've been in charge of daily operations since Ania passed away. Your bags will be sent to your new quarters. Would you like to see your new offices first or your rooms or perhaps a guided tour of our extensive facilities?" They opted to see their new quarters first.

As head of the ID, they took over Ania's old suite of rooms on the top floor of the dormitory. A side door led into the Admin building located conveniently by the elevators that could be taken up the ten floors to the top where Ania's office had been, now his. Their suite was plush and quite large, as befitting his new position. "Oh this is convenient, dear. My new weather offices are on the same floor as our suite. I can just take the side door and walk over to my office. Great," Karolina said rather pleased at the convenience of their new setup.

Throughout the Imperium, officials and workers usually wore the drab grey synthetic, unisex cat suits and soft soled shoes that were easy on the feet. Indeed, as one looked over the thousands who now worked and lived here at the spaceport, one hardly saw any variations in dress. They were cheap and easily synthesized to one's body shape at nearly every clothing machine on every world. Seldom even washed, when dirty, one simply tossed them into the recycling bin and their molecules would be recycled into another cat suit.

However, the Imperium had never been entirely able to dispense with women's fashions. Getting a woman to dress identically to every other woman was nearly impossible to accomplish. The Imperium made great strides by making the purchase price of "real" dresses and shoes prohibitively expensive, since these things nearly always had to be imported. Shipping costs alone jacked up their prices. However, Karolina came from a very wealthy family. Coupled with her amazingly good looks, she always wore designer outfits. After marrying Lech, she made him dress in a fine looking business suit as well, though he protested slightly at their cost, some three thousand credits each. Only when traveling by spaceship did they resort to wearing the uniform cat suits to avoid any possible damage to their expensive attire and shoes.

Now they waited for their dozen crates to be brought up to their room. Normally on a distant trip such as the one they just finished, passengers were allowed a single crate of not more than a hundred pounds. They had brought ten crates and paid the overweight fee of ten thousand credits. One held Lech's many suits and shoes. One held their imported Arcturian Satin bedding. The remainder held her many outfits and shoes. "There is nothing like walking and wearing a finely made leather shoe," Karolina insisted. Years ago after wearing such a pair she gave him for a present while they were dating, he agreed fully with her. Still, he thought she had gone a little overboard with nearly fifty heels in her collection. Most were stilettos with at least a five inch heel, superb in quality. "Dear, never wear a leather shoe more than a day without giving it a week's rest to breathe properly." She'd instilled that in him long ago.

When their crates arrived, they headed for their bathroom to wash the stench of the long trip off. Microspray economized on the water that was then recycled through an extensive purification process. Still, the shower's high intensity spray did its job, leaving one's skin feeling as if it had just had a massage thrown in as an extra. An hour later, she slipped into her silk nylons, fastening them to her garter belt and then donned her favorite light brown silk dress, form-fitting with a hem just below her knees. She put on her black patent, oxford style heels and then redid her makeup. Meanwhile, Lech dressed himself in a fine light grey tweed suit. He preferred bow ties, black usually. As he tied it, Karolina's words came into mind, "Remember, dear. Pride in your appearance instills confidence in others." He'd discovered her golden rule to be very applicable, especially in his line of work. It had been part of his rapid rise to this top post. Besides, she looked fabulous. Wherever they went, all eyes turned to them. As the new Sector ID Minister, he intended to look the part and demand the attention of his subordinates, just as Karolina captured the attention of all who saw her.

As they walked to his new office on their grand tour, both noticed the recycled air had that distinctive metal odor. As in all Imperium buildings, the perfect humidity and temperature was maintained at all times throughout the two huge buildings. Even the lighting was set up to Imperium standards using the high efficiency LED tubes that completely masked the dull orange-red coming from Ashford-5's sun. The idea behind all this standardization was no matter where you went in the vast Imperium, your living conditions would remain the same. Yet, what did the real atmosphere smell like? All planets had their own distinctive odor just as all had their own unique natural lighting and flora and fauna. They'd only gotten the briefest of glimpses while rushing from the ship into the building.

Geologist Minister Bolek gave them their tour and then privately met with Lech to bring him up to date on the latest Intel. He'd been sending dispatches to him ever since Lech's appointment was confirmed and most dealt with affairs on other planets. "So what has been happening on Ashford-5?" Lech asked of the fifty year old geologist.

"Nothing. As you know, it's a hands-off world. Our only contact is with Exchange City," he replied. He wore the standard grey cat suit and seemed truly bored with this whole business. Lech sensed he was more than glad to be finally done coping in Ania's place.

"That's good. Say, I have a little research project for you, Bolek. Can you go over all the geologic data since first contact with Ashford-5? I would like to see a report of all unexplained phenomenon or anomalies — anything far out of the ordinary," Lech asked.

Bolek raised his eyes. "Hum, well, now that you mention it, there have been some strange happenings. Ania fully documented them. Let me dig up her reports for you." He seemed slightly nervous, his hands twitched. Lech began to think Bolek was hiding something. Nervous people often did.

"Say, off hand, did Ania leave behind the password to her private documents? I've got several hundred of them I have been unable to open. They may or may not concern Ashford-5."

She hadn't and Bolek left to research Lech's request. Lech was now even more convinced whatever Ania had written in her secret documents had to be extraordinarily important. Yet did they concern Ashford-5 or entirely other matters? He quickly again reviewed all the other matters of the sector and could find no indications of clandestine activities. All seemed routine. Well, he'd wait on Bolek's reports. Meantime, he pulled up his own private document that outlined the strange, unexplained phenomenon on Ashford-5 to refresh his own thinking.

Days later, Bolek showed his findings. Over a century ago, the original refining station had a catastrophic explosion that knocked the planet's pole off center some thirty degrees. Further, it began wobbling madly like a child's top. "Sir, if you will compare the motions then with the motions now, you can see the wobble has ceased. While the pole is still off by thirty degrees, the wild motions have ceased. Now this is what I have been studying ever since I discovered it some ten years ago. Ania seemed to know about it, but she refused to enlighten me on any details, so I've had to work it out on my own. I've spent an enormous amount of computer time coming up with possible models of what it took to terminate the wild wobble."

"Did that wobble contribute to the reports of wild, erratic weather?" Lech asked, hoping to pin another fact down.

"Precisely. After the wobble died down, the wild swings in the weather over the main sections of the continent subsided. I found a report that initially Ania had the entire geologic department working on possible ways to undo the wobble and polar shift without causing a further deterioration of planetary conditions. They could find none. If you examine my empirical models here, you can see I've worked the problem backwards. Given the current state and the original state, my program has computed what forces would have had to be applied and where." He showed Lech his summary diagram.

Lech growled, he had no idea what the diagram signified or meant. Geology was not his thing at all. "What's it mean?"

Bolek realized Lech had no notion of what his carefully constructed diagram actually meant. He couldn't resist a small smirk; Lech wasn't all-knowing after all. "Just this. Nothing we have in the Imperium could have applied these forces in the manner indicated. Further, the forces are not natural in nature. That is, Ashford-5 ought to still be wobbling like mad, but it isn't."

"Really?" Lech asked, his eyebrows suddenly raised and

he looked sharply at Bolek.

"Yes, someone or something has stabilized the planet and it was not we of the Imperium. It had to be some outside force. Ania never mentioned anything about it, but I did find my predecessor got her at least to admit it was a 'miracle,' for whatever that may mean. In short, just how the wobble was stopped is a complete mystery. It should not have occurred, but it most definitely has occurred. No known natural law can account for it, period. Unexplained phenomenon, if you ask me. What troubles me is Ashford-5 is a primitive planet. The locals certainly do not have the knowledge to have so altered the wobble of the planet, let alone the means to apply such gigantic forces so precisely. I've been trying to work out plausible alternative means, but to date I've come up with nothing but a total blank on that one."

"Excellent work, Bolek, really first rate. Thanks. Yes, it is indeed a mystery. Well done," Lech replied. Compliments go a long way, which was his operating model. Bolek still seemed a tad uneasy. Wisely, Lech asked, "Is there something else that is strange?"

"Well, I don't know how to put this, but there certainly is. Can I show you a bit of video I captured from our geosat imaging camera?" Lech nodded and Bolek pulled up his file on Lech's computer. "Our satellite takes periodic pictures of the surface. The weather folks use the data to work out their forecasting models, as I understand it. However, I use them for geological surveys. Now I've pieced a number of images into a time-lapse sequence. You are looking at an area of these very mountains, about a hundred miles north of here to the west. The city there is Valen, Trujillo. I want you to watch this area here, the stone quarry. Watch." He allowed the time-lapse sequence of images to play back, a half second apart.

Small dust lines were visible, as if someone were cutting out stone blocks. Lech thought, *well that's ordinary, it's a rock quarry and quarrying is ongoing. Ah, there is the block being freed and lifted and moved. Ah, it is being placed on the side of a wall. Makes sense.* Then, he saw what he was missing. "Where are the workers, Bolek? What's the scale? Shouldn't the resolution be such that we ought to be seeing the workers?"

Bolek grinned broadly and relaxed fully for the first time in Lech's presence. "Precisely so! The workers ought to be very readily visible. There are none. I've studied this one extensively now. I have dozens of these recordings. All show clearly stone is being quarried and moved into positions. I even have comparisons showing the buildings increasing in size as a result. Yet, there are no workers ever seen at the quarry, though occasional images do show people there at other times, as if inspecting the site. No images ever show the scaffolding needed or workers on the buildings under construction. I ask you, ID Minister, how can this be? How can invisible workers cut through stone and move it without heavy equipment? I've done measurements from the sat images and can say that wall there is thirty feet above the ground — yes, just there where that new stone block is being placed. No scaffolding, no cranes, no nothing!"

"Incredible! Well done indeed, Bolek! Can you get me a copy of all these? Keep on with your researches!" Lech was elated. Here was visible proof something was going on here on Ashford-5, something the Imperium knew nothing about, unless it was hidden in Ania's secret documents. Certainly, Central Headquarters knew nothing about it. Something of this magnitude would have raised all kinds of red flags there. Bolek did so, walking out of Lech's office with his head held high. *Finally, someone appreciates my work!*

That night after supper in the commons, Lech showed the image clips to Karolina. She too was equally impressed. "Now we are getting somewhere, dear. There just has to be something going on here on Ashford-5! The weather, the polar wobble, now this stone quarrying. Unexplained phenomenon. I've found yet another weather anomaly today, dear. Let me show you what I found." She ran another short clip. Again, the massive storm took an unpredicted route, almost as if some giant hand had reached down and moved it a little.

"The question, my love, is how are we going to get out there to see it first hand?" Lech asked. She tossed her head and chuckled. The physical appearance of Rigel-3 bodies looked vastly different from the primitives. So yes, his question was key.

She then changed the topic. "Remember the reports we received about all Rigel-3 women who have been here on Ashford-5 for about six months who claim their breasts drastically grow in size? Well, I've been examining the many women here. The claim is not exaggerated one little bit. So I dropped by the medical facilities to inquire about it."

"You have a vested interest in that one," Lech chuckled, giving her a loving hug.

"Of course, dear. They explained to me they have isolated a pathogen in the air on this planet that is responsible for women's breasts to enlarge so greatly. Their operating theory is women's mammary glands have become so big to offset the food shortages that developed so nursing mothers always have plenty of milk for their children. Makes sense. They have been trying to filter that pathogen out of our air here in the two main buildings, but so far, they have been unsuccessful in eliminating it."

"Ah, so then you were wise in also bringing along all that extra material. You can then have your dresses and blouses altered," Lech replied.

She grinned, "You bet. If they do get huge, I don't want them to force me to wear those awful cat suits! Hideous apparel." He grinned and thought, *No she certainly wouldn't!* "So how are we going to find out what is really going on here, dear?" she said, sliding coyly up to him, holding her drink off to one side.

"If you keep on teasing me like this, I'll never get it worked out," he flirted back, sliding his arm around her waist, pulling her close to him. Whispering, he added, "I think it can wait until tomorrow."

Per the ironclad contract, the aliens, that is, those from the Imperium worlds, were not allowed beyond the edge of Exchange City. Even so, they were only permitted to go there for trading purposes or to make deliveries, save their security forces. Making matters more complicated, their physical bodies identified them as aliens instantly. No way could a Rigel-3 person blend in with the local primitives. To gain Intel, he could bribe some local traders and set them to spying for him. If he went that route, he knew the Intel would be dubious at best. Another avenue that might be worth exploring was the mixed-race offspring. It was documented two of the original ministers had gone native, marrying local men before the catastrophic explosion wiped out all the others from Rigel-3.

While those offspring were unknown, with the establishment of the Exchange City, men and women often exchanged more than trade goods. He knew every city had its own equivalent of the red light district, where sex could be purchased. In some cultures, such was encouraged, but in others, it was taboo but still practiced on the sly. Lech knew from birth records there were over two dozen mixed-race men and women living in and around Exchange City. Could they be used?

Unless their physical forms were vastly different from those of their Rigel-3 parent, they too would stick out as partially alien. Thus, they likely would not be able to work as effective field agents, assuming he could gain their loyalty for a price. No, even those would be a poor choice for the Intel he and Karolina really needed.

"Suppose for a moment I did bring in someone from the Imperium whose body would match the primitives here. I could send them out to gather my needed Intel," he spoke to his walls. That idea, while it got around the physical body form problem, was also out. This was a closed planet, what with the rigid enforcement of Imperial Directive #5. It would be totally illegal for his spy to travel beyond Exchange City. If he or she were caught, as Sector ID Minister, the blame and responsibility would fall entirely into his lap. While normally not a big deal, in this case, those to whom he reported would have his head for breaking the directive.

Countering all this was the nature of his new job, Sector ID Minister. He was obligated to obtain the key, critical Intel the Imperium needed to run effectively the sector and this planet. He had to find the answers to these mysteries, but the rules effectively prevented him from doing so directly. Lech was in a quandary. His own innate curiosity dictated he had to find out the underlying truth, regardless of the official rules and policies in force. Yet, how?

Even if he sent a spy out beyond Exchange City, he or she would need all manner of prohibited devices. Technology not possessed by the primitives was again prohibited by ironclad rules laid out in the signed lease agreement. Breakage of those rules would also get him fired or worse. He bit his lip. This, he absentmindedly noted, he always seemed to do just before he got a flash of insight into tough problems. "Time for a hot cup of strong black tea!" That was always his first answer to insolvable problems. Fortunately, Ania had a hot plate here and soon he had some water boiling. He'd brought a pound of high quality black tea, Amino Steel, with him — expensive tea at a hundred credits per pound, imported from Helios-3 in the Axos System. Soon, he sat back, put his feet up on his new desk, and smelled the heady aroma from his large mug. Then, he blew and sipped the delicious, hot brew, waiting for his grand idea to appear.

Formulator Mark V came to mind. "Yes, that would solve the first problem." This clever device in widespread usage within the ID created the illusion of whatever body form and shape that was needed. While the small pocket-sized device was activated, anyone looking at the wearer would see the desired image and could not tell it wasn't real. Using the Formulator Mark V, one of his Rigel-3 field agents would be completely indistinguishable from any other primitive. Unfortunately, this device was designed for brief usages and needed to be recharged every twenty-four hours. This would not work in this situation, because the field agent would need to use the primitive's mode of transportation to Valen, and travel time alone greatly exceeded this.

Now that he was thinking along these lines, he had an even better idea, though more costly. There was the Ring of Modulation. Looking like an ordinary, rather plain ring, it modified some physical characteristics of the wearer. Unlike the Formulator, the ring held its charge for a month before it needed recharging. It could easily alter the distinctive Rigel-3 skin tones to match those of the primitives. His chosen agents ought to be on the short side and a little overweight, from the Rigel-3 perspective, to not draw undue attention to themselves. "Yes, this ring is the answer I need. Bingo. Now to find the perfect field agent!"

He pulled up his roster of field agents who were on Ashford-5. He had twenty to choose from; most were disguised as either traders or policemen who were charged with maintaining order in Exchange City. Next, he checked their reports. *Curious, there is so very little in these. Mundane things. Something is not right here. Let me see the filings listing.* He brought up the entry log and noticed severe discrepancies. Each agent sent in a report file, which was substantially larger than the final report document on file, raising a big red flag in his keen mind. The more he checked the more the file size discrepancies he found. "These have been edited for content, severely I might add! Why?"

Now he had yet another mystery to solve. His field agents were reporting in all right, but Ania was somehow heavily editing them before posting the reports. Why? Well, they could be full of fluff. Agents often embellished their field reports hoping to gain favor with their boss. "Would all twenty do this on a routine basis for over a century? I think not! Something is definitely going on here!" He had two choices. One, he could bring in each agent and question them at length. Two, he could crack Ania's password protection. He decided to try the latter because at the moment, he did not want his agents to have any clues about his line of thinking. Something was going on here and he wanted and needed to know before he talked to his many agents. He'd have to crack her password, but how?

Lech had not risen to his high position in the Imperium Intelligence Division without gaining keen skills. He knew Ania's computer was networked to the port's main server. All her files were stored on the massive server. While all was secure, the server always kept a log of keystrokes sent from each computer. If Ania edited her files while they were stored on the server, she would have had to enter her password and those keystrokes would have been logged, along with trillions of others. He grinned; there was a way. He headed for the computer department.

An hour later, he had access to a three terabyte log file of Ania's keystrokes. Now he set to work writing a search program. He had it scan for repeated sequences. By setting a threshold for reporting of at least fifty occurrences, this would eliminate all but the most frequently typed sequences. Of course, articles like "the" would occur with alarmingly high rates, so he set a second threshold of at least eight characters, eliminating shorter words. After getting the bugs out of his program, he turned it loose on the huge raw data file.

A day later, the program began displaying results as it found them. Ashford-5 appeared and he task switched and tried that as a password. Invalid. One by one, he tried each sequence that appeared. Hours later, he tried the next one, AniaAnka42. The document opened! He killed his search program and let out a silent cheer, punching his fist into the air. "I didn't make Sector ID Minister for nothing! Now, let me see what she was hiding from the Imperium!"

He began with her oldest document and began reading. "My god! Doctor Zosia and Minister Dita Ewa became telepaths too! Ah, they were reporting highly sensitive data to Ania over the years. My god! Ashford-5 has evolved into a telepathic society! No wonder she wanted to keep this off the main grid!"

"What have you discovered, dear?" Karolina asked when they were in their quarters that evening. She always knew when he had come across something of great significance. The way his eyes looked, bright and shining, the curl around the edges of his mouth — even his bearing changed. She knew he'd found out something vitally important.

"You know me too well for your own good," he teased her. "Okay, this is *top* secret. I cracked Ania's password and now have access to all the Intel she has *never* reported on up the line to the Imperium."

"Okay, *out* with it. Does it explain all these strange goings on here?" she asked. "Especially the weather anomalies?"

"After the explosion that sent psi dust all over the continent, people began developing telepathic skills. According to Doctor Zosia, many people's pituitary glands greatly enlarged at the same time. That's what led to the experiments off-world that we discovered. Ania was having the Imperium conduct its own experiments with psi dust. Even I don't have high enough clearance to know the results of that one. Ania reports someone called Marisol Bolivar compiled a list of the telepathic skills that surfaced. The primitives call them *mentales* gifts. Evidently, one of these is the ability to control the weather. Your anomalies are caused by the primitive's intervention, dear."

"My god! That's impossible! Controlling the weather? Moving storms from their natural course? Dear god!" she exclaimed, sitting down before she collapsed. Her legs felt suddenly very weak.

"Yes, and apparently a whole lot more. Ania reports some of these primitives can kill another person just by thought alone! Now that *is* scary! And I've only gotten *started* reading her private logs!"

"We'd best keep *quiet* about this. If the Imperium finds out, they could try to intervene in a major way. Perhaps these people are not so primitive after all!" she suggested, growing somewhat frightened. People reading her every thought, people able to kill her by a thought — scary indeed!

"Well, they all don't have this telepathic gift. There is not any planet-wide census, but she estimates the some twenty percent do have the gift, but it is just a guess. They have also some kind of Rules to follow. I need to get a hold of that Marisol document and these Rules, somehow I must."

Days later, after reading through all Ania's private documents, he learned the *mentales* leaders built the eleven towers. Even more curious, he learned everyone who had the telepathic gift had their eye color changed to yellow with brown spots. Quite why, Ania had no clue nor had Doctor Zosia. Recently, Ania learned that around the turn of the century these towers forced all the various political leaders to sign onto something called the Brom Compact, effectively yielding political control to the towers. The many open conflicts and small wars had ended with the compact, but now the towers were expanding both in physical quarters and in members. Her last entry was simply, "Will an unlimited weapon truly lead to universal peace? Personally, I doubt it, but time will tell. All has been uncharacteristically quiet for twenty years now, and I like that, for I am getting way too old for this."

At last, Lech could choose his special field agents. Ania had edited out all traces of these things from their field reports. From the twenty that worked around the spaceport, he picked two: Jarek Lajda, a thirty year old agent-policeman, and Kassia Kunegunda, a twenty-nine year old "merchant." He summoned them both for a private meeting. As they walked in, he saw his choices looked right, physically that is. Jarek was far more muscular than the normal Rigel-3 man, five inches shorter than Lech, and he had kept fit, adjusting to the thinner atmosphere here on Ashford-5. His face was completely commonplace, a trait useful in the espionage arena, since he'd be seen but never remembered. Kassia shocked him a little at first. True, he had seen various women around the spaceport with their greatly enlarged bosoms, but seeing her close up and first hand rather startled him. Rigel-3 women were not known for having large mammary glands and hers were positively humongous. *Will Karolina's get this gigantic?* he wondered. Her face was plain and roundish, and she wore her hair similar to the way Ashford-5 primitive women wore theirs, long and with a bluebird clasp in the back. Both wore native clothing at this visit.

Kassia commented, "Like my knockers, eh, boss? Give your wife time, she'll have 'em too. We all end up with monsters. The real question is what happens to them when we leave Ashford-5? No one answers that one for me. If they don't shrink, I ought to put in for compensatory field damages, don't you think?" She was jesting and it brought a smile to Lech's face. She was also on the very short side and had evidently been working out to build up muscle mass in her arms and legs to better fit in with the natives.

"Amazing. Forgive me, Kassia, I've only been here a week and haven't seen women close up yet, except for my wife, of course. Yes, I'll sign it if you fill out the form," he continued the tease. "Now then, have a seat both of you. I've got a special assignment for you both. First, do you speak whatever the native languages are around here?" He recalled there were evidently three related dialects in use, but he was not yet certain which went where.

"Yes, boss. We call them after the areas in which they are primarily spoken, Westerlings, Midlands, and Easterlings. We both speak Westerlings and Midlands, but we've had little contact with anyone from the far distant Easterlings so we've not worked on that one," Kassia pointed out.

"Excellent. Now then, are you aware Ashford-5 has become a telepathic based society?" He thought he'd just see how much they really knew.

"Sir, you ought to get used to calling it by the local name, Tierra. Yes, we are. It can be quite tricky when someone with yellow eyes is around. They can read your thoughts. We have to be very careful about what we think about," Kassia answered.

Jarek added, "But not all have this gift. They refer to it as a gift, since they have needed such abilities to survive the cataclysmic climate changes that struck over a century ago. Ania was here during that early time period, and she claims most of the population would have perished had those with the gift not stepped in to help out everyone else. Ania says that's why she initially decided to keep the fact there are telepaths here from the Imperium officials. She told me about ten years ago it had been the right decision, because some of these telepaths now have ungodly powers. Sir, have you seen our report on the strange crystals most of them now carry around their necks?" Lech nodded he had. "We are not sure of their purpose yet. It's rather difficult to talk to them; they seldom come to Exchange City."

Lech decided to level with these two. "I hereby swear you both to Secrets Level 8." Both had very surprised looks on their faces, for this was an exceedingly high level of security. They were only classified at level 1. They swore their binding word, knowing if they violated it, they would be executed or if they attempted to flee such executions, assassinated.

"It is high time we learn more about these gifted people in the towers. They seem to be the top-most leaders of Ash — Tierra," he corrected himself. "Specifically, I would like to somehow obtain their book of Rules regarding these *mentales* gifts and a copy of the Marisol Catalogue of *Mentales* Gifts, as it is called. Further, I want to know what the devil is going on with the stone quarrying and construction in and around this Valen Tower. Let me show you some video." He played several of Bolek's geosat image collections.

"From here, it looks like they are magically quarrying stone and magically laying them. I want full details on this. I want you, Jarek, to travel to Valen and spy on the construction and quarrying. See if there is any way to obtain copies of the two books for me. Kassia, I want you to travel to this Haverhills Tower and see if you can figure out who there is altering storm paths as well as obtaining copies of the two books." He showed his wife's storm track anomalies to her. He added, "Yes, I know we are forbidden from going any further than Exchange City. I think these developments require close-up field analysis, so I am suspending that clause for you both. However, if you are caught, I will of course deny any such thing and be forced to administer appropriate punishments for violating the Lease Agreement and Imperial Directive #5. So don't get caught." He saw both beginning to protest and hastily added, "Yes, I know you cannot travel looking like Rigel-3 aliens to these locals. Hence, I am giving each of you a Ring of Modulation." Their facial expressions changed utterly to one of awe and respect.

"Now you are talking! With those, we can pass for natives. How long does their charge last?" Jarek asked.

"You have a month. Just don't take them off while you are out in the field and don't let anyone see you change when you put them on. These are rather expensive little devils, so don't lose them. Also, I am giving you each a handheld Navigator, since there are no roads on this world. Plus, I am providing small Communicators you can use to contact me, should the need arise. They are on a special frequency not monitored by the base here, and I have the only receiver tuned to that frequency. We ought to have secret communications. In case of real trouble, I will give you each a blaster too. Just be darn careful not to lose these or I will be in hot water myself. Draw some local coinage in Exchange City before you leave."

"Boss, one small problem," Kassia finally spoke up. "On

Tierra, women do not travel by themselves. They are always escorted by armed men. This culture is going to extreme measures to protect their women and to breed more *mentales* gifted children. Of course, we've heard it is far worse for women over in the Easterlings than here, but we have no data, just rumors that say the men there physically bind their women."

"Damn. Well, I admit I have not yet gotten familiar with all the cultural details of Tierra. Only been here a week. All women?" Lech asked. It seemed his grand spy plan was in dire danger. He really didn't want to risk everything on a single field agent. Two had a better chance of succeeding. Besides, if they got caught, he'd not be able to get away with spying in the future.

"Well, not exactly, boss. The Sisterhood women — they can travel anywhere. Strange bunch of women, though. They're operating out of the cultural normal for the planet and are looked upon as a total disgrace by the rest of the population. Those women alone can travel anywhere they wish unimpeded. Perhaps, I could hire some of them to 'take me' to Haverhills, boss. Would that be acceptable?"

"Ah, yes, make it so, Kassia. Again, I can see I have much more homework to do here. Forgive me, I've only been at it a week," he repeated his justification and continued. "Look, if you cannot find a way to procure those books for me, see if you can get a personal dispatch from me to the person in charge of the tower. I'll write out a formal request to meet with them in Exchange City. You can say you are supposed to return to me with their answer. That ought to not raise too many questions."

"Thanks boss for having confidence in us. We won't let you down. It feels great to finally get to do some *real* field work at long last!" Kassia said enthusiastically.

Equally excited about the prospect of real field work at long last, Jarek added, "Yes, under Ania, we thought we were just killing time and were about to put in for a transfer like nearly all the others have been doing. Turnover rates among agents is huge because we are so darn limited in what we can do. This is much more like it!"

Lech adjusted the two rings simply to alter the pair's skin coloration and eye color, leaving their black hair alone. He had the two look each other over to see if they looked like the natives. "I think we will pass now, boss," Kassia stated, a smirking smile appearing.

Chapter 3 A Meeting of the Minds

Both Kassia and Jarek needed to come up with local names. Fortunately, Kassia was able simply to alter hers slightly to Cassia. Jarek opted to go by the name Jacobo. Next, both had to acquire proper trail apparel, horses, and gear, all without drawing the native's suspicion. To avoid getting both of them caught at the same time, they spit up and went their separate ways in Exchange City.

The city that normally was home to a few thousand now swelled to closer to ten thousand. It was July 1st and the delivery date for the Imperium's lease payments to the kingdoms abutting their Plateau Grado. At these times, Valen, Haverhills, and Bedwurth sent large teams of wagons and soldiers to pick up the iron ore and gold and to protect the shipment. Likewise, many traders from numerous smaller kingdoms also chose this time to come to Exchange City to market their wares. Hence, the two found the streets packed with wagons, carts, and people, both natives and Rigel-3 personnel.

Jarek kept his persona in place, frequently staring at the tall, thin countrymen of his, just as the many native men were doing. After all, he was a trained field agent. From his prior fieldwork, he had good ideas where he could pick up the many things he needed. His first stop was the very crowded Trader Bill's store, packed with locals and visitors seeking bargains and possibly alien items. A sign over the door read: If it's available, you can get it at Trader Bill's. Here he picked up a heavy trail cloak, nicely oiled against the frequent rains. Adding a change of clothes and a set of saddlebags priced a little too high, he paid for his goods and headed off to see about getting a horse, the bags slung over his shoulder. His blaster was stuck in the top of his right boot; his Navigator, compass, and radio were in the top of his left boot. Both boots had been altered by making small compartments to house these. His pant legs hid the slight upper bulges.

As he approached Hilliard Stables, he realized the fatal

flaw in his plans. He had no idea how to ride a horse, let alone care for one on a trip across country! He knew he would need a saddle and bridle, but what else? What did the horse need while not in the stables? *Damn, why can't we just use a stupid shuttle! Primitives!* Now he knew he faced a serious problem. Nearly every native knew how to ride. How could he fake it? *Damn this place and its primitive transportation! Hell fire! What do I do now?* He calmed down mentally. *Focus, focus on the job at hand. Too far to walk. Need transportation. Say, all these wagons are in town to haul back their ore and gold. Maybe I can finagle a ride there on one of the wagons or hire myself on as a guard or something.*

He strolled around the town looking for prospects. He found it easy to tell those from the Westerlings from the Midlands people. Hair color and more colorful outfits gave them away, if not their language. Eventually, one wagon seemed to be a little shorthanded and he ambled up to the lone teamster, a man in his forties. "Hello. Looks like you have your hands full with this load of ore."

"Aye, that I do. Mighty fine ore I'm told. When it's turned into hard steel blades, then I will be more impressed. Hidalgo's the name."

"Jacobo here. Say, I'm a city dweller and unused to horses and the trail, but I need to visit Valen. Any chance you are headed that way?"

"Sure am. This is part of Venerado Amo Augusto Valen's payment."

"I wonder if I could hitch a ride with you and help out as I can? I can bring along my own food and will work for nothing more than passage to Valen," Jarek asked, keeping his fingers crossed.

"Well, I don't know. I could use the help since Diego up and got sick on me. I don't make those kinds of decisions though. It'd be up to the Amo Enrico; he's the boss, you see."

"Where can I find him?"

"He's over there with the alien men. Probably going over the manifest. He'll come this way when he's done. I'll get him for you. Sure could use a hand and the company. It's a three day journey with this heavy load." Jarek thanked him and the two chatted for a while. His plan was to seem friendly enough to Hidalgo so the teamster would put in a good word for him with the boss.

A half hour passed before the strikingly dressed young man came over to Hidalgo's heavily loaded wagon. "Hey boss, this here's Jacobo, and he is looking to get a ride with me to Valen. He says he'll work for his passage."

"Yes, I don't want to travel alone. Jacobo's the name. I couldn't help but notice Hidalgo here is shorthanded." He studied the man while he replied.

"Amo Enrico Valen. So you want to ride along with Hidalgo here and help him out in exchange for the ride. Are you prepared to help defend this shipment? It is extremely valuable as you probably know." He was perhaps twenty-five with curly black hair that just touched his shoulders. His black moustache was prominent on his stern face. While his attitude didn't reflect his look, his angular nose, square jaw, and raised eyebrows tended to give him that no nonsense look, whether he intended it or not. However, what Jarek saw first was his yellow eyes with the usual brown speckles and a stone covered in a fine silk pouch hanging from his neck. He wore a red shirt with a yellow waistband and brown pants with the usual tall brown riding boots so common in the Westerlings.

"Yes, I have my sword and am also good at unarmed combat," Jarek answered. *Damn! Just my luck a telepath is in charge of this group. Careful, think of nothing, Jarek.* He did so, believing that would be enough to block telepaths from reading his mind.

Enrico sensed something was wrong from the moment he approached Hidalgo and this stranger calling himself Jacobo. First, his manner of dress seemed a hodge-podge of styles, a formal shirt, work pants, trail cloak, and dress boots. Second, he spoke with a terrible accent, one that didn't fit those from the Midlands trying to speak the Westerlings dialect. Yet, the color of his skin and hair did fit a person from the Westerlings. Gently, he focused and touched Jacobo's mind, looking for surface thoughts. *How very strange! Is he a spy? Something is wrong with him. He is not what he proclaims to be. Well, time to find out.* He said, "Well, give me

46

a few minutes to think about it. Security protocols and all that. Stick around Hidalgo here and I'll be back shortly." Jacobo nodded and made a polite reply as Enrico walked on down the line of wagons, seemingly checking on them. Jacobo had already noticed all the wagons had two men with each of them. That's why he chose Hidalgo's wagon.

Once some distance from this Jacobo fellow, Enrico took the pod-silk cover off his crystal and activated it. This time, he sent his awareness deep into Jacobo's mind. *Damn! No wonder everything is slightly off! He's an alien, one of the Rigels, but he's somehow altered his body coloration. He wants to go to Valen? That's illegal! Best tell dad about this one. No way am I going to get myself into a treaty break!*

He focused and reached out for his father. *Dad. Enrico here. Something really weird has come up.* He went on to explain what had happened and what he'd discovered. *So what do you want me to do? Let him come to Valen and the tower?*

Well done, son. How very interesting. I wondered how long it would be before the aliens broke their own treaty. So it's happened. Okay, let him come with you, but keep a sharp eye out for mischief and/or trouble. I think he is mostly on a spy mission, but we'll see. I'll meet you when you get here and take over. So his skin looks like ours, not the grey the aliens always have. I wonder what they did to him? If there are lots of these imposters around, we could be easily infiltrated. Good job, son. He broke the connection and Enrico put his pod-silk covering back over his crystal. After inspecting the remaining wagons, he walked back to Jacobo and Hidalgo.

"Well, Hidalgo needs the help, so I've decided to let you tag along. Just be prepared for trouble. This is an extremely valuable shipment," Enrico told Jacobo.

"Thank you, sir. I will," Jacobo replied, hoping his great relief would not be visible to the telepath man.

"Climb up, Hidalgo, time to move out," he ordered and went on up the line issuing the same orders. They were transporting twenty-five tons of iron and two hundred fifty pounds of gold as Jarek well knew. It was evenly distributed between twenty-six wagons. Additionally, fifty mounted men accompanied them, along with a cook and his wagon plus one supply wagon. Jacobo joined Hidalgo in the tall driver's bench and waited the signal to begin, confident his mission was getting off on the right foot. *These telepaths are easily fooled,* he thought to himself.

Soon they began to roll westward along the special road carved from the bedrock by the great machines of the Imperium. Per the original lease agreement, Valen was provided an easy roadway across the Goza Mountains so that a second exchange city didn't have to be constructed to facilitate the exchange of iron ore and gold each year. Cut deep into the heart of the mountain, the road had only a shallow grade, easy for the wagons and their heavy loads. It ran just at the southern edge of the plateau and spaceport. For a time, Hidalgo and Jacobo talked about the alien spaceships they saw descending and taking off just to their right. Jarek could see that from this road, one would get a really good view of the spaceport ships. However, the tall security fence kept the inquisitive out. It was electrified and had sensors that monitored any potential breach, sounding an alarm if such happened. It had. The fierce Montaña beasts occasionally tore through the fence, but always had been repelled by the strong electrical jolt they received. Only one had actually gotten onto the base proper and was handled with blasters.

Enrico kept a covert eye on Jacobo during the three day trip to Valen. By the end of the first day of travel, it was clear to him this alien had not the faintest notions of how to handle horses, wagons, camping, navigation, or camp life. Several times, he smothered grins at how inept the alien actually was, though old Hidalgo didn't seem to mind helping the greenhorn out. As far as Enrico could tell, Hidalgo appreciated the man's company. He could not detect any subversive actions on the alien's part though he did not let his guard down during the entire trip.

How the hell can they possibly know where they are going? Jarek grimaced. They left the Grado Plateau area and entered the rugged foothills just west of the peaks. Here was a spectacularly beautiful land with craggy ridges, deep valley gorges covered often in dense pine forests or tall, rolling grasslands only to rise on the other side to nearly impassible rocky ridges once more. There was no road he could see, though Hidalgo pointed out the wagon trail they had made coming here. Jarek suddenly realized without the use of his Navigator device, he would be hopelessly lost! Yet, it was far worse than that. This inhospitable land of seemingly endless steep, jagged ridges that opened into another valley system continued on endlessly. More than once, they just seemed to be randomly heading out down and across a valley system, though how they could know where the rocky ridges ahead would allow passage of the heavily loaded wagons was beyond him. The ridges looked like monstrous teeth of the unforgiving and unyielding vicious Goza Mountains. The only safe route was west, down a valley system with its small, bubbling creek.

The first night on the trail Hidalgo was of immense help to him. He had no idea how to set up his bedroll or where to put it, until the older man told him to put it beside his beneath their wagon. Hidalgo later had to tell him to remove the rocks or he'd not sleep well at all. Dealing with the horses was a nightmare. "You've not been around horses much," Hidalgo pointed out.

"Er, no not ever. I've been a city dweller all my life. Never had to travel before. This is all new to me, but I am a fast learner, I hope," Jarek replied, trying to emulate Hidalgo's actions with the hobbling the horses and fitting their grain sacks over their heads, later swapping them for water sacks. At mealtime, he followed Hidalgo's moves closely, but he'd never eaten the primitive's food before. Tears swelled in his eyes from the hot spices the Westerlings loved to put on all their food. Hidalgo merely laughed at him and handed him the water skin. "Good! Hotter than I'm used to," he managed finally to squeak in a high voice. Hidalgo laughed even more. Jarek realized all his field training had not prepared him for such primitive conditions, not even remotely. Well, he'd learn fast, he told himself. In fact, by the time they arrived in Valen, he was adapting fairly well, in his opinion.

He had studied the geosat images of Valen, committing them to memory, but the two dimensional images were a far cry from the 3-d reality of the huge, sprawling city, cradled in the foothills of the Goza Mountains. The tower proper along with its castle sat high on the ridge line. A wide cobblestone road led straight west out over a small marsh area at the western edge of the city. The streets undulated up and down over the ground on which they lay. Houses were either pine or stone, but all had the typical red tile roofs so common in the Westerlings. He could not help notice nearly every home had a formal gardens or courtyard beside it, again quite typical of the Westerlings, who people loved to take time out from the hustle and bustle of the workaday world. Always there was at least a bench in the gardens, and sometimes, even more elaborate gazebos were present, but only at the wealthier homes, usually made of stone.

Off to the west, the valley opened up into huge, rolling grasslands with pine forests nearer the ridge lines, blocking his vision beyond perhaps a few miles. Again, without his handheld Navigator, he'd be lost within a few miles, though he did see what had to be a well-traveled track leading off westwards. As the caravan rolled up the wide street, Hidalgo pointed out, "This is called Valen's Way. Kind of spectacular, since it's several feet above the marsh. Ahead are Castle Valen and its tower, our destination." The streets were packed with people, all wearing colorful outfits, though the rain was threatening. Reds, yellows, and browns predominated in the Westerlings' apparel, including some tartans.

The weather had been uncommonly dry during these past three days. Hidalgo explained this was due to the Amo's. "It wouldn't due to have this valuable cargo mired down in the mud because of all the rain. So our *mentales* — they keep it from raining on us." Jarek was amused and a little awed at the same time. Here was this ordinary teamster who talked about those with telepathic skills as if it were commonplace and easy to move rain clouds away!

Venerado Amo Augusto Valen, the fifty-five year old leader of Valen and thus all Trujillo, met with his three Capo leaders of the three *Círculo de mentes*. Capo Amo Armando Valen, twenty-eight, was his eldest son, while Capo Amo Basilio, thirty-five, was his nephew, and Capo Amo Camilo, forty, was his cousin. He had carefully selected all three tower leaders, who focused and used the combined psi energies of the circle. They were totally loyal to Augusto, naturally, since they owed their immense power positions to him and him alone.

"Well, we certainly do have an interesting situation developing, though I am completely amazed it has not happened before," Augusto began, rubbing his right hand through his long black beard, which his wife Bonita and his consort Camila thought made him look more distinguished. It certainly had spiced up his bedtime activities. "It seems the aliens have finally gotten entirely too curious of us and have sent a spy into our midst. Enrico spotted him and has him under close observation as he brings him to Valen."

"The alien wanted to come to Valen? Why?" asked his son Armando.

"Yes, specifically here. Why? Who knows at this point? The alien thinks he is deep undercover, and we are not aware of his identity," Augusto pointed out.

"How can he possibly think that? They are tall, skinny, and have distinctive grey skin and coal black hair and eyes. He'd stick out to a blind man!" declared his nephew Basilio.

"Enrico claims his skin color matches ours and his eye color is altered too. He certainly doesn't know anything about horses and his accent is atrocious to say nothing about his mixed bag of clothing. Perhaps the aliens have been working on a breeding program of their own all these years, intending to alter some of them so they will fit in with our people," Augusto theorized.

"Dad, this is a major lease treaty break. Aliens are forbidden to go beyond Exchange City. What are we going to do about it? Are they after our secrets?" asked Armando.

Augusto commented dryly, "Hey, I told you it was just a matter of time before the aliens began spying on us. The question before us now is what do we do about it? We could play along with the spy and see what he is up to or we could apprehend him and interrogate him. We could also launch a formal protest with their leaders, demanding these actions cease at once."

Camilo growled angrily, smashing his fist hard onto the

table, jarring the mugs. "I'm inclined to the latter action. We cannot trust these aliens. After all, look what they did to our world centuries ago. I say we apprehend him and torture the information out of him and then file a formal protest." His anger quickly faded as he regained his composure.

"I don't think we should trust to luck and let him wander about spying on us, dad. That's too risky. He probably has all manner of alien weapons on his person. He could blast us with their guns, wiping us out," Armando pointed out, rather worried about losing their power base and grip on Trujillo.

"I agree son, we best not allow him to wander about. Still, apprehending him might force his hand and make him use his blaster weapon," Augusto wisely pointed out.

"We can form up our circles and hold him with our powers while you search him. None can withstand our forces, dad. I'd feel a whole lot safer if we had him totally disarmed before we interrogate him," Armando stated factually.

"I like that idea, son. Let's have Enrico bring him on into the castle proper along with the ore and gold shipment. Once within our walls, the circles can hold him, while some of us thoroughly search him. Disarmed, we can then question him at length, making darn sure he is not lying to us. I have a feeling we can make this work to our benefit. If the aliens want something from us and are going to such an extreme to get it, then perhaps we can *get* something we wish from them. Think of the *edge* we would have if we had just a *few* of their blasters. I still aim to take down Portillo Tower and then Duero Tower. We *Valens* ought to be in total control of the entire Westerlings, just as Adelmira runs all the Easterlings."

"Good idea, dad. I'd like to get my hands on one of their shuttle cars. It would greatly simplify our attempts to make one of our own," Armando suggested. All four smiled, imagining their mighty army flying through the sky to attack their enemy towers and forces. The strategic advantage would be huge. Although Valen had no choice but to accept the Brom Compact, Augusto had carefully bided his time, waiting for the chance to present itself. In his mind and way of thinking, it was wholly unfair of old Felix Brom to allow one tower to control all the Easterlings while dividing up the Westerlings into thirds. Valen ought to have been given total and absolute control over the Westerlings, with the other two towers subjected to Valen's laws as well. He saw no reason those two towers should not be subsidiaries of Valen Tower. To that end, the many new steel blades made from the alien's iron ore simply did not find their way into the lands outside of Trujillo. These blades were superior to those made from local iron deposits. Slowly but surely, Augusto was setting things up for his assault upon the other two towers to "put things right."

Sitting beside Hidalgo in the driver's box, Jarek rolled up to the impressive gatehouse, the sole entrance into the heavily fortified castle-tower complex. Again, his 2-d flat geosat images failed to do this complex justice. *Man am I ever the clever field agent! If I'd of come by myself, assuming I had not gotten hopelessly lost in the process, I'd never get past those guards, not without using my blaster. The whole caravan of wagons is moving right on through without any checking. Amazing luck! Wow, this place is really quite huge! Ah, there are the buildings that are under construction I need to watch.*

He spotted the two dorm wings or manor houses attached to the sides of the five story tall tower proper. Many men and women wearing crimson robes moved around inside the castle, and the wagons moved over to the right or south to where the large stables were located. He assumed these people had something to do with the tower and the telepathic endowed people, since they had the distinctive yellow eyes. However, from his position he could not see if they all had them.

As Hidalgo pulled on the reins halting the wagon, suddenly Jarek's body froze stiff. He couldn't move a muscle or speak. Fear swept through his mind. He sensed a foreign presence of immense power that was commanding his own body, freakish. *What's going on? What's happening to me? Help! This cannot be! I can't move!* Fear gave way to utter panic, but still he could not move a muscle. His involuntary muscles did continue to function; his body was breathing and heart pumping, albeit at an alarming rate. Now he felt a foreign presence soothing his own heart, calming it down.

A voice appeared in his head. *Relax alien. You will be searched, but not harmed. Not yet anyway. You can't move, so stop trying.* Although he fought against this overwhelming control, he simply could not move a muscle. Strong arms lifted his body down and he heard a voice saying, "It's okay, Hidalgo. He's having a seizure. We will take him to the healers right away. Don't worry; he'll be all right soon."

"Take good care of him; he's a friendly sort, though awfully ignorant," Hidalgo replied.

They carried him into the southern manor house, down a hall, into a well-illuminated room, and placed onto a chair. Several men searched him, stripping off his boots and clothing. *Damn! They found the blaster! Now I am defenseless against them! Oh no, not the Navigator, now I'll never be able to find my way back to base. Shit, there's the communicator too.* Though he still fought to regain control of his body, it simply did not respond to his will any longer. Next, they found the dispatch. Just when he thought all was lost, one of the men slipped the ring off of his finger, and he knew they now knew he was both a spy and an alien. The worst possible outcome had just occurred. There would be hell to pay back at the port now. He'd utterly failed his new boss, who would be pulling his hair out trying to clean up his blunders.

Four men surrounded him; one was older and had a full beard. He spoke sternly, "We are now going to release you, alien. Do not try anything or we will not hesitate to kill you." He nodded and Jarek felt free of that vice grip control; his body slumped now under his own control. "Welcome to Castle Valen, alien Jacobo or whatever your name truly is. I am Venerado Amo Augusto Valen, leader of this castle and country. You may put your clothes back on now."

Jarek did as asked, taking the time to regain his senses, dignity, and to size up his captors. *What will they do to me? Torture me most likely.* He looked at the four faces and decided to play the only card left to him. "While I am dressing, Venerado, please read that letter. I was ordered to bring it to you."

"That is mostly true," one of the younger men announced.

"My son, Armando," Augusto indicated. "My nephew, Basilio, my cousin, Camilo. Ah, here comes Enrico, another son. You've already met him."

Enrico just entered the room with a smile. "I see you have him. Say, how did his skin suddenly get grey? His eyes too — now they are black like the Rigels."

"It happened when I pulled this ring off of his finger. Don't know what else it may do," Armando replied with a grin at his younger brother. "Well done on spotting him." Enrico flashed him a broad smile.

Augusto opened the dispatch and read it aloud.

Dear Valen Leader,

The previous Imperium Sector ID Minister has passed away and I have taken her post. I am Lech Kuba. You have my representative with you now. His name is Jarek Lajda. I have sent him out disguised so as not to raise undo suspicions of everyone that we are violating our lease agreement.

Times have changed. People too. Old agreements perhaps ought to be revisited. I would like to set up a formal meeting with you for an exchange of ideas and such. However, I don't want to include all the other leaders at this time. May I suggest a private meeting between us two rulers? Jarek has a Communicator with him and he can help us arrange a time and place.

I see no reason for our two races not to at least talk to one another and perhaps exchange even more between our cultures.

Sincerely,

Lech Kuba

Imperium Sector ID Minister

"Well, we can't tell whether this document is a forgery or not, or whether or not this Lech is speaking truthfully," Augusto added. "So we can take it at face value. Okay then, Jarek, does your ring do anything more than alter your skin color? I remind you we can tell if you are lying or not." He fingered the crystal hanging around his neck. Jarek noticed all five men's crystals were glowing a soft blue light.

"Not as far as I am aware. Lech didn't want everyone to

see that I am, as you say, an alien to your world. I am short for my race and have been working out to build up my muscles so I do not look quite as thin as my people do," he replied, carefully picking his words. Whether or not they could tell if he was lying, he didn't know. After what he'd just experienced, he was taking no chances at all. These men were both dangerous and powerful, wholly unexpected. Did Lech already know this, he wondered, or did Lech suspect as much? He had no answer at the moment.

"Okay, here, put it back on then. I agree, we want to keep your alien status from the common folk. No sense starting wild rumors," Augusto said rather dryly. He did so and the five watched the amazing transformation. Once more, he appeared to be a thin Westerlings man.

"Now then, Jarek, were you sent to spy on us, to gather information about us?" Augusto asked directly, rather ignoring the document. While he could not sense what this Lech fellow intended, he had Jarek right before him. Their *mentales* gifts would alert them to any and all lies and half-truths.

"My boss just discovered there are some curious anomalies going on around here. One is the weather. Storms are not tracking where they ought to be and are sometimes pushed off their predicted paths. The second is the stone quarrying and construction going on here. He sent me to observe how you are quarrying the stone and laying the blocks. As the dispatch suggests, Lech would like to meet with you. What he wants beyond knowing what is behind these two anomalies, I really don't know. He's only been here on Ash — er, Tierra ten days or so. He's really new and is trying to learn about your world."

Augusto glanced at the other four who merely nodded as far as Jarek could tell. *He's telling the truth,* Armando sent his father. The others concurred. Augusto then asked, "Okay, so what are these things? This is a blaster?"

"Yes, I brought it along for protection in case I ran into one of those nasty cat beasts. Careful with it, please," Jarek replied, not liking how the man was handling it, especially the nasty grin that appeared beneath the beard.

Augusto laid the weapon back down carefully. "And

this?" he held up the small Navigator.

"It is my Navigator. It shows you where you are located and which direction is which and which way you need to go to get to where you are going," he answered keeping it simple. Jarek figured these primitives would not have any idea of global positioning satellites and polar coordinates.

Enrico laughed, "So your people can't even tell which direction is which without this thing?"

"Right. It's mighty easy to get all turned around out there in those hills we traveled, Enrico. I can show you what I mean." Augusto sensed the alien meant no harm and handed it to him. He activated it and the screen illuminated, showing their 2-d map of the area. A red dot indicated his current position within Valen. A green dot indicated the spaceport. "See, I am here, the port is there. I only need to travel on a line between the two points. The scale is on the right side."

All five men burst out laughing. At last, Enrico, trying to keep from going into hysterics, explained, "That is so wrong it is not funny. You cannot go in a straight line from here to there. Were you asleep the whole three days? Using this thing, you'd end up on an impassible ridge in no time at all!" The men roared once more while Jarek's face heated up as he realized the complete uselessness of his Navigator. Enrico was right, one could not travel in a straight line in these rugged foothills. Of course, in better terrain one could.

"That's my Communicator. If you like, I can call up Lech and you can talk to him personally and arrange a meeting," Jarek suggested, hoping to get their attention off him and his foibles. This whole assignment had gone so completely wrong that he was completely embarrassed.

"Does it do anything more than communicate? Nothing harmful to us?" Basilio asked.

"No, it only allows us to talk to each other," Jarek replied. *Well, I guess I would be as paranoid as they are if the situation was reversed.* "Perfectly harmless."

Given the go ahead, Jarek turned it on. "Agent Jarek calling Minister Lech. Over." He purposely used his name and not that of Jacobo. The two had arranged this benign way of alerting Lech to an incoming call. If he used his disguise name of Jacobo, Lech would know all was well and he was reporting in. On the other hand, if he used his Rigel-3 given name, Lech would know he'd been uncovered and to be very careful what was said.

Damn him, captured already! Shit. This is not going as I had planned. "Hello Jarek. All is well with you? Lech here. Over."

"Yes, boss. I have their leader here, Venerado Amo Augusto Valen. He's read your dispatch and wishes to talk to you about the proposed meeting. Here, when you want to talk, just press this button. Release it when you are finished speaking." He handed it to Augusto.

He gingerly pressed the button and spoke rather loudly, "Hello, Lech is it? Augusto Valen here. I've read your message, though you know you are in violation of several clauses in the lease agreement."

"Hello, Augusto. May I call you that?" Lech replied diplomatically. *Well, he's right. At least a half dozen clauses just went by the boards. Still, something useful may come from it.*

"Yes, Augusto is fine for now. So you think it is time we hold private talks?"

"Yes, I do, Augusto. My predecessor kept everything under a tight lock down here. I want to be more above boards and free in our relationship. Can we meet in person?"

"That would be ideal. Exchange City, say the first of August, ten o'clock in Mac's Pub. No tricks. I will be keeping your agent here with us. If you try any treachery, Jarek will be the first to be killed," Augusto answered sternly. *I hope that is enough of a threat. I don't trust these aliens as far as I can see them.*

"Perfect. Yes, keep him. You may keep the Communicator and use it to get in touch with me when you desire," Lech added as an afterthought.

"Thanks. We're also keeping the blaster and the Navigator thing for now. See you in a few weeks."

"Right. Over and out," Lech replied, turning off his receiver. "Damn Jarek anyway. I wonder what went so terribly wrong? It was a simple assignment. Travel less than two hundred miles and observe. How did he botch that up? Well, no second guessing. I best begin preparations for the meeting. One thing I have going, this Augusto fellow did not seem too concerned over the flagrant breaking of the lease agreement. Maybe I can find out what I need to know and make this work out to my advantage anyway."

"Well, Mr. Jarek, it seems you are going to be with us for a while," Augusto said sardonically. "While the accommodations might not be what you are used to, we will treat you as our guest unless you take advantage of that status. Please continue to wear that ring of yours. It is in no one's interest to advertise you are an alien. In the meantime, I will shortly assign someone to look after you. First thing, we simply have to get you properly dressed. You cannot go around Valen in that mixed up outfit. Enrico, watch over him while I go make some arrangements for his comfort and stay. Capos, take the blaster and Navigator with you. I'll hang on to the Communicator. I assume it will be safe for me to continue to hang on to it." He looked at Jarek. "It is safe, isn't it? No treachery intended?"

"It is a Communicator, but it, like all our devices, has a tracking chip in it so its exact location on Tierra can be pin pointed, much like the red dot on the Navigator. Other than that small detail, it is just a Communicator," Jarek decided to volunteer a little information. While he suspected Lech may use that tracking chip and he ought to, since he was ultimately responsible for having their technology now in the hands of the primitives, Lech probably could not use it to harm Augusto, merely to retrieve "lost" technology. Besides, they were talking as if he would not be held prisoner. Perhaps he could still gain the information he came here to acquire. The men left, leaving Enrico watching over Jarek.

Augusto headed to the upper floor of this manor house, which, like the other, was still under construction. This whole section held his large family. He found the women in the sunlit drawing room, embroidering some new dresses and chatting about the arrival of an alien and what that might mean. His wife, Bonita, was here along with his Royal Consort, Camila, who also bore him children. Her children were officially called fosterlings. He spotted Camila's eldest daughter. "Ah, Carmen, just who I am looking for. I have an assignment for you, my fosterling daughter."

As the Venerado, it was his responsibility to arrange proper marriages for his sons, daughters, and fosterling children. Arranged meant finding just the right man or woman so their children would inherit the powerful Valen *mentales* gifts, if not adding to them. He'd already married Enrico, Armando, and Consuela — his direct heirs. His three fosterling children from Camila, his consort, were still waiting for their matches. Carmen at twenty-three was the eldest of these three and she was also the prettiest of all his daughters by either woman. In a way, he had been holding out on her, trying to find her the very best possible match. Her incredible good looks deserved that, he always told her. Now a new plan formed in his mind.

He took her into his master bedroom. "Carmen, as you know, we have an alien with us. I'm going to hold him here at least a month, maybe longer. He is not a prisoner, but one of the alien field agents sent here to observe us. Well, observation goes both ways. I want you to be his personal attendant. Take him wherever he desires to go, except of course the tower or the other manor house. No sense in disturbing the circle members. For heaven's sake, get him properly attired and do work on his awful accent. Teach him our ways, that we are a highly civilized people. Use your feminine wiles on him."

Carmen grinned mischievously. "You want me to seduce him?" she asked directly.

"If it suits your fancy, please do. If you find him worthy of you, I will give my consent to a marriage. We both know what it will mean to have an alien closely allied with us, as the Wyth Tower had in ancient times with Dita and Doctor Zosia. This is a golden opportunity, but please, only if you are attracted to him. I only want the very best for my darling Carmen."

"Yes, my father, I will do as you bid," she again smiled coyly. She always got her way ever since she was a little girl. No one could resist that sweet, angelic grin of hers. Carmen was something of an historian and knew well the benefits the old Wyth Tower got because of their two aliens who had married local men. *If nothing else, they still had their two original shuttle craft. Think of the prestige I'll have if I have an alien as my husband! This is too good to be true. I bet he is a pig! Be my luck.*

He led her down to the first floor waiting room. "Jarek, this is my fosterling daughter Carmen. She will look after your needs, accompany you where you desire to go, teach you our ways, and whatever else you desire. She has impeccable tastes in dress, so my advice to you is to follow her suggestions. I will leave you two to get acquainted. We can chat more at the dinner table. You will join us for suppers, I trust." He bowed slightly to Jarek, motioned to Enrico, and the two men left.

Dad, are you suggesting Carmen seduce him? Enrico sent him when he saw his fosterling sister enter with his father. Why else would he bring the most beautiful woman in the castle to the alien?

I told her it is her choice. If she finds him attractive, she has my permission.

Enrico grinned at his father as they walked out. *You sly devil! If that happens, we will be the only tower who now has an alien connection! Devious.*

Jarek could not believe his eyes. Carmen could have been a super model on many worlds. She had thick lustrous black hair, long and straight, falling to just below her waist. Her eyes were yellow as well, typical of those with the gift. Her face was perfectly proportioned almost to perfection. Her nose was rounded and she had thick eyebrows and long lashes to match. Her form, like all other women on Tierra, was extraordinarily shapely, with breasts somewhat larger than her head, but her waist was thin; hips, well rounded. She was physically fit. Her face held a smile that could melt any man's heart. Jarek was nearly speechless.

"I do hope you will not be disappointed with me," she said both charmingly and disarming him completely.

"Oh no, no! You are an incredibly beautiful young woman. Your husband is a very lucky man," he replied, trying hard to gain control over his swelling emotions and awe.

She gave a flirting, coy laugh. "Silly, I am not married.

Dad has not given my hand to any man as yet. Come on; let's get you properly dressed. How did you ever get into such a total mixup of clothing? That tailor ought to be assigned to the pigsty! Follow me, Jarek." She offered him her arm, which he eagerly took. *I have him now! Men! So darn predictable!* "So is your real skin grey? I'm something of an historian. I believe your race has grey skin."

He stopped before the door. Closing it, he slipped off his ring. "Here's what I really look like. The ring only gives the illusion my skin and eyes match yours." He slipped it back on, adding, "I am short for a Rigel-3 man and way too bulky. I admit I've pumped iron for some time to build up my muscles to more closely match your men."

"Pumped iron? What's that? Something you eat?" she asked, unable to make any sense of his expression. He explained as they walked out of the manor house and into the main street of Valen. She wore a colorful light brown dress very heavily embroidered with bright, gay colors. She wore tall black boots of soft, supple leather. Of course, she had a pod-silk covered crystal around her neck.

A short walk later, they arrived at an elegant tailor's shop. By now Jarek knew this woman commanded the attention of every man on the street and they knew her on sight. Her fame rubbed off on him. Many asked who her charming young man was. She continued to giggle and reply demurely he was a distant relative from the Midlands and to ignore his improper dress. "Bolivar, we need Mr. Jarek here outfitted in one of your finest suits and also a riding outfit." She turned to Jarek and said, "You do ride well don't you?"

"Yes, Miss Carmen. Right away!" the middle-aged man replied, hastily taking Jarek's measurements and politely not listening to him.

"Er, well, not exactly, Carmen, but I would like to learn to ride well. I came with Hidalgo on his wagon. Friendly man, I might add."

"Well then, Mr. Jarek, we are just going to have to do something about that, aren't we? Plus, we have to get rid of your awful accent. Honestly, can't the Midlands' folk get it right?" she chatted on.

An hour later, he looked like he belonged with royalty. His new suit fit perfectly. *I feel so different, like I belong here now or something.* His pod silk shirt was a bright red, his pants were a dark brown, his jacket matched his pants, and he had a yellow belt contrasting sharply. His boots were tall and supple, quite similar to hers.

Of course you belong. That's the whole point. Besides, now you look far more handsome, she placed into his mind, rather startling him. Bolivar handed him a wrapped parcel containing his second outfit and he thanked the tailor, but wondered how the man would be paid. *Silly, dad's already taken care of it. He sent a message to Bolivar long before we left the manor house.*

"Come on; let's go for a walk and I'll show you around the castle proper. What is it you really came here to see?" she asked.

She was obviously pumping him for information, but he went along with it, since what he had to say was pretty much what he'd already said to Augusto. "We noticed large stones were being quarried, lifted up, transported from the quarry to the buildings under construction, that is your manor houses, and laid in place, but we saw no actual workers doing all this. Rather like magic or something. I was asked to come here and see if that is for real and, if so, how it is done."

"Okay, no real mystery there. Come on. I know a balcony where you can watch it and that place is not off limits to us." Again, she took his arm and led the way back into the castle complex. She took him up to the third floor and then on out onto an eastern-facing balcony. "Here we go. You can see the quarry there in the distance and look over there. Here comes another block now. Watch, it will be laid with perfect precision right up there." She pointed and he watched in awe as a huge block, perhaps three feet by two feet by one foot floated overhead, coming down onto the fourth floor wall.

"How can this be? Magic?" he asked again, pumping her for details. It was happening exactly as the constructed time lapsed images he'd seen; seemingly no human hands were at work here.

"The Capo uses the psi energies of his group to cut the

stone block free, move it into position, and set it. So simple really, a child could do it. It saves a bundle on the cost and time it takes to build the manor houses and it avoids all those accidents that harm stone masons and other workers. Safer really. It's the least we can do for our people who provide for us. Come on. We ought to go inside; it is going to rain soon. It often rains in the afternoons around here. Of course, in the winter, it's snow. We are snowed in here in Valen for some of the winter months. That's when we have our big festivals and parties. You do like to party don't you?" she fluttered her eyes and gave him a coy grin.

"Well, I've not had much time for parties. On the base, it has been all work mostly. Ah, that's not exactly true, Carmen. Try boring. I've had little to do for years now. I'm a trained field agent. I'm supposed to go out among the population and observe and gather intelligence."

"Oh how exciting. What kind of intelligence? How many soldiers and such?" she asked disarmingly.

"Soldiers, well yes, but rarely. No, the Imperium wants and needs to know how countries and their people are doing. How much excess food is available this year? How much ore could be mined if they had more workers? Then, there are the more exciting things like who is fomenting rebellions and who is planning a government coup? Those can be more interesting."

"So why is your Imperium interested in us? Per the lease, they are not allowed to bring in more food to help us from starving," she asked cleverly.

"That's true. I think it is because in the eyes of the Imperium, your people are seen to be very primitive and not technologically advanced. Hence, rather than totally destroying all your culture and civilization, they refuse to bring in technology your people could neither understand nor operate properly."

"Do I seem primitive to you? My, I wonder what your women must look like to not have that label," she replied in a coy, teasing manner.

"Oh no, not really, Carmen. It's clothes or the style of clothes you wear."

"Do I not look attractive to you? What is the difference in clothes anyway?"

Jarek felt his foot in his mouth. "Oh no, no, you are gorgeous. Well, clothes are not so important. It's reading and writing."

"Hey, I can read and write. So can most of us in the castle." She put her hands on her hips in a sexy-looking protest.

"His face was now really red and she enjoyed his discomfort. "Well, that's not it exactly either. I mean you don't have a proper education, mathematics, science, engineering. You don't know how far it is from here to the spaceport, for example."

"Ha!" She closed her eyes and focused. A moment later, she opened them, "Exactly one hundred seventy-six miles and fifty-two feet from where I am standing to the edge of your port. I just measured it."

Now his face was even redder. "Well, if you have a right triangle that is three feet on one side and four on the other side, what is the length of the longer side? That's geometry."

Again, she closed her eyes and focused. "Ah, five feet. I just measured it. But I admit I don't know how your spaceships fly or even your aerial cars or shuttles as you call them. I don't know how your blaster works. So does that make me any less?"

"Well, not really. You don't have any roads, no cars or trucks. You get from place to place on horses, wagons, and carriages. That's primitive by Imperium standards."

"Ah, but we don't have much metal on this planet to build such things. So that counts against us?" she asked, again flashing him her irresistible smile.

"Well, no it shouldn't, not really. I can see your point. You haven't developed space travel to the thousands of worlds out there."

"That's true. So your Imperium classifies any world that doesn't have spaceships as primitive?"

He sighed, "When it comes down to it, you are probably right. No space travel equals primitive cultures, I suppose. Not too fair is it? Your world couldn't develop nuclears either. No heavy metals. I admit your people are pretty constrained here."

"Couldn't that stuff be imported from a planet, which has them in abundance?" she asked.

"Sure, but what would you trade for them? Barter. Things of equal value to both sides. You are doing a small trade in various furs, but there is only a small intergalactic market for them. Likewise with your copper vessels, they are quaint, but there's not much of a market for such things." Then his mind struck upon the singularly valuable commodity Tierra had: psi-crystals, which, when refined, produced very high grade fuel for the Imperium's fleet of ships. Carmen picked up his thought, though she didn't reveal she had. *I'll let dad know that detail!*

"What about our telepathic abilities?" Carmen decided to probe him a bit.

"Well, throughout the galaxy, telepaths are really rare. From what I can tell, they are commonplace on Tierra. Now if you wanted to barter your telepathic people to the Imperium, I suppose you could garner top dollar for them."

"But isn't that more like slavery?" Carmen asked, knowing full well it was.

"Yes, I suppose so, though perhaps a few would like to trade their services for material things and a life off of this world. I think that is why the previous Sector ID Minister, Ania Anka, kept the fact Tierra had a lot of telepaths out of common Imperial knowledge."

"She should have. Honestly, after nearly destroying our world and then not making it right again, it's the least she could do. We'd of all perished if it had not been for us telepaths working together to make things better for our people," Carmen lectured him a little.

"That's why my boss is going slowly. He wants to know what the true nature of your telepathic skills is so he can protect you all better, I think." He added that last for her sake. He had no idea of the motives of Lech; he'd only recently met him.

"So tell me, have you got a girlfriend back at the spaceport?" Carmen asked, changing the subject to one, which interested her more.

"Not really. I've been pretty much a loner. My parents were killed in an accident when I was five. I was raised in an Imperium orphanage and got good schooling there. I excelled at observational skills and was told I'd make a good field agent. So I signed up and here I am. I admit I was terribly disappointed to find out I could not observe beyond Exchange City. I leapt at this chance to really get out and explore your world."

"Glad that you did, Jarek. Say, do you dance?"

"What?" he asked, slightly confused. "No, why?"

"Well, then I am simply going to have to teach you how along with everything else. Tomorrow, you are going to get your first lesson in horse riding. I'm a good rider, dad says so."

A few days later, Augusto met privately with his daughter. "Carmen, you've been doing a fine job with our alien Jarek. Thank you. So what do you think about him? Is he marrying material for you?"

"Thanks dad. He's an orphan and has been pretty much on his own his whole life. He doesn't have much allegiance to anyone or any place. He's naive with women but I think he'd make a good husband. We've been making sure there is a respectable amount of psi-dust in his food, so there is a chance he'll also develop the *mentales* gift, but as you know, that takes time. He's a wealth of information on the Imperium too, dad. I think the only people who really know about our *mentales* gifts are his boss and those few field agents he's entrusted missions to. He sent out a female agent to the Midlands at the same time that Jarek came here. So do I get to have him?"

"Are you sure you want this? He is an alien after all," he asked politely. *My god, if she marries him and if I can get her into their spaceport, then the key information she can obtain for us is beyond imagination. Besides, it opens the door to further relations, especially if I can find a way to keep it between this Lech fellow and the rest of the Imperium.*

"Oh sure dad. He's rather plain looking, but other than that, he's really a nice man. I could do far, far worse. Besides, I want to get married; you know that. I don't want to become an old maid, after all!" She put her hands on her hips and gave him her disarming, charming smile, one that never failed to melt the old man.

"Okay, then, let's see if we can get him willing to marry you." She relaxed, her plans were coming to fruition. If she could pull this off, she would enter a position of extreme power for a woman of Valen, far more so than her consort mother or Augusto's wedded wife. Carmen wanted power and respect, far more respect than she had as a fosterling daughter of a consort mother. She also wanted something else. She'd seen an image in Jarek's mind of Lech's wife, Karolina. She ached to obtain dresses and shoes like those this elegant woman she wore. At night, she imagined how she would look dolled up like that man's wife. Somehow, someway, she was going to get them.

Chapter 4 Deals

Carmen got her wish. Two days before they had to leave for Exchange City and the big meeting, she got Jarek to propose to her. A pleased Augusto made the arrangements for the trip based on this potential. Lech was more than willing to bring his wife to the meeting since Augusto would bring his wife and consort as well. He didn't mention the marriage proposal yet; he'd spring that one on the Sector ID Minister.

All rode their horses this trip because Augusto wanted speed in case of trouble. However, they also brought along numerous packhorses. Jarek, now a fairly good rider, rode beside Carmen, chatting about how they knew which way was the best route to travel. All wore their oiled rain cloaks, which were needed to fend off the late afternoon thunderstorms. Augusto brought along a hundred soldiers along with Enrico and his personal guards.

However, Augusto was very cagy. Knowing the Communicator could be used to locate his precise position, he took appropriate precautions. He didn't trust this Lech fellow, since he'd already unilaterally broken the lease treaty by sending a covert spy into his land. The meeting Lech agreed to was in Exchange City on the first of August at ten o'clock in Mac's Pub. The hour was such to give the women time to change into their formal dresses and look their best. The men too wanted to change from their trail clothing. However, Augusto secretly arranged for the meeting to be held at Ernie's Pub, three blocks away. This change he did not relay to Lech. The last night out, he handed off the Communicator to a guard, along with specific orders to be followed the next morning.

They arrived in Exchange City very early in the morning. While Augusto and his party headed for Ernie's Pub to change and get ready for the meeting, some of his soldiers fanned out and kept Mac's Pub under surveillance in case this was some kind of trap. Enrico and his private guards took up positions in and around Ernie's Pub. At five until ten that morning, the soldier walked into Mac's Pub, where he saw the aliens waiting somewhat anxiously for the Valen leader. "Are you Lech Kuba?" he asked.

"Yes, where's Augusto? It's almost time," Lech replied a little annoyed.

"Slight change of plans. For security reasons, the meeting will be held down at Ernie's Pub, three blocks south of here. I can escort you there if you do not know the way. Augusto and his party await you, sir."

"Damn, I hate change of plans. Okay, lead on soldier." Lech gave his arm to Karolina and they walked out of the pub. He hated to leave all his extensive preparations behind. He had installed five recorders to record everything that was said at the meeting, both audio and video. He'd put five agents in there disguised as waiters. He had another five milling around outside. *Well, I won't underestimate this Augusto again,* he vowed. It was a short walk to the alternate location, and he insisted on five of his agents accompany him as the two entered Ernie's Pub.

"Welcome Sector ID Minister Lech. I am Venerado Amo Augusto Valen, my wife, Ama Bonita, my Royal Consort, Camila, and our fosterling daughter, Carmen," he said, rising to his feet and offering the alien his hand. The older man looked impressive with his full beard and fine, gay-colored suit. The women were dressed similarly, wearing their most expensive pod-silk dresses, again in gay, bright colors, heavily embroidered. Jarek was standing next to Carmen and covertly holding her hand.

In contrast, Lech wore his finest business suit, a grey tweed pattern and polished black boots. At his side, Karolina wore her finest, light-blue, silk dress that fit tightly, following her every curve down to just below her knees, where her black nylon hose continued down to her black six inch spiked heels. Her dress was low cut and already had been altered slightly. Her breasts had begun to grow. She, however, stared at the enormous bosoms the other three women had, wondering how soon she'd look like they now did and whether or not she would like hers being that large.

"It is good to meet face to face, Augusto. May I call you

that? Ladies," Lech began, nodding respectfully to the three women. *Heavens, they have two wives in this land! Jarek looks none the worse for wear.*

They exchanged pleasantries for a few minutes before getting down to business. "We ought to have a regular exchange or meetings. We've kept our distance for a century and it's high time we learn more about you and your people. After all, I am responsible for the security of this planetary system," Lech suggested.

"Oh, I couldn't agree more with you. To that end, I have a proposal for you. It seems my fosterling daughter has fallen for your agent, Jarek, and he's proposed marriage." He watched as his intended bombshell struck.

"What? Jarek? Are you serious? You want to marry Carmen?"

"Absolutely, sir. She's a fantastic woman. I've gotten Augusto's permission, subject to yours, of course."

"Well, I can see why. Carmen, you are a very beautiful young woman indeed," Lech stalled for time to absorb this unexpected development. *Married to Augusto's daughter? Incredible luck. This is almost too good to be true! I'd have an inside track on the goings on in Valen at the very least! Jarek, you are making up for your mission failure.* "Well, there is no reason why they cannot marry, Augusto, if that is their wish. Of course, Carmen would then be granted Imperium citizenship as would their children."

"I would not expect anything less for her. Their children would also have Valen citizenship. I would expect the young couple would be spending part of each year at my court in Valen, and then spend part of each year here in your spaceport. I realize Jarek is in your employ, but if you will allow the young couple to spend part of each year in Valen, I will treat him as my fosterling son and teach him our ways and what else he might wish to learn."

"Oh, well, yes, yes, that would be ideal. I can spare him from the spaceport at least half of the year. It would bind our races closer, no doubt about that. Of course, he would need his Communicator and other devices to keep in touch with me while he is out in the field."

"Of course, it has already been returned to him. Jarek has been telling me what you really wanted to know about our *mentales* gifts. Might I suggest the women get together and discuss things of interest to them, while you and I discuss how we may assist each other?" Augusto cleverly moved the conversation in the direction he desired. He knew Carmen wanted a chance to talk privately with Karolina, and he wanted to go over the minister's request for key documents. The fewer who knew such details the better.

The women moved over to one side, giving the three men some privacy. Enrico, his guards, and those of Lech remained way over by the entrance, while the barkeeper began serving mugs of ale. "So you have captured the heart of our Jarek, Carmen. I can see why, you are extremely attractive," Karolina began.

"Thanks, but I truly love your dress and shoes. I'd give anything to have some similar outfits. We have nothing like them in Valen," Carmen replied. "I was so surprised when Jarek told me about your clothes. I am something of an historian and I thought all you Rigels wore those funny looking suits."

Karolina chuckled, "Cat suits, they are called. Hideous things. They smell and are so cheaply made you don't even bother to wash them when they get dirty. Just toss them in the recycle bin. No, I can't stand those Imperium outfits. Never could. Me personally, I go in for quality clothing and heels. You cannot beat a well-made, leather heel. I am so very pleased to meet another woman who shares my sentiments, though your dresses are very pretty in their own quaint way. If you get married to Jarek, I will see you get several complete outfits, my wedding present to you. Please wear them when you are around the spaceport, join me in attracting all eyes upon us. So many wear those awful cat suits it is not funny. I'll enjoy the company."

"Thank you ever so much. I most certainly will wear them, never those awful looking cat suits. Is there anything I can help you with?" Carmen asked, knowing full well there might be. She was picking up the alien's surface thoughts.

"Well, maybe so. I am a Galactic Meteorologist. That is,

I study weather patterns on many worlds. The idea is to be able to predict the weather, especially severe weather, in time to give warning to those who will be affected by tornados and monsoons. I am very good at it, never missing them, that is, until I came to Tierra. I've been studying your weather patterns and storms. Sometimes a storm takes a completely wrong path. I've spent all month studying the planetary forces in play and there is no way they should be following the path that some have. I call them anomalies. I've heard some of your people can control the path storms take. I'd really like to know how they can do that. So anything you can tell me or help me with that would be very much appreciated." She lowered her voice a little, "Also, your breasts. They are so huge and I'm told mine will also get huge and they are already nearly double what they were when I came here." She asked more personal things about them and Carmen was only too happy to answer her honestly.

Then she returned to Karolina's original request, "Yes, some of us can control the weather, moving a storm a different way. However, there is always a down side. While you are depriving your area of the rain, you are also giving that rain to some other area and that can cause them problems. So it is a tradeoff. We use it to help keep things on as even a keel as we possibly can." She explained a little more about it.

Next, Karolina whispered, "If you don't mind my asking, what's it like being a telepath and all that?" Carmen grinned and the two chatted even more intimately. Then Carmen had another thought, but kept this one to herself. She would put it into play when she was finally spending time here with Karolina at the spaceport.

"You see, to really understand your society and your towers, I really do need to know just what types and forms your *mentales* gifts take," Lech laid his cards out openly. After all, the yellow eyes of Augusto told him the man could read his mind anyway. "I've heard of this catalog of the gifts done nearly a century ago by some woman named Marisol. If I could get my hands on a copy, I could see better how extensive this gift actually is and how best to protect you from those in the Imperium who might wish to exploit you for them."

"The problem I have with that is what could possibly happen if that information went beyond you. While I trust you would not misuse it, I can see where others above you might want to come here and kidnap some of us and force us to use our gifts for their benefits. I cannot allow that to happen. If I could have an unbreakable pledge from you that you would return the copy to me and not allow the information to go beyond yourself and your wife, I could see my way to allowing that to happen, but I would need to have some ironclad safeguards built into such a deal," Augusto began to bargain.

"Oh, I assure you I would comply with those restrictions," Lech said hastily trying to mask his greediness over getting access to such confidential data.

"If shall we say some two dozen of your blasters, fully operational mind you, should somehow appear in my court in Valen, then I would have something with which to counter any possible breakage of our agreement over Marisol's book," Augusto suggested, completely masking his eagerness to get his hands on some. He added, "In the future, I can see no reasons why we cannot make other deals on the side. No one would be the wiser, eh?"

"Er, right. I can make a dozen of them disappear from our extensive stock. I'll send them along with Jarek. If they should ever be discovered, they cannot be traced back to me, though, just to the station here. One other small thing, is there a manual or rule book a new *mentales* gifted person is given or trained with?"

"Absolutely. I will see you also get a copy of that, Lech. Now one more thing, I hate to do this, but I simply must. You will understand, I would expect you would take similar precautions as well. If the Imperium does find out about the extent of our telepathic abilities and come here to kidnap our people and take them away to serve their kidnappers, you will experience a great loss of your spaceships. You see, we can very easily give the ships that are landing or taking off a shove in the wrong direction at the wrong time, resulting in a catastrophic crash and destruction of said ship."

Lech could not hide his awe and concern. "You, you can do that?" Augusto nodded. "Don't worry. I will not divulge the information. I'm just glad you didn't ask for a shuttle craft. I cannot hide the disappearance of something that big." The two men chuckled.

"I would love to have one, but I knew that would be an insurmountable problem. No, we are in the process of developing one ourselves."

"You are? Incredible. I'd like to see that when you get it working," Lech replied. His impression of Augusto continued to rise. Perhaps he'd been grossly underestimating these people. Just possibly these people were not primitives at all! The two discussed more details and then got back to the wedding details.

"We ought to have one of our Imperium ministers in attendance to validate the marriage," Lech explained. "How soon were they planning to wed?"

"Perhaps the smart move would be to hold the ceremony here in Exchange City soon. That would rouse far less suspicions. After that, they could return with me for another month and a half. By mid-September, the snows can pose travel difficulties. They could spend the winter here at your facilities, returning to Valen in the spring." *That would give Carmen time to execute her plans. If they only knew what she had in mind. Well, I'll give her credit; she's one clever and devious woman. Chip off the old block if I do say so myself.*

"Hey, I like that idea. Let's see if we can arrange it quickly." *I sure as hell don't want to miss this golden opportunity!*

A day later, the young couple was married in the traditional manner by a Westerlings Church of God priest in Exchange City. An official from the Spaceport bore witness and signed Carmen's papers making her an official citizen of the Imperium. After that, Augusto was given a small demonstration and training session at the spaceport on the care and usage of a blaster. When they departed on the fifth of August for Valen, two dozen blasters were packed in saddlebags and overseen by Jarek. Lech had his two coveted books; unfortunately, they were written in the Westerlings language, and he had to spend some days translating them.

Carmen was promised complete outfits would be waiting for her when she returned in six weeks, compliments of Karolina. Thus, for all concerned, this meeting of the races went extraordinarily well, for the moment at least.

Carmen continued her covert operation on the side, both known and approved by Augusto himself. She was putting a rather large dose of psi-dust into all the food Jarek ate. When she returned to the spaceport, she brought along more of it and began putting it into Karolina's food as well. Her objective was somehow to bring on the *mentales* gifts in both of them. In his case, she really didn't want a head blind husband, if she could do something about it. Besides, if he received the gift, then he would be even more obligated to them. With Karolina, she was being both kind and clever at the same time. She wanted to become good friends with this exceptionally beautiful and powerful alien. What better way than for her to have the *mentales* gift as well? She'd fit right in with Carmen and the people of Tierra. Also, it would help Karolina in understanding how storm paths could be changed, something Carmen found was consuming much of the woman's everyday thoughts and work. However, Augusto insisted she also bring along a supply of *bacal* leaves, just in case they underwent a bout of Verge Sickness. Neither had any idea if this would work or how soon.

When they arrived back at Valen, much to Jarek's surprise, he and Carmen found their new suite was already prepared for them. Occupying five rooms on the northeastern quarter of the second floor of the manor house, their rooms were freshly redone and smelled heavily of polish. "Oh my, dad is treating you with great honor, Jarek! We've got a whole suite to ourselves," Carmen explained rather excited about the sudden change. Before, she'd shared a room with her younger sister, Emiliana, but now she had spacious quarters. She had her own large drawing room and even a large living room where they could entertain guests. Examining the closets, Jarek discovered he now possessed six fine suits and an equal number of everyday riding outfits.

After getting settled in, Enrico came by. "Time for sword practice, Jarek. Dad wants you to be able to defend yourself well. Come on. I'll take you to our sword master. He'd quite good." When he returned a couple hours later, he complained, "I've got more aching muscles than I ever knew I had!"

"Oh come here, silly man. That's why you have a wife to care for you," Carmen teased him. To his great pleasure, she gave him a massage that left him totally relaxed and pain-free. She, of course, used a bit of her Regulator skills on his body, soothing out overloaded nerve channels and muscle tensions. Soon, he came to treasure her daily sessions with him. Before long, Jarek realized Augusto was indeed treating him more like a son and he felt very pleased. Until now, no one had shown him any real, honest affection, and by the time they had to leave for the spaceport, he began thinking of Augusto more as a foster father than Carmen's dad.

"Son, while you are at your spaceport, you ought to bone up on historical battles. One day, we may find ourselves at war with other towers, and I could use some good battle strategies," Augusto planted the idea into his mind.

"Sure, sir. I have computer access and can study every known battle on all the planets of the Imperium. It will give me something to do besides being mostly bored there. Thanks," Jarek replied, genuinely pleased to have a new goal and one that would give back something for all the older man's kindness he'd shown him.

Also during these six weeks, Jarek began teaching Carmen to read, write, and speak Imperial Standard. Once they returned, she would need it, because only a few at the port spoke crude Westerlings dialect and those were almost exclusively the field agents. True, one could go around wearing one of the squawk boxes, the ULAT, the universal language translators, but he just couldn't see her using one. When they arrived, she could read and carry on a basic conversation and knew she had to learn their language in a big hurry. Still, she could fall back on her telepathy to catch the ideas a person was thinking, but she also had to make herself understood. This was her biggest worry as they arrived. She would soon have far more worries.

Enrico and his group of guards escorted them to the

southwestern edge of the sprawling spaceport. Here there was a side entrance and the security forces were expecting them. After loading their things on an electric cart, Enrico took their horses on into Exchange City where they would be boarded until the spring. Carmen insisted she had a horse at hand, if she needed to leave the spaceport and Augusto agreed with her. Still, he was uneasy over her well-being so far out of his reach. Augusto had always been very protective of his own children and fosterlings.

On the drive across the seemingly endless stretch of concrete filled with spaceships of various designs, some landing and taking off, Carmen began to feel like she was entering an alien world. Indeed, here on the Plateau Grado, it was basically an alien world. Everything was set up to Imperium Standards for the convenience of the many off-world pilots, personnel, and passengers who came and went. If one examined every other spaceport on the many worlds of the Imperium, one could tell little differences between them, save this one had a particularly spectacular view of the mountains. Both looked out of place in their native clothes; every man and woman they saw wore the unisex, form fitting cat suits, which drew even more attention to the base's women and their enormous breasts. Nothing was left to the imagination in them. Carmen was very thankful Karolina had some "real dresses" waiting her.

Because her IS (Imperium Standard) was so poor, Jarek accompanied her as she went through all manner of arrival events. First stop was at the ID center, where she was photographed, fingerprinted, and a retinal scan done. The result of all that was spewed out of a machine: her ID card, which he explained would allow her to gain access to various places on the base. Next, she visited the medical center where she was stripped and given a thorough examination, culminating in another large printout that meant nothing to her. Jarek simply said everyone went through this and that the doctors said she was in perfect health. And so it went for a crazy two hours. At long last, he led her up to the twentieth floor to Lech's main office.

"Ah, here you are at last. Welcome, welcome, Carmen,

Jarek. I have taken the liberty of getting you appropriate new quarters, Jarek. You have suite 9D on the floor below us in the dormitory building attached to this building. The elevator is close at hand. I figure Karolina and Carmen will be going back and forth frequently visiting each other. It seems Karolina has taken a fancy to you, Carmen. I can see why. If you dress like my wife, you will attract the attention of every man on the base just as she does. Anyway, your bags were taken there and your ID badge will open your door. Have you explained to her she must carry her badge on her person at all times? That it is used to open the many doors around here?"

"We haven't gotten to all that yet, sir."

"Well, see to it. Again, welcome Carmen. I know Karolina is anxiously awaiting you, so come on. I'll take you to your new suite and then show you how to take the elevator up to our suite," Lech said eagerly. *As soon as she gets settled in, I need to have her help me translate these documents. What a hassle; here I have finally gotten them and can barely read them.* This, Carmen picked up and smiled at him, though she said nothing.

"Oh here you are, Carmen! I'm so excited and glad you are *finally* here. Lech, dear, do leave us women alone for this afternoon. Find something for Jarek to do as well. Go play pool or something." Karolina was very good at manipulating her husband, and Carmen didn't need telepathy to notice this. He hastily took Jarek into a side room, his private game room, much impressing Jarek who had never had this much personal attention from his bosses before.

"Never wear the same dress and shoes a second time until they have had a week's rest. That's the rule to follow with these extremely high quality leather shoes and silk dresses. Treat them with tender loving care and they will treat you well, that's my motto. So few women pay any real attention to their appearance. It's so disgusting. Now back on my planet, I ran in a circle of like-minded women, and we always took great pride in our appearance, just as you do, Carmen. If you have pride in your appearance and look your very best, then you have confidence in yourself as well. With that in mind, I am afraid I splurged a little on your behalf. Okay, okay, I admit I padded the order some. I just could not pass up adding some of the new heels to my collection and a few dresses as well. But honestly, Carmen, I must apologize. I look awful now. My breasts have grown considerably, and I can't find anyone who can alter them properly."

"Hey, I can sew very well, Karolina. I see what you mean, that's easily fixed. Let me do your alterations for you. Please, it is the least I can do for you. It must be terribly hard for you suddenly to find your breasts growing so much. Here, we just take it for granted they are going to become melons. Still, I kept outgrowing my dresses every six months when I was a teenager."

Carmen soon looked over a dozen new dresses in various colors and shapes. All were a good fit, since Karolina had taken her measurements during their first meeting in the pub. Each dress had a set of matching heels to go with them. A few heels were five inches, but most were like Karolina's, six inches tall. Although no two pairs were identical, each was made from the highest quality leather and craftsmanship.

If this were not enough, Karolina also took the liberty to purchase a case of cosmetics for Carmen along with purses to match the dresses. Of course, she had to teach Carmen how to apply them and now Carmen saw a purpose for the purses. Normally, she carried her few things in a small bag whose leather straps she kept fastened around her wrist. After getting Carmen appropriately dressed and her makeup done, Karolina then showed her off to the two men who were shooting pool. Carmen sensed the arousal of both men and smiled demurely, now absolutely certain of the effect she was creating on men. Carmen's motto: Why use the Command Voice when I can accomplish the same thing with the clothes I wear? She knew Karolina felt the same way.

The first few days were the worst for Carmen who was grateful Jarek seldom left her alone. Until she finally realized she could use a map of the spaceport and its buildings, she felt completely lost, though she always knew which direction was which, just not where anything was located. In their suite, she had to be shown how to operate everything. The bathroom facilities were a total mystery to her, especially the machine that formed the everyday cat suits around their bodies. At least that was one machine she dispensed with entirely, preferring to wear the real clothing Karolina provided her. Nothing was familiar at all. "I'm a horse trying to swim in an ocean," she tried to explain to him. *But I'll be damned if I am going to let this defeat me. I am not a primitive! I have to show him I am not!* Fortunately, Lech was all too familiar with culture shock and had allowed for this. That is why he allowed Jarek to spend nearly all his time with her this first week.

Perhaps the worst part of the initial experience was the sterile odor of the recycled air. Everywhere she went, room by room, the disinfectant smell was present: no resinous pine, no grass, not even the smell of unchanged chamber pots. She laughed as she found herself wishing for that last odor. Quickly, she fell into a routine.

Mornings she spent on the computer learning the IS. She was determined to read, write, and speak the alien's language fluently or die trying. Afternoons she spent with Karolina, at first making the needed alterations to her many dresses. Karolina did take her advice and had her only alter the seven dresses she intended to wear that week. "Look, when I was a teen, they seemed to grow enough each week so mom had to continually enlarge the tops. That was what she came up with — to just do the ones I would be wearing each week."

"Really? Well, that does seem like a plan. They do hurt so. Did yours hurt too?" Karolina admitted and asked.

"Yes. Here, let me show you how to alleviate it a little," Carmen volunteered. She removed Karolina's top and slowly massaged them, demonstrating the technique she'd found to relieve their nearly constant pressure-like pain.

Karolina sighed, "Oh, what a relief! I haven't felt this good since they started growing. You have a healing touch, Carmen. Soft and gentle. Thank you, thank you." A bit later, fastening her blouse shut, she added, "You know, I've been going over the medical records of all the women on the base. Based on when mine started to grow, I think it will be over in another two weeks or so. God, I hope so anyway. Can you give me one of your massages each day? It is helping so much." Carmen smiled and agreed.

"If yours get as big as the rest of us," Carmen pointed out, "we will have a problem altering all your dresses and tops. There isn't enough material in the seams to handle knockers like mine."

Karolina looked positively crushed. "I suspected that, Carmen, but I kept telling myself they wouldn't get that big. All my dresses will be ruined. What am I going to do? I do so hate those disposable cat suits."

"I know, we get creative, Karolina. We take one dress and use its fabric in the other's alterations. We just need to get the colors to blend appropriately. Come on; let's go sort out all your outfits and see what we can devise. We need a plan of action." That boosted her spirits and they set to work. In the end, Carmen did manage to accomplish the feat and Karolina's many outfits were altered to fit her new bust size, and they looked as if they had been designed to do that in the first place.

"Honestly, Carmen, you ought to be a dress designer. You have a knack for this and you could make a fortune. I know, why don't we set up a custom dress design company — you and I? I know the market and can handle the off-world sales aspects; you design and make the dresses. Really, there is not too much weather study work I have to do here. My predecessors have already worked out the prediction programs and all I have to do is monitor the occasional anomalies when they occur. What say you?" Carmen agreed tentatively.

By November, Carmen had their language down well; she was a fast learner, though the highly efficient computer system greatly aided her, as she later thought about her rapid progress. It noted what she knew, what she didn't, what she was uncertain about, and avoided needless repetition of words she already had down. She also began designing a few dresses, based heavily upon Karolina's tastes, figuring she knew what other women would desire, off-worlder's that is.

She continued her covert insertion of the psi dust into both Jarek and Karolina's food or drink, in the case of Karolina. In actual fact, relatively few people had ever been fed psi dust in an attempt to induce the *mentales* gifts in them. Ancient logs in the tower had suggested the psi dust from the alien refinery had caused the massive outbreak of the *mentales* gifts, particularly so since there were far more people who had the gift here near Plateau Grado than in the more distant areas. The Easterlings, for example, had very few with the gift. Likewise, along the western coast of the Westerlings, there were few who had it. The heaviest concentrations lay in the lands near the explosion and refinery site proper. Still, Augusto had experimented with this, and a few who did not have the gift eventually did so, once enough psi dust had been ingested. Still, Carmen had no clear models to follow, but she persevered with her covert project.

In late November, it worked. One morning, Jarek awoke with a high fever. "I've come down with something, dear. I'll go to the medical center first thing."

"My love, if they don't know what's wrong, promise me to come back here right away. I am a healer, you know. I don't want them doing crazy things to you," Carmen pleaded with him. He discovered he was so weak and dizzy that he couldn't make it there on his own. Hence, Carmen dressed quickly and helped him go down to the center. She had to sit in a waiting area while the doctors and nurses used their many machines on him.

At last, a doctor came to her. "You are his wife, right?" She nodded and asked what was wrong with him. "Well, we just don't know at this point. Whatever bug he has is not in our medical databases. We're giving him a general antibiotic and we will see how that goes." He looked even worse when they brought him back to her. She struggled to get him back to their suite, but she was determined not to ask for help.

Once there, she put him to bed and quickly brewed some *bacal* tea. Though she was not an expert, he did look like he had come down with Verge Sickness and if so, the tea would help. After getting him to sip the bitter tea, she waited nervously. All manner of crazy thoughts ran through her head. What if he really had contracted some unknown disease? What if he was allergic to something here on Tierra? Would they make him move off-world? She knew she simply could not leave her world behind. A very long half hour later, he began to relax and Carmen breathed a huge sigh of relief. He had the Verge Sickness and that meant he now had a *mentales* gift!

83

She nursed him for two days, turning away the doctors who tried to stop by and check on him. "I'm caring for him and he is getting better, so leave us alone." She was most insistent.

On the fifth day, he awoke feeling fine once more. "Boy, was I ever sick. I've never been that ill in my life. I wonder what I contracted?" Carmen woke up and leaned over to look at his face full of stubble; he needed a shave. A broad grin greeted his alert eyes. "What?" he asked sheepishly.

"Your eyes have turned yellow, my love," she said quietly but with a proud tone in it.

"What? Yellow? Can't be, can it?" he shot out of bed and looked in their full-length mirror. Rubbing his eyes, he exclaimed, "My god! They are yellow, just like yours. Does that mean. . ."

Yes, my love. You are now one of us, a telepath. You have the mentales gift as well.

Incredible! I do! I can hear you. Can you hear me?

Of course, loud and clear. You have much to learn now, dear. It is good you have me with you. I can teach you what you need to know. She did just that. *You need to quickly learn how to Block Your Thoughts and to Dampen Out Other's Thoughts or you can go crazy when you are in a crowd of people and hearing everyone's thoughts at the same time.*

Later that day, he reported to Lech who was shocked to discover his field agent had become a telepath in his own right. After recovering from the surprise, he began to see how utterly more valuable his field agent had just become and doubled his yearly salary as a reward. Carmen told him, "My people at the tower will work with him this spring and get him skilled with whatever form his gift takes as well as providing him with his own amplifying crystal like mine. No, it costs nothing; it is our obligation to do this for anyone who gets the gift."

Mid-December, Karolina also came down with the Verge Sickness. Again, Carmen intervened when the medical staff could not pin down her illness. By now, they learned Jarek had had the local Verge Sickness as his telepathic abilities appeared. This time, they studied the effects of the illness on Karolina, while allowing Carmen to work her cure.

A week later, Karolina was well again and looking at her eyes in her mirror. Lech had long gone off to work and Carmen was staying by her side, as she had been for the entire week. *Well, the yellow does go well with my black hair and grey skin. It could be worse and be orange or something.*

Of course, you look as radiant and beautiful as always. Only now, you will be even more you. Your senses will be heightened, especially when you have sex with Lech.

She flushed, *Really?*

Really. You will be in a close rapport with him and it will be the most intimate thing imaginable, second only to what it would be if he too were a telepath.

I don't believe it. How can it be?

The slightest touch will drive you mad with desire. I'll show you. Carmen's fingers ran ever so lightly down the sides of her mammoth breasts causing Karolina to moan in an ecstasy she'd never known possible. Before long, both women were in a deep rapport with each other, sharing an extremely intimate round of pleasure with each other's bodies.

I've never done this with a woman before. I am rather embarrassed by it.

I know. I know as you know, but among telepaths, this is quite common. We share and give pleasure where we can. Now you can compare this to what you experience with Lech. You and I can share something that he cannot. You will see. Of course, you must come with Jarek and me to Valen in the spring. We will get you both trained to use your new skills properly and give you your own crystal too. It won't take too long, maybe a couple of weeks.

I don't know what to say but thank you Carmen. I do love you so.

I love you as well. We can do this as often as we desire. Let's!

When Lech discovered his own wife had now become a telepath with the *mentales* gift, he was overjoyed. *Now I have two with me! Incredible and extremely valuable. What a wife I have!* He eagerly arranged for her to travel with them in the spring. Then he had another thought. If he took her there now in a shuttle craft, she could be trained months sooner, Jarek too. He used the Communicator and discussed this incredible turn of events with Augusto, who did not tell him that he long ago knew about both of them from Carmen.

"Certainly, I agree. Secrecy is vital. Come at night. If you can really home in on this communication device, then I will leave it out in the open courtyard where you can land your ship. We cannot say how long it will take, but usually basic training seldom takes more than a couple of weeks. To get them fully adept with whatever gifts they might have, now that takes far longer and is highly variable. We can do what we can and report back. If it will take too long, we can postpone the more advanced training until spring. How does that sound?"

"Absolutely prefect, Augusto. I am amazed you are doing all this for us and there is no cost involved. You have my utmost respect sir and my heartfelt thanks," Lech poured it on a little heavy, but for once, he was being sincere, especially since one was his wife. Of course, Augusto already read this from his thoughts.

He brought the three back to Valen flying there late at night, avoiding others seeing the shuttle craft. After leaving them and again thanking Augusto, he returned alone to the port and impatiently awaited their call to return to pick them up. That call came three weeks later along with a detailed report from Augusto.

Karolina's gift lay with the weather, as one might expect. From this point onward, she always knew just what the weather would be each day over any area of the world, just by looking there. Later on, with some training, she became able to affect the path that storms took; her long unanswered questions were finally answered. She knew now how the anomalies were caused, since she was able to cause them herself. She also had the gift of empathy with other women, but not so much with men.

Jarek's gifts lay in an entirely different route. While he could Move Objects, more important than that, he could Disguise Himself. No longer did he need a ring to appear as a Tierra native. Rather, he could appear in any number of body forms. He had heightened physical senses and an awareness of dangerous situations too. These would greatly assist him as a field agent.

Neither Jarek nor Lech minded that their wives also had a strong sexual relationship as well. Lech had always had the greatest admiration and respect for Karolina and now even more so. He continued his practice of having her attend his meetings, only now she relayed others unspoken thoughts to him. She and Jarek had become the most valuable assets in his line of work, intelligence gathering. As long as she remained faithful to him and no other man, Lech allowed her to obtain additional pleasures with her new friend, Carmen. Jarek, on the other hand, by virtue of now being a telepath himself, understood the two women and their bond and did not let that affect their relationship. That both men and both women had moved into a different moral and ethical scheme — that of a telepathic society — eluded them. Things just happened and they accepted them.

Chapter 5 Trials of Women

Twenty-nine year old Kassia Kunegunda ran the Swap Shop, a second hand store where aliens and natives alike came to swap or buy or sell personal articles, such as clothing, boots, saddles, knives, and so on. Located next to one of the many brothels in Exchange City, she often got many customers who were in a hurry to make an exchange before ducking into the next door establishment. Sex was always a good business on any world, though quite why men and women could not find suitable arrangements elsewhere without having to "purchase" them, Kassia didn't know. Such was merely another fact of life on all worlds, which she accepted without further thought. Kassia had one of those totally forgettable faces, the kind no one could recall having seen — plain but not ugly, for ugly would be memorable by others.

Of course, within her own race, she was also considered rather deformed because of her incredibly short height, barely five-five, almost unheard of for a Rigel-3 adult woman. Her embarrassing nickname as she went through her teens was "tiny teen" and she'd entered the ID field agent training in hopes of getting around her liability. Perhaps on some other world she would better fit in, and thus she'd leapt at the chance to come to Ashford-5. Now in her ninth year here as a field agent, she was doing rather well for herself, having become well established as a down on her luck owner of the Swap Shop, where second hand merchandise was sold and bartered daily. So profitable was her small business that she now had two local female assistants. Still, she provided a valuable tool for the Sector ID Minister. Occasionally, someone from Rigel-3 would be tempted to trade her contraband items. While she accepted the trade, she also turned the person over to the Security Forces along with the contraband items, such as compasses, Navigators, and even once a blaster.

At least on Ashford-5, she was no longer called tiny teen. Mingling with the local women on a daily basis, she fit in well, though her skin color always gave her away as alien. Still, Kassia was more content and happy with her life these past few years than ever before, but there was no romantic element to her existence, and she assumed there probably never would be because of her extremely short stature.

She was highly trained in personal close quarter's combat, both unarmed and with a knife, as fitting for this world. However, when her breasts began expanding, her annoyance turned to a disgust with her malformed body, though she often made fun of herself to others, as she had done during that initial meeting with her new boss. Now acutely aware of her body, she compared her bosom to others from the spaceport and even the native women. To her continual dismay, hers seemed proportionately larger. The taller Rigel-3 women carried theirs well, even though their breasts were commonly as large as their heads. She on the other hand looked more like a native woman, except hers were even larger than the normal native's, half again as large as her own head and the native's. Worse, they upset all her fighting skills; her balance was now way off. "I'll never be able to see my feet again," she lamented, rather exaggerating it.

Thus, when Lech summoned her to the meeting and gave her the assignment to go to Haverhills, she was a very troubled young woman. Still, she coveted this opportunity to do some far more valuable field work and had eagerly agreed to do it, before working out the means by which she could carry it out. She knew she dare not travel across the countryside alone; women just did not do that on this world. However, the Sisterhood women were the sole exception to this ironclad rule, but she was well known to the three local Sisterhood women. Often they had come by her shop to pick up clothing and other useful items cheaply. She could not go to them wearing the ring of disguise. They would be sure to recognize her. Kassia needed another plan, but what?

She made arrangements for her assistants to run her shop for her, telling them soon she'd have to attend a lengthy training session on the plateau. Kassia had her bag packed, keeping it to the minimum: a change of clothes, a waterskin, and a used bedroll. Still without a plan, she began wandering the streets of Exchange City, hoping to get inspired. Specifically, there were a very large number of strangers in the city because of the annual ore and gold exchange. Perhaps she could book passage with the Haverhills ore caravan. With her saddlebag slung across her shoulders, she began walking the streets in search of that bright idea following some undefinable hunch. Kassia always had hunches and more often than not, they had panned out. She sincerely hoped this one would, for she needed it to work out; her job was on the line.

"Hey mom, there's one of the aliens now. Come on. Let's see if we can talk to her. You wanted to meet one," Gina called out. Kassia heard it and for a second glanced around looking for an alien before she flushed. The woman must have meant her. Oh well, she thought.

The one who spoke pulled on an older woman's arm and a trio of trail-dressed women moved towards Kassia. She saw an older woman and two younger women about her own age, she guessed. As they drew closer, she noticed their earrings, double horse heads and knew at once these three women were members of the Sisterhood, the very people she needed to take her to Haverhills. She grinned involuntarily.

"Hello. I am Gina Lucca Brom e Thorn, my free mate, Molly Thorn e Lucca Brom. This is my mother, Savina Lucca Brom. Mom has never seen an alien and really wanted to see their spaceships. Do you mind chatting with us for a few minutes?" the brown haired woman asked. All three had yellow eyes with brown speckles and Kassia knew at once they were telepaths as well. The two free mates were quite pretty, Kassia noted, and wore their hair rather short, falling to their shoulders, while Savina's grey streaked hair was braided in two long braids, which fell to just above her ankles. Their trail clothes were rather dirty, indicating they'd just arrived, probably on horseback. They carried short swords around their waists, rather as the local men did. Something about Savina's skin color was slightly off, but Kassia couldn't place it right away.

"Hi there. I am Kassia Kunegunda. I run the Swap Shop several streets over. Pleased to meet you, Gina, Molly, Savina. Well, now Savina you can say you met a woman from Rigel-3.

Am I what you expected?" Kassia asked with a broad, teasing grin.

"Not really. I thought your people were really overly tall and very thin," Savina replied. "I am very pleased to meet you, Kassia. I've traveled Tierra extensively, but before I died, I wanted to see the aliens for myself and to see their spaceships. My daughter, Gina here, insisted we come around the ore exchange time so there would be more opportunities to see things. I do hope you are not offended if I am staring at you some."

Kassia laughed. "Not in the slightest. I hope my Midlands is clear enough for you. I'm told I do have a bad accent though. As far as your notions of our race, you are right. I am not typical at all. Every Rigel-3 adult that I know is at least a foot taller than I am and drastically thinner. I am considered super ugly by my people for being so utterly short and fat. Plus now I am really hideous with these knockers that are even larger than yours."

"Well, I couldn't help noticing that, Kassia. Yours are the largest I've ever seen. There is a reason the Goddess Ariana altered us women so drastically. With the horrid alteration of our climate and so many babies dying and with food so scarce, she wanted our babies to have the best possible chance to survive. I myself only had one child, Gina here, and I speak from experience, she had more milk than she could drink." All three chuckled and Kassia joined them.

"Well, I'm not likely to have even one. I am so ugly that no man will bed me. They are just a huge nuisance," Kassia replied.

"You can say that again," Gina broke in. "They really do get in our way lots of times. But then we can also have fun with them," she winked at Molly, who grinned back at her. Kassia sensed they shared some intimate thought with each other via telepathy. For a second she was a little envious of the two women.

Kassia decided to change the subject. "So you want to see the spaceships taking off and landing?"

"Yes, but we can hear them from here, but I've only caught glimpses of them way up in the sky. Is there some place

where we could get a good view or at least a better view?"
Savina asked.

"Sure is. Follow me. On the western edge of Exchange
City where they are handling the ore exchanges there is a look
out that is perfect to see them fairly well. Of course, if you had
the time to travel along the road to Valen that just touches the
southern border of the port, from there you can get a close up
view," Kassia explained.

The four pushed their way through the crowds and
headed westward. Before long, they passed the outer edge of
homes and saw long lines of wagons, men, and aliens, dealing
with the transfer of the yearly lease payment of iron ore and
gold. Here security was very tight and many were being
challenged and moved back. "Stick close to me. They won't
bother me or you if you are with me," Kassia suggested. The
three did as asked, pressing as close to Kassia as they could.
She was right, Savina noted. Although she was shorter than
the other alien men, no one challenged her right to walk along
the roadway beside the many wagons loaded with the ore.
Many men, however, stared at her and she heard many calling
out very nasty phrases directed towards the three Sisterhood
women behind her.

"Just ignore them," Savina whispered to Gina and
Molly. "Remember your training. Don't give them any reason
to accost us. I just want to see the ships."

After walking the gauntlet to the observation overlook
— that's what it felt like to the four women, but for two
different reasons, one alien, one Sisterhood, they reached the
best location in Exchange City from which to view the
spaceport off to the west. While Kassia had no interest at all in
the ships, she watched the three Sisterhood women as they
stared in awe at the sleek, silver ships descending or taking off,
accompanied by the roar of their engines. Kassia tried to think
just how she might get these Sisterhood women to take her
down to Haverhills, but other than directly asking them,
which, as an alien, she could not do, she could think of no legal
way.

Savina asked a number of routine questions about the
ships, where they were going, what cargo they were carrying,

and similar all too familiar questions Kassia had heard for the last nine years. She dutifully answered each to the best of her ability. None of what she said was in any way classified information and the three women relaxed and enjoyed her company and chat.

In time, Kassia's eyes shifted from the Sisterhood women to the caravan lines of wagons. She noted those from Haverhills were not more than a hundred yards from them, all lined up and in the process of being loaded by aliens using their mechanical scoopers as they were known. She toyed with the notion of just walking up and asking one of the Haverhills men if she could get a ride with him, but tossed that one away. She would have to put on her special ring that would change her skin color to that of the Tierra locals. That she could not do in front of these Sisterhood women, let alone all the other men who occasionally stole glances their way.

Kassia and the trio had been standing watching the ships for about an hour when all of a sudden a fight broke out not more than a hundred yards from where they were standing. In the chaos accompanying the altercation, Kassia noted two things. Suddenly, a man and a woman totally vanished from sight not far from where another man, armed only with a short sword, was valiantly fighting off a half-dozen similarly armed soldiers from Haverhills. The man with short black hair cast a quick glance at the four and then the alto voice called out, "Sisters! Help!" In that instant, Kassia realized the man was not a man at all, but a woman!

At once, Savina, Gina, and Molly did not hesitate. They drew their swords and raced towards the greatly outnumbered woman, as another dozen men swarmed down on the battle. Kassia drew her sword and followed the three women. She saw the alto-voiced woman down three of her assailants, though at least one had cut her left leg. The trio smashed into the line of men, swords clashing, steel upon steel, and then she too entered the battle. Kassia dodged a sword and retaliated by kicking the man in him groin, he crumpled to the ground and she stepped over him, forming a battle line to the alto woman's left, while the trio pushed back the soldiers on her right side. A blaster shot fired into the air, creating a deafening noise, ending the battle instantly. Swords were not even remotely effective against an alien blaster.

As the Security Force men, all holding blasters, rushed up, Kassia barked to the men, "I have these four. You take those men." To Savina, Gina, Molly, and the unknown woman, she barked, "You four, come with me now!"

Honestly, there were few other options for the four women, who stared down a dozen tall, thin alien men all holding blasters. They backed up and began to follow Kassia, who whispered, "Follow me. I'll get you out of here fast." She did just that, ducking down the first side street and then veering down the next side street and on into a quiet alleyway. "Okay, you are safe here. No one is going to follow us. Shit, you are bleeding like mad!" She noticed the strange woman's leg was gushing blood and was leaving a blood trail right to them.

"I've got her," Savina spoke up. "Lay down. Let me at it." She uncovered her pod-silk covered crystal. As Kassia watched, the crystal began to glow as Savina's fingers reached towards the woman's bleeding leg. Her fingers just barely touched the leg and, as Kassia watched completely fascinated, the gushing blood subsided and then stopped. Still Savina kept at it. Kassia glanced up and saw Gina and Molly had their swords out and were standing guard at the entrance to the alley.

"There, how does that feel?" Savina finally spoke about fifteen minutes later.

The alto voice said, "Thanks! It's sore but healing well. I owe you a big one. Thanks for coming to my aid. I'm Feliciana Evita. We've got big problems now."

"Yes, I assumed it was you. I am Savina Lucca Brom. My daughter Gina, her free mate Molly, and our alien friend Kassia. Glad we were close enough to help you. That was a bad leg wound. You should take it easy for a week. Let it heal fully," Savina replied, covering her crystal with its pod-silk bag.

Kassia finally noted Feliciana had yellow eyes as well, but her chest was as flat as a man's. How could this be, Kassia wondered. *Could it be some women were not affected with giant mammary glandular growth?*

Feliciana noticed Kassia staring at her chest and said,

"Thanks for helping us, alien Kassia. *Castinto*." That last was supposed to convey all there was to say about her lack of breasts, but Kassia had never heard the word before and looked confused. Feliciana thought, *Shit! Ignorant alien.* "My breasts have been cut off — *castinto*, get it?" She looked up at Savina and said to her, "We have a really big problem. I am invoking the All Hands Clause. I need your help."

"We'd better move from here; you left a clear blood trail that can be followed," Gina called out. "We are with you."

"I know a safe place. My shop, come with me," Kassia spoke up. She led the way across town to her shop, taking them into her private quarters at the rear of her shop. All the way, though, she insisted on Feliciana leaning on her to take the weight off of her leg. The woman had allowed her to help, but Kassia also noticed she kept her hand on her knife in case Kassia tried to lead them into a trap.

While Kassia put the water on for tea, Savina asked, "Okay, Fel, what is going on? Why pick that fight with the Haverhills men?"

"It's all gone completely wrong. It was supposed to be a simple snatch and run operation. Hells fire, what the devil did happen there?" Feliciana cursed. "Okay, it's Sara Haverhills. She has the gift and called out for help to the Sisterhood in Haverhills for help. She wants to join us and flee from her impossible situation there, but she was too heavily guarded at her home. Her father sent her along with the caravan wagons to Exchange City where she was to be sold to her betrothed, a Mark Benton of Wye. We arranged a simple snatch and grab. I was to snatch her just before that fight broke out, and together we would flee the city, but something went horribly wrong. Just as I was about to make my move, one of the guards moved over to her and touched her shoulder. She cried out and the fight broke out, just as that man and Sara completely vanished! It is now a matter of honor that we retrieve Sara from her abductors and give her the chance to join the Sisterhood."

As Kassia leaned over the table, setting a teacup before Feliciana, she commented, "Damn, Kassia, you have the largest knockers I've ever seen!"

95

Her crass comment came wholly unexpectedly and Kassia felt a sudden overwhelming shame and embarrassment. Although she didn't know it, she was fairly screaming her shame to everyone in the room. Savina sent Feliciana, *You had better handle that.*

Feliciana put her hand gently upon Kassia's which was still on the teacup. "I'm sorry, padrona, I meant no offense; rather you should be proud of them. They make you a woman, what I no longer am."

"It's just they are too huge. I'm sorry too. How can we help you find Sara?" Kassia desperately tried to change the subject. Something about Feliciana's touch on her hand sent an electric wave through her body, something she'd never felt before, but she felt better because of it.

Savina spoke up, "We four saw the man and woman disappear too. It could only have been the use of the extremely rare *mentales* gift of teleportation. If so, that means he could have taken her at most a couple of miles from that spot. But why would someone kidnap her?"

"Good, you saw it too. I don't feel like such a fool then. Teleport? I think you are right. Give me a minute and I will see if I can locate where Sara is right now." She uncovered her crystal. Again, Kassia watched fascinated with the cool, comforting bluish glow from the germanium crystal. A bit later, Feliciana let go of it and the glow faded. "Damn, they have pumped her full of *bacal* tea, but I was able to get through to her. She's tied to a horse and they are heading east, but not on the main track. Have you got horses?"

"Yes, we can be ready to go as soon as we get trail food supplies," Savina replied.

"I have that here in my store. Come on. Help yourselves. I'm coming with you, but I'll need a horse. I can ride," she said looking squarely at Feliciana, challenging her.

"We will owe you then, padrona. Aliens are not allowed beyond Exchange City," Feliciana said factually.

"True," she activated her ring. "Now I look like one of you, except for the earrings. Like I said, I'm coming with you," Kassia declared. "I can hold my own in a fight."

"Why?" demanded Feliciana.

"She's been very friendly to us. Let her come if she wants to. We need all the help we can get with this teleporting man. It will be tricky to capture him," Savina took a gamble on Kassia. She too often followed intuitive hunches she could not put into words. If asked why she thought Kassia should come, she really could not offer any other justification than what she'd just said. Hunches are that way.

"Well, so be it. I take no responsibility for the alien woman," Feliciana declared.

Savina explained hastily, "What she means is you are not a Sisterhood member nor are we under your employ. Thus, we are not responsible for your safety or what happens to you if you come. However, your help is very much appreciated, Kassia."

"Good. I am my own master. Come on; let's load up whatever supplies you think we need and get going. It will begin to rain soon and that'll make tracking more difficult. I assume one of you can track? I'm sorry, I can't."

Feliciana laughed. "Of course I can track. You heard her. Let's get moving; we've already wasted too much time." The women gathered up what they thought they would need and Kassia's two assistants helped them pack them into saddlebags. Kassia told her assistants she was going now and to watch the store for her. Once back in her quarters, she slipped on the ring, once more having her skin color match that of the other women. She followed them, with Feliciana leading the way. They stopped at the Sisterhood house, retrieved their horses, and rented one for Kassia. While she was waiting, Kassia quickly sewed the sword cut in Feliciana's pants for her, which brought a flash of a smile her way.

Kassia studied the four women carefully, since she was about to head out into the field with them. Feliciana cut her hair very short, like a man's. She had muscles that seemed well-toned and she carried herself well, like a cat ready to pounce. Her face always seemed stern, as if she carried the weight of the world on her shoulders. Perhaps she had, Kassia thought, wondering what awful thing had happened to her breasts. Whatever it had been, it must have been horribly painful.

Savina was fifty-nine and the slowest of the group, showing her age. Yet, she seemed to have more wisdom than the others did, and even Feliciana bowed to her suggestions. Gina and Molly continued to chat among themselves; they were gay and lighthearted, but they too were solidly built with strong muscles. Kassia guessed all four were trained fighters and that came as a relief to her. She didn't have to also worry about protecting one of them should trouble arise, which it most likely would.

Savina, why are we bringing an alien woman along with us? Feliciana asked, while she was saddling her horse.

I always trust my hunches, Feliciana. I can't explain it, but she wants to come and she has already gotten us out of a tight spot back at the battle. We ought to have been arrested or something. I am not sure how deadly fights are handled in Exchange City, but I am sure she broke all kind of laws helping us duck being arrested. I also think she is following her own agenda here. There is something more about her than she's allowed us to see. I will keep an eye on her, though. I will take the responsibility for bringing her along, Feliciana.

Okay then, I bow to your greater wisdom. I do hope you are right. She handled herself well in the fight, I'll give her that. Plus, she has a quality Haverhills sword. Now if she can only ride well. She flashed Savina a quick grin. *I've heard of you. Aren't you Felix Brom's daughter?*

Yes, mom was an Easterlings bound woman who returned there right after the attempted assassination of dad. I've heard of you as well. You are supposedly the best fighter in the Sisterhood. I hope we don't let you down.

You three held your own in the fight. Thanks again for the quick healing. Well, let's see how the alien rides. "Kassia, here's your mare. She's not too spirited. Fasten your saddlebags and bedroll on back. Keep your oiled cloak on; it will likely rain on us before much longer." Kassia did as asked.

They mounted up and headed out of the Sisterhood stables into the crowded streets. It took a half hour to finally clear Exchange City. Feliciana led them about a mile east of the city before asking them to fan out and search for the trail. "When I glimpsed them, they were not following the main track, so we get a break there, if and only if we can pick up their trail. Kassia, you stay with Savina, unless you are also a tracker."

"Okay, I don't think I qualify as one of your trackers," she replied. *But I am a field agent and a trained observer. Picking up a trail left by horses can't be that difficult. Let's see if I can find it.*

The group fanned out, half moving northwards from the main, well-worn path, half going south of it. Dark clouds were gathering and Kassia knew rain was imminent. Still she trained her eyes on the rocky ground, where bits of grasses fought for life. They were high in the foothills of the Goza Mountains and great ridges sloped downwards towards the east. Far off in the distance, she saw pines and denser patches of grass. Still, riding north-south would be quite a challenge; the ridges were almost natural barriers, traversable only by knowing the precise route horses or wagons could travel, the latter were very few and far between.

"Hey, I think I found something," Kassia called out. Savina moved her horse closer and called out to Feliciana, who trotted over to the two.

"Well, that certainly looks like a fresh trail. We'll take it for a while and see. Nice job, Kassia," Feliciana actually complimented her and then studied the signs. Shortly Gina and Molly joined them and studied the ground as well.

"Looks like a woman's boot here, drag marks too," Kassia suggested.

"A number of men certainly stood around here for some time," Feliciana pointed out. "It's within range of the man's teleport I suspect. Probably brought Sara here and forced her onto a horse."

"*Bacal* leaves, Feliciana," Gina pointed to a small batch of leaves that had been dipped in boiling water, seeped, and then discarded.

Kassia whispered to Savina, "What are *bacal* leaves used for?"

"It turns off the *mentales* gifts for a time, making a telepath head blind as we call those who do not have the gift. That way, her abductors don't have to worry about her using whatever gifts she may have to fight them or delay them. It is a terrible thing to do to one of us who has the gift, much like a rape."

"Okay, this is their trail heading off eastward. Come on, the game is afoot," Feliciana called out. Kassia fell in behind Savina, who brought up the rear. Feliciana set off at a loping canter and then the rains began. A bright flash of lightning followed by rolling thunder announced the afternoon's rain. All five hastily donned their cloaks, pulling the hoods over their heads and continued onwards. Kassia suspected the rains would wash out all traces of the trail they were following and she was right. Late that afternoon, Feliciana was forced to call a halt. "Trail is washed out. Have to try to pick it up tomorrow. Let's find us some place to camp."

Feliciana led them into a dense patch of pines. "This will do. I'll rig the shelter; you deal with the chow. Kassia, lend me a hand with the shelter. Gina, Molly, you two handle the horses. Let's get cracking, only got an hour of daylight left before the sun goes behind the mountains." The other three went about their tasks with a speed and efficiency that Kassia assumed came from many years of camping out. She followed Feliciana's orders and soon began to see what kind of shelter the woman had in mind.

They tied a branch between two tall pines, about five feet off the ground. Next, two other dead branches were laid at either end with their bottoms on the ground. Across this form, she and the *castinto* tied an oiled canvas tarp, their roof. Finally, they tossed several rocks out from beneath it and scooped piles of pine needles inside the shelter. By the time they were done, the others had a light supper waiting for them and a crackling fire.

As they sat around the fire sipping their after-dinner, strong tea, Savina felt like chatting so Kassia asked, "I've heard the name Brom before, but I am not certain I know its full implications."

Savina explained, "Felix Brom discovered these crystals and how to join telepaths together to make them more powerful. His grand idea was to have we of the gift become so ultra-powerful that wars would end, since normal men could not stand any chance fighting against us. He set up the eleven towers as the rulers of all Tierra and made every political ruler sign on. It's called the Brom Compact. Well, I suppose it has worked for a time, but you know men, they will always find ways to fight." Feliciana chuckled and heartily agreed with her.

"So if there have been no wars, how come you are in the Sisterhood? Forgive me if I am asking something I should not ask," Kassia asked politely.

Savina sighed, "Long story. We women are bound, one way or another. My mother was a physically bound Easterlings woman. I grew up being bound myself. The women there always wear these fetter skirts that are so tight you can only take a two inch step at most. Then a woman's arms are chained at her elbows to her waist so only her lower arms are free to move. If that isn't bad enough, at night, they bind her lower arms behind her back. I lived like that for several years as a little girl. When Felix brought us back to the Midlands, he undid mom's bindings, but her shoulders were almost frozen in place. She couldn't move her upper arms much at all."

"My god! Why do they do that? Why do the Easterlings women put up with it?" Kassia asked rather shocked to hear this vivid description.

"Attention. They do it for all the attention their men give them. Mom once told me Easterlings men dote over the women in their family, spending many hours with them each day. She said at least a quarter of each day, their men were with them caring for them, while back here in the Midlands, the men pay so very little attention to their wives and then mostly at night before bed when they want sex. The Easterlings women embrace their physical binding and have gained the full attention and caring of men. Do you realize if a woman there was having some physical problem while out say shopping, she'd have a dozen men rushing to assist her. Total strangers. It is a hideous crime in the Easterlings to hurt or injure a bound woman. You can murder men and get away with it, but just striking a bound woman is tantamount to having every man in the village coming at you with their swords. For a long time, I too longed to go back to the Easterlings and be bound once more," Savina admitted.

101

She went on, "Here in the Midlands, women are not physically bound, but are bound in many other ways. At first, Felix had me convinced that here I would be a free woman. Not so, not at all. No, here men arrange the marriages for their daughters. It is even worse if you have the *mentales* gift. Men breed us to get better gifts in their children. We are nothing more than brood mares for the males in our lives. I just could not take it when they tried to marry me off to breed more children. I abandoned my entire heritage and joined the Sisterhood," Savina admitted.

"Sisters are not free either," Feliciana spat out rather disgustedly.

"She's right," Savina added quickly. "We are considered the scum of the earth. Everywhere we go, we face constant ostracism and hatred. Sisters are treated like fourth class citizens, barely tolerated. Only because we force ourselves to become superior fighters do we hold our own. No, I found not freedom in the Sisterhood, but I did find barriers I could personally live with. Later on, I truly wanted children and I took a free mate, Sam Wycombe, who was also gifted. He was Gina's father, but he died several years ago."

Gina took this opportunity to speak her mind. "I followed in mom's footsteps. She made me visit the Easterlings and see for myself what physical binding was all about and how much adoration and attention I received from males. She's right about that, they dote on us, but honestly, I hated every minute of it. For a time, she had me in one of the towers and they even tried to force me to marry a man just so our children would have potentially certain *mentales* gifts and for no other reason! I refused utterly so then they tried to turn me into a circle member, working long hours in the towers flowing my energies to the leader who in turn used it on their many projects. While that was fun for a short time, it was exhausting work and I got almost no reward for doing it. I will say it did have one huge benefit. I met Molly while I was in the tower. She and I fell passionately in love and together we joined the Sisterhood so we could be free-mates. We've never regretted that move, though the looks of hatred we sometimes get would fry an egg!"

Molly added, "She's right about that. My dad insisted and demanded I marry Sam, who I utterly detested, ever since I was a child. I ran off to the towers, knowing they would give me a life free from that as long as I worked as one of their circle technicians. For some women, that is enough, but it wasn't for me. Thank god I met Gina! I was about ready to take my own life because everything was so utterly futile and pointless for me as a woman. Gina saved me, but we both want to have a child one day soon. We haven't found the right man yet. We figure we'll flirt with him into bedding us on a one-night stand and he'll never be the wiser." Both women chuckled at that.

Savina said, "Now Feliciana here has an even worse horror story, but she never talks about it. She's the best fighter in the entire Sisterhood, world famous. Few men can stand against her fighting skills. As you can see, men have done terrible things to her, let's just leave it at that."

"You had better leave it at that," Feliciana growled. She hated even this much of her life being discussed, let alone with a stranger. Instead, she changed the topic. "Sara Haverhills is in a similar situation. Her father has actually sold her to some man from Wye. He kept her under lock and key in his home until the sale, which was to be consummated back there at Exchange City during the ore transfer. She used her gifts somehow to contact a Sisterhood member who contacted others. Eventually, I was given the assignment to snatch her before she could be handed off to this fellow from Wye. It was supposed to be an easy snatch, wholly unexpected by all, an in and out trip. And it would have been had that guy not kidnaped her right before I was about to snatch her away! I swear I will kill that man when I get my hands on him!"

"The question is, Feliciana," Savina began but was interrupted.

"Fel, I prefer just Fel. The other reminds me too much of my past. Fel, just call me Fel."

"Okay, Fel. The question is why did someone go to such extremes to kidnap her? Men who can teleport are extraordinarily rare. Hiring him must have cost a fortune. So why? If someone wanted to grab her, why not do a simple snatch and grab like you intended? Could it be that the man who was buying her wanted to get her without paying for her?"

Gina pointed out, "Mom, that doesn't make sense either. The amount he would have to pay the teleport man probably is more than he originally paid for Sara."

"Point taken. So why?"

"I have a very bad feeling about this," Fel lowered her alto voice to a whisper. "I haven't said this before cause of Kassia here. She's an alien."

"Hey, please go ahead and say whatever you want. I assure you that I won't take any offense," Kassia hastily suggested.

"Well, there have been some alien abductions of *mentales* gifted men and women, women mostly," Fel said quietly.

"What? Aliens? Us abducing some of you?" Kassia asked shocked utterly.

"Well, yes, Kassia. *Your* people. We know of five such cases over the last ten years or so. We've documented them. Your people snatched and grabbed them and took them off-world," Fel explained.

"How do you know they went off-world?" Kassia asked, still trying to come to grips with this news. It flew into the teeth of everything she knew.

"A telepath can make contact with another telepath anywhere on Tierra. One can be on the western coast of the Westerlings and the other on the eastern coast of the Easterlings, and they can communicate as if they were standing in front of each other. But no one can reach those who have been taken off-world, the distance is too great. In one case, the abducted woman was able to send an image of the place where she was being held. It was inside one of your spaceships. She felt it taking off and was telling her mother about it when she literally faded out when the ship got too far from Tierra. It happens."

"Damn! That's highly illegal! When I get back, I will look into it and see if I can find those responsible and have them tried for their crimes," Kassia vowed.

"Don't make promises you can't keep, Kassia," Fel

admonished her and Kassia became silent. "We've chatted too much. Time for sleep. Long day tomorrow."

The five women lay on their bedrolls, crowding close to one another for warmth. Kassia took a long time to fall asleep. She'd never slept out in the open before, let alone on such hard ground. At last, listening to the breathing of the others, she finally drifted into an ill sleep. Her mind was plagued by the awful accusation Fel had made.

Her people were abducting some of the telepathically gifted people of Tierra! Could it be widespread? Similar to the makings of the disaster of the first settlement over a century ago? The implications were mind boggling. Why had the Sector ID Minister not known of these gross crimes? Had he known? But he was so new. Had old Ania known? Why had she not stopped it? What should she do? She dreamed she was revealing all this to the Supreme Court only to have them smile at her and order her immediate execution. As she was being hauled away physically, she saw one of the abducted women chained to one of the judges who smiled at her. She awoke in a cold sweat.

Fel had her arm over her, snuggled up tight against her, just under her large bosom. How strange that felt, she thought and tried to wipe the sweat from her forehead. She knew she couldn't sleep anymore. Instead, she let her mind drift over everything she had ever seen or heard that might be relevant, no matter how slight. She was a trained observer after all. That's how she made her living, noticing what others might not. Kassia wished she had her computer terminal right now. So many things could be checked, unscheduled departures, unchecked cargo, even diplomatic flights. In the vast Imperium, telepaths were a real rarity and a good one could earn a fortune. What if someone out there learned Ashford-5 was full of telepaths? Certainly, they'd make arrangements to come here and recruit. With the total restriction of the Imperial Directive #5 in force, they would have to resort to nefarious means to obtain the telepaths. Why hadn't she seen this sooner? Wasn't this sort of thing in the province of her boss, not herself, a lowly field agent?

A low growl roused her. The morning sun was just

rising in the east, casting its peculiar red glow over the wet landscape. A large black bear was sniffing them at the front opening of their lean-to. Just as Kassia was about to panic, Molly sat up and scratched behind the bear's ears. "It's okay, he's just curious. I've told him to go look for some honey," Molly whispered. She added, "I've a knack with animals. Guess it's time to rise. Did you sleep well, Kassia? Oh, I can see you didn't. We probably should not have mentioned the alien abductions to you last night."

Is she reading my mind? My thoughts? Kassia wondered. "Is it that obvious?"

Molly grinned and rose, disturbing Fel, who pulled hard on Kassia's waist, snuggling her tightly. Almost at the same instant, Fel woke and realized what she was doing. "'cuse me. All right, rise and let's get cracking everyone," she barked orders, though Kassia sensed she did so to avoid facing her. Kassia rose and rolled up her bedroll.

She marveled at the efficiency of these four women. In less than an hour, they were again on their way, having had a quick breakfast, handled the horses, and broken camp. She wondered if they had done this together before, but then suspected not. Fel seemed known to the other three only by reputation. After mounting, Fel issued her orders. "Okay, to find the trail, we are going to fan out from this last known point. Molly and Gina will go off thirty degrees from either side of due east. I'll go due east. Savina and Kassia, you to veer off say fifteen degrees to either side of me. Holler as soon as you pick up signs of a trail. Also, they probably camped perhaps a few miles from here. They had barely two hours head start on us and unless they really pushed their horses, they ought to have camped no more than ten miles from here. Let's go everyone. Sara is depending upon us."

Riding a little north of Fel, Kassia spotted the remains of a camp in another grove of pines, just as Gina sent Fel a telepathic message. *I've picked up a trail heading northeast.* Fel turned around and met up with Kassia, verifying the camp and then ordered everyone to join up with Gina. "Kassia found their campsite. Gina has their morning trail. Come on; they cannot be but a few hours ahead of us now. Let's crack some leather." Kassia didn't know what that expression meant, but as Fel broke into a canter, she presumed it meant something like go fast.

At first, the trail was very plain, hoof imprints in the grass and soft, rain-moist earth, but as they closed the distance towards the rugged ridge line that ran nearly due west-east from the Goza Mountains, the grass patches gave way to sparse pines and rugged, large and jagged boulders. Around noon, they were definitely nearing the ridge line, and Fel called a halt to rest the horses and let them graze a bit on the last patches of grass. "Break out some food. They cannot be but an hour at most ahead of us. I think I know where they are headed."

While Savina handed out dried venison and an apple to each, Kassia asked, "Where?"

Between bites of her apple, Fel explained, "If I am not mistaken, there is an old abandoned psi-crystal mine up there, a relic from the early days when the aliens were paying miners to mine for psi-crystals. I took refuge there once when I got caught in an unexpected blizzard. Winters are bitches in these foothills. It would make a good place to hold up, but why would they want to hold up? Hurry up," she added, growing impatient with the needed delay.

Before long, they hit the trail once more. The going was rough, but their horses seemed to be able to pick out a safe passage in and around the massive boulders, which lined the steeply rising ridge line. Kassia surmised it could only be crossed at a very few places; it was almost too rugged for the horses. She was glad they were going up and not down and she clung to the front of the saddle. Their saddles were basically a rounded frame over which leather was tied, and it was to the frame she clung. The others were not and she could not figure out how they were managing to stay in their saddles without slipping off its back.

Upwards they climbed, though the going went progressively slower by the minute. Kassia could no longer spot the trail, but Fel still seemed to be able to see it and continued leading them. "Keep quiet, we are getting close," she whispered and Kassia felt adrenalin begin to flow. Surely, they were headed into a grand fight for sure.

A little further on, they came to the base of the ridge itself. Ahead and a little to the east a large talus slope was clearly visible, though a few resinous pines now thrust their scraggy trunks upwards through it, as if sending a clear signal they were recovering the mess left by the ancient miners. However, that is not all they saw. Kassia gasped, but not at the several dozen horses tethered in a long line, tied between two scraggly pines. No, what shocked her was seeing one of their shuttle crafts parked there. It was one of the two-man crafts, small, sleek, and silver colored. No one was around but all could see the dark opening of the entrance tunnel just above where the horses and shuttle were parked.

Fel immediately back tracked them a quarter mile. Whispering, she explained, "We don't want the horses whinnying to each other alerting those inside to our presence. Tether them; we go on foot." A few minutes later, the horses handled, the four followed Fel, who led them back to where they first saw the tunnel. Crouching down, Fel surveyed the scene. Kassia bemoaned the fact she'd left her blaster back home. Going out in the field among the primitives, she'd decided a blaster was too alien and way too powerful a weapon. *If the natives use swords, so can I.* Well, now she regretted her decision. Her people who came in the shuttle craft undoubtedly had blasters and very likely the PDS's, the Personal Defense Shields, that acted like a force field that kept even bullets from hitting the person, but not a blaster shot. How many of them could there be, she wondered. Two at most, maybe only one, if he were planning to take Sara back with him. The craft would only hold two people.

Kassia whispered to Fel, "Probably only one Rigel-3 person is in there, but he will have a blaster in all likelihood and a PDS, a Personal Defense Shield, which will prevent your swords from hitting him, projectiles too."

"Damn you aliens! How can we take him out?" Fel asked very antagonistically.

Kassia ignored Fel's anger, for it was obviously not directed at her per se. "Its weakness is that it is more like a cone. He has no protection for a strike that comes up from below his feet. If we can get him to fall over, you can get at him from his feet. Or if you can slowly move your hand inside the field, you can turn it off by pressing the large red button on his belt. It won't stop a slow moving object like your hand, but it will stop it if you try to punch him with it. Of course, the blaster is beyond deadly."

"Okay, let' see if we can sneak inside and see what is going on and work out a plan," Fel suggested. "Use telepathy, no talking. Damn, Kassia can't. Well, think your thoughts to me, Kassia, I'll relay them to the others. Keep damn quiet. I go first and I'll handle any guards."

Walking over the rough ground was challenging. More than once, Kassia slipped and ended up on all fours trying to keep from taking a bad spill. Fortunately, the others fared little better. At last, they reached the dark opening. Fel slipped inside first, sword drawn. *Wait here,* she sent to all. Fel moved quietly inside, pausing a moment to let her eyes adjust to the dim light. She heard voices up ahead, but saw the back of one man who was supposed to be guarding the entrance. He looked very bored and was smoking a pipe while on duty. Like a cat on the hunt, Fel slipped up behind him. One hand slipped forcefully over his mouth, her other drove her blade deep into his back between his ribs. Then she twisted it and wiggled it until she felt all resistance in the man fail. He slumped to the ground dead. *Come on in quietly,* she sent and moved further into the tunnel.

She knew there was a large open area just ahead. It was where she'd taken refuge years ago to wait out the blizzard. Stealthily, she moved down the tunnel to where it turned slightly and opened up into the working chamber. She noted the tunnel itself was near collapsing and added that to her cautionary messages to the others coming up behind her. Soon, the others reached her and they peered into the well-lighted chamber. A dozen lanterns were hung around the perimeter; the chamber was roughly circular about twenty feet across. Farthest away from them was Sara. She was bound in chains. From the way her legs were chained together, Fel guessed she could barely walk in them. Her wrists were chained together and then chained to her waist, making her completely helpless. She had a cloth gag tied around her head and her teeth were biting down on the gag.

The alien man was sitting on the very rock Fel had once sat upon years ago. Four other men, well-dressed, were equally spaced on either side of him. Six guards were lounging against the back wall to their right and another six to their left. Another man stood before the five and was talking. "Okay, everyone is here. The bidding for this *mentales* gifted woman shall begin."

"I still protest. I bought her fair and square!" One of the men to the right of the alien spoke up. Kassia guessed this was the man from Wye who had tried to buy her from her father.

"No one is disputing that my good man. However, you can always get a refund. I have her now and that is all that counts. If you want her, then be the highest bidder."

From the man's clothing and accent, Fel and Savina knew he was from the Easterlings. In addition, one of the bidders was also from the Easterlings as well. This one spoke next, "But how can you expect us to outbid the aliens? They have unlimited money. This is not a fair deal. You were hired to abduct gifted women for us, not for the aliens."

"Deals change. The bidding starts at ten thousand silvers. Who'll open the bidding for this fine *mentales* gifted woman?" the man sneered. Fel guessed most of the guards belonged to the speaker, who she recognized as the man who teleported Sara away from the caravan just as she was about to snatch her herself. She sent this recognition to the others, though Savina also recognized him and also the fact most of the guards were Easterlings. They had curved scimitars and wicked daggers slung at their sides which gave them away to her. They would be fierce opponents, fighting with two blades, unless they could be somehow disarmed first.

Fel knew this too. For once, she was stymied, uncertain how to proceed. There were just too many of them for the five of them to handle, ignoring wholly the alien and his strange weapon and defenses. "Ten thousand five hundred," an Easterlings man called out. The alien raised him another five hundred.

We need some help, Molly sent and proceeded to focus

and her crystal began to glow. Meanwhile, Kassia thought quickly. The alien was her problem; he should not be here and he was violating so many rules she couldn't count them.

How about a bluff? Let me see if I can handle the alien, Kassia thought, hoping Fel would pick up on it. Fel turned her head to look at Kassia.

Stall for more time, please, Molly sent.

"Twenty thousand silvers from the alien. Going once. Do I hear more? Going twice. Come on, gentlemen. Are you going to let this ideal telepath go to the alien?"

Kassia saw the bidding would be over shortly. The other four men looked downcast and were grumbling over the exorbitant price the alien had bid. She decided to act and stall things a bit. She slipped off her ring and at once her skin returned to its olive color showing clearly she was also an alien like the winning bidder. She stepped boldly out into the edge of the circular cavern and into the lantern light.

"I am from the Sector ID Minister's office. You are all under arrest for heinous crimes. You, sir, have broken so many Imperium laws in this matter, you will be lucky if we merely deport you off-world. A battalion of Drugi is just outside this tunnel entrance. For you primitives, Drugi are our top Security Forces. I order you to throw down your swords and you, your blaster, and turn off your PDS. If you do, the Drugi will not blast you to smithereens." Kassia played her role well. She sounded totally official and believable. A number of the guards did just that, casting glances at their leader, the teleport man. Kassia added, "You there, teleport man, the Drugi outside are waiting for you to jump out. They are begging for some target practice. You'll do fine."

The Easterlings man gave her a look that could kill, but lowered his hand from his crystal. The alien spoke up, "I know you; you are that pathetic field agent Kunegunda. Don't you know the Imperium has sanctioned the abduction of likely telepaths for the last fifty years? No one is going to do anything to me over this. I flew in at night unseen by all. So no visible breakage of the lease agreement. No one has ever traced the abductions to us, and they never will. She's bluffing, gentlemen. There's no Drugi outside."

111

As she spoke, Kassia slowly moved into the chamber, edging closer to the alien. Her notion was somehow to disable his PDS giving the others a chance to get to him. Fel moved silently behind her. Savina knew what Molly was doing and carefully backed outside and took up a position near the horses. She guessed the teleport man might try to make a break for it and jump out to grab a horse and flee. If so, she would be waiting for him, sword drawn.

Five black bears came slowly ambling up to the tunnel entrance and then moved on inside, pausing for a moment at the dead body, giving it a sniff and shove. Both Molly and Gina pressed their bodies hard against the side of the tunnel, giving as much space for the bears to pass as possible. Molly knew they would not harm them, since she was in control of them. *Don't bother the three women in there, please,* she sent to her new friends.

"She's bluffing, I tell you," the alien said and began to draw his blaster. At that instant, all hell broke out, as the bears came growling and howling into the confined space. Two of the bears plowed into the guards on either side of the cavern, while two more pushed around Fel and Kassia heading for the bidders in the central part of the cavern.

The alien man finally got his blaster clear of its holster and aimed it at Fel, guessing that she was the fiercest fighter. Besides, she was lunging towards him. Kassia had a fraction of a second to act. She knew if he fired that weapon, Fel would be disintegrated. She, as a field agent, was responsible for these native women. One of her race was violating the legally binding lease and was guilty of many crimes against these natives. She had to act. She dove and threw her body in front of Fel's just as the man fired his blaster at Fel. Flying through the air before Fel, Kassia felt a sudden, intense pain in her arms, pain like she had never felt before. Then the rocky floor smashed into her head and all went totally dark.

Fel heard the concussion of the blaster ringing in her ears and saw Kassia taking the brunt of his attack, sparing her. The two bears plowed into the bidders, knocking them back towards the helpless Sara, who was trying to scream but couldn't, nor could she move. Fel moved quickly. The alien was knocked off his feet, and she dove into the melee thrusting her sword up from the direction of his feet as Kassia had told her. It cut into his lower abdomen and groin, and Fel ruthlessly twisted and sliced her blade around his innards until the alien fell unconscious. Then, she pounced on other bidders, while trying to avoid the bears, who seemed to give her room. Molly was concentrating heavily on her bears, making sure they didn't harm the women by accident.

The teleport man, who they still had no name for, jumped out of the cavern, using his *mentales* gift. He didn't have time even to use his crystal, but it wasn't needed; he only wanted to get to the horses and get away from this mess. He arrived outside where Savina was waiting. She grinned; she'd guessed right, the man was basically a coward. She attacked him while his back was turned and he never knew what killed him. Then, she dashed into the tunnel to help inside.

One of the Easterlings bidders saw his chance. With confusion everywhere, being the closest to Sara, he moved over to her, picked her up and threw her over his shoulders. Then, dodging bears and guards, he made his way towards the tunnel that led outside. Two of the guards managed to avoid the bears and made a break for the tunnel where Gina and Molly were standing. Molly was still deep in concentration controlling the bears, and Gina was protecting her. The two guards merely bowled the two over, throwing their bodies into the two women, knocking them over. Stumbling over them, they continued their race for life. The Easterlings man carrying Sara followed nimbly after them. Gina tried to stop him, but only managed to cut his leg slightly. He didn't stop. The two guards then plowed into Savina, knocking her over, and the Easterlings man took advantage of this lucky break as well. His *mentales* gift was one of incredible good luck.

Knocked senseless, Molly's concentration broke and so did her control over the bears. The bears howled and growled a little and then turned around and ambled out of the cavern and tunnel, eventually loping off over the rocky hills, ignoring the frightened horses who were straining to break free. As they ambled off, one of the bears wondered why he didn't stop for a meal of a horse, but decided he wasn't that hungry at the moment.

Fel was still busy with one of the guards and didn't see the alien struggle to his feet, bleeding profusely from his lower abdomen. He picked up his blaster and saw it was crushed and useless. Then he realized Fel didn't know that. "Stop bitch! I've got my blaster back. I ought to blast you into atoms! But I won't. Tell that bitch Kunegunda there that when I get back to base, I will report *she* was abducting *mentales* gifted women. There will be a price on her head for sure!" His laugh was more of a snicker or sneer, and he too left, leaving a bloody trail behind him. During the lull, the guard that Fel was fighting took the opportunity to flee for his life as well.

Silence fell in the cavern. Only Fel still stood, though a groggy Gina and Molly soon rose and looked around at the carnage. Holding her slightly bleeding head, Savina walked in as well. No one said anything for a moment, taking stock of the scene. Then Fel acted. She went to the fallen woman who had saved her life and lifted her up. "She's alive! I don't know how, but she is. Come on. Give me a hand with her. God, she's lost her hands."

About the only good thing one can say about a blaster hit is that it is both sterile and searing. The shot had struck her arms just above her elbows, disintegrating everything below that point, while also searing the two wounds from its high heat. Only a small amount of blood was oozing from Kassia's two stumps, but she had also taken a nasty cut on her forehead from the rocks on the floor of the cavern, which she had hit full force.

"Put her down there, and I'll see what I can do for her," Savina suggested, wiping the blood off her own forehead.

"Mom, let me fix you up first," Gina ordered and proceeded quickly to mend her mother's small gash.

"That's enough, dear, thanks. I really need to work on Kassia. Help Fel. I killed the teleport man outside by the horses," Savina said, pushing Gina aside and leaning over the unconscious Kassia.

"Come on; let's drag the bodies outside and see what's what," Fel ordered. The three women set to work dragging the men outside, though Fel insisted on searching them. She found a small fortune among the dead bidders, as she suspected she would. Outside, Fel noted three horses were missing along with the shuttle craft.

The Easterlings bidder had gotten away taking Sara with him, though Gina pointed out the small blood trail. "See, he's bleeding. So we know he took the horse that was here and headed off that way. We have a clear trail to follow. He must be carrying Sara with him on the one horse. Chained as she was, she could not sit on a horse by herself."

"Good going, Gina. Okay, back to work," Fel ordered. *Damn! I was so close to rescuing Sara a second time and he got away again! I ought to go after him right now. I probably could easily catch him and rescue Sara, but damn it! Kassia! Now I there is a life between us! I am honor bound to serve her until my debt is repaid! I cannot desert her right now, shit! Well, she did save my life back there. Damn, how inconvenient. Well, mister Easterlings man, I will come after you and get Sara if it is the last thing that I do! You have my sworn word on that!*

An hour later, they had the dead bodies hauled some distance from the tethered horses and had their own brought up and tied into the line. Inside, Gina and Molly had set up a temporary base and had a meal cooking. Savina finally ceased her healing work on Kassia. "There, that is as much as I can do for her. Her head wound is healed fully and I have skin growing over her exposed stumps. I will work on her some more every day until I have her in as good a shape as possible, Fel. You know there is a life between you two now, don't you?"

"Hell yes and an alien one at that! She saved my life. I never expected an alien would ever do that for one of us, but she did. Thanks, Savina. I owe you another one," Fel replied. "Look, she's coming around."

Kassia moaned a little. The darkness began to lift and her eyes fluttered and then opened. "What happened?" she whispered. Then, the images came flooding back into her mind. She looked down at what remained of her arms and shrieked.

"There, there, you are alive, Kassia. You saved my life. Now I must repay you for that," Fel whispered.

"Did, did we win? Sara?" Kassia tried to formulate a coherent thought, suppressing the horror of her arms, but only barely.

"No, damnable Easterlings man snuck out with her, but Gina wounded him. Left a clear trail to follow. We'll get her next time," Fel answered her.

Kassia now recalled the Rigel-3 man. "The alien? His blaster? Did we?"

"I wounded him pretty darn well, thanks to your tip. He was bleeding like a pig, but he too managed to escape in his shuttle craft. Oh, he told me to tell you he is going to make a full report saying it was you who had been abducting the women. He said they will put a price on your head. Is that true? Will they believe him and come after you?"

Kassia could not take any more losses. She broke down and began bawling. It wasn't enough the man had mutilated her for life, turning her into a helpless cripple. Now he was going to convince them she was the guilty party. It would be her word against his and they'd believe a man over a woman any day. That was just how it was. She cried and cried. Wisely, Savina indicated to the others to allow her to do so.

In a soft voice, Gina called out, "Supper is ready. Come and get it. I'll feed Kassia this time, Fel."

Even though Kassia only wanted to continue to cry, Gina kept putting a spoon to her lips and she found her body eating almost as if she had nothing to do with it. Finally full, Gina held a mug of hot tea to her lips. The sip felt so good. Then Kassia came out of it. "Fel, if he does that, they can find us. Please, go to my saddlebags. I have a Communicator, a Navigator, and a compass in there. Bring them to me; we cannot keep them with us. Damn, the arm chip. Fel, I need you to cut the ID chip out of my left shoulder. They can track me anywhere with it."

"What the hell? A chip? I'm sorry. I don't know what you are talking about," Fel answered. Kassia tried to point to where the doctor had inserted the chip, but ended up crying again, unable to point properly.

Savina came over, having overheard their conversation. "Okay, Kassia, I think I get it. The aliens have put some kind of thing in your left shoulder that they can use to locate your body, right?"

Sniffing, Kassia said, "Yes, it is very small and just beneath the surface."

"Okay, don't try to point, dear. I can find it." She uncovered her crystal and focused. Ah that soft, comforting bluish glow appeared and Kassia looked deep into it. So warm, so comforting. She knew she could get utterly lost in it.

Ah, there it is. I see it now. Okay, let's move it on up to the surface. I could cut it out, but I think I can just move it. Yes, this is going to work. She's undergone enough trauma for one day. Just a bit more. Ah, there it is, just beneath the skin. A tiny bit more. "Ah ha. There it is, I have it removed."

"But how? You didn't cut it out," Kassia asked, baffled and braced for more pain.

"Part of my gift, Kassia. I moved the foreign object up and out of your skin. Shall I toss that tiny thing into the fire?"

"Please do. Fel, find those other three things and smash them into bits please. I can't have them tracking us. They are signed out to me and as soon as that man reports me, they'll come looking for me following the tracers in those three things," Kassia whispered, trying to keep from breaking down once more.

A half hour later, after some stomping, and rock bashing, the three small devices were rubble. Kassia looked relieved. She then bravely said, "So how soon do we go after Sara? I insist on coming with you. I know I am now a helpless cripple, but if this is the last thing I ever do, I have to help you get Sara rescued. Then, you can abandon me anywhere you like."

"I can't abandon you, Kassia. There's a life between us now. I am honor bound to look after you until that debt is repaid and I somehow save your life," Fel stated factually.

"Okay, then the best chance you have of doing that and getting free of me is to take me along with you and rescue Sara," Kassia declared. *Then, I can just die somewhere by myself. I have to get Fel free from this obligation.* Promise me you will take me with you and go after Sara now?"

Fel chuckled. She'd heard Kassia's unspoken thoughts,

but wisely chose not to react to them. "We can't right now, silly. It's nighttime and it is raining too. We'll get started at first light."

"Promise me you will take me with you until we rescue Sara, promise me that Fel," Kassia insisted with the last of her rapidly fading will.

Fel sighed. That was the last thing in the world she wanted to do. Taking Kassia along now would hinder her enormously. Savina sent her, *You have to do as she asks. She'll die otherwise or even try to come after us by herself. You know that, Fel.*

Again, the *castinto* sighed. "Yes, Kassia, I give you my sworn word we will take you with us when we go to rescue Sara. Now get some sleep, my padrona." Vaguely Kassia's mind tried to translate padrona. Did it mean mistress? She slumped down and fell into a deep sleep.

Again, Kassia had dreams. This time the entire garrison at the spaceport was searching everywhere for her, though she continued to try to hide from them. The only comfort she got was that fascinating blue glow from the germanium crystals. Slowly she slipped more and more into that warm glow. It felt so good, so comforting, so right.

"My god, she's burning up with a fever!" Fel said as she awoke the next morning. As before, she'd lain beside Kassia, cradling her like she was her daughter. "Savina, come have a look. She must have gotten an infection from her wounds yesterday."

Wiping the sleep from her eyes, Savina commented, "I'm getting too old to sleep on the hard stones. Okay, let me see her. Gina, Molly, breakfast please." Savina undid the pod-silk covering of her crystal, focused, and examined the unconscious Kassia.

A bit later, she looked terribly puzzled. "Well, is she dying?" asked Fel, holding her breath. If she died, then she would be relieved of her honor-bound duty to Kassia. Yet, she really didn't want Kassia to die, though she didn't quite know why.

"I can't say, but I can find no trace of infections in her. Then again, she is an alien, and I've never examined one before her. Maybe it is something with her body I don't know about. Let me eat and think, please," Savina replied.

A half hour later, Savina was back at it, again going into a deeper rapport with the unconscious woman. She found Kassia was wholly absorbed in the images she had in her mind of the blue glow from her crystal. Savina felt what Kassia was feeling, the warm comforting energies. Slowly she backed out of the rapport and on a hunch, used her fingers to open Kassia's eyelids. Then she sat back rather astonished. "Well?" Fel nudged her.

"I'd say Kassia has come down with a bad case of Verge Sickness," Savina reported. "Look at her eyes, they are changing." Fel did just that, prying first one and then the other open. Both were slightly yellowed.

"My god!" was all Fel could say. "What the devil do we do now? Verge Sickness? But she's an alien!"

"Not any more. She's becoming or trying to become one of us Fel. I've handled a few cases of Verge Sickness, but she doesn't fit the pattern. Usually, children get it when they reach puberty. You know, sexual arousals block the same nerve channels that our psi energies use, causing the high fever. She's not had sex; she's a virgin still, and she's as old as Gina, I'd guess. You didn't pleasure her the other night did you?" Savina asked.

Fel flushed. "No, she's an alien." Gina and Molly chuckled to themselves.

"It must be caused by the severe trauma she'd undergone. Worse luck, we don't have any *bacal* with us. Why don't you search all those other saddlebags? See if you can find any."

Fel, Gina, and Molly did as Savina requested, but found none. Evidently, the Easterlings man had taken the horse whose saddlebags had the leaves in them to keep Sara under control. That made sense to Fel.

"Gina and I will do what we can. We'll try to keep her nerve channels open. Probably have to do it every hour or so. I'll go first, Gina, you spell me in say an hour," Savina ordered.

Meanwhile the Easterlings man is getting further away with Sara! Fel moaned silently to herself. She was caught in a quandary. She was obligated to rescue Sara; she'd given her solemn word on that. Now she was honor-bound to assist Kassia as well and Kassia was deadly ill and could not be moved. Fel wanted and needed to go into action, but simply could not. She was frustrated, more so than she'd been since that horrible day when she became a *castinto*.

Chapter 6 The Chase

For a week, Savina and Gina tended to the feverous Kassia, soothing her frayed nerves, unblocking her nerve channels, and lowering her body's excess heat. Such only lasted for a short time before the blockages returned and her fever rose again. At night, Fel slept beside her, talking soothingly to Kassia. "Padrona, you can beat this. Don't give up. Fight it, my padrona with the most fabulous knockers I've ever seen. Come on. Fight it my padrona."

At last exhausted herself, Savina became more desperate. "Okay, she's obviously not getting any better and we have no way to get *bacal* leaves here. There is one more thing I can try, but I'll need a circle. All of you, we need to merge into rapport with each other and then you all funnel your energies to me and I'll try this one last thing. It's risky without having someone act as a Regulator for us."

"What are you going to do to her?" Fel asked, growing a little concerned.

"She is continually stuck in the glow of my crystal; she is trying to absorb its comfort, and she will simply not let go of it. I have to somehow pry her out of that."

Fel reached a decision. "Look, it could well kill her. Let me do it. I'm responsible for her now. Her life is in my hands. It is only right I make the attempt, Savina."

She agreed and the four women activated their crystals. Savina joined with her daughter and then with Molly. That was the easy part, for they'd often shared such an intimacy with each other. Now came the hard part, adjusting to the fighter that was Feliciana, whose personality was quite different from the three. It took Savina nearly a half hour finally to drag Fel into rapport with them.

Fel suddenly felt the combined power of four telepaths, a power rush she'd never felt before. So imitate and yet such wondrous power! It took her a moment to adjust and focus. At last, she reached out to Kassia. There she was, embracing the soft blue glow of the crystal, oblivious to all else.

Kassia my padrona, it is time to let go of the blue light.
I can't. I'll die.
No you won't my padrona. I am here with you. I won't
let you die.
I can't. No one loves me. I am forsaken by my own
people. I'm a hopeless cripple. The only comfort in the whole
world is this beautiful, soothing blue energy.
Padrona, you must let it go. It's killing you.
Perhaps that is a good thing. How can I live with my
body so destroyed?
I am here to help you, my padrona.
Let me die and you are free of me.
I can't. That is not honorable.
But you will be free of me.
I, I don't want to be free of you, Kassia. I am falling in
love with you, my padrona. Please come back to me. In
desperation she added, *It is time we go rescue Sara. Please*
come back to me so we can rescue her, please, Kassia. You
and I, we have to rescue Kassia.
You love me?
Yes, you have the most gorgeous set of knockers I've
ever seen. Please come back to me.
Sara! Yes, I promised to help you rescue Sara. You will
take me with you, won't you, Fel?
Yes, Kassia, I promise. I know it will be hard for you,
but we will manage, if only you will let go of the blue light
and come back to me, my padrona. I love you, please.

Kassia's body sighed. She let go of the only thing that
gave her comfort until Fel had spoken to her. She drifted into a
darkness of no thought, no feeling, and no emotion. She fell
into a deep, relaxing sleep and Fel slipped out of rapport with
her.

"You did it," Savina whispered, feeling Kassia's
forehead. It was already noticeably cooler. Fel smiled, but
knew those three had felt everything she had and had heard
everything she and Kassia had thought. That was the liability
of telepathic rapport; nothing could be kept a secret. Wisely,
the three said nothing to Fel.

For several more days, they nursed Kassia back to

health. She was dehydrated and half starved, but she recovered rapidly. She now had very yellow eyes, with the brown speckles of course. "I'm a telepath now? How can that be?" she looked at her eyes in Savina's small mirror.

"Psi dust was the original cause and you were living in an area that was covered in that dust. That's my best guess, Kassia, but who knows," Savina explained. "Now we have to train you some. An untrained telepath is a liability to herself and to the others around her. That's one of the rules. Ordinarily, we should take you at once to one of the towers to be trained."

"But you can't! We have to go rescue Sara first, and I'm an alien and a hopeless cripple too," Kassia protested, adding, "and likely a wanted criminal too, if that man does what he told Fel he'd do to me."

"Points taken, but we have to train you for all our sakes. I've had some experience in the towers, but it's been a long time ago. I will endeavor to train you, Kassia. Then as promised, we'll go after Sara."

"I don't see why, but I will cooperate, Savina." She did just that. In a couple of days, she was able to Hide Her Thoughts from the others and to Block Out Other's Thoughts. Next, Savina worked on trying to figure out in what direction her *mentales* gifts lay and just what her inherent skills might be.

"Mom, wouldn't it be easier to do if she were attuned to her own crystal?" Gina asked.

"I think so, dear. Let me get one of the spares we always carry with us."

Kassia looked at the inert greyish germanium crystal about two inches in size that Savina produced. She had it tied securely to a leather strap and placed it around Kassia's neck for her. "Now then, we are going to activate it. Each of us radiates our psi energies at a slightly different frequency. What my dad discovered was they can be attuned to one specific frequency. Once that's done, when you touch the crystal, it amplifies your own psi energies a hundredfold. Here we go, Kassia."

Slowly, Savina slipped into rapport with Kassia and

then the two focused on the inert crystal. Suddenly the crystal began glowing bright blue. "There, that's all there is to it. Now you have your own crystal. Don't ever let someone who is not in rapport with you touch it. If you do, you will get a really bad shock. If the crystal gets destroyed, it can give you a horrid shock. I've heard some have even died when theirs was broken. Normally, we keep ours covered until we need to use them. In your case, you can't get yours uncovered, so I think it best to leave it open. All you need to do is touch it with your arm and it will activate."

Kassia touched it with her right upper arm and watched it begin to radiate the comforting blue glow. She smiled, very pleased indeed. She wanted a sip of tea and suddenly her mug floated up to her lips. "Oh my! How did that happen?" She took a sip anyway.

Savina smiled, "Well, there is one aspect of your gifts. It looks like you can move objects around by thought. That's going to be valuable for you, Kassia. Let's see what else you can do. I wish I had a copy of Marisol's big list of gifts."

"Say, that's what my boss, well ex-boss, wanted to get from the tower in Haverhills. What is it anyway?"

"A complete list of all known forms gifts have taken. A compendium of skills. Oh, wait a second, I see you are using another skill."

Fel looked at Kassia and didn't see anything unusual at first. Neither did Molly or Gina. "What?" Fel finally asked.

"Look at her skin color. It's not olive any more. She can change her skin color. I think with some training, she can change her body into other forms, but let's leave that one for those in the towers to handle."

"Okay, is she ready enough to travel? We need to get going after Sara," Fel broke in, growing impatient once more.

The thought of Sara caused a reaction in Kassia. Suddenly, she was looking out of Sara's eyes, rather startled by her strange vision. Fel noticed something was wrong with Kassia and slipped into rapport with her and saw what she was seeing. Then she slipped back out and brought Kassia back to the present. "Well done, Kassia. She can see from another's eyes. She saw Sara. She is still chained but is riding in a wagon, so at last we get a break. Horses can go faster than a wagon any time. Further, I recognized that landscape. They are somewhere near Wycombe, heading east towards the Easterlings, naturally. Way to go, Kassia. This is going to be a big help in catching up to them!"

For the first time since the battle, Kassia felt a tiny bit of self-pride. Perhaps, she wasn't a hopeless basket case after all. She could help them get to Sara. "When do we leave?" she asked.

"First thing in the morning. Pipercity is not too far from here. I'll lead the string of horse there and get us some provisions and supplies and catch back up with you. The rest of you, keep heading due east," Fel answered, highly enthused, terribly eager to get back on the trail once again.

"How is she going to ride?" asked Molly.

"On a horse," Fel replied without thinking. "Oh shit! Damn. I see your point."

"I had to cling to the saddle before, now I can't," Kassia added, tears swelling in her eyes. She rubbed them with what was left of her arms.

"You are supposed to grip the horse with your legs. I thought you said you could ride?" Fel asked.

Kassia blushed. "Oops. I guess I am not as good a rider as I thought. I can try, someone can lead my horse, can't they?"

"This is so humiliating!" Kassia admitted the next morning as she stood beside her mare ready to mount but was unable to do so on her own.

"At least you have your figure. Everyone thinks I am a man at first, now that *is* much more humiliating!" Fel countered, lifting her up onto her mare. "Remember to grip with your legs this time."

"What else have I got to grip with?" Kassia replied trying to make light of it. She was very nervous and fearful, sitting astride the horse but unable to hold on if needed.

Daunting, my padrona, but you can do it, Fel sent her and Kassia did smile back.

Savina took the mare's halter lead and led Kassia's horse, while Gina and Molly rode on ahead of them. Fel waved and led the long string of horses off, heading slightly to the south. At first, Gina led them south to the valley's floor before turning east. As they rode along, Kassia said, "Savina, thanks for everything. How is Fel going to find us?"

"You are welcome, dear. We are going to go due east. All she has to do is head north from Pipercity and look for our trail. If she doesn't find it, she waits for us to catch up to her. If she finds it, she catches up to us. You'll see her before nightfall, if I know Fel. She's fallen for you in a big way, you know. Well, I've really only known her personally as long as you have, Kassia, but I've heard many, many stories about her before. She's always been a loner and a terrific fighter. Now she is positively doting on you, that much I can tell." She then decided to educate Kassia a bit more about her psi energies and how they used her body's nerve channels, especially their sexual channels. Slowly, Kassia began to understand, but realized she now had much to learn and vowed to do so, somehow.

When the late afternoon rain began, Savina stopped to put Kassia's cloak over her. They glanced to their rear and saw no one. "I hope she shows up soon or I will have to pick our camping spot. I think it might snow tonight; temperature feels like its dropping too much." An hour later, Savina did just that, halting them at the edge of a small pine forest. She tied up the horses, while Gina and Molly began working up another lean-to style shelter. Kassia marveled at how inventive these women were, seemingly making a shelter out of nothing in the middle of nowhere. Kassia felt utterly useless, as she watched the three women working efficiently. All she could do was stand and not get in their way. Depression began to take hold of her again.

Just as the resinous fire began to crackle, Fel came riding up, leading a string of two pack saddled horses, each heavily loaded. "Hi ya, miss me?" Fel called out, rather cheerfully. Her horse was lathered and Kassia presumed she'd ridden hard to catch up with them. "Gonna snow tonight," she added.

"Savina guessed that already. Glad you found us. I was getting worried," Kassia replied.

"Come here, padrona, and help me unload these beasts of burden," Fel said.

Kassia walked over to her and the horses. Whispering, she said, "Fel, haven't you forgotten something? I don't have my hands anymore."

"No, I figured I'd load things over your shoulders and you can walk them into the camp for me. Then, you and I can walk them a bit to cool them down. Here, hold still." She slumped a heavy saddlebags over each of Kassia's shoulders and motioned for her to take them to the shelter. Kassia did as asked. After making several trips, Fel put the lead rope of one beneath her armpit and told her to clamp down on it and lead the horse around the grassy are before the pines, while she took the other two herself. Although the rope slipped a little, Kassia managed to get the horse walking and felt a little pleased she could do a little bit to help out.

Once out of ear shot of the others, Fel whispered, "I know, padrona, it is going to be difficult adjusting to the way things are, but I know you. You aren't the quitting type. You and I, we will just have to find ways you can do things. Be brave, my padrona." Kassia smiled. Around Fel, she felt safe and somehow wanted.

Again, she used her new found ability to move objects to feed herself, amazing the other four women who saw the fork or spoon seemingly rising up and down as if by magic. Just as they were about to turn in and well after dark, Kassia heard the telltale hissing sound. She glanced up and saw a shuttle craft approaching their camp as the drizzling rain changed to large snowflakes. "Aliens!" she called out.

"Shit! What do we do now?" Fel cried out. She could handle men, but flying ships? No way. Just then an energy beam shot down at them, narrowly missing their shelter, hitting a pine tree trunk that exploded with a loud popping sound.

"They must be after me," Kassia cried out, moving out from the lean-to and attempting to draw their fire away from the four women. "You bastards!" she yelled up at the ship, knowing full well whoever was inside couldn't hear her. She waved her short arms futilely in the air, mostly just wiggling her cloak. Again, the ship fired down at her, narrowly missing her. "Damn you!"

She moved her right arm up and felt her skin touch her crystal. *Focus. Focus, that's what Savina says. All right, I'm focused!* As the four women cowered within the scant protection of the lean-to, they watched the alien ship being pulled towards the ground. Its engines began to whine as the pilot poured on the thrust to overcome intense pull Kassia was making. With its engines straining to their utmost, it began to pull free of her tugging hold. She let it go and the shuttle backed off rapidly and fired another shot at her once more. Then it began to move swiftly towards her. This time, Kassia took a different approach. As it flew at her, she gave its front a strong downward push. The shuttle's nose pointed to the ground and hit it. A blinding explosion resulted, knocking Kassia off her feet.

Fel came running out to her. "Kassia! Kassia, are you hurt?" She lifted her up in her strong arms and sat her on her feet.

"Thanks, no, just lost my balance there. I've got no way to keep it now. It's really strange wiggling my arms and hands when they aren't there. But I got him!"

"Way to go hot shot! How the devil did they find us?" Fel asked.

Kassia replied sheepishly, "I must still have something with my stuff that has an ID tag in it. Come on. You've got to help me go through everything I brought along and find it or they'll be back!"

Although all five searched, they couldn't find anything. "Okay, we'll burn every damn thing I brought along with me, clothes and all. I hope someone's got something I can wear," Kassia declared, very much annoyed she couldn't find it. "If I had an RFI tag locator I could find it in a second." Before long, they were all getting in on the action, tossing item after item of Kassia's onto their campfire. Each of the others loaned her a bit of clothing. Although a hodge-podge, she was warm and dressed for the cold. They even burned her saddle and bridle. When they finished, there was nothing of the original Kassia Kunegunda remaining except her physical body.

Then sipping tea afterwards, Kassia asked Savina to thoroughly go over her body and see if there might be another ID tag imbedded in her. Savina did so, but found nothing. "Thanks. Okay, if they find us again, it isn't me that's giving away our location," Kassia stated factually.

Later, they turned in for the night as the snow continued falling lightly. True, it would melt off by early morning, but it was symptomatic of the wild weather patterns Tierra experienced for the last century plus. Fel snuggled close to Kassia, holding her firmly as if she were her child. *Thanks for saving us again, my padrona.* Kassia fell into a relaxing, deep slumber; she felt totally safe again.

In the morning, Fel asked Kassia to use her gift to see where Sara and the Easterlings man were at so she could get a better feel on the direction they ought to travel today. "My god, what has he done to her?" Kassia exclaimed a little later. Fel and Savina quickly went into rapport with her and saw what she had just seen.

Savina smiled, "Welcome to the Easterlings binding traditions, Kassia. He has her bound in their usual manner, fetter skirt, arms chained at her waist. But having her lower arms bound behind her back in that leather tube is only supposed to be done at night and only when the skirt is removed. He's making sure she is immobile and cannot get herself out of the wagon. Oh, yes, he's tied her lips shut to keep her silent. Four rings in each lip is their usual way to handle recalcitrant women."

"That's inhumane!" Kassia countered.

"Well, she should not have her lower arms bound behind her, but other than that, the rest is typical of the Easterlings," Savina countered.

"At least I can recognize where they are at," Fel interrupted them, getting them back on track. "They are now east of Wycombe and that tells me he has picked up their pace. Perhaps he can sense we are now on his trail. Let's get moving."

Fel's strong arms lifted Kassia up and onto her saddle. "If we go too fast for you, let us know, my padrona."

"It's scary, Fel, *really* scary, but I *have* to manage

somehow," Kassia whispered. "I feel so helpless."

"I'd love to say otherwise, padrona, but I cannot. Instead, I can suggest it is a state of mind. The Easterlings women manage to do all their daily chores while bound. With them, I know helplessness is just a state of mind, only you have more constraints than they. Be brave, my padrona." Kassia flashed her a quick smile. At least I can think about that, she thought.

With Gina and Molly leading their packhorses and Savina leading Kassia's mare, Fel rode point, setting a swift pace. The horses were well rested and already the light snow was melting. Far off to the north and south the great barrier ridges of the foothills broke the skyline. Patches of resinous pines broke the rolling grasslands of the valley they were following. Occasionally, they could see smoke from chimneys of small hamlets, which Fel skirted. They wanted no delays now.

Kassia did think about her situation. She knew the Imperium did have great prosthesis for those who lost one or both of their hands. However, with the additional loss of one's elbow, the prosthesis was only marginally useful. *I might as well have lost all my arms for all the good the doctors can do for me. Hell, I can't even get the doctors to work on me now, not as a hunted woman. What's left of them is nearly completely useless. Well, I have a compensating gift of being able to move things, so that will have to compensate.* Still, she felt quite depressed. *How could my situation have gone so utterly wrong?*

For three days, they continued their eastward chase. Fel continued to bypass all major settlements, though more and more farmsteads appeared as the foothills were giving way to the rolling farmlands, dotted with nut trees. Once this had been the breadbasket country, but with the change in climate, the farmers planted new crops that could survive these colder and wetter days of summer. One of these new crops was various nut trees, whose nuts, when ground, made a passable substitute for flour. The actual breadbasket these days lay some five hundred miles to the south.

Based on the visions Kassia had each day, Fel guessed

they were gaining about ten miles on their prey each day. Fel had no doubts now the Easterlings man had picked up his pace and she continually wondered how he could know they were hard on his trail.

The fourth day found the five approaching the outer farms and hamlets of the greater Wycombe area, the Kingdom of Wycombe as it was called. The original fifteen kingdoms had long ago disintegrated into hundreds of smaller political units that still retained the title of kingdom. However, the ground situation changed for the worst. They entered an active combat zone.

Smoke clouds rose into the cloudy skies as they neared the hamlet of Wise, cradled in a small valley with many small farmsteads dotting the landscape. Low stone fences marked the boundaries of the fields, picturesque under normal circumstances. Today it was hellish. "My god, what's happened here?" Fel said to herself. Shells of the hamlet's buildings and homes were all that remained, many still smoldering. Just to the north of the hamlet, dozens of fresh graves were plainly visible, the black earth mounds in sharp contrast to the green of the grass, crops, and pines. A few people were milling around just outside of the hamlet and Fel stopped to ask what had happened.

"The towers were supposed to protect us from this!" one older man complained angrily.

Another added, "Haverhills and Bedworth Towers are fighting it out, both claim these lands. Two days ago, their armies fought here and destroyed the town with magical fires and stone eating acids. Hardly anyone was spared, excepting the nearby farms. Moved on eastward, they did. You be careful; they'll kill anything that moves!"

"Hit us with terrible magical weapons they did," a third man volunteered. "Tower folks caused more destruction than the soldiers did. That's what I say. No offense Sister."

"None taken, sir," Fel answered.

They continued onward. Savina commented sarcastically, "So much for dad's dream of ultimate weapons bringing peace to Tierra. Lasted what? Maybe two decades? Ha."

Molly added, "That's just like men. All they can think about is fighting! Kassia, is that true of your Rigel men?"

"Yes, they are quick to fight. Ours are called Drugi, heavily armed shock troops. Not all men are that way though, Molly. Lord, I hope so anyway."

Late that afternoon, they came upon a large field encampment of soldiers and several guards rode out to intercept them. "Ah, Sisterhood fighters. Come with me. General Skaggs will want to speak with you," the captain ordered Fel.

Shit, now we are in for it. Don't give them any reason to harm us, Fel sent to everyone. She turned her horse south towards the many tents. She estimated several hundred soldiers were camped here. The captain led them to a tent that flew a red banner. A well-dressed man stepped out. "Ah, captain, you've found us some more volunteers I see. General Skaggs here, Sisters."

Fel dismounted and then helped Kassia get down, much to the dismay of the general. Seeing the helpless state of Kassia rather changed his mood. "We are on a mission, general. We've not come to fight," Fel then said. A light rain began to fall and she raised Kassia's hood over her head for her, taking advantage of the general's discomfort around Kassia.

"Well, I accept that. We've taken a lot of wounded. Perhaps if one of you is a healer you could spare a little time to help out our tower healers?" he asked politely.

Fel saw no way out of this one. By law, Sisterhood women who had healing skills were obligated to use them when asked. It was part of the agreed upon regulations the towers and the Sisterhood had set in place, giving the Sisterhood the worldwide recognition that it desperately needed. In effect, the agreement had legalized the Sisterhood, but it brought obligations such as this to the women. "We have two who have such skills. If we are permitted to camp at the edge of your encampment, I will send the two to your tower healers, general."

"Yes, that will be acceptable. See to it the others remain at the edge. I don't want any trouble from my men," he replied solemnly. Fel knew what he meant. Soldiers often loved to engage Sisterhood fighters to prove they were better than the outcast women. Other times, they attempted to rape them when they could get away with it.

Fel helped Kassia back up and then led her group to a suitable spot at the northern edge of the camp. While setting up their camp for the night, Fel reminded them, "Remember, don't look any of the men in their eyes. That can be construed as your flirting with them and thus giving them permission to rape you. Don't pick any fights either, no matter the provocation. Savina and Gina, you two be extra careful and don't over tax your energies. We'll keep supper hot for you."

The two healers headed back into the camp, ignoring the whistles and catcalls from many soldiers. "Will they be all right?" Kassia asked, growing more alarmed by the moment. "Do you think the men will try something against us?"

"Safe? Probably. They need healers so probably they will be okay. There are only two of us who can fight now, so Molly, stay alert and don't respond to their taunts," Fel ordered. "We'll make a saddle lean-to for tonight." Kassia had no idea what that was and watched as the two unsaddled the horses. Fel and Molly used the saddles as the entrance poles to their lean-to that was just enough to allow them some room to slip under the canvas roof. "Going to be a little hard for you to get beneath it, Kassia, but there's no other options here."

A while later, Fel gathered the two to her. "Okay, there are no options. We have to get some firewood and a bucket of water. We can scrounge for firewood back there beyond our camp, and the water can be brought from their water wagon over there. I can get the firewood and Molly can get the water. The questions are what do we do with Kassia and do we leave the camp unguarded?

"We can't go off and leave it unguarded. I'll be all right here alone," Kassia said determinedly. She hated Fel had to always consider her helplessness. It hurt, but she knew Fel had to think of her now.

"You sure, padrona?" Fel asked lovingly.

"Yes, I'll watch over things. Don't be too long, please." Fel gave her a hug and the two left in opposite directions, Molly carrying a large canvass water bag. Kassia decided to take this opportunity to observe the soldier's encampment. Her field agent nature kicked in.

While she was taking note of how it was laid out, noticing its weaknesses should they be attacked, three soldiers came walking up to her. One said, "Well, well, what have we here? A lone sister. Maybe she'd like some company."

Another boasted, "Maybe she'd like a whole lot more than company." He laughed wickedly. His intentions were quite clear to Kassia, who didn't need telepathy to know what he meant.

One reached for her and she stepped back a ways. "Hell, this one doesn't have any arms! We can take her right now." He moved towards her menacingly. Kassia felt her own distinct vulnerability but thought, *I'll not go down without a fight!* As he drew close to her, she brought her left leg up and socked him a good one in his groin. The man doubled up in pain, collapsing onto the ground, howling. The other two looked momentarily stunned, but one called out, "Let's teach this armless bitch who is her master!" He moved quickly towards her. She ducked, avoiding his out stretched arms, and gave him a swift kick in his rear. He lost his balance and fell flat onto his face. The third one grabber her from behind and held on to Kassia as she struggled to get free.

Just then, two other Sisterhood fighters carrying steaming pots walked up. "Well, well. What have we here? Three grown men trying to take advantage of an armless woman! Shall we make them armless too or just emasculated, Sally?"

"Oh, why not both, Ann?" the other replied, sitting down her pot and drawing her sword as well. The three men facing the two fighters decided not to push their luck.

"We were just having a little fun with the cripple here. No offense intended, sister. We be on our way. Come on, boys," one said, helping the first man up. He was still in pain and could barely walk.

Once they moved off, one of the women said, "Hi, I'm Sally. This is Ann. We heard some fellow Sisters had come by with some healers, so we thought we'd bring them a hearty stew laced with honey. When they finish their work, they will

134

be craving food and calories. Sorry about the men, but you know men."

"Hi, I'm Kassia. Feliciana and Molly are out gathering firewood and water. Thanks, I guess you can put it down anywhere. As you can see, I'm not much good."

She did and then Ann asked, "How did you lose them?"

Kassia thought fast. She didn't dare tell them about the alien and his blaster. "I had a bad accident not too long ago. Fel is looking after me for the moment."

"Not Feliciana Evita, is it?" Sally asked.

"Yes, that's her. Why?"

"Wow! She's famous! The best fighter in the entire Sisterhood! Mind if we stick around and meet her?" Sally asked.

They chatted a bit and Fel came back carrying an armload of dead branches. Sally and Ann introduced themselves and explained how they'd rescued Kassia and that they brought stew for their healers. Fel was obligated to chat with them while she laid the fire. When Molly returned, Molly began fixing their supper, leaving Fel to continue to chat with the two fellow fighters.

Sally explained, "We are from the Bedwurth house. It seems Haverhills has not been recognizing the official boundaries between their lands and Bedworth Tower's lands. Last month, Bedwurth Tower launched an offensive to drive the Haverhills men back across the border and then some. I think they are trying to teach the Haverhills a lesson. Been pretty fierce fighting the past two weeks though. The tower folks are really helping out. They were able to wipe out entire small hamlets where Haverhills soldiers were holding up. Beats us having to go building by building rooting them out and taking enormous casualties in the process. Still, we are mighty glad for the extra healers."

"How did they burn down the hamlets?" Kassia asked, quite curious.

"They've invented some kind of acid bombs. They use simple catapults to fire their containers at the stone walls. When they strike, they break splashing the caustic acid all over. It really does eat through stone! Amazing, if you ask me.

Of course, it eats through flesh and bone just as readily. They also have invented fire bombs that work similarly. I heard rumors the tower is perfecting a flying car, something like the small alien flying ships. Then, they will be able to fly over the target and simply drop their bombs on them. Drastically safer for all the attackers. I like that idea. I am trying to keep my skin whole. It must be awful trying to survive without your arms, Kassia. You have my sympathy."

Fel came to her defense, "She's adapting well. She's very brave."

"Well, there's the dinner gong. We got to be going. Very pleased to meet you, Feliciana." Sally and Ann shook her hand and then left.

Well after dark, Savina and Gina returned, utterly exhausted and starving. Fel dished out the honey laced stew and the two ate ravenously. Once finished, Savina finally related what they'd seen and done. "The towers have invented new weapons of mass destruction. Acid bombs and fire bombs. We've been treating some of those who were wounded by them. Hideous scarring. My god, one man's face is nothing but a massive scar now. At least he is alive, lost an eye and both ears and most of his hair too. The destruction has taken on a whole new level, Fel, almost beyond belief."

Gina added, "Kassia, you are not alone. I handled a dozen men who've lost one or two arms, one or two legs. Grim. They won't have much of a life now. Men don't take care of other men, not like we women, who will always be there to help you out, Kassia. No, those men might be better of just dying. God, I'm tired. Fel, let's get out of this place as early as we can in the morning!"

They did just that, leaving at the crack of dawn, forgoing breakfast that they had a bit later while on the trail. Fel decided to travel further north, hoping to bypass more of the armies. This was a wise move, only later did they hear of more vicious battles, which they would have encountered. Eight days from the last alien shuttle craft attack found them some forty miles east and twenty north of Wycombe. Unfortunately, Sara and the Easterlings man were now drawing close to Wye, where the mighty Wyndl River was joined by the Wal River spur forming a giant Y in the river. They'd narrowed the gap between them to about five hundred miles thus far.

Fel estimated they would overtake them in thirty days, if they continued to push hard, less if the Easterlings man slowed down. Her real question was what route would he take once he crossed the river at Wye? He could continue eastward to Northend before striking south to Matruk. He could follow the Wyndl River mostly southwards until he reached Matruk. Or he could cut southeast towards Matruk. His unknown destination would be the key. Was he headed for some place in the breadbasket land of Matruk or was he headed further into the desert lands of Alba or Arad?

For the next two days, Fel carefully monitored his directions, utilizing Kassia's gift. At last, she had a good idea. "He's heading east by south, directly towards Adelmira at the southern edge of the Buku Hills. Where he goes after that is anyone's guess. But considering his choice of directions, he's heading straight for it. We can shave some distance off if we strike for the river just east of Leedsburough and head straight for Adelmira. Probably save us seven days, maybe more." They agreed to her plan.

Unfortunately, that night, the situation changed. Just as they were about to turn in for the night, Kassia heard the drone of shuttle crafts. Looking up, she saw three of them flying just below the cloud level. The rains would not come this evening for a change. "How the hell are they still finding me?" she cried out. The three were still a mile away. Kassia thought quickly. If she stayed here in the camp, her new friends would surely be killed as well. She couldn't handle three ships at one time. Kassia got up and raced out into the open grasslands away from their small camp beside a stand of nut trees.

Fel looked up and saw the ships. As she turned, she saw Kassia running out away from their camp and she knew why. "Damn her, she's sacrificing herself! I'm still responsible for her." She dashed off after Kassia, yelling for her to stop. Kassia didn't. Molly, Gina, and Savina turned and saw the two dashing off from the camp and then saw the three ships drawing close. Before they could do anything, they saw brilliant arcs of light, the blasters or disintegrator beams firing from the ships towards the two running figures.

"How on earth?" yelled Savina, shocked the aliens still managed to find Kassia. "Don't they ever give up?"

"Mom, get down! They're shooting at them!" Gina pulled her mother down and back into the nut trees, hoping to get some protection from the dense stand.

They watched in horror as a series of bright energy beams shot from the ships, blinding their vision partially. Suddenly, the ships ceased firing and hovered over the area where the two had been running. Savina blinked her eyes and stared, but could not see either Kassia or Fel. She rubbed them again, but saw nothing.

"Where'd they go?" Gina whispered, afraid the aliens in the ships might hear her and blast them too. After hovering momentarily, the three ships suddenly accelerated and rose up into the clouds and vanished, leaving a total quiet in the valley.

"Come on. Let's see if they are all right," Molly whispered. The three women got up and raced out onto the open grasslands where they'd last seen Kassia and Fel. They passed several burned circles of grass where the beams had struck, but found no sign of either Kassia or Fel. "My god! They've been disintegrated!"

"Murdered!" added Gina, horror struck.

"Butchers!" Savina screamed, waving her arms defiantly in the air. "You filthy butchers!"

All three searched further, but found nothing at all and headed back to their camp in complete silence. Finally, Savina spoke, holding back her grief, "They are gone. The choice is ours now. Do we continue to follow them and try to rescue Sara or do we abandon this chase and go our way?"

"We, we owe it to Fel to finish. She gave her honor-bound word to rescue Sara. We must take on her quest, mom, if only for the sake of the Sisterhood," Gina answered, but then broke down and began sobbing on Molly's shoulders. Her mate put her arms around Gina and allowed her grief to flow too.

Later, Savina whispered softly, "Let's get some sleep and get an early start tomorrow. We will do as Fel last suggested and cut diagonally, shaving a week off our chase. One way or another, we'll rescue Sara."

Chapter 7 Business

"Sector ID Minister, your presence is requested in the infirmary," the intercom spoke up noisily.

"Damn thing. It's way too loud," Lech complained. "I thought the techs were going to get it adjusted. I'm not deaf!" He pressed the send button and said simply, "Coming." For a moment, he wondered why he was needed in the infirmary. Was one of his agents ill or wounded? He'd not yet heard from Kassia and that bothered him. Jarek has made a mess of his assignment. Still, both were competent field agents.

"Ah, there you are. I'm just finishing up here on Marik. He came in badly cut up and near death. I've saved most of his organs, but he won't be having children anymore," the doctor addressed him. "Here's his chart. I'll wake him in a moment."

"My god, what happened to him? It looks like someone ran a sword or something up his rear."

"That's precisely what he said before I knocked him out to work my miracle cures on him. I'll let him tell you about it shortly, firsthand." He finished his work and then gave a small injection in the side of the man's neck. Marik stirred.

"There you go. I've fixed you up as best I can. You will be a little weak for a few days. We can talk more about your recovery later. I've taken the liberty of bringing the Sector ID Minister here. You can make your report now. I'll leave you two alone." The doctor left the emergency room.

"What the devil happened to you, Marik? Is it?" Lech asked. He still only knew a handful of the thousands of personnel here at the spaceport.

"Yes, Marik. I'm afraid one of your field agents, a Kassia Kunegunda attacked me and very nearly killed me. I was working on Project Gemini when she interfered and attacked me."

"I'm sorry, Project Gemini? Sorry, I've only been here a short time and I am not at my computer."

"Project Gemini is a secret project. We seek out Ashford-5 telepaths who are willing to travel to other worlds and work as Imperium telepaths, highly paid, I might add. We are allowed to only extract one a year, per the Imperium Council's orders. Don't want to raise suspicions of the locals, you see. Anyway, I was just about to transport the latest volunteer when Kassia set upon us, screaming all manner of nasty curses. She went berserk and attacked me. While I had my protective PDS activated, she managed to knock me off my feet and then rammed the sword up my rear, where the PDS doesn't protect us. She left me for dead and ran off with the telepath."

"Oh dear god."

"So what are you going to do about it? We need to stop her. If she goes public with what we are doing with Project Gemini, that could cause all manner of major problems for the Imperium, what with this being a Imperial Directive #5 planet," Marik pointed out, looking for more leverage.

"Okay, let me see if I can contact her and get back to you. I'll review the details of the project too and see if there are protocols in place for this sort of thing. I am glad you survived, Marik."

"Thank you, minister." A troubled Lech turned and left, heading rapidly back to his office on the top floor. Once seated, he punched in his access code and brought up Project Gemini, marked Top Secret — Clearance Level 10. Well, he had clearance and opened it.

"Damn. What has Kassia gotten herself into this time? Hell, for a breech such as this, there is only one protocol. Damn, damn, damn. Now my project is wholly dependent upon Jarek." He buzzed Marik and gave him the clearance codes. "Make damn sure you only take the shuttles out at night when they cannot be seen by the locals. We don't want them claiming we are violating the lease agreement, even though we obviously are. And do keep me posted on the results."

Late evening he got more bad news. The ship Marik had taken out to execute Protocol One had somehow crashed! He ordered two more to go check out the crash site the next night. "Make damn sure nothing of the shuttle remains for the locals to find! And find me Kassia!"

The next night he got even worse news. "Minister, she's

141

removed her ID tag and all the tags of the equipment she took with her. We have no idea how to locate her."

Lech spent the day thinking about this problem. At last, he came to the conclusion Kassia must be traveling somewhere and on horseback. "Send out three shuttles and have them begin a systematic search pattern. We know the original direction they were traveling, due east of here, so use that as your initial heading."

Days passed by with no further word from the scout ships. Lech began writing up a formal explanation for the violations of the lease agreement, fully anticipating the day when Kassia would break this damning news to the locals. Finally, many days later, he received the final report. Kassia had been spotted and disintegrated. No trace of her body remained. Lech smiled and brought up Kassia's personnel records. He made a single entry: Deceased while in the field. "Well, it looks like we are off the hook, unless she's told the locals about this. Since I've not heard anything yet, I'll keep my fingers crossed that we have plugged this leak soon enough." After a few more days went by, Lech put the whole matter out of his mind and began worrying about Jarek. His entire mission now depended upon him.

Chapter 8 Choices

As Fel raced out onto the grasslands after Kassia, she thought as fast as she was running. *Against three of them, she doesn't have a chance! I owe her a life, but how can I repay her? These are aliens after all! Yet, my honor tells me I have to save her. How?*

A ship fired an energy beam at Kassia, but it missed. Fel knew there was the secret sect of healers who were the High Priestesses of Lysandra dwelling at a mystical place called Matera. She'd heard they provided a safe haven for women who were in dire need, and that the Goddess Lysandra worked her miracles there. This was secret information that was given to each woman after she'd been in the Sisterhood for three years, that is, after the House Mother was convinced the woman was not about to change her mind and flee the Sisterhood. Fel also knew stories suggested Lysandra, the Goddess of Life and Death, always demanded a major sacrifice from those women on whose behalf she intervened. Indeed, even when Fel was undergoing her own massive mutilations, she refused to call out to Lysandra and Matera. She didn't hold much with gods and goddesses who no one could see. Fel was a realist, a practical woman, a fighter. She bore her mutilation and went on.

Now the game was altogether different. She was honor-bound to save Kassia, and, if she did nothing, Kassia would be dead in seconds. Fel did the only thing left to her. *Lysandra of Matera, it is I, Feliciana Evita. I really don't know how to pray or do this. I am honor-bound to save Kassia. Please, you must help us or we will be killed by these alien ships. I am begging for your intervention. I will do anything you ask of me, only save my Kassia.*

For a moment, Fel thought time itself had stopped. Her body was frozen mid-stride, the three ships didn't move, though one of its energy blasts seemed frozen halfway down to the earth before her. A ghostly, shimmering form appeared before her, though it was really in her mind. *Will you and*

Kassia do as I ask?

Yes, I will and I am sure I can get Kassia to agree too. Lysandra?

Yes. Then I accept your pledge and I will save Kassia and yourself now. A bright light flashed and Kassia and Fel found themselves standing in a darkened room. A dingy oil lamp provided the only illumination. It was hot, exceedingly so. Strange odors filled the air. "What's happened? Fel? Where are we? Are we dead? Is this what it is like to be dead? I tried to keep you from being killed too. I am so sorry they killed you too, Fel."

"I don't know. I was trying to save you, my padrona. I prayed to Lysandra and something happened," Fel whispered back, uncertain of her whereabouts. She felt her body to see if it was real and Kassia, seeing her doing it, moved her stumps about. Her breasts were still real, but she couldn't reach much more. Just then, the door opened and an old woman made her way very slowly into the room. Both Kassia and Fel blinked and stared in disbelief.

The woman wore no blouse; her massive bosom was prominently visible. She was old, probably in her late sixties, her twin braids lined with grey. She wore a fetter skirt that was so tight that Kassia could see every curve from her waist on down to her sandal shoes, allowing her to take a two inch step at most. Her upper arms were bound by chains to her waist, allowing only her lower arms to move. Her fingernails were at least six inches long. Her face was lined and her skin, loose, though once, Kassia imagined, she must have looked fairly attractive. Her eyes were yellow. It took her a minute to close the distance from the door to them and at last, she spoke.

"Hello. I am Ama Alessia, the High Priestess of Lysandra, and leader of the secret Matera Sanctuary for Women. You are now in our waiting room here at Matera. Lysandra has answered your prayers, Feliciana. Now it is time you honor your pledge to do whatever the goddess asks of you and Kassia. Are you and are you, Kassia, willing to do this? If not, she will return you from whence you came."

Kassia said, "I, I don't understand. I was being shot at by alien ships, and now I am here, but I don't know where here is nor do I know of this Lysandra. What must we do?"

"My padrona, it is my doing. It was the only thing I could think of to save you. I owe you a life and I am honor-bound to repay you. Lysandra is a goddess and I asked her to help us. Now we must do as she asks of us," Fel hastily explained.

Ama Alessia added, "She's right. Lysandra is the Goddess of Life and of Death on Tierra. She has heard Feliciana's prayer and answered it, transporting you from that battlefield to our waiting room here in Matera. You are not supposed to know where Matera is at; no one but we priestesses of Lysandra know where this place is at. And no men are ever able to even see it, as Lysandra has hidden us from the sight of all men that we women may dwell here in total sanctuary. What must you do for her to repay her? That has yet to become known. If you both agree to do what she asks of you, whatever that sacrifice may be, then I will summon her and we will find out."

"Anything is better than being dead, I guess. If I don't, then Fel's going to be killed along with me. I will do what she asks, Fel," Kassia replied. "Only, it can't be very much. I don't have any arms now." She raised her short stumps for Alessia to see.

"I am sure what she asks, Kassia, you will be able to do. With your agreement, then I shall summon Lysandra that she may ask of you what she will." Kassia watched the High Priestess closely, expecting to hear some arcane chanting, some magical words spoken, some wand waving. However, Alessia did none of these things. In fact, Kassia could not see her doing anything at all.

Suddenly the glowing, yellowish form of Lysandra appeared in the room. She wore the thinnest of gauze over her body. Kassia noted she too seemed to have the overly large breasts and took a bit of comfort in that small thing. She spoke, but Kassia really heard her in her mind.

"I have heard your prayers and have answered them. You are both safe. In return, I ask this of you. Lord Damiano Domenico has become an evil mis-treater of women and I am answering their prayers. I have given him a warning that his downfall will be at the hands of a man who is not a man. You are to go to Lord Damiano, kill him, and bring his tortured harem wives back here to Matera. My High Priestess will give you the details. You will appear as a man until you draw your sword, Feliciana. Will you accept?"

"Of course, I hate men who mistreat women. I will slay this beast of a man, I so swear," Fel declared.

"I'll help too. It is not right that men should torture women, wives or otherwise," Kassia spoke up. *Though I haven't any idea how I can do it.*

"Thank you." Lysandra's glimmering form vanished leaving them in the dingily illuminated room.

"If you will follow me, our women will serve you and I can outline the assignment," Ama Alessia said softly. She turned and began her slow shuffling steps. Kassia thought she was taking forever to move such a short distance and realized they must somehow be in the Easterlings! How they got here gave her something to think about as they followed slowly behind their hostess.

They entered a dining room and several other women were in the process of bringing in trays of refreshments, dressed and bound as Ama Alessia was. Tea, honey, biscuits, dried fish, dates, and figs lined the trays. "They are all naked," Kassia whispered to Fel.

Ama Alessia smiled. "No dear, we are not naked. Women in the Easterlings never wear tops when indoors; it is just too hot. If we go outside, then we do don a very thin, silk blouse to keep from burning our skin, but nothing more. Come, be seated and I will explain further what Lysandra needs done."

"We have had our attention on Lord Damiano for some time now. He has been warned several times, but he continues to add new women to his harem and tortures them as well. He lives at Fakir Oasis in a well-guarded compound that could withstand a siege, though not these new acid bombs. We'd rather not risk harming the women any further. So here is the plan. As you can see, Fel, you appear as a man at the moment. Even your voice is disguised. When you draw your sword, the illusion will end and your true self will appear. The only way you can get an audience with the Lord is to bring him a new wife. Kassia will be the woman that you will be bringing him. She will be dressed as a normal Easterlings woman. When you present yourself at his complex, they will grant you access to him. Bargain with him and he will dismiss his guards, leaving you alone. He does not want anyone to know the price he pays for his wives. At that point, you may kill him. Assuming you are in his private chambers, the wives are located in the gardens to the south if it is day or the royal bedroom to the north if it is night. You are to bring the wives back here to Matera."

"But Matera is invisible," Fel pointed out.

"It will not be to you and Kassia. You will take her there in a wagon so you have the means to bring the wives safely back here."

"Okay, but I don't know the land here or where this oasis is located. Nor do I know how to travel in the desert."

"The oasis is five hundred miles from here and it will take you many days of travel both ways. We understand this, and will send along a Sisterhood guide, who will drive a second wagon with your supplies. She is not to be involved in the killing; she is only there as your guide. She may help you with the needs of the many wives on your return trip. Her name is Tecla Fina e Fulva e Brom. Take care of her, she is sixty-one, but very knowledgeable of the Arad."

"Since Kassia will be dressed as an Easterlings woman, you, Fel, will be responsible for her needs as though you were her husband. We know you are not familiar with our customs and traditions, so you will find that at any time, you will just know what must be done for Kassia. Now, please dine and then we will bathe and dress Kassia appropriately. You begin your quest in the morning when Tecla comes with the wagons."

"Thank you, High Priestess. We will not fail you or the goddess. This lord must die," Fel replied. She began feeding herself and Kassia, who decided not to use her gift before these women. She was unsure whether or not such would be acceptable.

Later, Kassia was taken to another room and bathed

and her hair washed. Somehow, her hair had grown substantially and her black tresses fell to her ankles, much as it did with the other women who were tending to her. That done, they helped her into a fetter skirt and fastened it securely around her waist. Next, they put a belt around her waist and fastened the chains to her stumps using silk covered leather bands, tied snugly. Now she couldn't even move what was left of her arms. Kassia felt petrified, but sat quietly as the women braided her hair exactly like theirs. Next, they numbed her lips, inserted four copper rings in each of her lips, and then inserted a leather tie strip, sealing her mouth. Finally, they asked her to rise and to practice walking. Two women moved to her sides and helped her keep her balance as she tried to take the tiny steps they all took. One woman said, "Be patient. We have to have you looking good enough to tempt Lord Damiano." Kassia could only nod.

At this point, Ama Alessia and Fel entered. "You look very pretty, Kassia. Well done, ladies. Now it is time for Fel to learn to walk with you and to assist you as needed. Fel, walk her around this first floor, into and out of any room. When you feel comfortable with her and she has the hang of walking, then you may retire for the night in the room you have been shown. Again, when you enter for the night, you will find you inherently know what must be done for Kassia. I bid you good night and good luck." She bowed to both and left, as did the two other women, slowly shuffling their way out.

Fel looked at Kassia and sighed. "I'm sorry you have to endure this, my dearest padrona. Be brave and I will not fail you. I do love you, you know that." Kassia tried to smile, but her tied lips prevented it.

Instead, she sent, *I will be brave for you, Fel. I love you to. I feel truly safe when I am with you. I hope I don't let you down. You look so much like a man. It is amazing.*

You won't let me down, my dearest padrona. I just know you won't. It is so weird, Kassia, I have male organs and they are doing strange things to me. Well, come on, you need to practice walking and I have to learn to keep pace and assist you. Together, they began a slow shuffle around the room.

Fel found it very helpful if she slipped her arm around Kassia's waist, giving her far more support. They practiced for an hour before both felt tired and eventually entered the small bedroom for the night. *Now what?* Kassia sent.

"I see images in my mind. I am supposed to unbraid your hair and brush it out. How did it grow so long, my padrona? It is so lush and thick. I really do like your hair this long. Look how full it is."

It feels so silky. They put some oils in the water, I think. Smells so strange, spicy like.

"Now, I would bind your lower arms behind you. That's one thing we don't have to do. Then I untie your skirt. Okay, here we go." Soon she had the restraining skirt off Kassia.

God, that is a whole lot better. I wonder why these women insist on wearing them?

"Oh, now I am to take my clothes off and help you into bed. My god, look at me and this thing I've got down there! Well, your breasts and hair really do turn me on, padrona." She helped Kassia get into the bed, adjusting her hair for her, as she would any bound woman.

Can we do it? Can we satisfy your urges and mine too?

I'd give anything if we could, my padrona. I've been wanting to pleasure you for days and days. Are you sure?

Yes, all this has me excited too. Let's, please.

An hour later, the two finally snuggled together and fell into a most satisfied slumber. Morning came too soon. Again, Fel's mind was filled with sequential images of what she must do for Kassia, beginning with the impossible, untying her lower arms from behind her back. Next, she braided Kassia's hair and then her own. Next, she helped Kassia into the tight skirt and finally dressed herself. Just then, a woman knocked and told them breakfast was ready.

After a long walk (time wise) to the dining room, Fel had more images. Now she untied Kassia's lips and set to work feeding her. Again, Kassia thought it wise not to use her gift to feed herself. Once they finished, Fel again tied her lips shut. She'd barely finished when another woman announced their guide was here with the wagons.

After the slow walk outside, they met Tecla. "Hello, Fel,

Kassia. I am Tecla, your guide. I've brought you proper
weapons; they are just there. You should put them on now.
Yes, I am staying bound too. It will cause fewer problems with
the locals, who detest us sisters vehemently when we go
unbound. I hope you know how to deal with us."

"Hi Tecla. Thanks. I have images that appear showing
me what to do. If they are insufficient, coach me please. We
need to make this happen!" Fel looked at the two wagons, but
both looked strange to her eyes. Each had four tall posts at the
corners and a thin silk canopy stretched between them.

"It gives us some shade from the searing sun's heat. The
desert is always hot, except late at night. I have plenty of
supplies, more than enough, I believe. I will drive this wagon.
Kassia can ride either with me or with you, but it might be best
if she rode with you. I am supposed to be just a guide."

She's naked too.

"Aren't you supposed to be wearing a top or
something?" Fel asked.

"I'll have you put the blouses on us later on when the
sun becomes scorching. Right now, I'm comfortable. You
should lift her up. She can ride either in the bed or beside
you."

Beside you, my love.

Fel lifted her up and sat her in the driver's seat. "You
sure do look like a man, just as the priestess said." Fel tried to
ignore her comment. "It's going to take us a little over twelve
days to get there, if we push it. We have to make about forty
miles each day, but that's constrained by always being at an
oasis at night, whenever possible. Those will be the most
dangerous times for us, but as long as I remain bound, that
will minimize the hassles. Besides, I am rather old and not a
likely rape target any longer. That's another reason I was
chosen. Okay, head off that way," she pointed with her fingers
to their right. Their trip out into the desert of the Arad began.

As they rode along the desert tracks that often
meandered around the great sand dunes, Tecla chatted away.
They learned she was the daughter of a Sisterhood woman and
the famous Felix Brom. She related how he'd come here in
search of the germanium crystals that the three wore around

their necks. Kassia paid close attention, she was learning a great deal about these people, well her people now. She knew she could never go back to the spaceport. That would mean her instant death.

Ask her why she has such long fingernails, Kassia sent.

"No need to always go through Fel, Kassia. You can send to me directly. I am here to help you both. With our arms so bound, having longer nails allows us to do some things more easily. Think of them as finger extensions. I'll show you tonight, both of you. However, there is political significance in them too. The lowest Castas have short nails, it being illegal for them to be any longer than an inch at most. The Lords Castas, that includes us who have the *mentales* gifts, are supposed to let ours grow to about six inches, but a wife's nails should never be longer than her husband's. We know Lord Damiano has his at six inches, so that will give you a combat edge, since he won't be able to grip his scimitar and dagger as well as you."

But why do you put up with these awful physical bindings?

"Tradition, Kassia. Women do not mind being bound because our men here, for the most part, spend many hours of the day with us, far, far more than they do in your lands or so my mother told me. Here, a husband will spend a quarter to a third of each day with his wife, helping her, loving her, caring for her, and so on. Women relish the fact they have their husband's and other men's full attention for three or four hours during the daylight hours, ignoring completely bedtime hours. Do you know it is a high crime for a man even to slap a bound woman? This Lord Damiano has actually tortured his wives, but he is such a powerful man that he has gotten away with it for nearly five years now. Hopefully, no longer! That's one thing, Fel, you are going to have to be alert for: anytime you see a bound woman who needs some assistance, you need to rush over and help her, even if she is a total stranger. That's the custom here."

"Another way for outsiders to look at it, mom told me once, is here women are physically bound and well cared for, whereas in other lands, women are mentally bound but not well looked after — you know, arranged marriages and all that. At least we in the Sisterhood get to choose our bindings, though there are still enough mental bindings around, particularly if we go around unbound." Tecla chatted on and on, eager to have the chance to chat.

Around dusk, they pulled into an oasis with several hundred adobe homes surrounding the life-giving waters. Tecla said, "A man will ask for a silver for the water. Do not pay him more than two silvers. We will be allowed to camp near the waters. That is the custom in the desert."

Fel did as asked and haggled with the man, eventually handing him the two silvers. He pointed out where they should park their wagons and camp. Fel now had images coming again. He lifted both women down and began setting up their camp. Tecla was an old hand at this and, in spite of her physical restraints, efficiently got their camp setup and their supper cooking. True, she did have Fel lift things down from the wagon for her. While she was cooking, she had Fel prepare their bedding, placing them on the packed sands beneath one of the wagons. "We will sleep together at night for warmth."

Fel noticed a number of people from time to time watching them from a distance, but they all stayed back. "Cause I'm in the Sisterhood," Tecla explained. "They'll keep their distance, I hope. Now you need to tie my hands behind my back using that leather collar and then unbraid and brush out our hair. They will be watching to see you do it." Fel complied and in the pale moon light noticed the locals seemed satisfied and retired into their homes.

"Do we sleep naked?" Fel asked, embarrassed again. Maleness was again causing her a problem, as he took off the women's skirts.

"Usually. That's why we have the blankets. Help us get snuggled in and let's share some pleasure. We need to calm your maleness," she teased him. She added, "Kassia, can you sense him and his needs? That is something we telepaths cannot hide from one another. It is best for everyone if we satisfy male needs when they arise, just as it is best if they satisfy ours, though we women are often slow to rouse." Both Kassia and Fel realized she was explaining this wholly for their benefit. Both had been broadcasting their needs all day long and she wanted some mental quiet.

The days passed slowly. During the heat of the day, Kassia sweated heavily, great balls of sweat trickled down her chest and back, sometimes tickling her, but she could do nothing about the itch. When perspiration got in her eyes, she had Fel wipe her off a bit, but he too was drenched. Both carefully followed Tecla's regimen of drinking lots of water and taking salt frequently. Just riding in the wagon was physically exhausting and both were glad they did not live in this country.

It was even worse for Fel, who knew the countryside of the Midlands like the back of her hand, having traveled over most of it at one time or other. Here, she was out of her league. Worse, she felt the distinct lack of the trail-sense, which Tecla had, and praised her often about it. The tracks led around great dunes and Fel knew she'd be lost utterly without the certainty of Tecla. Miss an oasis and you could well forfeit your life. One thing Fel was confident about was it was not five hundred miles as the crow flies to their destination. Indeed, they seemed to be following a very meandering route, often doubling back some distance. Again, the oasis locations dictated their path out here in the Arad.

By the twelfth day, the two had more or less adapted to their current environment and roles. Fel was efficiently handling the women's needs now and both knew when they needed water or salt. Further, they both knew why these people used such exotic spices: it helped mask sweaty bodies, for baths were very infrequent. It was way too much trouble to fill a bath barrel at an oasis. Instead, Fel gave the women sponge baths every other night.

"There it is, Fakir Oasis. We should make it by late afternoon. We have to go around the dunes to get there; that'll slow us down. The lord's fortress is on the north side of the oasis proper, abutting it, naturally. We should spend the night on the south side and you make your attempt in the morning. If we do it now, we can't get far before nightfall. When we get there, you probably should tie my lips too, after we eat. Anything to lessen possible confrontations with the local men."

"At least we don't have to contend with hostile local women," Fel teased her. She was silent for a moment and then said seriously, "The flaw in this goddess's plan is just how do we get the wives safely out of here after the deed is done? Won't his guards and others counterattack us? How can we possibility escape that host of men bent on revenge or maybe even stealing the women for themselves?"

"Based upon the scanty reports we've had, I don't think any man will covet his wives, not in the condition they are supposed to be in. I think we are safe on that one. Revenge? Well, that is another matter. You know men as well as I. That's a likely action. Ideas?"

At the moment, Fel had none, but she continued to ponder this detail off and on until morning came. They entered Fakir late afternoon, just as Tecla predicted. Fel quickly estimated there were about a hundred adobe homes arranged in a roughly circular pattern around the central water pool and its nearby palms, dates, and figs. Like all the other oases they'd encountered, most of the inhabitants were poor but proud. The women were bound as expected though Kassia saw only a couple of women whose lips were tied shut. Most looked up at the arriving two wagons and then ignored them. They were not a supply caravan, just three weary looking travelers. Fel followed Tecla's suggestion and made for the southern edge of the water and, as expected, a man came out asking for a silver for each wagon, which Fel paid without haggling.

Quietly, the three made their camp, cooked, and ate their supper, after which Fel did as Tecla asked, lacing her lips shut before binding her lower arms behind her. He helped them out of their skirts and did their hair for them, before they turned in on their blanket beneath one of the wagons. The two women fell asleep quickly, leaving Fel to ponder the morning's actions. Fel was certain she could get as far as killing Lord Damiano, but the rest seemed impossible. Thus far, no one had said what tortures he'd inflicted on his wives, only that there were twelve of them now. Well, she'd handle that when the time came. No, how to elude all the guards who would be sure to come after them seeking revenge — that would be the real problem. Wouldn't it be a matter of honor for them to obtain justice for their Lord's killer? Fel took Tecla at her word that they would not be after the wives, seeking some of them for themselves. Still, what could be so wrong with them that other men wouldn't still desire them? Fel had too many unanswered questions and sleep came late for her.

At dawn, Fel roused the others and was amazed "his" handling of them was now mostly an automatic reaction. Her mind still dwelled on their escape. After feeding them breakfast and breaking camp, Fel lifted Tecla up into her driver's box. Fel already knew what her plan was. She'd pretend to be arranging their supplies for a time and then drive her wagon over to the complex, hopefully in time to help load the wives into the two wagons.

"Are you all right, padrona?" Fel asked, noticing Kassia looked a little different this morning.

Just a little nausea. I think it's my nerves. We are about to head into real danger and I'm so utterly helpless like this. I want to help and I will, somehow, Fel. Let's do it! Fel lifted her up and climbed up. Before starting out, he looked her over, making sure she was looking her best in the Easterlings fashion. Everything depended upon getting Lord Damiano enticed into bargaining for her, at which point he would excuse his guards from the room, giving Fel the chance to do the deed. Kassia looked attractive, at least to Fel, and she took up the reins for the short trip around the waters. She glanced at her scimitar and then her dagger, hoping she could manage these weapons half as well as she could her trusty short sword.

Minutes later, she pulled up at the entrance of a walled compound. Stone blocks were set in a re-enforced pattern forming a fifteen foot tall barrier around the complex, which had this single heavily guarded, entrance gate. Four muscular fighters answered her knock. "I have brought a potential new wife for Lord Damiano Domenico to consider. May we enter and show him the goods?" Fel said. Their eyes scanned Kassia and one of the men nodded, swinging the gate open. Fel drove the wagon inside, holding her breath.

At once, her fighting skills kicked in as did the field agent in Kassia. Off to the north was a stable. They were in a small courtyard that led to an ornate main entrance of the single story stone main building. A smaller bunkhouse for the guards lay to her right, along the southwestern corner. Some twenty feet separated these main gates from the main entrance to the lord's home. Two men armed with a scimitar and dagger each stood before that door. One motioned for Fel to bring the wagon over to the door and she did so. After stepping down, he correctly lifted Kassia down and heard some hushed whispers from the two guards. One said, "Boss might really like this one. Look at the size of those boobs and she's got no arms to interfere." Fel took these comments as a good sign and put his arm around Kassia, guiding her towards the door, as if she was reluctant to enter.

Inside, Fel noticed another pair of guards who took over for the first two, leading them down the hallway to a pair of mahogany double doors. He knocked and said something to the guard just inside, but Fel couldn't hear what was said. Then these doors opened and the two got their first look at Lord Damiano and his so called "throne room." Elaborately colored silks were draped around the walls. There were no windows, but matching mahogany doors opened to the south and north, that is, to their left and right. He sat on a slightly raised block of stone on an elaborately carved mahogany and silk cushioned seat.

Lord Damiano appeared to be around forty. He sported a goatee and a moustache with curved ends, both deep black. His eyes were not yellow and both Fel and Kassia were relieved he was not a telepath. He wore a scimitar and dagger strapped to his waist. His silk shirt was loose fitting and thin. His pants were baggy and short, revealing his black sandals with their typical pointed toes. Both shirt and pants were spotlessly white. His eyes were black and cold. When he spoke, his voice sounded both condescending and sneering. "Well, what do we have here?"

"Lord Damiano, I have found this lovely woman and brought her to you, thinking she would make you a fine new wife."

"Ah, presumptuous are we? Well, no matter. I like men who show some initiative. Let's see the merchandise." He rose and both saw his nails were at least six inches long. He moved close to Kassia, his eyes boring into her, as he looked her up and down. He raked his long talons over her massive bosom and Kassia pulled back slightly. He only grinned. He raked his talons on down her right arm, feeling her scared tip, just above where her elbow had been.

"Have you ever seen such tits?" Fel said crudely. "Largest I've ever seen and no hands to interfere with your will. Such a bargain, do you not think?" Lord Damiano didn't reply, but continued to examine Kassia as if she were some horse he was about to purchase. Fel glanced over the empty throne and was surprised to see a message somehow burned into the wall, etched into the stone: Lord Damiano will fall at the hands of the man who is not a man. Someone had tried to erase part of the message at one corner, but had failed to do so. Fel inwardly grinned; Lysandra had been right, she'd sent him a warning some time ago.

Lord Damiano's talons lifted one of Kassia's long braids and let it slide through his nails until it had slipped back down, nearly touching the floor. "Such thick, lush hair," he mused.

Fel's *mentales* gifts kicked in. In a flash, she knew how he preferred to fight: let his guards do it. He'd only draw his sword as a last resort and then use it to back stab. He'd rarely fight fair. Her analysis was interrupted. Lord Damiano said, "I'll take her for five hundred silver."

"Ha! Surely you are teasing me!" Fel countered. "Such a fine woman, so unique, why I can't let her go for anything less than ten thousand silver."

Lord Damiano chuckled. He walked back to his throne and sat down. Would he bargain? At last, he spoke, "Guards, leave us. We will bargain for this exceptional woman. Once the door was closed, he said, "Five thousand silver." Thus the two began haggling over the price he would pay for Kassia, who felt terribly demeaned by this, but was helpless to even utter a word let alone do anything about it.

They finally settled on nine thousand five hundred silver. "You drive a hard bargain, but indeed, you are right.

Never have I seen one so delectable, so delicious as this one is." He turned around to his back wall and moved a tapestry aside revealing a locked door. He took a key from his neck and unlocked it. Here was his treasury and both Fel and Kassia were momentarily stunned by the mass of shining coins and gems inside.

Then Fel acted. She drew her sword. "I am the man who is not a man!" She lunged at the evil lord. He was fast and drew his scimitar and dagger, Fel had forgotten to draw her dagger. The Easterlings, she knew, fought with two weapons, a very deadly combination. Although his long nails gave him troubles, he was nevertheless a highly skilled fighter, and he refused to summon his guards, partly because he was too embarrassed that somehow this woman had so completely fooled him. He dashed around slicing at Fel with both weapons. Fel was in the fight of her life and she knew it. She didn't even bother to try to draw her dagger.

As Kassia watched the two, she saw Fel was slowly losing the battle. His two weapons were no match for her single scimitar with which she was unfamiliar in its use. Kassia had to act, to save her lover somehow. Her eyes fell on Fel's dagger still around her waist. She focused and slowly drew the dagger out of its sheath. Lord Damiano's back was to her and she moved the dagger behind him and brought it up to his neck. In one swift motion, Kassia moved it in front of his neck and made a slicing motion, severing his jugular veins. Blood splashed everywhere and he dropped both weapons, grasping at his neck trying to keep the blood from gushing out. Fel then stabbed him in his heart and he collapsed over his own throne.

"Now what the hell do we do? The guards are coming! I hear them calling out!" Fel gasped somewhat out of breath. Her eyes darted around the room looking for some place she and Kassia could hide. The guards were opening the door now and soon she'd have to fight all them!

Again, Kassa acted. Using her gift, she lifted Fel and her own body and moved them to the ceiling some fifteen feet above them, pressing their bodies tightly against the roof. Just then the door burst open and two guards rushed in, scimitars and daggers drawn. They saw their dead lord with his splattered blood dripping down the etched message in the back wall. The blood dripped down over: Lord Damiano will fall at the hands of the man who is not a man.

Fel took a gamble and placed a thought into one of the guard's mind. He looked up and saw the opened treasury closet. In an instant, Fel knew how to deal with the guards. The two looked greedily at the treasure and headed straight for it. Soon, they yelled for the others and shortly a dozen men were greedily stuffing all the coins and gems into their pockets. Several ran off to find some bags. A half hour later, the men fled, leaving an empty closet. Slowly, Kassia lowered them back to the floor, nearly losing her balance and falling. Fel quickly kept her from taking a hard fall, thankfully.

Quietly, the two made their slow way to the southern door, Kassia inwardly cursing her skirt that made this impossibly slow. Not knowing what to expect, Fel opened the door slowly and peered inside. She saw a beautiful formal garden with a pond in its center. Sitting around the pond on ornate benches were a dozen women. One tall, unarmed man stood silently watching over them. From his demeanor, she guessed he was a eunuch and in charge of the women's needs. She was right.

"Halt. You may not enter the harem," he spoke in a high-pitched voice, confirming Fel's suspicions.

"Lord Damiano is dead, killed by the man who is not a man, me. You are now free of your charge here. The guards have already raided his treasury and have fled. Go take what you want and leave, sir. We will be taking charge of the women here. Go on, step outside and see for yourself." She tried to get him to move. At last, somewhat confused by the sudden news, he stepped forward and came over to where they were standing and peered around Kassia.

He spoke again, "Death is too good for him. I leave the women in your hands." He bowed to her and made a very hasty exit. Now Fel and Kassia took a good look at the women who were rising, but unable to speak. A dozen eyeless faces attempted to detect where Fel was standing.

"My god! He's pulled out their eye balls!" Fel exclaimed. All the women were wearing their skirts, of course. All had their upper arms chained to their waists as expected. However, all their lips were tied shut, all were blinded, all had their hair unbraided, as if ready for bed, and all had their lower arms tied behind their backs. The latter two were wholly inappropriate for the morning and should never have been done, a total disgrace to these women. There was more, but just now, neither could see that.

As Kassia looked at the women, the man's wives, she suddenly wondered where all their children were. *Fel, their children. What about them? We can't leave them behind.*

"Right. Okay, first thing ladies, I am Fel, and Kassia is with me. I've killed Lord Damiano at the request of the Goddess Lysandra. She has ordered me to bring you to her at Matera and that's what we are going to do right now. I have two wagons waiting us outside. It is morning, and you should be prepared for the day. Kassia has no lower arms, so I am going to free her upper arms so she can walk you outside to the wagons. You will be free to speak whenever you desire. I'll get to each of you as quickly as I can." *What a mess, Kassia.*

She untied Kassia's lips and unfastened her chains so she could at least more her arms again. Then, Fel went from woman to woman. She untied the woman's lips, untied her hands, and braided her hair rapidly. Then, she had Kassia lead her towards the doors. Since it would take them a long time to travel that distance, Fel had time to spare. As she worked on them, she began to notice other tortures the women had endured. Several were missing fingers and thumbs. More than one woman begged Fel to kill her humanely, but Fel refused, saying she should talk to the goddess about that. Several asked about who would be their husbands now, who would provide for them. Again, Fel had no answers, save to ask the goddess.

She did find out there were no children. It seems Lord Damiano's seed was worthless. That's why he had taken so many wives, trying somehow to have a son and heir. He refused to believe the problem was his and not the women's. Both Kassia and Fel were greatly relieved to hear there were no children to handle as well. These dozen blind women were going to be enough of a problem as it was.

Almost an hour later, she finally got to the last wife.

"You are awfully young. Hang in there while I untie your lips. There you go. . ."

As soon as her lips were free, the young woman started talking. "Thank you, thank you. I am Renata Raffaella Lucca Brom. I am young, eighteen to be precise, when I was kidnaped by those awful men and just after mom died too. You killed him, that lord man, my supposed husband?" Fel again said she had. "Okay, then, according to our centuries old tradition, I demand *sesso disposto* with you as proclaimed by Wystan the Bold. Then, you can accept me as tradition dictates. I can do it right now, please."

"I'm sorry, I — oh my god! He's cut off both of your hands right at the wrists!" She'd gotten the leather binding off her arms only to discover the young girl was handless too besides being blind. The skin was still tender and pinkish. Fel guessed it had happened fairly recently, probably several months ago.

"Well, yes, but since you killed him, I demand *sesso disposto* with you right now," Renata said very determinedly and feistily.

"Hold on. We have to get all of you safely out of here and back to Matera and the goddess who asked us to do this. Besides, I don't know what this *sesso disposto* is," Fel explained, trying to brush out her hair to braid it.

"I mount you and show you I am a willing and able and can have sex with you, then you will take me as your wife," Renata explained almost as if Fel were a little child. "It is one of our oldest traditions. When a man kills another man, what happens to his wife who is dependent upon him? If she is able to perform successfully *sesso disposto* with the man, then he is to accept her as another of his wives and support her. So I demand *sesso disposto* with you right now. I can do it."

"What a second, Renata. I am not a man. I am a woman!"

Renata tentatively felt Fel with her lower arms. "But you do not have breasts and your hair is short, like a man's."

Fel flushed crimson. She hated her appearance, but what could she do about it? "*Castinto*, I'm *castinto*."

"But how? Did it hurt like it did with my hands? I don't

feel them anymore though." Renata didn't give up her child-like fire.

"Bad man and yes it hurt like the devil. No more of that, please. I am not a man so no *sesso disposto*, okay?"

"No, not okay. I can still show you I can give you much pleasure anyway. Women sometimes marry, I'm told. I demand *sesso disposto* with you right now so you will know I mean it."

"I am a Sisterhood fighter, Renata, and I hope to soon have Kassia become my free-mate. We marry for love not for obligations or traditions. Besides, Renata, I am not an Easterlings woman. I come from the Midlands, where no woman is bound like you Easterlings women are. I don't even speak your language."

Kassia made her slow way back to Fel and Renata. She had been ushering each of the others out to the wagon where they were waiting in a line for Fel to come and lift them aboard. She'd overheard much of the conversation, considering how long it took her to cross the spacious gardens room.

"Yes you speak it fine."

"That is because of some magic of the Goddess Lysandra, who has asked us to come here and get you. There, your braids are done. Now up you go. Kassia is here and she's going to lead you out to our wagon. She lost her lower arms at her elbows so don't be surprised if she cannot hold you well. I've got to get the others up into the wagons." Fel rose, blew a kiss at Kassia, and breathed a sigh of relief. Renata had a way of embarrassing her more so than anyone else ever had.

"Come on. I will guide you with what's left of my arm. You can put yours up against my waist if you like. Here we go, Renata."

"You are her free-mate, yes?"

"Yes."

"So I demand *sesso disposto* with you *and* with her. You must let me. It is our oldest tradition. You must. I can give you great pleasure, really I can," Renata pleaded.

"I'm sure you can, Renata. First, we must get you to safety. Right now, there are a whole lot of men who may try to stop us and harm you women further. Let's get you to safety first, then we can deal with this *sesso disposto* thing," Kassia defused her.

"Well, okay then, but you must help me make Fel listen and allow me to do it to both of you, promise me you will do that," Renata pleaded.

"Okay, I will talk to her about it, but only after we get you to safety. A little to the left please."

Outside, Fel untied Tecla's lips and lifted her aboard. One by one, she lifted the other eleven women up and into the wagon bed, helping them get properly seated. She put six in Tecla's wagon and five in hers. By then, Kassia and Renata came slowly towards them. Fel whisked Renata up and into the wagon bed, against her protests that she wanted to sit beside them in the driver's seat. Finally, she lifted Kassia up and then slapped the reins. Behind her, she heard Tecla doing the same.

As they began rolling through Fakir, she saw they had a large audience. Half of the town was now out on the streets watching them. Some tossed curses at her, others merely smiled and waved. These she ignored. The men who were saddling up — these she kept a close eye on as she drove the wagon though the streets and finally reached the edge. "Did you see those men mounting?"

"Aye, Fel. Looks like you were right. Some are going to come after us. I'm going to unbind myself and get ready to help defend us if they come after us," Tecla replied. Fel glanced back a few times to see if she could manage it. She wiggled a lot but got out of her restraining skirt. Already she'd undone the waist chains. A bit more wiggling and she got a pair of white pants on and then retrieved her short sword from beneath the seat. "Okay, I'm ready, Fel. I suspect they will wait a while before attacking us. Probably they don't want to do it so close to their oasis. That will give me time, I hope."

Fel didn't know what she meant but urged the horses into a trot. Already Fakir was no longer visible, hiding behind the great dune just south of the oasis. Fel hated these winding tracks, because she couldn't just go in a straight line like she was used to doing, putting some distance between them. The sun rose higher and the day grew hotter as always. Sweat dripped down her face. She looked at Kassia and saw she was drenched, sweat again trickling down her bare chest. *You look sexy, my padrona. Hot though.* Kassia giggled a little, but she was really worried about the attackers.

Several hours later, they rounded a bend and were back at that first location from which they got their initial glimpse of the oasis over the two intervening dunes. As she looked back, she saw the dust cloud from the riders. Evidently, this was far enough from Fakir, and they were riding hard to close the distance. "Shit! Here they come," she called out to Tecla.

Tecla was already holding her crystal and focusing. "What's she doing?" Kassia whispered.

"Dunno, but I hope it's good," Fel whispered back.

"I know what she is doing," Renata called up to them. She couldn't see whether or not they were waiting on her, so she continued. "She's summoning up a tempesta di polvere."

"What's that?" Fel asked, confused. How could this blind woman have any idea what Tecla behind them was doing with her *mentales* gifts?

"A tempesta di polvere, silly. Don't you know anything?" Renata asked in disbelief.

"I am from the Midlands. I have no idea what you are saying. What is a tempesta di polvere?" Fel replied a bit testily.

"A dust storm. She's summoning one up. I can hear it in the sands. Soon you probably can see it, though I can't anymore," Renata replied, though her enthusiasm died off at the end of her thought.

"Keep an eye out back there, Kassia. I have to watch the track ahead."

"My god! She's right! There's a huge dust storm blowing up behind us!" Kassia reported and Fel turned to look back.

"There, that will slow them down," Tecla yelled up to Fel. "Keep going at this speed or we will get sucked into it too!" Fel didn't slow down.

"The dust sometimes can cut the skin off of a dead horse, leaving behind nothing but bleached bones," Renata again began chatting. "I saw that once. We should not get caught in the tempesta di polvere. Of course, if we do, we should cover up with blankets, though I worry about the horses. Maybe you could hold up in the lee side of a dune and hope the horses don't get covered up. I saw that once too. The dune shifted and totally buried a whole wagon of supplies. We had to dig it out. Sand was in everything, though, kind of gritty to eat, even after we washed the dates off good."

On they rode with Renata continuing to chat merrily away behind them, as if nothing was threatening her safety. Fel forced herself to focus on the path ahead, taking verbal directions yelled to her from Tecla. Finally, she had to hold the horses back; they were sweating profusely. After walking them a stretch, she got down, watered, and salted them too, following Tecla's advice. She took this opportunity to also water the dozen women, giving them a little salt as well, before continuing.

"Think the storm stopped them?" she asked Tecla.

"Don't know. Let's get going, I'll take the lead this time." Once more, they were off, only this time she set a pace the horses could handle in the heat of the day, barely a walk. Tecla thought, *Well, the storm ought to have completely wiped out our tracks. However, that does us little good. We have to make a watering hole tonight and there's only one possibility. So even if they lose the trail, they would head there anyway. This is going to get downright nasty before it's over! Lysandra ought to have thought this through.*

Late afternoon, she spotted the oasis far off in the distance. They would make it before dark. However, she stood up on the wagon, looked behind, and saw the telltale dust cloud of the riders. They survived the storm, and she guessed they intended to overtake them before they got to the oasis. If they could get there before that, she figured they'd be safe for the night, but they'd likely be waiting for them just beyond the oasis when they left in the morning. Tecla felt slightly trapped.

Fel called out, "They are overtaking us. Any more tricks up your sleeve?"

Just as the band of riders seeking revenge approached the two wagons, they saw the wagons simply vanish from sight. Poof! They were gone. They halted and studied the ground. Deep wagon ruts and horse hoof prints simply stopped. They rode around the area for a while before heading back to Fakir.

Tecla was looking back over her shoulder at the riders when suddenly they vanished, as did the dunes. Instantly, the land was more open. Off to the right she saw the eastern cliffs of the Buku Hills. Ahead she saw the oasis of Matera. "My god! We've arrived at Matera! What magic is this?"

"What just happened?" yelled Fel, looking in all directions. The entire landscape had changed as she too recognized their original starting point.

"These people have very powerful *mentales* gifts!" Kassia whispered, very much awed.

"What's happening? Where are we? I don't hear them coming after us any longer," Renata called out, turning her head in several directions trying to pick up recognizable sounds.

Tecla headed to the main building where she'd waited for them with the two wagons. As she pulled up, the door opened and two women shuffled out to greet them. Ama Alessia stood in the doorway. "I see you have been successful."

"Aye, that we have. Thanks for whatever just happened," Fel called out, pulling her team to a stop. "They very nearly got us."

Ama Alessia smiled, "Welcome ladies. I am Ama Alessia, the High Priestess of Lysandra. You are all safe and sound at the secret Matera Sanctuary for Women. Come on inside, you too, Tecla." One by one, Fel helped each woman down, though Tecla helped out this time. She then tied the two teams to the hitching rail and fell in behind the line of women. Several other priestesses came out and were now guiding the women inside.

"No, Fel and Kassia are leading me," Renata protested when one of them took her arm. "I have demanded *sesso disposto* with Fel and Kassia, and they promised me this when we got to safety, which we now are, I think."

"Come on, Renata. It's me," Fel said, putting one arm around Renata's waist and the other around a grinning Kassia. Tecla smiled and followed them inside.

They were taken into the large dining room and were

seated around it. Ama Alessia moved to the head of the table and folded her hands together. Fel assumed she was praying or somehow contacting the goddess and she was right. Everyone present suddenly saw the shimmering, glowing figure, but each woman heard a different conversation.

Eleven of the rescued women heard similar words. "I am Lysandra and you are now safe in my Holy Temple. I have heard the prayers of one of you and have responded. Now it is your turn to make your choice. You can remain here safe and sound for the rest of your lives, helping other women as best a blind woman can or you can be returned to your previous home there to live out your life or I can restore your sight if you pledge to devote your life to helping us heal other women in dire need. Your choice?" Eleven had their sight restored, as suddenly their original eyes were remade in their empty sockets. Neither Fel nor Kassia nor Renata nor Tecla heard them gasp for joy, praise Lysandra, and then being escorted out of the room.

"Tecla, as always, I am in your debt. You have again shown the mettle of your Sisterhood. Go with my blessings and my grace, dear child."

"We live to serve all women, goddess." Tecla smiled as the image in her mind vanished. She wanted at least to say goodbye to the others but did as Ama Alessia beckoned; she left the room for now.

"Renata Raffaella, I have answered your prayers. You are free from Lord Damiano forever. I cannot allow all that he has done to you to go unanswered. I give you your eyes back, my child, as I am doing to the other wives. Your hands will be a sufficient sacrifice. Will you now choose to spend your days here at Matera helping my priestesses with other women who are in need?"

"Is it truly my choice, goddess?" Renata asked, without the slightest humility or awe at the presence of a goddess in her mind.

"Truly, dear child. You always have free choice. What would you choose?" Lysandra had a hint of curiosity in her voice. That humans were not always so predictable gave her great pleasure as well.

"I wanted to follow the traditional *sesso disposto* with the ones who slew my husband, as is our custom. I know they are women and Fel says Kassia is to be her free-mate, but I want to follow our ancient ways."

"But what if they do not wish this? They are not Easterlings and do not understand your ancient tradition. They will be returning to their own lands where women are not bound as you are. Will you be happy with women and not a true husband?"

Renata sighed, "Well, if I can't convince them, then I will stay here and help the priestesses, but I want to try to fulfill our ways. It is important to respect the old ways. We have but honor that we can call our own."

"You are wise beyond your years, child. You will get your chance then." Lysandra vanished from her mind.

"Oh, I can see again, thanks Lysandra!" Renata exclaimed, rubbing her eyes with her two stumps. Then, she looked around the room and noticed the other eleven women had gone.

Fel saw the image of the goddess again and heard, "Thank you, Feliciana Evita. You did as asked bringing honor to the Sisterhood once again. I am well aware you have asked nothing of me for yourself, only for Kassia. Hence, knowing your most secret desires, know that they have been fulfilled. She bears your child now, a daughter, part of you and part of her. Raise your daughter well, Feliciana Evita."

Fel flushed to the roots of her hair. How did the goddess know that was what she most wanted in the entire world? The impossible, yet somehow Lysandra had joined the two. She realized it must have happened when she had the illusion of a male body, but she said it was part of her, so it could not have been an illusion. Fel was confused, but extraordinarily happy. When she was roused from the meeting, what she saw then shocked her more that.

Kassia again saw the Goddess Lysandra. "Hello. I've never believed in gods or goddesses. Yet there you are again. I've seen more unexplainable miracles in the last couple of weeks, so you must be real. Are there more of you, gods and goddesses? Am I allowed to ask this? I have not talked to the others about this, though, but you probably already know that."

"Ah, now you have found your voice, Kassia Kunegunda. You may ask, Ama Alessia can tell you about us gods and goddesses. Yes, I am very real. I want to thank you for what you've done for my women. I know you were born alien to this world, and came to Tierra as an alien. Yet, you are no longer an alien; you are as Tierran as anyone of us. No longer will you need to hide the color of your skin, for it will be as ours. For your sacrifices and unquestioning help, I am giving you back your arms the aliens took from you."

"Thank you, Lysandra! That is a Holy Miracle if I ever heard of one. Not even the Imperium can do that. I mean they have prosthetic limbs but they are not very satisfactory really. I thought about trying to get some but decided they wouldn't help all that much. Can you help Fel? I mean she has been so horribly wronged by men who cut off her breasts. Can you give them back to her? I know it would mean a whole lot to her."

Lysandra smiled. "I understand your desires, Kassia. I have given Feliciana what she wanted far more than her breasts restored. She will tell you about that shortly. Now I must go. There are other women in need calling out. I fear in the future far more women will be in the greatest of peril and need. Look out for them if you can, dear child."

"Okay, I certainly will, Lysandra. Thanks again for your miracle." The goddess vanished and Kassia looked down. There were her original hands! She wiggled them and moved them around excitedly. She looked up at Fel, "Look! She gave me my arms and hands back!"

Fel looked more serene than Kassia had ever seen before. "Padrona that is nearly the best miracle ever! I am so happy for you! Did she not tell you the rest?"

"Er no. I'm sorry, Fel. I did ask her to give you your breasts back, but she said she gave you something that you wanted far more. She didn't say what. You look the same though."

Fel leaned over and whispered, "You are carrying our child! When we did it; Lysandra joined part of me and part of you to make our daughter. You are going to have our daughter.

That's why you felt so nauseous these past few mornings; you're pregnant! Please, will you become my free-mate?"

"Oh yes, yes. Wow, two women? I never knew that was possible. Wow, oh Fel! We will have a daughter! Incredible. I want her too. I want you so badly it hurts sometimes. I don't care anymore what anyone else thinks about us. I love you, Fel."

Fel turned to Ama Alessia and asked, "Can you perform the free-mate ceremony for Kassia and I?" She smiled and said she would be honored.

Just then, Renata roused and rubbed her eyes. "I can see again! Oh, which of you is which? Oh, you are Fel and you are Kassia. Okay, I am ready to perform the ancient ceremony of *sesso disposto* with both of you now. We are safe and you promised me."

Ama Alessia raised her hands halting the rapid fire flood of words from the young Renata. "Dear child, these are Midlands women, and they do not know what it is you are asking of them. Allow me to explain it fully and please allow them the decision." Renata looked a little miffed, but nodded.

"Here in the Easterlings, women have been bound for centuries, reaping many wonderful benefits from their men as a result. Perhaps you two have experienced a little of this, perhaps not. However, as bound women, they must have a supporting husband. When theirs is killed, tradition allows the grieving wife to perform the *sesso disposto* act. In essence, she herself mounts the victorious and demonstrates to him that she is willing to satisfy him sexually. If she does so, then the man is obligated to accept her as another of his wives, if in fact he can support her. If she does not do this ceremony, then she is sent back to her parents in total disgrace. The ceremony is a way for the wives to be able to continue to survive despite the loss of their vitally needed husband."

"But we are not men," Fel complained.

"I know, yet, Renata still wishes to perform the ceremony and is willing to accept being your free-mates. That in itself is another problem entirely, since free-mates have only one mate, not a harem like we have here. There are no threesome marriages on record. Be that as it may, you are not

Easterlings and will be returning to the Midlands soon. If she was accepted by you, she would likely have to become an unbound woman. As I understand it, no women are bound in your land."

"Right, she'd be looked on as a freak or something. Besides, here the land is rather flat. Where we come from, the land is so rocky and rough that she couldn't walk a foot. We'd have to carry her everywhere she went if she continued to wear the skirt," Fel explained, hoping this would help convince Renata to desist in her desires for the ceremony.

"I am willing to become an unbound woman if that is what my husband-women's desire of me," Renata countered Fel's thought, almost as if she could anticipate Fel's notions. "They would be my husband-women, High Priestess. I would be bound to them both, but only as a *second* wife should be." Again, Alessia had to explain the significance of the numerical order of the harem wives.

Renata didn't like the feelings she was getting from both of them and decided to play her last trump card. She was most determined to achieve her goal. "I know why they don't want me. They see me as a helpless cripple, a woman with no hands, someone who will be utterly dependent on them for everything. They don't want a cripple to join with them, that's it, isn't it, Fel and Kassia?"

Damn, she didn't have to say that! Kassia said, "Fel, why don't we give her a chance to show us her intentions. I think she really and truly wants to be part of us." Fel nodded, not daring to meet Renata's eyes. That was a low blow she'd tossed at them both, but she picked up Kassia's thoughts and reasoning and she agreed.

"Okay then it is time for you to be bathed and fed. Then you may retire for the night and allow Renata to perform her *sesso disposto*. In the morning, I will wed you both and ask for your decision on Renata's situation. After that, I will help get you back to your original quest. Again, I thank you both for your service to the women of Tierra and bid you good night." She left and another priestess led them to the bathtubs, where the other eleven were just finishing up.

Clean for the first time in days and well fed, the three

entered their small bedroom. "You should prepare Kassia first always before me, Fel. We must be proper. Tie her hands behind her first, then remove her skirt, and then undo her hair. Then do me."

A while later, Fel helped them into the single bed. After she finished loving Kassia, Renata did her very best to pleasure both women. All three slept very soundly that night. In the morning, Renata was unusually cheerful and hovered over Fel, making sure she did everything right and proper for Kassia and then herself. Then, they made their slow way to the dining room.

As she'd promised, right after breakfast, the priestess performed the free-mate ceremony, uniting the two women. All the other women here, well over thirty, were on hand to witness their uniting. By mutual agreement, Kassia wanted to be hereafter known as Cassia Kaylee, since she was abandoning her old life and race forever. Kaylee meant slender woman which, because of her race, she was just that.

High Priestess Ama Alessia began, "Ladies, we are gathered here today to bear witness to the joining of two lives together solely out of a deep love for each other. Seldom are marriages formed from love alone. Yet, it is the sole basis for all free-mates. We are joining Cassia Kaylee and Feliciana Evita together. They share a bond of love and compassion for each other that none may shake." She went on with the ceremony and ended with, "I now give you Cassia Kaylee e Evita and Feliciana Evita e Kaylee." The women clapped and cheered, while the couple shared their first kiss as free-mates.

A bit later, Ama Alessia took the two aside along with Renata. "It is time. Have you made your decision about Renata?"

"We accept her with us and will be her husband-women," Fel said formally. No one in the room knew precisely what that meant, but Renata did not care, she was jubilant.

"Thank you! Thank you! Thank you!" she bubbled with joy.

"Okay, now down to your original quest. Your three companions have not given up the chase and are closing in on the kidnaper and the woman called Sara. They believed you were both killed by the alien ships and hence have not tried to communicate to you. I can see that you are there with them now, if that is your choice."

"That would be great. I don't know how you can do it, but I am honor bound to fulfill that mission," Fel replied. Alessia nodded, folded her hands, closed her eyes, and chanted something. The next instant, the three found themselves standing on the open roadway in front of Savina, Gina, and Molly, who were riding along the well-marked road. Fel didn't see the energizing of an enormous germanium crystal network in the basement of the Matera Tower.

Chapter 9 Rescues

Savina, Gina, and Molly picked up their pace after the dramatic and tragic loss of their two companions. Savina, in particular, felt the weight of Fel's mission on her shoulders. She was the eldest Sister, and she ought to have handled this better, taken more precautions, something, anything. Unfortunately, she had no idea what else she could have done. Their attackers were aliens. Instead, she pushed her daughter and Molly on hard, covering nearly fifty miles each day.

They did lose a half-day trying to find safe passage across the Wyndl River far south of the usual crossing at Wye, where the Easterlings man had forded. Following Fel's suggestion, she'd led them diagonally, hoping to cut some days off their chase. However, they had to travel down river for half a day before they found a ferry crossing.

The trio had covered some six hundred fifty miles since that horrid night that took their two friends from them. Based on her best guess, the last thoughts she'd picked up from Sara, the Easterlings man was heading due southeast, making for Adelmira. Savina hoped to catch them at Brownsville at Brooks River, some two hundred miles south of Northend. Today, they finally hit a partially graveled roadway, a main line that ran from Woodhill far south of them, paralleling the Brooks River, up to Brownsville and then on up to Northend. Before the climate change, this whole area had been part of the breadbasket of the Midlands, but now shepherding had replaced the old cash crops this far north. Woodhill, however, still thrived and was considered part of the prosperous croplands of the Midlands.

The sun ducked in and out of the building cumulus clouds, and Savina predicted a late afternoon thunderstorm, but no snow was likely. The temperature was too warm, approaching eighty, thank goodness, she though. Just then, three women suddenly appeared smack in the middle of the gravel roadway. The trio had just enough time to rein in their horses before colliding with them. "Oh my god! Fel? Is that really you? Kassia?" Savina rubbed her eyes. It certainly looked like Fel, except the clothes she wore were so foreign, white shirt, baggy white pants that seemed too short, and strange curved sandals. They saw two bound Easterlings women with her, save one looked like Kassia, sort of, but this woman had intact arms and hands, unlike Kassia.

Fel grinned, "Savina! Yes, it's us. We're back! Thank god, you continued after Sara. I owe you one."

"Is that Kassia with you? It can't be. We saw you disintegrated by the alien ships," Savina questioned and then challenged them.

"Long story. Yes, this is Cassia only she's been healed and is my free-mate now, Cassia Kaylee e Evita. I do hope you still have our spare clothes with you. We have to get out of these things, especially Cassia. Oh, she's now pregnant with our daughter! Mine and hers, for real!"

Savina had never seen Fel this happy; her face was radiant, quite unlike the usual stern look she remembered. "Free-mate? Pregnant? What the devil happened to you? We thought you were dead! Yes, we have your things on one of the packhorses." They dismounted and Savina hugged Fel and then looked at Cassia, who grinned sheepishly. She did her best to hug, though her arms were still bound.

"I really want to get out of this skirt and chains pronto, please. Can we afford to heat up some tea with honey too?" Cassia asked. "We have quite a story to tell."

"Sure, Molly, Gina, bring up the packhorse and see if you can make a quick fire for tea. Golly, your arms look real, Cassia," Savina said, feeling them.

"Oh, this is Renata Raffaella something," Cassia turned to introduce the eighteen year old young girl with them.

"Renata Raffaella Lucca Brom. Please to meet the friends of my husband-women," she said eagerly and without any bashfulness. "I suppose they will want me to be unbound too. Well, I will do as they ask, since this place does not look much like my homeland. They killed my husband for me, you see, and I performed the *sesso disposto* ceremony on them, so now I am their number two wife, you see."

Savina didn't see, but wisely didn't say so. Rather, she

was stunned by her last name. "Did you say Lucca Brom child?"

"Yes, ma'am. Lucca Brom," Renata replied, standing tall and proudly.

"Who are your parents? Forgive me for prying. You don't have to answer if you don't want to," Savina corrected herself. She was being rather impolite with a total stranger, but the name shocked her.

"Oh, that's okay. Mom passed away last year. She was Annetta Lucca Brom. She had a free-mate husband, Raffaella, but he took off and got killed when I was little. I was on my way to Adelmira Tower to be trained when I was kidnaped and given to Lord Domiano as his twelfth wife, you see. He tore out my eyes, as he did to all the other wives, so I slapped him hard and punched him in his balls. I think maybe I should not have done that though, cause he got really mad at me and had my hands cut off. But I prayed to Lysandra, and she sent Fel and Cassia to rescue me, and she gave me my eyes back and Cassia's arms too. Now I am their number two wife, you see." Renata would have chatted on even longer, but she finally saw Savina's wide-open mouth and stunned eyes and stopped momentarily.

"Annetta? Oh my god! She's my little sister! I've never seen her, though. That makes you my niece, Renata. I'm Annetta's older sister, Savina Lucca Brom. Felisa Lucca Brom is my mother and Annette's too."

Now it was Renata's turn to look shocked. "Aunt Savina? Really? Mom told me she had a sister who stayed behind in Brom when she and grandmother returned to the Easterlings. Grandma always told me to be proud of my Easterlings heritage and to honor our ways. I have been trying to do it, but now I have to change because I am number two wife. I hope that will be all right."

Savina began crying and hugged Renata tightly. Gina came up and gave her a hug too. "That makes us cousins. I'm Gina, mom's daughter. This is really fantastic, Renata. You look good and a lot like my mother too, since your mother and mine had the same parents."

"Will someone please get me out of this torture outfit

176

please?" Cassia teased. Fel laughed and began freeing her. Molly brought up saddlebags with their spare clothes in them and quickly the two changed. Renata was so excited about her relatives that she didn't pay much attention to Fel unbinding her and dressing her in spare clothes culled from Gina and Molly's packs.

"Oh! I feel so naked like this!" Renata suddenly exclaimed, finally realizing she was unbound and dressed like the other Sisterhood women. She had on a loose fitting blouse, warm leather pants and soft trail boots. Her long hair was brushed out and a spare bluebird clasp held much of it together by the back of her neck.

Everyone roared with laughter. Between laughs, Fel explained, "You are wearing warmer and more clothes than any woman does in the Easterlings and yet you think you are naked?" She laughed some more.

"Well, sort of. I can move my arms and take man-steps. Naked. No braids. I feel naked like a man must feel," Renata tried to explain to all.

"I truly understand, Renata. I got quite an education in Easterlings culture from mom," Savina replied. "Come on. Let's have tea and please, Fel, tell us the *whole* story! I am really keenly interested in the Goddess Lysandra and the role she played in this."

"You know about the gods and goddesses?" Cassia asked. "I kept wanting to know about them, but there wasn't any chance to ask anyone. Things just happened so fast and then my lips were tied shut and I couldn't speak for days really."

The group sat on a low stone fence around some farmer's field sipping tea, while Fel related what had happened to them. The trio found their tale fascinating and quite illuminating. "Only a goddess could have restored your arms, Cassia, and your eyes, Renata. Of that I am as certain as I am that I exist," Savina said as they finished up. "You three have really been blessed by the goddess. Pretty impressive, if I say so."

With a twinkle in her eye, she added, "And Fel, I am amazed at what your gift from Lysandra was! I would never have guessed."

Fel blushed beet red. "Well, what of it?" she said a bit defensively. "I'll never hook up with a man; I'll die first. Almost did once." Savina had a hint of her past and didn't press her on this.

Gina, on the other hand, had a coy grin. "Molly, it looks like we need to get a special wedding present for Fel and Cassia." Molly added her grin to her mates and Fel felt a little uneasy. What were those two planning?

"So who are these gods? What are they? How come we've not seen them before?" Cassia ignored them and asked.

Savina replied, "I don't know much about them, save some believe that they exist. We've got some very scanty records in Brom Tower. There is supposed to be an ancient penta-pantheon of gods and goddesses who were quite active in ancient times, though hardly anything remains of their works," Savina explained. "Lysandra is the Goddess of Life and of Death. She hears the prayers of women and only those who are in the greatest need, presumably because of men's evil actions against them. Of course, it is always said she demands a sacrifice from those who she helps either by giving them a merciful death or restored life."

"The strongest is the neutral Alleric who sits at the top of the pentagram, all powerful, but seldom mixing in our affairs. Some believe Lysandra had him to do something to fix up the terrible weather, which used to be destroying the world. From all I have learned, the weather is substantially better now than it was centuries ago. Calder is the God of Waters. I'm told he used to be worshiped by those who make use of the oceans and rivers, but those are few."

"Wystan is the God of Battles and Warriors. He is the men's god and he loves to create conflict and strife so men fight and he can watch and enjoy. Some say he is perverse. What with the wars we have seen springing up again, I suspect he is again active somewhere in our world. Finally, there is Ariana, the Goddess of Fertility. When the awful climate change struck and so many people died, Ariana became active again. I personally think she is responsible for women's boobs being so huge, giving our babies a better chance of surviving infancy. Does this help, Cassia?"

"Well sort of. What do the others do? How do we see them? Where are they? Do they have temples somewhere? I have lots of questions," Cassia laughed.

"I don't have any other answers, Cassia. We in the Sisterhood know of Lysandra and her temple, which you were highly privileged to visit, there in Matera. None of us knows how to find Matera. It's said it is wholly invisible unless the High Priestess or Lysandra summons you there and that no male can even get close to the invisible place. Beyond that, I don't know more," Savina answered. "I suppose we need to get going. Sara still has to be rescued."

"I guess I best do my thing and see where she's now at," Cassia volunteered. Grasping her crystal, she focused and contacted Sara for the first time in nearly two weeks. "Oh dear, they've run into another big battle! Fel, look."

Indeed, the Easterlings man and his wagon were racing along towards Brownsville, fleeing a charging bunch of cavalrymen. She saw many other families in wagons loaded with possessions fleeing along with them towards the city. This Cassia could see happening through the eyes of Sara and via her, Fel.

"Damn men and damn the towers anyway!" Fel cursed. "Another bloody battle just ahead. Okay, if the Easterlings man is smart, he's going to get across the Brooks River as fast as he can and will not stay in Brownsville. So let's play it smart and cross the river as soon as we can manage it. Come on. We'd best get riding."

"Hold on, how's Renata going to ride?" asked Savina, worried Fel had forgotten Renata had lost her hands and couldn't hold the reins.

"I can ride, I think. You can't leave me behind, husband-wives," Renata protested slightly while looking at the horse. "I used to ride in wagons before," she added, but didn't say she could ride a horse before she'd been harmed.

Cassia took heart, "You can do it. You have more arms than I had and I managed to sit on the horse while Savina led it. Grip with your legs, Renata." She helped Renata mount and gave her some pointers. Then they were off, though Fel kept them at a walk, while she rode on ahead looking for a likely ford or a ferry crossing. Several miles ahead she found a shallow ford and soon they crossed over, leaving the well-marked gravel path for open country once more. Fel felt more at ease in the wilds than she did on the main road.

Seeing Renata was managing, she picked up the pace gradually. She found the teen enjoyed cantering, but hated trotting and smiled at that. On they rode as the sky darkened. Before the rain came, Fel halted briefly, allowing everyone to don their oiled cloaks. Then she led them onwards.

The rains came down, a late afternoon torrent. "Wow, the sky is falling!" Renata yelled. "It's hitting me on my head!" She'd never seen rain before, Savina realized, and explained to her that it did this nearly every day. Still Renata enjoyed the lightning and thunder, claiming the gods were speaking to them. Savina recalled her own childhood when she moved from the Easterlings back to Brom and how strange and unusual the weather had seemed to her. She smiled back at Renata, who was very excited, though still trying to keep on her horse somehow.

Before long, they spotted smoke clouds and then an army of soldiers with some wooden machines moving up the road towards Brownsville, the very road they had been on. Fel smiled; she'd made the right call by crossing over. Here the river acted as a natural barrier between them and the army that was approaching on Brownsville. Soon the large town appeared, most of it lying on the other side of the river. A great wooden bridge arced over the Brooks River, and at the moment, it was packed with men, women, and children on foot, on wagons, on carriages, and horses. Some even pushed handheld pushcarts of belongings, fleeing the coming battle. As they neared, they could see soldiers wearing green uniforms hustling around the outskirts of the city, setting up defenses. Now the problem was to find the Easterlings man among all this confusion.

Fel thought, *What would I do if I were him?* She had an immediate answer, *get the hell out of the way.* He would need to avoid all these people, most of who were fleeing south towards the village called Thornton. No one, save themselves, were riding parallel to the river. Just as Gina called out, "Which way?" she had a reply.

"We keep paralleling the river." They did so, but had a devil of a time getting through the line of evacuees heading in an almost solid line southwards blocking their path. It delayed them nearly a half hour to get past this bridge and path. At last, they moved on up the river, leaving the chaos that was now invading Brownsville behind them. As it was getting dark, Fel had to make a decision. Did they continue on or should they stop for the night and try to close the distance tomorrow? "Hold up a second," Fel ordered and dismounted. In the dim light, she studied the ground and smiled.

"Gang, they are only a little ways ahead of us, fresh wagon tracks and horse dung. We'll take them tonight! Come on." Fel was enthusiastic now. Her prey was close at hand; she could feel it. She led them on, albeit slowly. She didn't want to risk losing the trail if he veered off to find a suitable place to camp.

An hour later, it was full dark, but now she spotted the glow of a campfire ahead. The man had chosen to camp along the riverbank. Well, in a way that would have been an ideal spot, water was nearby, and he could fish if low on provisions. "What's the plan," whispered Molly, eager to get this over with and return home to Brom.

"Let's ride into the camp. You three circle around so he has his back to the river and no direction to flee. I think we'll try a simple bluff first," Fel suggested. She could have opted to slink into his camp while he was sleeping and slit his throat, but that would not be an honorable fight. She wanted him to know fully kidnaping women of the Midlands would not go unpunished. Besides, there was one of him and six of them, if she counted the handless Renata.

A few minutes later, they rode into his camp. His horses were tethered to a willow tree. He had bedrolls laid out beneath the wagon. Sara was sitting on a rock, fully bound and still gagged. He was busily cooking their supper over the fire when the six rode into his camp. He rose quickly and drew his scimitar and dagger, moving in close to Sara.

"Well, we finally caught up to you. Remember me? We

wiped out the alien and the other bidders. But this time, we don't need the bears to help us," Fel said in a commanding tone while she dismounted and drew her sword, squaring off to meet him.

"You!" he cried out, suddenly recognizing Fel. "Damn you!"

"No, damn you for kidnaping a young Midlands woman," Fel countered. "Let her go and I may be lenient with you."

"Come one step closer and I'll slit her throat!" he sneered at her, his eyes following the others, but only Cassia had dismounted, joining Fel but taking a position on the other side of his campfire from her.

"Sir, if you harm Sara even slightly, I will make sure you endure the worst torture imaginable, and I can imagine a good deal. I've just slain the Easterlings Lord Damiano Domenico, and he was a far more deadly opponent than you. I again ask you politely to release Sara to us unharmed."

"If I do that, what's to keep you from attacking me anyway?"

Fel sensed he was sizing up his options and there were not many of them open to him. "I give you my pledge as a Sisterhood woman to allow you to continue on your way unharmed if you release Sara there to us unharmed. I give you my pledge to torture you mercilessly if you do harm her," Fel said domineeringly. Would he give in? That was what Fel wanted to know. She'd rather bluff Sara free from him than hazard a fight in which Sara or one or more of them might get injured.

"Damned Sisterhood anyway. You bitches make life hard for the rest of us." He spat on the ground.

"Men like you give all men a bad reputation. Kidnaping helpless women — you are the scum of the earth. Make your choice. I'm getting hungry."

He needs some persuasion, Cassia sent Fel. She touched her crystal and focused on the man's dagger. She began to move it slowly towards his crotch. He felt her force, and, as he realized where she was intending that dagger to cut, he strained his arm against her! Sweat poured from his forehead as he fought to keep the dagger from his privates. "Okay, okay, I will do as you order, but I want my wagon and team."

"You may have them. Cassia, get Sara out of the way. When she's clear, you can pack up and leave here unharmed. Try anything and you've had it. Last warning," Fel ordered. Hastily, Cassia moved to Sara, who was shaking from fright. She picked the bound woman up and carried her behind Molly's horse out of the way. At once, she untied her gag and began unbinding her arms.

Meanwhile, Fel and the others watched the Easterlings man as he hastily packed up his gear and hitched his horses. Fifteen minutes later, he climbed aboard. "Clear out and don't try to sneak back tonight. We will be expecting you," Fel added. He cursed her again but slapped the reins and headed off into the darkness along the river's edge. "Molly, tail him; make sure he doesn't double back right away." She nodded and rode after him at a safe distance.

"How is Sara?" Fel asked, sheathing her sword.

"She's alive, but her arms are in a bad way. They are numb; he's kept her bound like this the whole way. Now what? Camp here?" Cassia asked.

"Not if we can avoid it. I don't trust him. I don't want to risk our lives standing guard all night long. We can't go back the way we came either. Wait here, see if you can find her some decent clothes to wear."

"But she is wearing decent clothes, very proper like," Renata protested, and then retracted what she'd said after seeing Cassia's glance her way. "Proper for the Easterlings, that is," she amended herself.

"Who are you anyway?" Sara asked Cassia.

"We're from the Sisterhood. Fel was the one who was supposed to snatch you back in Exchange City, but the teleport man beat her to it. We've been following you ever since. Took us a while to catch you though," Cassia answered her. Savina and Gina brought her some clothes and began to dress her. She'd been beaten some, Savina noted grimly, as if being helplessly bound was not enough. She wished the man would have tried something!

"Okay, the river current isn't strong and it's not too deep here. We'll get our feet wet, but we can cross. Easy does it; let your horse make its own way. Single file. Someone stay close to Sara and Renata. No accidents. Come on. Here comes Molly back," Fel ordered.

One by one, they followed Fel and her horse into the dark river waters. She was right; they could cross but the water came up over their boots soaking their feet. Soon, they climbed up the bank on the other side, but not before both Sara and Renata nearly fell off their horses as they lurched up the bank. "Now what?" Savina asked.

"One good thing about a nice river is there are usually a lot of small towns along its banks. We'll ride on upstream and see if we can't find a village inn. We could all do with a hot tub and a good meal."

An hour later, they rode into Waynesville, a small village of five hundred on the northern bank of the Brooks River. They found the single inn and Fel made the arrangements. Before long, the women were enjoying a hot tub bath, pitchers of ale, and a hearty meal, warmed up by the innkeeper's wife.

While they were bathing, Savina kept a close eye on her niece. She sensed Renata's depression creeping back as she found she couldn't bathe herself at all and had to let the others bathe her. Sara couldn't move her arms and willingly allowed them to help her. Now Savina could see the numerous black and blue marks on her body. She cursed the kidnapper once again.

As they sat down for their warmed over stew, Renata insisted on trying to feed herself and she managed somewhat by holding the spoon between her stumps and leaning over her bowl. She kept refusing Cassia's offer to help her. Meanwhile, Fel pumped the innkeeper for news of the battle taking place south of here in Brownsville.

"Haverhills and Oakham Towers are fighting over just who controls this territory. There's no clear boundary, you see. We were supposed to be Oakham's but the Haverhill's think we belong to them. Don't think they will come this far east with their fighting, leastwise, I hope they don't. Bad for business," he explained.

Then, she asked about any news further north. "Oh, Bettingham and Bedwurth Towers are disputing much of the lands up there. Best be careful if you go that way too. Only safe place is to go further east. Can't go south, Rusden and Oakham are battling over who controls the land down to the Wyndl," he added.

Back in their room, Fel looked at her crude map of the Midlands. They were boxed in, with battles going on all around them. Eastward was the last direction she wanted to go. She'd had enough of their bindings to last her a lifetime and she hadn't been bound. For a moment, she glanced lovingly at Cassia, who was feeding Sara, admiring the courage and bravery of her lover who had endured so much without complaining. Then, she returned to her map. At last, she worked out a route she hoped would be safe. They could back track down the river, skirting the fighting at Brownsville, and when far enough away, cut due west to the Wyndl, crossing somewhere south of Leedsburough, and then follow that mighty river up to Wye and on into the Kingdom of the Angels, eventually home to Brom.

Savina, on the other hand, thought about her niece. *I'm responsible for her now and she is so young and inexperienced. Yet she has the Lucca Brom spunk in her. Now her life is practically ruined. Without hands, she's doomed. I can see she is fighting back her grief, but for how long? Damn men anyway.* Then, she remembered Aurora and Ally and how the aliens had given them prosthetics hands that worked reasonably well for them or so all the stories Lilly had told her said so. They lived in the Wyth Tower, a hundred fifty miles south of Brom Tower. *What has happened to those hands and the medical machines of Doctor Zosia? Are they still around? Cassia is an alien. Perhaps she could work the machines and get the hands working for my niece.*

That night when Cassia was brushing out her now much longer hair and still wondering how it had grown so much, Savina broached the subject with her. After explaining what she wanted and about Aurora and Ally, she asked, "If the machines and the hands are still there, could you possibly work them and help my niece?"

"I'm not a trained doctor, Savina, but I do know some about it. Field agents have to be able to tend to wounds in the field and all that. I can try. Besides, it doesn't take a doctor to operate those machines. Sure, I'll give it a go," Cassia answered, and Savina felt greatly relieved. Perhaps there yet might be hope for Renata having a worthwhile life.

By morning, Sara's arms had some feeling back in them, and she could just barely move them a little, giving her a morale boost. After a good breakfast, Fel and Cassia visited several stores and bought more supplies for the return trip. Around ten, they headed back downstream, crossing where they'd crossed the night before. Their spirits were high, for they were headed home at last. At least Renata didn't feel badly having to have someone lead her horse, likewise Sara, who rode beside her.

"I am going to become a tower technician working the crystal networks," Sara explained. "Dad first wanted me to marry a guy I detested. When that fell through, he let another stranger buy me, paying him ten thousand silvers. Can you believe that? Well, I was determined not to go along with that. I sent a message for help to the Sisterhood in Haverhills to help me escape and get to Bedwurth Tower. But then, that man touched my shoulder and I ended up kidnaped. I was so scared, especially when that alien was bidding for me." She chatted merrily away and Renata returned the chatter, telling her about her life as well.

Their mood changed as they passed the southern edge of the battle at Brownsville. Acrid smoke filled the air. They watched as the siege engines hurled fire bombs and acid bombs into the city. The fire bombs were directed at the flammable structures, while the acid bombs were directed primarily towards the opposing troop concentrations. The hideous screams of men in pain and dying could not be drowned out, turning a gay morning into a nightmare for the travelers. Instinctively, Fel urged them into an all-out canter, hoping the two women could stay on the horses somehow. Several miles away, she slowed back down, the girls, ashen-faced, had made it, but Renata asked to stop. She vomited up her lunch; Sara followed suit. It was a very somber group that continued on downstream.

Kyle and Mary Smythe, thirteen and fourteen, lived in the small village of Miller's Crossing, along the Brooks River. Their father was the local miller and their mother had died some ten years before while giving birth to their brother who also didn't survive. Sam had refused to listen to the village midwife who claimed *mentales* births needed special handling. "That will cost us far too much money. She can get by like the rest of the women in the village!" She had the gift and thus had already given it to Kyle and Mary, but even today, both were wholly untrained telepaths.

Sam was a miser and he beat the children mercilessly whenever they didn't instantly do as he asked, which was frequently several times a week. It didn't matter he was asking them to do something even an adult would find difficult. Rather, it would save him a pretty copper.

"Money is everything! How many times do I have to scream that into your silly heads!" That line the kids had heard a hundred times if not more. Mary liked animals and wanted to train dogs, but Sam would not hear of it. "They eat up all your profits and give you nothing back in trade." He'd squelched that one in the bud. Still, Mary took care of other folk's animals there in her village and was known to have the "knack" with farm animals, having saved several who had been injured over the years.

Kyle, on the other hand, wanted to be a chemist. Already he knew a dozen home remedies. "I'm taking after the ancient witches and healing the sick," he proudly told Mary when their dad was not around. Indeed, many villagers came to him for help when Sam was not present. His specialty was curing headaches by using a leaf he found in the woods not far from the village. He had no name for the *bacal* leaf, but it worked wonders on people's headaches, and he was never without some on him, usually stuffed into a pocket of his heavily patched pants. Neither child could remember when they got their last set of new clothes. Always it was "patch it up, save a copper."

As the kids grew older, the beatings grew harder. He'd broken Mary's right arm so badly, even Kyle could not set it to rights. After that, her right arm was mostly useless to her and she was beaten even harder for failing to sew up the holes in their clothing. Two years ago, he'd broken her left leg rather badly. Kyle worked his magic on her, but now she walked with a distinct limp, barely able to get around. "Don't worry, Mary, I'll never leave you, not ever."

Then two weeks ago, the large army of Haverhills came marching through their village, demanding to be well fed. Of course, Sam saw no profit in giving away all his hard earned grain. As the heated argument broke out, Kyle and Mary headed into the storage bins to hide from the soldiers. He feared they would rape Mary and abduct him into their army, at least that's what they were threatening Sam with doing. As they peered out, they watched as the soldiers torched the mill and ran their father through with a sword. They then headed to the storage building to take all the miller's grain. Kyle and Mary crept out a back door and fled for their lives, heading into the forest nearby, where they hid.

"Now what do we do?" Mary asked, sobbing. Their only home was up in flames.

"Well, mom says we have a gift or something. She always said when we get old enough we are to go to a tower to be tested. I think we are old enough. We should go to a tower and at least ask for help." Thus, the two with nothing on their backs but their patched clothes, set out on a twelve hundred mile walk to Rusden Tower. Of course, to Kyle, the tower would by just over the next hill. Neither had ever been further than a few miles from their village.

With Mary's heavy limping, they could only make a few miles each day. Water they had, as Kyle kept them close to the river, but food they had not. Kyle scrounged for mushrooms and odd tubers, but they slowly began to starve and grew steadily weaker. Then making matters worse, they both got deadly ill, running a high fever. Delirious, the two lay beside the river where they last drank.

Fel called out, "Hold up. Something's wrong ahead. Kids, are you okay?" She saw two utterly filthy young teens, a boy and a girl, lying face down on the bank. Their clothes had more patches than original cloth. Neither moved or responded. She dismounted and went to check on them. "Savina, we have two deathly ill children here. Little help please."

Savina and Gina dismounted and joined her, rolling the two over. "My god, they are burning up! Okay, set up camp here. This is going to take some time. We can't just leave them, they'll die." She and her daughter activated their crystals and began to examine the two, searching for the cause of their high fever.

At last, Gina forced Mary's eyes open. "My god, mom. Verge Sickness! Him too."

"Damn! I'll get a fire going so you can brew some *bacal* tea," Fel responded to the ill news.

"We'd best strip them and get them into the water some. We have to lower their fever soon," Savina ordered. Unfortunately, their threadbare clothing mostly ripped when they tried to strip them. In doing so, Gina discovered Kyle's cache of his headache cure.

"Mom, look, he'd got a big stash of *bacal* leaves!" Gina exclaimed. "What a stroke of luck, cause we are plumb out!"

"You can say that again, I've only got enough left for one pot. Okay, you brew it, and we'll get them in the waters and bathed. Cassia and Molly, see if you can find something for them to wear in our supply packs. Never thought we'd end up being a clothier this trip," she jested.

An hour later, both teens had been washed, dressed in a mix-match of pants and tops, and had some *bacal* tea poured into their mouths. Fel had taken pity on the lad and donated one of her tops, since the women's tops all had space for their huge breasts, and the lad would look awfully silly wearing one of those. "So what do we do now?" Fel asked as she sipped her strong tea.

"We wait. Their fevers should break sometime today. Then, if Gina and I keep at it, we ought to get them over this bout of Verge Sickness fairly quickly. However, look at their muscles. I'd swear they haven't eaten a square meal in a long time. Worse, the girl is in a bad way physically. Look at her right arm and left leg."

"Cockeyed?" Fel suggested.

"Right, both have been badly broken and have not mended properly. I suspect the girl walks with a noticeable limp and probably has little use of her arm. See how her fingers are so atrophied? I wonder what has happened to these two?" Savina answered and wondered aloud.

Late that evening, Mary roused. She sat up weakly and looked fearfully at the group gathered around their campfire. "Please don't rape me or hurt my brother," she mumbled. "Don't kill us like you did dad. Please." She was whispering in a whimpering, yet pleading tone.

Savina rose and came over to her. "Dear, you are safe with us. We're all women, so you need not fear that. You and your brother have gotten very sick, Verge Sickness. We've gotten your fever broken and I think you'll soon recover. What's your name? Where can we take you? Are you lost?"

"Mary Smythe, he's Kyle. Soldiers came, wanted to rape me, killed dad, burned down our mill, and stole all dad's grain. We ran away. Kyle is taking us to the tower in Rusden to be tested and helped," she replied. "Can I have something to eat?"

"Sure, but only light food tonight. When was the last time you ate a good meal?"

"I don't know, may be before we ran away. Couple weeks ago? I don't know." Savina sighed, lifted her up and fed her some of the broth Gina had simmering, waiting for the two to wake. Before long, Kyle woke and was shocked to see so many adults around the campfire. Savina repeated her explanations and Kyle wanted to eat as well.

"Good thing you had that stash of *bacal* leaves in your pocket, Kyle. It saved your lives."

"My what? Oh, you mean my headache remedy. I am going to be a chemist, like the ancient witches were. I can cure a dozen things now, including headaches," he answered proudly. "I even got Mary sort of patched up after dad broke her arm and leg. They were really bad breaks, but I got her healed. I'm taking us to Rusden Tower. Mom said we are supposed to be tested. She died ten years ago though. It's just over that next hill, I suppose."

Fel stifled a laugh. "Over the next hill? I'm afraid it's a bit further than that my lad. Try something like twelve hundred miles give or take a few."

"Is that far?" Kyle asked naively.

"Take it from me, Kyle, it is a very long way to go on foot. You might make it by next year." He looked surprised and then downcast. "Don't worry; we'll get you to a tower on horseback long before then. Rest, get your strength back, son."

Then he noticed Renata and exclaimed rather startled, "She doesn't have any hands!"

Renata flushed. "Nope, a really bad man cut them off after I punched him in his privates."

"That's worse than Mary. She can sort of use hers," Kyle replied. "What's happened to our clothes?"

"Sorry, but they ripped when we took them off of you. We'll get you some new clothes when we get to a town or village, Kyle. Now rest up. We need to hit the trail as soon as you two can manage to ride," Savina answered him.

"Thank you for helping us. See, Mary, women are nice; it's the men who are bad," Kyle pointed out to his sister. He didn't get a counter-argument from this bunch of women nor did he see the missing fact he too was male.

They stayed put another day allowing the teens to build up their strength and to make sure their fevers didn't return. Meanwhile, the teens asked numerous questions, particularly about the towers and the crystals that many in the party wore around their necks. "I had one too before that bad man stole mine," Renata explained. "I supposed now I can't ever get another one, since I don't have any hands."

"Of course you can have another crystal, Renata. It doesn't need hands to activate, just the touch of your skin. I'll get you fixed up later on," Savina replied. Renata's face beamed with pleasure. Naturally, Kyle wanted to know what the crystals did, and Savina found herself launching into an area in which she was terribly ignorant, wishing she'd paid more attention when she was a teen in the tower among those who knew such answers.

The teens rapidly recovered and the next day they hit the trail again. Kyle was pleased Mary didn't have to walk.

Already, everyone had seen how badly she limped and knew she could not walk long distances. Riding was the answer for both of them.

When the river took a big bend to the south, Fel again cut across country shaving several hundred miles off their trip home. She decided against going to Rusden Tower. There were too many battles going on in and around there at the moment. Instead, they headed up the western bank of the Wyndl River. Five hundred miles ahead lay Wye and another five hundred beyond that lay Bettingham and the Kingdom of the Angels. Of course, Brom Tower lay eight hundred miles beyond that. Twenty-five days later, they pulled into the tower at Bettingham without further incident. Here they left Kyle and Mary to be trained and given new lives. Then they headed not to Brom but to Wyth, arriving there some twenty days later. It was now mid-September. This far north, the first winter storms came and they were very glad to be back before the long winter really came.

Their first stop was at the Wyth Sisterhood house, where they reported in and Fel counted out the Sisterhood's share of their profits. It was considerable since they'd taken nearly twenty thousand silvers from the men who were bidding on Sara. Always, the women gave a quarter of their profits to the Sisterhood to help support the various houses throughout Tierra. Fel then divided the rest among all present, including Renata and Sara, figuring those two needed some financial assistance. Each woman received about two thousand silvers, a tidy profit for their long summer's work.

While Molly and Gina headed into Wyth to do some shopping, Savina, Fel, Cassia, Renata, and Sara headed to the tower on the Bettingham estate north and west of the town proper. Savina intended to get Sara tested and trained here if possible. Plus, they wanted to find out if the old prosthetic hands were still around and workable.

The original tower and Bettingham estate would have been no longer recognizable by Alford and Aiden Bettingham. The original tower some fifty feet tall and a hundred feet round was now invisible. An even larger tower had been built around it, measuring two hundred feet across and rising to a hundred feet. The manor house was gone, replaced by a giant manor house, capable of housing two hundred people. Surrounding the estate that had sprawled to the north was a thirty foot tall massive outer wall, heavy on defensible positions and features, complete with a single huge gatehouse offering the only entrance.

Now in their fourth generation of cousin marriages, all the leaders could trace their lineage back to the original four couples: Aurora and Aiden Bettingham, Ally and Alford Wycombe Bettingham, Dita and Norwood Ewa Wycombe, and Doctor Zosia and Able Wiola Smith. Currently, the top leader was Venerado Amo Al Wycombe Bettingham, thirty-one. His wife, Betsy, five years older, ran the entire manor house. Other top lineage personnel were the Capos or the top leaders of the three circles, which operated in eight-hour shifts. The continuous inbreeding was beginning to take its toll here. Miscarriages had now become commonplace and Venerado Al was anxious to interject fresh bloodlines to the tower.

Ordinarily, Fel and Savina would have reported their adventures to their Sisterhood house up in Bettingham and Brom, respectively. However, what they'd encountered had to be relayed firsthand to one of the kingdom's Venerado. Since Savina desperately wanted to help her newfound niece with the possibility of reusing the ancient prosthesis hands, they decided to meet with Venerado Al and let him relay the information to the other three towers in the Kingdom of the Angels.

Venerado Al was thin and rather weak, a direct result of the four generations of inbreeding. However, he had a keen mind and powerful psi energies. "Well, I got your message, Sisters. I am a very busy man, but out of deference to the Sisterhood, I will hear you out. Please be seated. I know some of you, but not all. My wife and manor house steward Betsy." He graciously motioned for the women to have a seat in his large meeting room. Betsy poured them all some freshly brewed tea.

"You know me, Venerado Al, I am Feliciana Evita e Kaylee. My free-mate, Cassia Kaylee e Evita. You know Savina, of course. This is her niece, Renata Lucca Brom from the

Easterlings. Outside is Sara Haverhills Benton who would like to be tested, and, if found worthy, trained here. Now then, where to begin. First, Cassia Kaylee is an alien from Rigel-3."

"What? Alien? She does not look remotely like an alien, Feliciana. What are you trying to pull off here?" Al grew very much annoyed.

Betsy touched her crystal and corrected him, "Dear, she speaks the truth, though this must not be her given name." He calmed down somewhat, but stared at Cassia.

"No it is not. Originally, she was a field agent for the Sector ID Minister. Her given name then was Kassia Kunegunda, and she looked very much like all the aliens you see around Plateau Grado. Let me tell you what has happened," Fel tried to steer the discussion back to her tale.

"It all started when I accepted the assignment to snatch and grab Sara Haverhills Benton," Fel began. An hour later, filled with many interruptions for clarifications, she finally finished up.

"Betsy says you are telling the truth, but honestly, gods, goddesses, Cassia without her arms and then getting them back, you must be hallucinating and that's why you are not registering with her gift. You believe is what happened to you," Al attempted to squash the vast majority of her tale. "Mass hallucinations, that's what it was. Perhaps it was something you all ate. The aliens have always lived up to the letter of their lease agreement. Now, if you will excuse me, I have more pressing matters to attend to. Oh, yes, we will test Sara and Renata and if worthy, we will accept them here at Wyth Tower for training. Deal with them, Betsy." He rose and left.

Fel was fuming, fighting hard to keep her angry thoughts contained and not broadcasting them throughout the manor house. Betsy was evidently used to Al's often rude handling of visitors. "You must forgive him; he's under a lot of pressure. The Brom Compact division of lands is very troublesome. Now then, you mentioned, Savina, something about those prosthetic hands of our ancestors. I suspect they are somewhere in the basement storage area. We pile all the unwanted gear there, kind of like pack rats we are. You are most welcome to go down there and search for them. If you can find them and if they will work for poor Renata, you are welcome to them. Only please return them when you are finished with them. I will show you the stairs, but running this huge manor with over two hundred people here is very taxing."

She rose, showed them the dark stairs, and left them to their quest. Fel took the stairs three at a time, trying to find a vent for her outrage. "Idiots. Men!" she finally cursed and opened the door to an enormous cellar piled high with all manner of unused stuff. Chairs that ought to have been thrown out, ripped couches, old clothes, mountains of discarded things greeted their first view.

"Light the lanterns and let's get searching," Savina said hopefully. "What a mess."

"Aunt Savina, I don't think I want to stay at this tower," Renata timidly spoke up. "He was rude and frankly stupid; besides I don't want to leave my husband-women."

"We'll try Brom Tower. First, though we need to find those hands and the medical machines," she replied. The four spread out and began rummaging through the mountains of accumulated junk. An hour later, they had uncovered the medical machine, the solar powered recharging units, and the two pairs of hands, which were in a nice glass display case, buried beneath a pile of moth eaten quilts.

"She did say we can take these things with us," Savina pointed out.

Fel grinned. She and Cassia lifted the heavier medical machine and carried it up to the first floor. Savina carried the generators and Renata carried the display case cradled in her arms. Without further words, they carried them outside to their borrowed wagon and deposited them. Fel felt responsible for Sara, however, and insisted on checking with Betsy about her.

"Oh she is doing very well indeed. Al has accepted her and she seems positively delighted, Fel." Betsy was all kindness, but Fel didn't trust her, but thanked her and left. *If Sara doesn't like it here, she can contact me telepathically.* She left and drove the wagon back to the Sisterhood house. The four carried their equipment into their large shared room, now filled with the new outfits Gina and Molly had purchased.

195

While Fel angrily related how it had gone with the two, Cassia began tinkering with the medical machine. Renata watched her quite interested in the strange apparatus.

"It needs to be recharged. Okay, let's set these units in the window here where they can catch the sunlight. These are solar cells, which convert sunlight energy into electrical energy that recharges the batteries. If we get the hands working, Renata, then once every few months you will need to recharge the hands in a similar way," Cassia explained. Once setup, there was nothing more Cassia could really do except study the machine's settings.

Fel busied herself with making arrangements to take everyone on up to Brom and the tower there. Since it was already snow season, she needed to plan carefully. While blizzards were uncommon in September, they were not unheard of and travelers had to be prepared or die. Fel was always prepared.

By evening, the medical machine and the hands were half charged, sufficient for Cassia to begin to operate them. First, she ran an internal diagnostic check on the hands. Both pairs performed well within tolerances. "Okay, the hands are operational. Now for the hard part."

"But my stumps are too big for the holes in them," Renata pointed out.

"Yes, the machine, if I can get it working, will modify your stumps to fit them perfectly."

"But won't that hurt like the devil?" Renata asked, becoming suddenly very worried and scared. "I've never felt such pain before. I don't know if I can take it again."

"Don't worry, Renata. If I get it working right, you won't feel a thing. Imperium medical procedures are pretty advanced. Let me study these menus a while. I'm not a doctor, but this is really a computer and those I can run," Cassia replied confidently. *I hope I can figure this out.*

Cassia played with the menus for over an hour and worked out the proper sequence. She inserted the hands and the machine took their measurements. So far so good. Next, came the hard part. She double-checked the menu sequence and then had Renata sit down and insert her right arm into the

196

machine. "You may feel a slight pressure and pin prick, but nothing more." *I hope so anyway.* She pressed the Activate Sequence button and held her breath. A tiny needle injected a local anesthetic that numbed her entire lower arm. Then, the machine began carving up the end of her arm, forming a perfect fit for the prosthetic right hand chosen. Once done, the sequence reverted to heal mode, rapidly healing up the surgery.

"How long will this take? When is it going to start?" Renata asked becoming rather bored with all the waiting. Nothing seemed to be happening at all. "Maybe it isn't working."

"There, the green light says it is done. You can pull your arm out now."

"Oh my god! Look at it!" She saw the end of her lower arm was now aesthetically tapered conically to barely an inch across at the tip where her wrist had been.

"I guess I have it working. Let's get the left arm done," Cassia said rather proud of her work. A short while later, Renata's left arm looked just like her right one.

"If nothing else, Cassia, they look rather attractive now," Renata complimented her work.

"Now for the acid test." She inserted each hand onto her stumps. A tiny vacuum pump began sucking her skin to the hand. "The way these are supposed to work is you just pretend it is your real hand and try to use it as you would if it were real. Go ahead; see if you can move the fingers, Renata." She did, first her right fingers and then her left. The look on Renata's face told Cassia she had just given the teen back her life. The relief was staggering, especially as she began to pick up things and even tried to write a little.

In the background, Fel beamed with pride in her free-mate. *You've salvaged her whole life, padrona.*

I know, I can see it in her eyes.

Savina had to wipe her eyes; tears came involuntarily and she thanked Cassia repeatedly. Renata then had to show Molly and Gina her new hands. Before it was time for bed, all the many women in the house were given a demonstration by Renata. The house mother sent a round of her finest ale to the group, allowing them to celebrate a little.

The next morning, while everyone was packing a wagon with their things — the alien machines, and supplies — Sara came trudging through the snow. She'd walked the two miles from the Wyth Tower. "Fel! Good, I caught you in time. Please, can I come with you to this other tower? I don't like the people at Wyth Tower. They were unfriendly sort of, I don't know. It doesn't feel right to me there. Please, can I?"

Fel grinned, "Sure Sara. I had no idea it had gotten this bad. Lend us a hand stowing our gear and off we go." They made a quick stop to purchase Sara some warmer clothing, a down parka, and fleece lined boots. Already the temperatures were just barely above freezing and at night, it would be well below freezing.

They rolled north out of Wyth along the slippery, rocky, and winding path that led north and somewhat west to Brom Tower, nestled very near the Goza Mountains, high in the foothills and touching the mountains themselves. This route would become nearly impassible in another thirty days, remaining so until the spring thaw came. "Don't worry, we'll be staying at two small inns and three safe houses along the way. Be there in five days, barring the weather," Fel explained. *Damn, I have been putting this off for far too long. I hate to have to do this, so humiliating, but I've got no choice. They'll see it when we get there. Damn.*

Fel had an Achilles heel, emotional and physical, one that had helped define who she was, the amazon fighter for women. Now, despite her intentions, she was returning to her original home and had to face the people there once again. While she could do it, she found it hard to reveal it to her free-mate and to her other friends. Well, Savina and her daughter probably knew it or mostly. She sighed and announced, "Okay, gang, Cassia, there is something I have to tell you — about me — really personal and I *don't* want you to tell anyone else, but I *have* to tell you."

What's she saying? She's got some deep dark secret? I'm the one full of secrets, alien and all, thought Cassia.

Where to begin, Fel thought. *Perspective, keep it in perspective.* "You have seen the leading edge of it back there in

198

Wyth Tower. Inbreeding. You see, those in power positions in the towers have been practicing a breeding program. Their idea is to keep their precious *mentales* gifts in their direct descendants, to add more gifts to their line, and to increase the psi potentials of their descendants. Cousins are marrying cousins, once even brother and sister. They are into the fifth generation of inbreeding now. Anyone can tell only trouble is coming. Venerado Al is an example. Their breeding women are now having more and more miscarriages. Some of their children are not surviving into adulthood. Yes, yes, they continue to have their powerful psi gifts, but in my opinion the cost is *far* too steep."

"They get awfully snooty," Sara added. "Stuck up, like they are the only ones who are important. I didn't like them much. Are all the towers like that? If so, maybe I don't want to go to a tower after all."

"All of them have been doing it, as far as we know," Savina answered her. She had the broadest viewpoint and had traveled widely in her sixty years.

"Even Brom Tower has done it, but to a far lesser extent. They have one disadvantage the other towers do not. They are so far north and in such an inhospitable area that only the very hardy go there. Thus, they tend to draw in more outside bloodlines, taking in many who don't like the other towers. However, when the original towers were formed over a century ago, one of the founding women was Drina Esteban, who had a rare and different gift, due in part, some think, to her physical condition. She was born without any arms in Benito, Trujillo. Her gift was she always knew what someone desperately wanted to know. She had three children and her abnormality, which some call bad genes, carried on to her children. All three were also armless, but her son died before reaching adulthood. Elena and Filipa not only ended up with their mother's uncanny gift to know what another wanted, but had one of the rarest gifts of all: the katalyein gift, the ability to unlock a person's inherent *mentales* gifts that were blocked by trauma. Some call them catalyst telepaths and they are *really* rare. Anyway, Elena was terrified her children would be born without arms and for a time considered not even having a boyfriend. Then, she also got kidnaped and encountered the goddess Lysandra, or so the story has been told. Until now, I thought it was just that, a story someone made up. Anyway, she used her gift to help bring Lysandra and her temple back into operation. Lysandra gave her the promise that her children would not inherit her genetic defect and she and her sister then got married."

"Their children did have arms, were perfectly normal, but lacked one thing: the katalyein gift. When they married, Elena moved to join her husband in Brom Tower. As you can imagine, the leaders were dismayed that the extremely rare gift had been lost. So Brom Tower did what all the other towers have been doing: inbreeding Elena and Filipa's children, cousin to cousin marriages for five generations now. Their goal has been to bring back that lost gift: katalyein."

Fel sighed, now came the emotionally difficult part. "I am the product of the fourth generation of their inbreeding line. I go back directly to both Elena and Filipa. One of my younger sisters died of Verge Sickness. Cousin Basilio is insane. Infertility and miscarriages are commonplace in our line now, but it gets worse. My older brother and sister were forced to marry my cousins and another pair of cousins married. They finally succeeded. Each of the three marriages has produced children who have a strong katalyein gift, powerful I'm told. However, now the breeders face new problems. All six children are girls; all six are armless. While they finally got what they wanted, it seems to me the line is now dead; there are no male offspring. The oldest is seventeen, but what man in his right mind would want to marry an armless woman expecting her to bear his equally armless offspring? Yes, they have big problems now."

"Oh my god! That's awful!" Cassia interjected.

"Worse, they wanted me — no they *ordered* me to marry my cousin who is already married and has two of those girls. They were desperate for a male in order to continue their breeding program. That's when I rebelled and got the hell out of Brom Tower. Of course, I was foolish and have paid dearly for that." *No way am I going to tell them about how I became castinto!*

"Anyway, for all that, I love my nieces and play the role of Aunt Fel to all six, even though only four are really my nieces. I guess to be truly fair, the other families at Brom Tower have been careful not to inbreed and to bring in new bloodlines when possible. It's just my lineage that is so fouled up. That's why I will never accept a man. I refuse to bear armless children. Don't worry, padrona, with your alien genes, I am hoping and praying our daughter is normal."

Savina replied kindly, "Thank you, Fel. I suspected as much, but as you know, no one at Brom is talking about it — only that you abandoned your heritage and duties to the tower." She already knew much of this, but not how Fel felt about it. Many pieces of Fel's history began to make some sense to her.

Fel explained, "When you get there, you are going to meet a whole lot of de la Cantara's and del Fuego's. My birth name, that I abandoned when I entered the Sisterhood, is de la Cantara. I chose to be called Evita after that. Our heritage is of course Westerlings all the way down the five generations."

"Well, they ought to think more kindly of you, Fel, now that you have me and a daughter on the way," Cassia suggested hopefully.

"Maybe." She laughed, "They certainly would if it was a son instead." After moment, she added, "Don't get me wrong, my six nieces are beautiful young women, bright, cheerful, and radiant. I love them and honestly I have missed them."

Savina pointed out, "In my opinion, those in Brom Tower are the most level headed and considerate of any of the towers. Don't judge them too harshly because of their one not-so-smart move."

Fel gave her a frown, *You didn't have to deal with them, I did.* "Oh, I should warn all of you, my nieces are fully independent so don't embarrass them by volunteering to do something for them. If they need assistance, they will ask for it. Also, they can be very persuading and almost always get what they want." She flashed Cassia a big grin and her free-mate knew that Fel, in spite of everything, loved her six nieces dearly.

Cassia asked, "Will we be staying there with them in the

tower or will we find accommodations in a Sisterhood house in Brom?"

Fel shrugged her shoulders. "To be really honest, Cassia, I don't know. I drop by for visits as often as I can, several times a year."

"Maybe time has mellowed them, Fel. Perhaps with all that has happened, they will think more kindly of you," Savina wisely suggested. Again, Fel merely shrugged.

Chapter 10 Reconciliation

The tiny village of Brom had grown considerably in the last hundred years. With three active circles and plenty of stone all around, construction had mushroomed. To appreciate the layout of Brom, one has to understand the lay of the land. Here against the Goza Mountains as deep into the foothills as one can go, the land was anything but flat. Rocky protrusions were the rule, with only the banks of the Wyndl River here at its source being at all level ground. Hence, the village and the tower complex were built upon many different layers or heights. It was not uncommon to have the house next door have its doorway three feet above your door, for example.

All of the buildings were stone block construction, heavy and solid enough to withstand the harsh winter's twenty feet of snow. The only access to Brom was from the east, its tower and castle stretched up the flank of the mountain behind it. Brom's population had grown to over five thousand hardy souls. One had to be hardy, because from November through February travel into or out of Brom was nearly impossible due to the depth and ferocity of the snow and storms. Half of the transportation animals were now trained reindeer. Sleighs provided the only risky winter access to and from Brom.

Brom castle and tower lay on the western edge of the village, slowly but surely building its way up the side of the mountain. Its outer walls were rugged, thick, and rose and fell following the bedrock beneath it. The original tower still stood, but was dwarfed by their new tower that rose a hundred fifty feet and was nearly three hundred across. Inside the walls, an enormous manor house was attached to both towers so one did not have to go outside to travel from one to the other, a necessity in the winter. A large stable was attached to the eastern side of the manor house, leaving a very large open courtyard. The women had small flower gardens close to the walls of the manor house, particularly gorgeous in the springtime.

The party arrived late morning on the twenty-fifth of

September 1131. Savina had alerted them that they were arriving, allowing them to be ushered into the courtyard without a challenge. Fel pulled up before the main double door entrance to the manor house. Twenty-five year old Tom Waters, their Chief of Security, met them at the door with a welcoming smile. "Hail Savina. Fel, it is good to see you again. Everyone is in the Great Hall. Ally's got hot cider waiting." Ally was his wife and Chief Steward of the manor house. The two were kept very busy with so many living here.

Fel led them inside the doors, down the short hallway to the Great Hall. As soon as she opened it her nieces came dashing up to her. All six wore sack-like dresses and sandals. "Aunt Fel! We missed you! Going to stay longer this time? It is winter. You have to stay with us and play," her namesake Evita, sixteen, gushed. One by one, all six threw their left leg up and around Fel, giving her their special hug. She gave each a solid squeeze in turn.

"We'll see," Fel whispered and looked up at the large gathering waiting on them. All members of the three circles were present, along with the top leaders and many of their children, who were at least twelve years old. Venerado Simon Bolivar, the forty-five year old leader of Brom, smiled at the enthusiasm the six teens displayed for their aunt. Indeed, the six wanted for nothing, the most highly prized people here at Brom. No other tower had six proven katalyein and most had none at all.

"Come sit with us," Evita suggested, pushing her body into Fel's trying to nudge her toward their table. The other five nestled around her pushing as well. Fel broke out into a fit of laughter.

Venerado Simon, smiling broadly at the antics of the teens, called out, "Better do as they insist, Fel."

"Evita, got room for my free-mate here?" Fel asked, knowing that would further excite the six teens. It did, they cheered and called out "Fel's married" as if the others had not heard it. Cassia got caught up in their enthusiasm as three pushed their bodies into hers, nudging her along after Fel. Simon motioned for the others to take the empty seats where hot cider had already been set out for them.

"Welcome to Brom Tower. I am Venerado Amo Simon Bolivar. Fel, Savina, will you do the introductions please."

Savina, now sixty, took charge. "You all know my daughter and her free-mate, Gina and Molly. Fel's free-mate is Cassia Kaylee e Evita, but she is an alien from Rigel-3." She watched Simon's eyes as she tossed out her bombshell.

Evita sitting beside Cassia exclaimed, "But she isn't grey. I thought the aliens were very grey and tall and thin."

Fel spoke up, "She is an alien, Kassia Kunegunda originally. She is now carrying our child, hers and mine. We've had an encounter with the goddess Lysandra. Trust me, Evita, she was an alien, but now she's one of us."

"Also with us is my niece, Renata Raffaella Lucca Brom," Savina continued, unleashing a secondary shock. Many here were related to Savina and thus to Renata and an audible gasp resounded. "Finally, this is Sara Haverhills Benton. Yes, we do have a tale to tell and yes, I did get to see the aliens and the spaceships on my supposed vacation that turned into quite an adventure. I will let Fel and Cassia tell most of it."

Fel said, "Simon, you might want those who can detect lies to pay attention. We told this to Wyth Tower, but they didn't believe a word of it even though their soothsayers said we were not lying." He nodded and Fel began to relate their adventure, beginning with her accepting the Sisterhood assignment to snatch and grab Sara, rescuing her from an impossible situation.

After about an hour, Fel finally finished up with, "Cassia has gotten the old alien medical machines working and Renata is wearing the prosthetic hands Ally Wycombe Bettingham used to wear. Plus, we brought all that equipment here with us." To emphasize it, Renata raised her hands, proudly showing her new artificial hands.

Fel had been carefully watching the reactions of Simon and her parents, Javier and Gabriella de la Cantara, sixty-five and sixty-seven respectively. While they were now retired from tower duties, their opinion counted with her. For the first time in her life, her father seemed pleased with his daughter. *Is it because I'm going to give them another grandchild and they think it might be another armless katalyein,* she wondered.

Cassia added a little, "I really was born on Rigel-3. I am extremely short for my race, plus I worked out and built up my muscles over the years. I am not your typical tall, thin alien, so that's why I got the field agent assignment. My body shape looks more like yours."

Simon spoke next, "Well done, Sisters, well done indeed. On behalf of all Brom Tower, let me welcome you here and thank you for a job more than well done. Yes, Feliciana we believe you. You forget we have a great respect for Lysandra, who so greatly assisted Elena and Filipa over a century ago. Sara, Renata, we would love to have you here at our tower. Your training will begin as soon as you desire. Plus, Cassia, you ought to be tested and trained as well. Fel has said you have not taken the Sisterhood oath as yet, so we would like to extend the same offer to you. Stay with us a while and get trained. Fel, Savina, if you like, you are welcome to stay here in the tower this winter as well. I will send the request to your guild house so stating, if you desire. I suppose Gina and Molly would prefer the guild house, if I recall."

"Thank you Venerado Simon. I would like that. I aim to see my niece gets off on the right foot, so to speak," Savina replied. "Right now, I long for a warm fire and hot cider. My bones can't take more of these adventures," she jested, bringing a smile to many of the others of her age group.

Fel looked at her parents before replying. Her father, Javier nodded to her. "Okay, I will stay too, as long as Cassia needs to be here. I want her to get the best training and to have the best care for our child. She will be a first, you know, woman by woman."

"Good, dear. I will have your things brought to your childhood suite. I know the six teens will be overjoyed to have you so close to their rooms," Ally spoke up. As steward, room assignments were hers to make. It also meant she would be close to her siblings as well.

Simon then said, "Fel, we would like to talk with you further about the battles you've witnessed, but your family would like some time with you. We'll talk later." He rose and the large gathering was over.

Celestina, Carmela, Duncia, Elena, Evita, and Gracia,

the six teens, surrounded Fel and Cassia, volunteering to lead them to their suite. Ever chatty, Evita said, "So you are our aunt too, now, Aunt Cassia. It is really great that we have an alien for an aunt. No one else has that! Will your daughter be like us or will she have arms like you? We don't really need them much, except sewing, and we don't like to sew anyway. Aunt Angelica did all this fancy embroidery on our dresses."

"Girls, let us get a word with Fel and Cassia too," Alano, Fel's older brother, interrupted them. "Welcome to the family, Cassia. I'm Alano, my wife Benita. Doncia and Elena are ours. Adora here is Fel's oldest sister, Bolivar is her husband, and Evita and Gracia are theirs. Her cousins, Andres and Camila and their two daughters, Celestina and Carmela. Oh, here is Fel's younger sister, Angelica who isn't married yet, but is a circle technician at the moment." He added, "If you see someone wearing a gaily colored outfit and who has black hair, that's one of the de la Cantara or del Fuego clan. We all hold with our Westerlings traditions. I know we are a whole army to meet all at once, but give us time; we want to get to know you too. None of us ever expected Fel to get married, let alone have a child. Fel, you've made mom and dad's day. Did you see how pleased they looked? Maybe some of the burned bridges can be mended before it's too late."

"We will chat more later," Fel replied non-committal in tone. In her mind, there were far too many burned bridges to ever be mended. As the teens began ushering their aunts down the halls, Fel pointed out the doors to Cassia. "Notice all the doors have sliding latches. That's so the girls here can open them. When they were born, Simon had all the doors fixed up this way, fearing the they could get themselves trapped in some room in this huge place. As you will soon see, these nieces are mighty independent young women."

"Of course we are, Aunt Fel. We don't need arms. Great-grandmothers Drina and Elena sure didn't and neither do we," Celestina pointed out, primarily for Cassia's benefit. "Cassia, if Lysandra had not given you back yours, don't worry, we could have shown you how to do everything." Cassia smiled, but didn't reply.

"Did you bring us any presents this time, Aunt Fel?"

Evita asked what she'd been dying to ask since Fel walked in the front door.

Fel laughed, "When have I ever not brought you six a present? This time, it's bluebird hair clasps with gemstones for their eyes. I know how you all love your long, black hair." The girls responded with thank you's and giggles, impatiently wanting her to hurry up.

A bit later after the six girls dashed off to try on their new hair clasps, Fel and Cassia were finally alone. "So this is your childhood bedroom?" Cassia asked. Fel nodded. The room had a soft bed, a lovely couch, a table, two chairs, a tall clothes closet, and a commode. The wood was highly polished and stained pine. Nothing pretentious. Two high, but small windows provided outside light. A fireplace was already lit along with a number of lanterns. The large overhead array was not lighted, mostly because the six teens who'd cleaned up the room ahead of time could not reach them.

In her light rapport with Fel, Cassia sensed the flood of childhood memories returning to her free-mate and wanted to allow her private time. She'd never see her childhood home again; it was light years away. She'd never be on a spaceship again. That last, she didn't mind, space travel always made her slightly sick. "I like it, dear. It's cozy. If you don't mind, I'm going to set up the medical equipment by the table. I want to make sure they are fully charged in case Renata's hands need a backup, though according to Celestina, Renata really doesn't need them."

"Oh, that's just the girls' way of trying to make you feel more at ease around them. I have to admire them for making the best of an awful situation over which they had no control," Fel replied, remembering the girls as they danced around her when she returned for a visit some five years ago. They were delighted to see her but even then, she sensed how they really felt. Now they were older and better able to keep their true feelings masked from those around them.

Cassia played with the machine a while and then discovered something else. "Hey, here is a strange menu item. I didn't notice it before because I was looking only for how to fix her arms for the prosthetic hands. It says Messages. What can this mean?" She experimented a little and let out a shriek. "Fel! Look at this! Here are all the secret documents the Sector ID Minister wrote! These go back a hundred years! Look, there are recent ones by my boss! How in the world am I getting these?"

"More importantly, what do they say?" Fel asked, shaking off past memories and coming over to look, but she was unable to read the script written in Rigel-3 characters.

"Hey, there is a flagged note, the very first one." She opened it and read it before explaining, "Dita Ewa planted a worm on our main server that sends decrypted documents to this medical computer once each week. For years now, it has been storing them up waiting for a connection. When I powered it up, it sent hundreds to us. Dita says she doesn't trust her people to abide by the Imperial Directive #5 and is monitoring the Sector ID Minister, since she controls everything about Ashford-5, that's our name for Tierra. Okay, I am going to read the recent ones by Lech, my former boss."

"Well, it's just as we thought. The man that was bargaining for Sara got away and got permission to hunt me down and kill me. Lech okayed it. Ah, they sent out three ships doing a visual search at night, following the original path we took. So that's how come they kept finding me. Ah, I am officially dead, Fel. Off the books, deceased. Well, they won't ever be looking for me again, that's some comfort," Cassia relayed the essence of what she was reading. "Hey, listen to this, they are abducting no more than five young women per year so as not to arouse suspicions and taking them from widely scattered locations."

A bit later, she said, "Hey, the other guy he sent out, Jarek, he's now married a woman from Valen Tower, the daughter of the leader's consort, Carmen. Ah, mysteriously somehow Jarek now has the *mentales* gift as well as Lech's wife, Karolina. Plus, she and Carmen have become good friends and even lovers according to Lech, and now Venerado Augusto is inviting the aliens to come to Valen. He's working out some private exchanges that include giving Augusto blasters! This is getting worse."

"Simon needs to hear about this! I'm getting him now,"

Fel exclaimed, growing more and more worried about just what the aliens were doing. Within a couple of minutes, Simon knocked and entered.

"What is so dire that you needed me here now?" he asked sternly.

"Cassia has just intercepted a whole lot of the Sector ID Minister Lech's personal logs. Some of it is frightening news," Fel said. She was white as a sheet, images of her fight with the alien man who was nearly invincible raced through her mind. If the bears had not knocked him over, his blaster would have killed them all.

Cassia explained what was happening with the doctor's machine and Dita Ewa's role, done perhaps a century ago. Next, she read the relevant documents to Simon, who also became white as a sheet. Then his color changed to a reddish hue as his anger surged above his fear. He'd cleverly seen Fel's images of her battle with the alien and just what his blaster had done to Cassia in that split second.

"It's not bad enough the aliens have been abducting our female telepaths and taking them off-world, but this is tantamount to treason! Augusto getting blasters, alien technology — those weapons will make his forces and tower stronger than all the rest of us. Cassia, keep monitoring and keep me posted on any more developments! *Extremely* well done, you are a credit to us all, Cassia. I've summoned my Capos and we will meet now to decide what avenue to take. I assure you we will take action, *strong* action!" He whirled and left the room rapidly.

By suppertime, Cassia's news had reached everyone in Brom castle, down to the maids and cooks. Everyone was talking about it and speculating on what Simon would do about it. When everyone had gathered in the Great Hall to eat, Simon rose and explained to everyone.

"As you have all heard by now, the aliens have been systematically abducting up to five telepaths each year and sending them off-world. Worse than that, Augusto of Valen has admitted aliens to his tower and set up illegal trade with them, receiving alien technology, some of which are blasters. He's married off his consort's wife's daughter Carmen to the alien field agent Jarek, who sometimes goes by the name Jacobo when he is appearing as one of us. Further, somehow Augusto has turned Jarek into a *mentales* gifted man as well. This spring the aliens will be spending time there in Valen Tower being trained in our telepathic technology. This cannot be allowed to happen!"

"I've been in communication with all the Venerados of the other towers. They now know all we've found out. We've decided tomorrow morning we will take appropriate action to put an end once and for all to this deceit and treason. I will keep you abreast. In the meantime, we owe a huge debt of gratitude to Cassia Kaylee e Evita for discovering all this for us and notifying me at once. Let's give her a round of applause." The room exploded in a thunderous applause, rather embarrassing Cassia.

Fel was dying to know what they would be doing, but she had rejected the towers when she joined the Sisterhood and was now on the outside. Later, her brother, Alano, told her about it.

Promptly at nine, all three *Círculo de mentes* joined together into one massive unit. Then one by one, each of the other ten towers merged with them. Finally, with the combined power, almost incomprehensible in magnitude, Simon executed his plan. Simultaneously, his image appeared before Augusto at Valen and Lech on the twentieth floor plush office in the spaceport.

"Lech Kuba, Augusto Valen. This will be your only warning. We know you have been kidnaping telepaths and taking them off-world, away from Tierra, for many years now. No more than five per year and from isolated areas. We know Augusto has accepted an alien as Carmen's husband and has setup an illegal trading deal for alien technology, some blasters for starters, and has plans to train your alien telepath Jarek at Valen Tower in the spring."

"Yes, this is a projected image from the combined power of the other ten towers, Augusto. If another woman is abducted and taken off-world, we will begin destroying your precious spaceships as they land or take off. If you do not believe we can do this, ask Augusto. We certainly can do it at any time. If you trade illegal alien technology to Valen Tower in the spring, if Valen Tower trains Jarek, we will also begin destroying your spaceships as well as launching a combined assault on Valen Tower, wiping it out. We will be watching you from now on. If you persist in these illegal actions, we will take prompt action. We will not warn you again."

In his comfortable office, the man's image vanished from sight leaving Lech dub struck and, miles distant, left Augusto terribly upset. Both men had nearly identical first thoughts: *How could they have penetrated my security measures? How could they possibly know these things?* Even more interesting was their nearly identical conclusion: was there a spy in his midst or was there a traitor among the aliens/primitives? Neither man knew which, but had to figure it out and fast, before spring came. Both men wanted this new relationship with the aliens and natives to progress at all costs.

That evening, Fel's parents came to her room for a private meeting. Fel insisted the Cassia stay, fully intending not to either get upset with them and cause yet another in the seemingly endless stream of upsets with them or to allow them to make further demands upon her, though she had no idea what that might be. *Stay, my padrona. I need your iron will.* Cassia quietly moved to other side of the room and fiddled with the medical machine, intending to read some of the more ancient documents written by the former ID minister, Ania. She got a good look at both her free-mate's parents, though. Javier was sixty-five and really showed his age. His once thick black Westerlings style hair was both thin and grey, cut very short. He still had a black moustache, streaked with grey. His back was bent and he walked with some effort, she noted. If he had been a Rigel-3 man, he ought to have reported to the Rejuvenation Center years ago. It was common for their people to live well into their hundred-twenties.

To Cassia, he seemed to be a man who felt somehow lost and she listened in to their conversation. Her mother, Gabriella, looked far older than her sixty-three years. Frail and thin boned, she did not look at all well and Cassia wondered if she had some illness beyond their healer's ability to cure. The thought struck her, should she try the medical machine on

Gabriella? *Best ask Fel first.* Her hair too was grey, though a few streaks of black hinted at her once fine hair. She had it tied in a bun, quite unlike the other younger women who wore theirs long, falling down their backs and fastened in the back with a bluebird clasp. From her angular face, she suspected that long ago, Gabriella was a force to be reckoned with.

"Dear daughter. This is hard for me. We've come to make our peace with you. I know we've had serious disagreements in the past."

"Disagreements? You call those simply disagreements?" Fel found herself quite unable to restrain her emotions and spat out her intense feelings. *Maybe this wasn't such a good idea to stay here.*

Javier fought hard to suppress his usual outburst reactions to his most wayward daughter. None of the others ever had the audacity to talk back to him, not ever, only Fel. "Call them whatever you like. You know as well as I that your mother and I were just following the five generations of efforts to regain the precious katalyein gift that was lost so long ago. Yet, now we have seen that perhaps, just perhaps, we were far to harsh on you, Feliciana. It was not our intention or desire to have you exiled to the Sisterhood."

"Exiled? I went freely to escape your domination over me, dad," Fel shot back antagonistically.

"From our viewpoint, it seems exile, for you are no longer part of our powerful tower here at Brom or any other tower. Such must seem like exile to you."

"Hardly, I have freedom of choice, something that certainly isn't present here anywhere. Just look at what you've created, dad. Six charming women who are forced through no fault of their own to live horrid lives. Don't you have any idea how hideous and miserable it is for Evita and the others to try to live in our world without their arms? Have you even thought how they must feel? Have you even thought about how they feel about having children of their own being as armless as they are?"

Javier flushed crimson. Fel knew she'd scored a point. Her mother, on the other hand, began weeping quietly, holding a handkerchief to her eyes, hiding it from view.

"Hindsight, Feliciana. Your mother and I are nearing the end of our days and we look to the future. Our grandchildren, our future." He sighed and Fel sensed the great effort it took for him to say this, "We may well have been misguided and wrong in what we forced upon our children. There, I've admitted it. What more can I say or do? It is done. The six grandchildren are as they are. I cannot undo it no matter how I might desire to do so. Isn't it enough to have to see them, our future, each and every day and continually face what we've done — all we parents?"

He's admitted it! After all these years, he's admitted it! Good god! Fel's harsh viewpoint of her father softened a little. "I've always known it; the six and I are very close, dad, very close. They tell me things they'd never dare tell their parents or their grandparents. I've known how they feel all their lives, ever since little Celestina came to me asking why she was so different from everyone else. I cried but had no choice but to tell her she and the others were very special girls. I've never had to do any as hard as that ever."

"We can only thank you for having done that, Feliciana dear," he replied, choking back tears of his own. "If only we could turn back time," he voice trailed off leaving the unsaid unsaid. "I know we drove you out, but can we at last at least make peace with you, dear daughter?"

"Why? You want to make designs on your newest granddaughter next year? Maybe she will have the precious gift, but will she have arms or not? Wondering that, are you?" Fel replied antagonistically. She suspected ulterior motives in the old man's professed conciliatory words.

"Would that be so bad to have a daughter with the most precious gift of all, katalyein?"

"Well, no, not that, dad. You know what I mean. If she does have it, everyone here in the tower will begin to make breeding plans for her when she is one week old!" Fel spat out her greatest fear about her unborn daughter.

"Point taken, Feliciana. I would be lying if I said otherwise. But can you not see the larger picture?"

"Larger picture? Ha. Male's larger picture. That's what's wrong with you, dad, and everyone else in the towers. Males get the choices; females have no choice, no free will. That's wrong, dad, wholly and completely wrong. That's why I fled you and the towers and all it. Women have as much right to their own lives as men do! At least in the Easterlings, men are totally above boards with it. Women there are physically bound, but don't have to suffer the even worse mental bindings that you men chain us with here in the Midlands. Just see how Renata does, why don't you. She's been raised as a traditional Easterlings woman, and she's given that security up for a chance to get tower trained. Let's see how she likes trading physical bindings for your mental chains." Fel retorted.

"Is it truly that bad for you, dear?" Gabriella finally spoke up. "I had no idea." She added, "I've always accepted your so called mental chains for the peace of mind and physical security that your father has always provided for me."

"All well and good, mom, but do you love dad, I mean really deep down, is he your one true love?" Fel stung her.

"I've grown to appreciate Javier's many good qualities, dear. What more can a woman ask?"

Fel knew it was pointless to argue with her any further. "Well, I married out of a deep love for Cassia. I admire her and respect her above all others in this world. That to me is what marriage is all about."

"But will Cassia have the security of a fine home, a warm hearth to sit beside during the long, cold winters, food in plenty, warm clothing?" her mother countered. "Or will she be bounced from one Spartan Sisterhood guild house after another, with none to call truly her own?"

Her words dug deep into Fel. She wanted the very best for Cassia, which is one reason she chose to bring her here to Brom Tower to be trained. Fel flushed and did not answer her mother. Cassia sensed the terrible unease from Fel and decided to intervene a little. "Ama Gabriella, I am too much like your daughter. I am a fighter too, all my life. I am used to living in dung holes with only the clothes on my back to call my own. I really would not know how to live in such luxury as is here in Fel's old bedroom. There are things worth fighting for in this wide universe and that seems to be the path I am always traveling. That's why I love your daughter so much. We are so alike in many ways. We will fight for what it truly right, especially for us women. Your world is not alone in the way it treats women. I've seen similar things on many other worlds; some have far worse treatment than I've found here. Security, warm hearth, these are things I might like in my old age, not my youth. There's a war to be fought first."

Gabriella laughed, clearing the air. "Cassia, you are *so* like my Feliciana. I can see why she is so in love with you. I do hope you will let us at least see and visit our newest granddaughter. We promise not to 'arrange' things for her."

"Of course, Gabriella, I would never deny you that, unless you attempted harm to her."

"We pledge we will never do such a thing. May we play our roles as grandparents-to-be then, Cassia?"

"Er, sure, but I don't quite know what you mean by that," Cassia admitted and looked to Fel for help. She was no help, she only laughed.

"We will see you have baby blankets, baby clothes, toys, and a host of diapers ready when your time comes," Gabriella explained.

"Now that would be most helpful. I have to admit I know nothing about motherhood. I never ever expected to get married, let alone have a child of my own. You see, in my world, I was about the ugliest woman on Rigel-3. Shorter than short, uglier than ugly, my prospects were non-existent."

Javier spoke up, "That doesn't say much for your people, Cassia. You are an attractive young woman here on Tierra and don't let anyone tell you differently." Fel appreciated his quiet diplomacy. "Fel, can we at least be friends?" He held out his hand.

A bit reluctantly, Fel held hers out and shook her father's hand for the first time since she fled Brom Tower years ago. He then gave her a hug and said, "We best get going. If I know Gabriella here, she will want to get a head start on all the baby things. May Day will be here before you know it." Fel laughed. It would give her mother something to do and to look forward to as well.

The next afternoon, her brother and two sisters came to

see her. Alano was tall and handsome, though rather thin. Like all her relatives, he had the rich black hair and eyes that marked his pure Westerlings lineage, unbroken through the century of inbreeding. He too wore a nicely trimmed moustache. He had a beaked nose that gave him a bird-like appearance. Adora, her older sister, had rich, long black hair that equaled Cassia's, reaching to her ankles. She had a round face and enchanting eyes, but she too was terribly thin, Fel thought. Her waist was a little flabby from having two children and four miscarriages. Angelica, her younger sister, barely twenty-seven, looked much like Adora, but she had bangs, which touched her forehead, giving her a charming appearance. Fel had already explained to Cassia that Angelica was sterile, always had been, and as such, would never marry. Men wanted wives to give them offspring, which Angelica never could. Instead, Angelica threw herself into the psi network technician work and was now irreplaceable in her circle, one of the best network technicians at Brom.

"Well, whatever passed between you and dad has sure changed him, sis. Dad's been, well far happier and kindlier since yesterday," Alano began. "Thanks for whatever you said to him and mom. You know they are not doing at all well. They are beyond healing powers now."

"I could tell. How long do they have?" Fel asked mechanically.

"Who can say, but I'd be surprised if they see a winter after this one. Anyway, I've arranged for Angelica to train Cassia," he reported.

Fel smiled broadly. "Thanks. You are making sure she gets the very best training."

"You bet, sis. Everyone knows Angelica is the best psi-technician in Brom and maybe many other towers too."

Angelica flushed. She added, "As if that would make up for my sterility. I envy you, Cassia, Fel. I'd give anything to have a child, but then, maybe not!" She didn't have to say why, not while in front of Alano and Adora, who had begat four of the six special children. Fel knew what Angelica left unsaid, so did Alano and Adora for that matter, but they gave no outward hint.

"Well, I know nothing about childbirth or caring for
newborns or even raising them. I hope you don't mind if I rely
on all of you for guidance in that area," Cassia said
diplomatically. That brought genuine smiles and they chatted
for some time. Fel felt closer to her siblings than she had for
many years. It was a good feeling, she decided.

That night at bedtime, Cassia had just finished brushing
out her hair. She had on her cotton nightgown and had her
long hair draped over her right shoulder, ready to climb into
bed with her short haired free-mate, when they heard a soft
knock on their door. Fel answered it and Celestina opened it
with her foot and slipped timidly inside. She too wore her
nightgown and had just finished with her hair, now draped
over her right shoulder as well. Like all the women here, she'd
never had it cut; only rarely trimmed split ends, and it fell to
her ankles similar to Cassia's.

Cassia looked at the seventeen year old young woman.
Already her breasts were mostly filled out and were quite
large, though nowhere near the size of Cassia's. Her shape
looked streamlined as she walked barefooted up to the two
who were sitting on the edge of Fel's bed. "Aunt Fel, can I talk
to you?" Celestina asked timidly. Fel lifted her up and sat her
on the bed between her and Cassia.

"Aunt Fel, do you love Cassia? I think you do, and I
want to know what love is like? How does it feel? Mom and
dad keep telling me love is nothing to concern myself about,
that when I am to marry, in time I will learn to like the man,
but I don't think that is love, is it?"

Fel had a choice. She could go along with the opinions
of the tower folk or she could tell her niece what she felt.
Damn if I will follow the party line! "Celestina, what is love?
That's a good question and one I thought I would never have,
until I met Cassia here. Analytically, dear, it is having a really,
really high admiration for someone coupled with an equally
high respect for that person. Emotionally," she grinned, "that's
a whole 'nother thing. I can't get Cassia out of my mind. I
think about her all the time. I dream about her. I want her
close to me, as close as we can be. I want to hug her, kiss her,
and make her feel pleasure. I feel I can't possibly live without

her with me. Makes me kind of nuts, doesn't it?" she tried to put a little levity into the mix.

Celestina grinned too. "Mom and dad don't feel like that. I know, I can sense their minds easily. But how come you love Cassia? She's not a man."

Fel flushed, "Well, that's a really hard one to answer, Celestina. It just happened that way is the best answer I can give you. When I first met her, I thought I despised and hated her; she was an alien, you see. Then as time went along, I got to know her, to see her good points and bad ones too. Then she saved my life, and my honor told me I had to protect her until that debt was repaid. Until that time, no one in this world ever did such a thing for me. Cassia intended to give up her life that I might live, me the *castinto*, the disfigured, breastless woman. My admiration and respect for Cassia only grew and grew after that. Plus, well maybe I shouldn't say this to you, Celestina." Fel hesitated.

"Oh you can tell me about how you love her massive breasts, aunt. I can read your mind easily," Celestina explained in her matter-of-fact girlish manner.

Fel flushed, "Well that too. Aren't they just the most gorgeous pair of knockers you've ever seen?" Cassia blushed this time. "Yes, that too, Celestina. It just happened, like it must have happened with Gina and Molly too. As you well know, normally women fall in love with men, not with other women. In our society, such unions are allowed as free-mates. Why are you so interested in love anyway? Have you got a boyfriend?"

Celestina giggled, "No. I am trying to figure it all out for us, for the six of us. I'm the oldest. We already know our parents and the Capos and even Venerado Simon are arguing about whom we should marry or even if we should. But we've been watching Gina and Molly and now you and Cassia too. All four of you are in love, real love, which is wholly lacking here at the tower. We've sensed all the different couples, you see. They live with each other and have babies and all that, but the passion isn't there, except for the little affairs our fathers sometimes have with other women. You four have it and we want it too, but," her voice trailed off and Fel knew what she wasn't saying.

"Let's be honest, Celestina, but you are worried about having children who are like yourselves, right?"

Fighting back tears, she whispered, "Yes."

"Well, Celestina, I wouldn't let that worry you or even concern you much. If you marry for love, then love conquers all. You will love your children whether they have or don't have arms or legs. You just love them and they love you and so will your husband. If he truly loves you, your physical limitations will not matter in the slightest."

"Cassia, doesn't Fel's missing breasts matter to you?" she asked timidly, trying to follow Fel's reply.

"It matters that she endured such an awful torture at the hands of wicked men, but whether or not she has them doesn't make any difference to me, not really. I love her as she is, Celestina. That's the way love is; some say love has no eyes. When you find the right man, he will love you just as you are," Cassia tried to find a proper way to put it to her.

"Really? He won't think I'm weird or something?"

"It won't matter in the slightest, just like it doesn't matter if you have a flake of dirt on your nose. It won't matter," Cassia insisted, while wondering if there was another way to explain it to her. She added, "In my race, I am considered extremely ugly. I am the shortest Rigel-3 woman on record and now am over weight in my arms and legs, positively fat by our standards. Yet, none of this matters in the slightest to Fel here."

"Nope, I see the most gorgeous woman on the planet," Fel teased her.

Celestina grinned and seemed satisfied now. She added, "Fel, I want to go on an adventure too, like you do. Can you take me one day? They hardly ever let me out of the castle. I only get to go into Brom a couple times a year, and then they surround me with so many guards I can't even see the shops. Please, can you take me with you on an adventure? I can manage. I am not all that helpless," she pleaded.

"Celestina, I dare not do that, not without Venerado Simon's permission. My god, dear, if I did that without his permission, he'd send the entire garrison of guards after me and kill me for doing that."

"But why don't we six ever get to do anything we want to do? Why? We want to live too? Don't we have that right? Or are we only kept girls?"

"You are kept girls all right, much like I was, Celestina," a trace of antagonism in her voice. Her words brought up old, unhealed wounds. "I ran away from that and sought freedom in the Sisterhood as a fighter, but you can't do that, Celestina and you know it, don't you?"

Celestina fought back tears. "Yes, but we don't want to be kept girls. We want to live too."

"I promise you, Celestina, I will speak with the adults and see if I can get them to see reason. Don't count on anything happening; you know how valuable they believe you are. After all, they have been working for five generations to get the katalyein gift back. They are now being overly protective of you because of it. Perhaps, we can get them to see reason and allow you six a little more freedom. I can't promise you anything more than that."

"Okay, thanks, Aunt Fel, Aunt Cassia. I best get to bed before someone figures I snuck out. I'll tell the others, though. They all wanted to know the same things." She grinned and planted a kiss on Fel and then on Cassia before slipping off the bed and scampering out of the door.

The next morning, Cassia's extensive training began, leaving Fel to wander the halls rather aimlessly. That lasted only a few hours. Simon summoned her to his private study.

"Fel, I have another assignment for you. I have already cleared it with your guild mother. I know winter is fast approaching and this assignment will be a rather nasty one. I need another snatch and grab, if persuasion fails."

"Another woman being mistreated by you men," Fel said rather harshly.

Simon laughed, "Not this time. It's a seventeen year old boy. As you know, wars are breaking out all over, and every tower is trying their best to make a flying car. You know why too. From the air, they can drop their various bombs on the enemy troops and fortifications. With the treachery of Valen, we have to step up our own attempts before it is too late and we ourselves get attacked. Lord help us if that happens. Anyway, we've just gotten word there is a boy called Gabe Jeffery, who lives high in the foothills down south, halfway between Haverhills and Oakham, on a remote estate run by his father, *Jefe* Amos Jeffery. Your assignment is to bring Gabe and his inventions back here as soon as possible. He does have the gift, so start with a plea to have him come here to get his training, if he has not yet had it. You are authorized to snatch and grab him if there is no other way to get him to come here. Complicating matters is that we also want his inventions brought back, so that means you will have to take a wagon. With winter coming, this makes it a hazardous assignment and thus triple pay, if you accept it. It's about a thousand miles there, two for the round trip. My guess is you'd be gone some three months. Will you accept this assignment?" he asked formally as required of a Sisterhood member.

"You know how I hate being cooped up like this. Okay, it sounds simple enough. Do I go alone?" Fel asked.

"That I leave up to you and your Sisterhood guild. My personal advice, though you never seem to take it, is I'd take some others with you for safety's sake. You know how terrible the winters can be here in the foothills."

"I accept. It will take me a couple of days to get prepared. Will that be acceptable?" He agreed. Fel donned her heavy parka and headed off through the light snow into the village proper, making for her Sisterhood guild house, wondering which women were present at the moment.

"Just like your crystal amplifies your psi energies a hundredfold, these networks of crystals perform similarly," Angelica explained to Cassia, who had just begun her training. She was now inside the smaller of the two towers. "Now these here, set into the shape of a cube, form the long distance communications network. Benita there is currently attuned to the network, listening for messages from the other towers, who have similar communications networks. We can instantly know what is happening at every tower. She will work a two-hour shift, and then another technician will take her place. It is monitored at all times, day and night. You can also come here

222

and request a message be sent."

"Sent to other towers only?" Cassia asked.

"No, you can direct it to a specific person, but that is not always successful, especially if they are currently behind a communications barrier network of crystals. Now this network is the smallest of all them. I've vastly more powerful ones to show you. With those, it takes a whole *Círculo de mentes* to handle the humongous volume of psi energies they generate. One wrong move and a person can easily get fried! Some are used to cut stone blocks for castle construction and the setting of said stones. Some are used to search for and bring rare ores to the surface from miles below the ground. Some are even used for teleportation, though there is a weight limit on that operation. We are going to begin by getting you able to operate the water network, Cassia. That network of crystals brings water up from the ground, heats it up, and sends it through the pipe network so we all have hot and cold running water. Once you have mastered that one, we'll put you on the wood network. That one handles the felling of great trees, chopping them into firewood cords. With the long winters here, we go through cords and cords of firewood, far too much to expect local men to cut for us. Recently, we've uncovered a deposit of coal and the inventions section is working on ways to make use of coal as a substitute for firewood. I hope it works out. Come on. Let's get you going on the water network. It's really a simple one and you should not have any trouble mastering that one."

"Will I get to be a part of a *Círculo de mentes* at some point?" Cassia asked.

"Yes, once you've mastered the simpler networks and they finish analyzing your inherent gifts," Angelica explained.

"This is going to be incredibly cool!" Cassia exclaimed, very much excited about what lay ahead for her. Then she added, "But it won't hurt my baby?"

Angelica laughed, "Absolutely not. Believe me, they will never ask you to do something that would in any way pose even a slight danger to your unborn child. Children are precious to us, far too precious sometimes." She was alluding to her own situation and the six with the katalyein gift.

She explained more, "Now on this floor is the Water Network. As you can see, we have dozens of crystals laid out in a three-dimensional network array and they are all attuned together and act as one unit, equaling the power of an entire circle, yet operable by a single person, Ally there in this case. Hi Ally, Cassia's here to learn how to run the Water Network." Thus began long training days for Cassia, who eagerly took to it. She was learning vast knowledge she never ever suspected to find on Ashford-5.

Chapter 11 Flying Machines

"They must be really, really desperate to hire us with winter coming on," Sally Weathers said to Fel. She sat beside the fighter on the large wagon, now loaded with supplies and covered with a heavy oiled tarp. "Been a while since we went out together," she added. Sally was thirty-three, a brown haired, blue-eyed Sisterhood fighter and Ama in her own right. Fel had picked her because of the nature of this assignment that paid them both triple. Sally had basic healing skills, an ability to start small fires, but an uncanny skill at controlling the weather. With the harsh blizzards that often struck high in the foothills during winters, Fel was taking no chances.

She had stowed away three spare parkas, five complete heavy sets of winter clothing. No telling when they might get soaking wet. In the freezing temperatures of the high foothills, this would be deadly. Hence, Fel opted to take no chances at all. They had ample food and a good deal of cooking peat-charcoal as well as a portable stove and plenty of lantern oil, along with the usual axes, shovels, and shelter tents, to say nothing of several bales of hay and some grain for the two reindeer who pulled the wagon.

Fel had opted for the reindeer instead of the horses primarily because they would be traveling due south in the high foothills, where snow depths sometimes reached upwards of twenty to thirty feet. Only reindeer could navigate in such situations and then only barely. Horses would never be able to make the long journey through the dead of winter. For the tenth time, Fel went over all their supplies, trying to make sure she'd forgotten nothing. Most of them came from the castle proper, where she'd parked the wagon for a day while the men loaded it with her lengthy list of items. She could not help recalling her parting, passionate kiss with Cassia. She loved every minute of her training. Fel could tell from the bright light in her eyes. She smiled but Sally didn't say anything.

"Yes, very desperate." Fel outlined their mission to her companion once more. It was late September and the early winter storms had already put down a layer of the white stuff, but not enough really to hinder them. At the moment, the sun was out turning the previous night's accumulation into a watery slush beneath the hooves of the reindeer, which were raised and trained by the Sisterhood up in Hilliard Heights, far north of Brom.

"It will snow again tonight," Sally said, noticing the gathering clouds over the Goza Mountains to their right. "Not a lot, though, too early for a big one, though I reckon we will see a big one before we're home again in late January. So tell me, how is your free-mate doing?" The two chatted as they rode along and Fel filled her in on their last adventure. The more who knew the truth, Fel felt, the better.

They made good time that first day, covering some forty miles, ten more than she'd initially estimated. They'd found a suitable camping spot at an abandoned safe house. At various locations in these high foothills, small safe houses had been built by the locals who lived in this harsh environment against emergencies, such as being caught out here in a blizzard. Four walls and a roof with fireplace, the crude cabin didn't offer much except barest survival. Although there was a small supply of wood, Fel refused to use it. "Leave it for someone who is desperate. We've brought enough along with us. You get the stove going and fix us something while I handled the reindeer and chop us some firewood," she suggested.

Sally teased her, "Ah, so you will be twice warmed. Okay, I get the easier job. My cooking hasn't improved much, though." Fel laughed and headed for the wagon. She untied the covering and began unloading the few things they would need. Suddenly, she saw something wiggling beneath their pile of spare clothing.

"What's this?" she said, curiously and began pulling the bundles out of the way. Soon two legs appeared. There lay Celestina!

"Hello Aunt Fel. I came along for an adventure. I hope you don't mind too much," she said rather timidly.

"Good god! Does Simon know you are here? Your parents? Celestina, what have you done?" Fel gushed, sensing all manner of ire shot her way.

"No, I snuck away and wiggled under these clothes. They would not let me come even if I asked them. You know that. I had to sneak away, if I am ever going to see the world and have an adventure of my own," Celestina replied a touch of hostility directed at the tower folk.

"I have no choice, Celestina, but to report to Simon immediately. Lord knows how your parents are frantic with worry wondering where you are. Did the aliens kidnap you? Gosh, they must be frantic with worry about now. Come on, inside with you." She helped the teen out of the wagon and marched her inside.

"What have we here? A stowaway?" Sally said seeing Fel ushering a young girl inside. "Oh no! One of the katalyein girls! Oh hell, Simon will have our hides over this!"

"I know. We'll be lucky if that's all he demands from us. I'm going to reach him now. Watch over our stowaway, Sally."

Fel pulled out her crystal and uncovered it. She focused and reached out, concentrating on Simon. She felt the tug of his mind. *Simon, we just discovered a stowaway among our gear in the wagon. Celestina. She claims she wanted to see the world and have an adventure. I told her she is in big, big trouble.* She also sensed a huge relief coming from him and guessed she had been right.

Thank god. Is she all right? We've been searching the entire castle from top to bottom for her. The other five would not say where she was, though we did threaten them. Hold a second while I alert the others, Fel. There. You didn't have anything to do with this did you?

No sir. Sally and I discovered her a minute ago as we were unloading the stove for tonight.

No wonder she didn't allow us to make telepathic contact with her this afternoon. Her parents are sick with worry. They even began to suspect the aliens had abducted her. Tell her to make contact with me this instant. Fel did so and Simon kept Fel in contact with him as he joined with Celestina. Fel blushed as Simon said some very harsh words to the teen. To Fel's amazement, Celestina was un-phased by his diatribe.

You never let us see the world. You never let us even go

shopping in Brom. So why should I ask you for permission? You would never grant it in the first place! I'm a grown woman and you can't control my life forever, Venerado Simon.

Fel grinned. She liked the teen's feisty defiance. It reminded her of her own self, when she was much younger. *If you make me come back now, I'll just sneak off another time,* Celestina added.

The Sisterhood woman then appropriately sent, *Should we abandon our trip and return in the morning with Celestina?* She knew she had to say this; it was the only honorable thing she could say. No sense getting the Sisterhood into deep trouble over a teen's rebellion within the tower.

Simon sent, *Damn it anyway, Fel. You know how critical this mission of yours is. Let me think. I guess I'd rather have her tagging along with you than with someone else. Fel, are you willing to take full responsibility for Celestina and her safety?* Celestina sensed where this was going and nodded her head up and down vigorously, as if this would help convince her aunt. *Let me see if I can talk some sense in her first, Simon. I'm sorry we didn't notice our stowaway sooner.*

"Celestina, I understand why you are doing what you are doing, but do you realize how physically challenging this is going to be on you? You use your feet where we use our hands. Yet, it is winter and you are going to have to wear heavy, warm socks, and thick boots to avoid freezing, to say nothing of heavier clothing."

"You just don't want a helpless cripple along, don't you, Aunt Fel," Celestina began crying.

She knows your buttons well, Fel! Sally sent her as she watched Fel's face begin to melt.

"Celestina, you know that's not true. If you are a helpless cripple, then I am a cur dog! But I see what you mean by that, Celestina. Still, you know very well Sally and I will have to do many things for you that you would ordinarily do for yourself back in the warm castle. That's what I meant by physically challenging for you and you know it."

"But I really *do* want to come along and see the world

even if it is only a little bit of it. I will do my very best not to put too big of a burden on you both. I will try my very best, Aunt Fel. Please, just this once, let me have a chance to be out in the real world and not locked up in the tower until I die."

"She has a point there, Fel," Sally pointed out with a smile. The teen had just struck a chord in Sally, reminding her why she'd abandoned the tower and joined the Sisterhood.

"Okay then, but you be on your best behavior and do precisely what Sally and I tell you. Agreed?"

Her face lit up like a lantern. "Yes, yes. Thank you, thank you." Fel contacted Simon again and told him what they'd decided and he went along with it.

I think we need to re-evaluate how we are treating the six, he sent.

I think that would be wise of you, Simon. You nearly lost this one to the Sisterhood. Fel really didn't know if the Sisterhood would accept Celestina or not, but wanted to strike a blow for Celestina and her five nieces anyway. Maybe this would lead to more personal freedom for the six, Fel hoped so.

"Okay, scamper inside and see if there is anything you can do to help Sally fix our supper," Fel ordered and headed off, axe in hand, to scrounge for firewood. *She's lived a sheltered childhood, but out here, she's going to see the world is a whole lot tougher for her to handle. I hope she isn't crushed utterly by it.* She felt a rush of sympathy for her niece.

Loaded with a large stack of wood, Fel returned to the shelter of the rickety, one room shelter. "It's snowing already." She saw Sally had the portable stove resting on the floor and Celestina was hovering over the pot handling the cooking. She dumped her pile of wood by the fireplace.

Sally said, "She insisted she is a much better cook than I am. What all have you been telling her about me, Fel?" Sally teased her, a big grin on her face. Celestina looked proudly up at her aunt, announcing that supper was ready.

Fel really didn't know the full extent of Celestina's capabilities, only those she'd seen her use around the manor house and castle. To her amazement, Celestina activated her crystal and used her gift to put her heavy sock back on and then her boot. Unseen hands moved the pot off the stove and the unseen hands filled up three waiting plates. She then used her gift to move her spoon to feed herself.

"I thought you had to use your feet to eat," Fel said somewhat impressed.

"Normally we do, but I can't here. My foot got too cold. I'm doing it the hard way," Celestina replied.

"Okay, I can take a hint, Celestina. I will wait until you tell me you need some assistance with something," Fel replied. The young teen smiled, for she'd scored another small victory with her aunt. Her small victory soon gave way to far more needs for assistance than Celestina ever imagined. She had to be heavily dressed for the cold and that she was unable to do for herself. Walking on the slippery snow-covered and uneven rock-strewn landscape caused her to fall more than once, though the two adults were slipping as badly, but they had their arms to help them from taking a spill. Getting into and out of the wagon proved more difficult than she had imagined.

By the end of the third day out, Celestina finally admitted, "Fel, I'm sorry. I didn't know I was going to have so many problems. It is really hard for me, isn't it?" She fought back tears. "We really are cripples aren't we? We've been pretending we're just like everyone else, but we are not like everyone else. We are freaks."

Fel put her arms around the young teen, pulling her head up against her scarred chest. "You are confronting the reality of the barriers in life you must face, Celestina. I won't say it is going to be easy, because it isn't. You are not a cripple and don't every let anyone tell you that you are. It is just you six girls have different barriers than most people have, that's the truth of it, dear, *different* barriers. I, for example, can never nurse a baby, if I ever had one, whereas you certainly can. What matters most, Celestina, is for you to accept your body as it is, be happy with what you do have, and find ways to get done what you must. Be inventive when you can, as you always have, and ask when you can't. In the end, people will only judge you by what you have done, for good or bad. There is nothing for you to be ashamed of — you had no say in the creation of your physical body, no more than the rest of us had. Play the cards you were handed and play them well.

Remember always, Celestina, you are not your body. You are a spiritual being with a body. What you do have that is all your very own is your honor. That is my guiding light: being true to myself and sticking by my honor."

She continued, "For example, when Cassia took that blaster shot aimed for me, saving my life at the risk of losing her own, my sense of honor told me I had to return the favor. On this trip, I have agreed to go find this boy and bring him to Brom Tower. This I will do somehow or die trying. I have sworn to keep you safe and this I will do or die trying. In your case, you told us you wanted to see the world and have an adventure of your own, that you are a grown woman, and that the Tower folks can't control your life forever. Now you have to be true to what you said. See the world. We are having an adventure. Be grown up and take the responsibilities that come with being one of us adults. No one could ever ask more of you than that."

"I promise, Aunt Fel. I will. I guess traveling in the winter time is not such an easy thing for me to do, is it?"

"Nope, it is tough even for us and dangerous too."

"Thanks, Aunt Fel. Can you brush out my hair a little? It's too cold for me to use my bare foot." Fel smiled and did so. After that, she and Sally saw a marked change in Celestina. No longer did she go around trying to prove she could do things, but simply did what she could and politely asked for help when she couldn't.

The one thing she did well was cooking. "Best trail food ever, Celestina," Sally complimented her a week later. "Fel, we need to bring Celestina along with us as our cook more often."

Fel agreed with her. "Never ate so well before. Sally, you best take some lessons from her. Well, tonight we will be in Wyth, so a stop at the Sisterhood house and a hot bath is in order."

"A real guild house? Wow! Will they let me in?" the teen asked.

"As long as you are with us, they will. Mind you, it's going to be crowded and crude by your standards," Fel cautioned her. Celestina didn't quite know what her standards were and took a wait and see approach. She was more excited about being inside the one where Fel often stayed.

Late afternoon, they pulled into Wyth. Snow was swirling around them, but it would come down far heavier this evening, Sally predicted. Fel halted at a weather-beaten, large stone building with a small sign hung over the single door. It read: Sisterhood. Fel knocked and a young woman not much older than Celestina opened the door. "Feliciana Evita e Kaylee and company asks for a night's shelter," she said formally.

"Who is it, dear?" a voice called from inside.

The young girl replied excitedly, "It's Fel. She wants to stay the night."

"Oh such silliness. Tell her to park around back; she knows the way. She doesn't need to be so formal with us."

"That's the guild mother, Martha," Fel whispered to Celestina. Around back, Sally hopped down and untied the gate and Fel drove the wagon inside the small stables. After handling the reindeer, putting them into the only open stall and feeding them, Fel and Sally picked up a couple of sacks containing some clean clothes and headed in the back door, where Martha had come to greet them formally.

"Fel, Sally, good to see you again. My, who do we have here?" the older woman, dressed in a rather plain dress asked. She offered her hand to greet her.

"Celestina del Fuego, ma'am," she answered politely. "I'm sorry, but I don't have any arms to shake, but a hug will do nicely."

"My word, Fel! Not one of *the* del Fuego girls?" Martha exclaimed rather shocked.

"None other. Simon's Okayed her to come on this little adventure. She's out seeing the world and I promised her a warm bath and good company."

Martha gave her a hug and replied, "Well, that she certainly will have! We've heard all manner of strange things about you from the tower here. Is it true? That you've found a free-mate? Come on in — here I am babbling like some old woman. Come in."

"We'll share whatever room is available, and then bathe. After that, if we can pry a hot meal out of you, I'll tell you all quite a tale," Fel promised the older woman.

"I'm sorry, Ama Celestina, we are nearly filled up, only have one old room on the second floor that's empty. Hardly fit for the likes of you, Ama," Martha explained.

"I'm sure it will be fine. It beat the shanty houses we have been staying in all week. Thanks for letting me stay," she replied politely.

As they walked the narrow hallway to the equally narrow stairs, the smells of fresh bread and supper cooking along with the musty smell of the old house greeted Celestina's nose. Many women opened their doors as they passed by, some greeting either Fel or Sally. More of the same happened as they walked the long hallway upstairs to their room at the far end. The room was small and only had one bed, but a young girl was hastily putting clean sheets on it as they entered. She nodded and hustled on out of the room, an awed glance first at Fel and then wide-eyed one at Celestina.

They took off their parkas and Fel explained, "We take off our dirty clothes and pile them there by the door. One of the sisters whose turn it is to do the laundry will come by and take them, returning them to us in the morning nicely cleaned. We carry our clean clothes on down to the bathing room at the end by the stairs. Don't worry, there aren't any men in here, just we Sisters."

Celestina needed some help getting her heavier pants and shirt off. She stood there naked until Sally soon joined her. Finally, Fel sighed; there was nothing to do but remove her shirt. This she hated, but had to endure it. "Oh my god, Fel!" Celestina exclaimed as she got her first ever look at her aunt's badly scarred chest.

Fel tried to take it in stride, though she had sworn never to have her nieces see such a ghastly sight. "Come on. Water's getting cold." Carrying her clean clothes and Celestina's, she headed down the hall, glad no one opened their doors to peek. Inside the bathing room, there were two tubs with steaming water. Fel pinned up Celestina's hair and helped her get clean first. Then to her surprise, Celestina used her feet to help scrub her own back. Finally, the three dressed and Fel led them downstairs to the dining room, where most of the women had already gathered. Word spread Fel was going to tell them about her last adventure and that one of the special Ama from Brom was with her.

The table was well worn as were the chairs. Unfortunately, none was low to the ground, and Celestina used her gifts to feed herself, much to the amazement of the gathered women who did stare at her at first. The young girl who had met them at the door whispered, "She really doesn't have any arms at all!" Other women told her to be quiet. Celestina grinned.

Once they ate, Fel spent an hour relating the events of the past summer and early fall. The women tossed out comments here and there and were extremely pleased Fel told them what she did. One woman spoke up afterwards, "Every word she said was the truth." Fel suspected at least one soothsayer was staying here, and she smiled. Her comment only added to the impression she'd made.

When they left the next day, four inches of new snow had accumulated, but again, some of it would melt as the orange-red sun rose in a clear, morning sky. Of course, clouds would be returning by afternoon, Sally pointed out. A week later, they reached Bedwurth and again stayed at the Sisterhood guild house there. Sally pointed out to Fel on the quiet, "You know some of those passes are going to be darn near impassable in this wagon by the time we head back."

"I know, but we'll find a way," Fel replied, she already knew that, hence the triple pay. She changed the topic, "Celestina, in two days, we will be going through Exchange City and you can get a good look at some aliens and probably see their spaceships too." That pleased the teen who was really looking forward to this experience.

If nothing else, those few hours meant everything to Celestina, as she sat between the two women while they rode slowly through Exchange City. Already, she had seen a couple silver ships landing and two blasting off into the sky. Now her eyes spotted a number of the tall, thin, grey-skinned aliens walking about, covered with their synthetic coats, which didn't keep them warm at all. This she sensed from their minds that were wide open to her. While there was a guild house here, Fel chose not to stop. She feared word might reach the aliens that

Celestina was here and they might make a snatch and grab for her. Instead, they pushed on and camped in their canvas tent that night. By morning, they had to brush off another six inches of snow accumulation before they could even get to their wagon for their supplies.

Two days later, they passed through Haverhills and again stayed in the guild house there. Now came the difficult part, and why Simon had hired Fel over all other possible guides. They had only a crude map of the foothills south of Haverhills and somewhere up some rocky valley lay the Jeffery estate. In the summer, it would be much easier to locate. In the winter with the snow that had not melted already six inches deep and more on the way, locating the estate would be tricky at best. Even if she could find the right valley to head up, there was no guarantee they could get through the snow. Often many of these isolated estates were snowbound during the winter. Fel hoped this was not going to be the case here.

She counted on the one thing in their favor: this far south the heavier snows would be later in arriving. That way, they could get in and then out again before becoming snowed in. She was right, south of Haverhills, the weather warmed a little and the snow accumulation slowly disappeared the further south that they went. Two weeks later, Celestina suggested they had gone back in time. "It is back to fall. All the colored leaves are out. It is really beautiful here. Remarkable. How can this be, Fel?"

"We are much farther south, Celestina. The further south we go, the better the weather. We are nearly in what's called the breadbasket zone, where they grow corn, wheat, barley, and vegetables galore. Even further south, it gets too hot and dry for anything to grow, becoming the vast desert of Bashir. Meanwhile, keep your eyes open for Montaña beasts. Up north they are in their caves for the winter, but down here they are still on the prowl in these foothills."

"This has been worth seeing. My sisters won't believe all this." Fel grinned, her adopted niece was getting her wish to see the world.

When Fel thought she was getting close enough north-south wise, she began stopping at every farmstead or hamlet asking for directions. At first, no one knew of this Jeffery but late October, they got their first break. A farmer said a shepherding rancher of that name lived at the head of the valley they were crossing. Encouraged, up the valley they rode, passing several more sheep pastures, nestled between great forests of pine and bare, jagged rocks, typical of these foothills.

As they rode upwards, the temperature began to drop once again and Sally predicted snow by nightfall. Fel hoped so because the reindeer were have major problems with these warmer temperatures. Suddenly, Celestina called out, "Look there, up in the sky! Darn I can't point." Once more, she felt badly; she'd spotted a strange thing in the skies but couldn't quickly show the others.

"What? Where?" Fel called out. Then she and Sally spotted it. "What is it? Some kind of huge flying beast? It doesn't look like a roc, but it is much larger than one."

"Dunno, but look how it soars," Sally pointed out.

"It flies so gracefully. Wait a minute. I sense a person is up there!" Celestina exclaimed. "Yes, there is a person, but it doesn't look like a person. What is it?"

Gabe Jeffery was again doing what he loved to do: fly. Soaring on the thermal currents like an eagle, he was free, the best and only true freedom the seventeen year old lad ever had. The sixth son, he knew he'd never inherit any land. The best he could hope for was to work like a dog and scrape up enough to perhaps form his own sheep spread in some other uninhabited section of the foothills, but he hated shepherding. His passion was flying. For the last couple of years now, he had his father's permission to guard the flocks from the air. Montaña beasts were a constant threat here so close to the Goza Mountains, especially in the late fall when they wanted full bellies for the long winter hibernation times.

How strange, a wagon with weird beasts pulling it. They are headed up dad's valley. I wonder who they are? Let's take a pass over them. He shifted his weight and his glider responded. Now he soared high over them and on down the valley before turning back for a second pass. As he did so, he spotted a Montaña beast crouching on a tall outcrop off to their left. The wagon riders didn't seem to be aware of the giant cat yet. *I've got to warn them!* Again, he shifted his position and now the glider began dropping, picking up speed as it dove towards the wagon.

"Look! The flying thing is diving on top of us!" Celestina called out. Fel twisted her head to see. Sure enough, it was losing altitude and coming straight for them. Was it attacking them, she wondered?

As it drew closer, a youthful voice yelled down to them, "Montaña beast! Montaña beast! On the top of the rocks to your right! Look out! Montaña beast!" The contraption swept past them and again seemed to rise upwards before circling around a third time.

"Hell! Just what we don't need!" Fel cried out. Sally drew her sword, but knew if the beast attacked them, her sword would be pretty useless. The reindeer were slow but sure and could not remotely outrun the giant cat. At least Fel thought the cat would go after her team first.

"I'll take care of the cat," Celestina called out. She activated her crystal and focused. Fel and Sally saw the giant cat suddenly standing up and stretching. Miraculously, it turned and loped on up the hill off to their right. The glow from her crystal died out. "There, I told the cat it was sleepy and off it went to take a nap somewhere."

"Kid, you did well! I didn't know you could handle Montaña beasts. Well done, Celestina. You saved our reindeer at the very least," Fel praised her and she meant it. She slapped the reins and got the wagon moving again on up the valley in the direction the strange flying machine had gone.

They spotted sheep grazing on the last patches of grass before the winter came. Soon, they saw several men and women with crooked staves walking among the sheep, slowly herding them up the valley. "Is the Jeffery estate ahead?" Fel called out. Several nodded and pointed on up the valley.

A couple of miles further up, the stone manor house with its huge stone fenced stables appeared about as far up the valley as one could travel. Its back was against the mountainside proper. Smoke curled from two chimneys and out in front of the building was that strange flying machine with a lad doing something with it.

As they approached, Fel called out, "Is this the Jeffery estate?"

"Yes, *Jefe* Amos Jeffery. That's my dad. I tried to warn you about that Montaña beast, but it looks like it ran away. You were lucky. I'm Gabe." He was tall and spindly, not yet filled out. His brown hair was curly and fell to his shoulders. His eyes were yellow and told all to these three. "Come on. I'll take you to dad," he volunteered.

"Is that your flying machine? We saw you flying, I think," Celestina asked.

"Yes, that's one of them. I love to fly and dad's letting me. I play lookout for the Montaña beasts that come down for a last meal before the winter snows come. Going to snow some tonight."

"Yes, I can tell," Sally replied, pointing to the gathering clouds. Shortly Fel pulled up before the manor house that held five extended families. Jefe Amos and Gabe's five older brothers and sisters and their wives and husbands all lived in this one house and handled the large flock of sheep. An older man stepped out onto the front porch as Gabe walked up and the wagon pulled up beside the porch.

"*Jefe* Amos Jeffery, I take it?" Fel said. He nodded, "Feliciana Evita e Kaylee, Ama Celestina del Fuego, and Sally Winters. We've come from Brom Tower to speak with you, sir."

"Brom Tower? Isn't that way up north somewhere?" he replied. Fel nodded. "Well morning, come on inside. Gabe, go tell the women to heat up some tea. We have an important guest." Fel picked up at once he meant Celestina. He gave Fel and Sally a look of either distrust or disgust, she couldn't quite pin it down without mentally prying. Fel lifted Celestina down after Sally hopped to the ground and began tying the reindeer to a post. All three took off their cloaks, leaving them in the wagon. Hastily, they followed their host, who covertly stared at Celestina.

"Mom's making tea — oh!" Gabe had come running back to tell them that when he stopped short facing Celestina and suddenly saw she had no arms at all, giving him a shock. Already Amos had seen this detail and was wondering what the devil was going on. Had these Sisterhood women harmed this Ama? If so, would there be a reward if he captured them and turned them in?

They entered a spacious living room, but the furniture was definitely second rate and quite worn, though well-polished in spite of its age. Fel guessed at once money was tight here. "*Jefe* Amos, I have come from Brom Tower on behalf of its leader Venerado Simon Bolivar."

"This is highly unusual. I barely know of its existence. How can they know of me?" he asked guardedly. *What is going on here?*

Celestina's crystal activated for a second and then died out. "Excuse me, Fel, but I will take it from here. *Jefe*, Simon wants to hire your son for a couple of years. He is to bring his flying machines with him. The pay will be excellent, but we know your son will be sorely missed around here. I am to offer you a thousand silver for each year your son is away from your ranch so you can hire others to take his place. We do not want to place any undue hardship on you while we hire your youngest son. His pay will be five thousand silver per year. Is this acceptable to you?" She spoke quite forcefully, as if she'd done this sort of thing all her life, when Fel knew for a fact she'd never done anything like it before!

A huge smile formed on the older man's face. "Well Ama, this is quite an offer, most generous indeed. Yes, I will accept those terms, but mind you, I expect to be paid, even if the lad is a complete bumbling idiot, which I am warning you up front he is. You cannot get a fair day's work out of him. Never have, always a dreamer, this lad is. That said, when will I get my silvers?"

What are you doing? Fel sent Celestina.

Trust me, Aunt Fel. I know what I am doing. She spoke up, "Will later today be acceptable to you?"

"Most certainly so, certainly so! When do you want Gabe here to go with you?"

"The sooner the better. It is going to snow, Sally and Gabe has said — so soon. Perhaps tomorrow?" Ama Celestina replied formally.

"Son, go start your packing! You behave yourself there and don't embarrass us!" *I don't want to lose all this silver!*

"Oh Gabe, you will need to bring along your flying machines. Can you show them to me?" Celestina asked.

"Sure, they are outside. Come on. Oh, is it okay if I show her dad?"

"Yes, but you watch out for the Ama there; she's very handicapped son, if you can't tell." *It would be my luck the bumbling idiot will accidentally hurt her. She must be completely helpless, the poor thing. Brom must be in a bad way to send such a helpless young thing here in the company of such disreputable women.*

Once outside, Celestina halted for a moment on the porch. "One second please." She focused and sent a message to Simon. "Okay, that's done. Silver is on its way. Come, show me your amazing flying machines. You looked so incredibly cool up there, soaring like an eagle. Is it hard to do? I'd give anything to fly like that! Oh, I'm Celestina. Forget the Ama title. I don't go in for formalities much."

"Okay, Celestina. Did it hurt much? I mean when you had that really bad accident? Was it a sword fight?" Gabe asked innocently.

"Huh?" Celestina flushed when she realized what he as asking. "Oh no, I was born without them. I used to say who needs them anyway, but this trip I have really missed having them. Now even more, because I saw you needed your arms to fly your machine, so I can never fly like an eagle I guess. Chalk that up to another thing I'll never be able to do. Come on; show me them. We need to take them back with us. I don't know why Simon wants to hire you, but he really does." She chatted away and walked up to his huge machine.

"It's light as a feather, has to be if it is going to stay aloft. If you watch the thermals, you can stay up for hours and hours. This is my second one. It can carry two people, but around here, only my brother's kids want to fly with me. The other one is in the barn. I can take you up for a flight, if you want."

Her eyes lit up and then darkened, "But I can't hold on."

"You won't have to hold on. I have a harness I strap the kids into when I take them up with me to watch for Montaña beasts. Come on. This will be lots of fun."

240

"Okay, thanks. Let's!" Gabe undid several straps and then fastened the harness around her securely.

"See, you don't have to hold on or anything. Now I get myself in here like so. Okay, here comes the tricky part. We have to walk over there to that cliff edge. Then we jump off and I take it from there."

"But that's a hundred foot drop off!" Celestina cried out a warning. Looking down, she saw rugged boulders at its base.

"Trust me. We won't hit them. We need to get an initial lift. Okay, run with me off the cliff. I'll do the rest. You'll see." Together they ran. Celestina took a deep breath and activated her crystal. If she fell into the boulders, she'd use part of her psi gift to save them. She felt rather sick at her stomach as she began falling off the cliff. Just as she was about to panic, she felt a heavy tug from her harness and was lifted up, missing the boulders. Before she could do anything, she was floating through the air way above the ground, though they were slowly descending. "I'm looking for a thermal. There's one over there." He pointed and she looked but didn't see anything but a shimmering from the heat. He headed straight toward the shimmering, and she suddenly felt a lurch upwards. Before long, they were circling several hundred feet above the manor house.

"I'll take us higher, because it's safer the higher we go, more room for a miscalculation, you see," he called out. She didn't, but trusted him.

"Wow! I am soaring like an eagle, Gabe! This is utterly fantastic. How high are we?"

"Oh I reckon we are about a thousand feet up. We could go higher, but there's no need. I'll circle our fields below. Keep your eyes open for Montaña beasts. If we spot one, I'll let them know. Honestly, it doesn't do them a whole lot of good. What the Montaña beast wants, it gets. But they can run for their lives. John, my older brother, once got a nasty cut from one of its claws. Bad scar."

What are *you doing?* Fel and Sally had come out to check on them and saw they were nowhere to be found. She noticed the flying machine was gone and looked up, spotting them.

I'm flying like an eagle, Aunt Fel! It's fabulous! Gabe says it's perfectly safe. I am in a harness and can't fall.

"She's up there with him," Fel whispered to Sally.

"Well, she is a young headstrong woman. You ought to have guessed she'd take the first opportunity to fly," Sally teased her. They watched them fly for a time.

"When we land and your feet touch the ground, pretend you are running. I'll do the rest." After doing lazy circles slowly descending, Gabe brought them in for a landing. She felt a little silly, but did as he asked. When her feet touched the ground, she tried to get to them and run. Eventually she did and then Gabe's feet hit the ground. Shortly after that, they came to a stop. Quickly, he unfastened her harness.

"That was super! You have to take me up lots of times!" Celestina insisted.

"Ah there you are," Fel pretended nothing had happened. "We need to pack this flying machine, Gabe."

"Okay, it breaks down into quite a small package really. I'll show you. You could easily lift it," he said to Celestina and then flushed.

She hastily added, "Yes, if I had arms. I bet I could." He felt better and began disassembling it. He was right, when he was done, it formed a small, compact package, a foot deep, three feet wide and five long. It would fit in the wagon, Fel observed. He headed to the barn and brought out another smaller one and a carrying case for the larger one.

"They fit in these cases so I can carry them with me, which I often do. Don't tell dad, but I take them with me when I am supposed to be watching the sheep way down the valley where he can't see me flying."

"Do you have many other things to pack, Gabe? We'll be gone some time," Fel asked trying to get the teens back on track. He nodded and dashed off inside to pack.

Finally alone with her, Fel asked about what Celestina had done with the boy's father. "So what was that all about, with *Jefe* Amos, Celestina? Is Simon behind it?"

"Not at first, but he went along with me. I used my gift to know what Amos wanted. I could see he hates the Sisterhood and wasn't about to listen to what you were going to propose. So I offered him what he most wanted: to be rid of Gabe and to have a pile of silver to replace him. He doesn't think much of Gabe at all. Simon will have a circle teleport the silver here in a while."

"Celestina, you are really good! Excellent thinking and good work," Fel praised her. "Only don't go scaring me like that, flying about. Who knows how dangerous that can be?"

"He said it is safe and I trust him, Aunt Fel. I wanted to give him a thank you kiss when we landed, but do I dare do that? Mom always says to be very careful of that sort of thing. Men get aroused easily, she says. So I didn't."

"She's right about that. Men sometimes mistake even looking them in the eyes as a sign that we are flirting with them and that it is okay for them to pursue us. We don't know anything about Gabe, so play it safe with him."

"But I like him. That's okay, isn't it?"

"Sure, thanks again for your quick thinking with Amos. Saved us a big hassle. The sooner we get going, the better. I sure as heck don't want to be snowed in here!" Celestina giggled.

Jefe Amos and an older woman came outside, she carried the tray. "Please, have a seat here on the porch. We have quite a view. Last of autumn's glory. Martha here has our tea." They took seats on the various odd chairs on the porch. Martha began serving the tea, but stopped as she approached Celestina, wholly unsure of just what to do.

"Thank you, please just sit it on the porch. I will lift it from there. I'm used to such things. I was unfortunately born this way. Such a lovely view you have here. I'd like to sit here for hours, don't you?" Celestina defused the momentary awkwardness of Martha and Amos, as well as told them what they really wanted to know, but thought better of asking.

She did as asked. "Yes, child. I love to sit here too. Springtime, the valley is one enormous blossom, but then here in autumn, the colors are so lovely. Almost makes up for the long, cold winters. We do get so much snow around here and not many visitors. Honestly, you are the first visitors all summer. Can you stay a few days?"

"No, we are from up north. There the heavy snows have

already begun. We must not delay or we will be snowed out from getting home," Celestina replied. "Oh! Here comes your silver now. Fel, can you help me with my tea?" she asked politely. While the others watched the miracle of a thousand silver coins appearing in nice, neat stacks on the porch, Fel smiled and held the cup for her. Fel knew she didn't need the help. Rather, she was putting on a believable show for the lad's parents.

As the coins piled up, Gabe came down carrying his two bags. "Oh my gosh, dad. It's the silver! With that, you can hired some extra hands and fix the place up while I'm gone. I'm packed. I hope two bags here isn't too much. *It is all I have.*

Amos bit into one coin, making sure it was real and smiled. "You mind your manners, Gabe. Make your father proud of you this time, will you? And behave yourself."

"Yes, dad. I will."

"Your bags are fine, go toss them into the wagon, Gabe," Fel suggested.

When they finished their tea, Celestina thanked them again and said, "We had best get going. It's going to snow. I don't think *Jefe* Amos wants us stranded here all winter." She laughed and saw that was precisely what the man was thinking, and he too laughed with her. Now that he had his money, he'd rather they go now than stay the night, during which something might come up to make this deal go sour. Gabe gave his mother a hug, nodded to his father, and followed the three to the wagon.

Celestina said, "Gabe, can you lift me into the wagon bed? You can sit beside me and show me the sights of your ranch as we go down the valley." Fel smiled. Celestina was certainly making the best of her "adventure." Soon, they were again on the move, retracing their path up the valley. The reds, oranges, and browns contrasted with the pines and the grey stone of the rocky outcrops and were amplified by the hue of the orange-red sun overhead, but a heavy cloud bank was slowly moving in from the southwest, bringing the first snowfall to this southern valley cradled against the Goza Mountains.

At first, the teens chatted about the valley, the sheep, and the weather. Then, Gabe began wondering what he was being hired to do. "I've been to the Oakham Tower two years ago and got my crystal, but dad needed me on the ranch. To be honest, Celestina, I hate shepherding. I'm an inventor really. I saw an eagle soaring over our valley when I was five and I wanted to soar with the bird. That's when I started inventing my flying machines. The first ones barely worked, but these last two work super, don't you think? I do hope the tower people will let me fly some days. What do they want me for anyway? Not that it really matters. I am so glad to be gone from the ranch! But I hope I can do whatever they want of me. Dad will have my hide if I mess this up. He needed the silver, you see. He really doesn't need me there."

"I think they want to learn about your flying machines, Gabe, but I am not wholly certain. They don't tell me much."

"Say, are we going to be safe with these Sisterhood women? Dad doesn't think much of them, but I've never met any."

"Fel is my aunt and she's the very best fighter around. We couldn't be safer."

"But she looks so much like a man," he whispered, unwilling to come out and say what he was thinking.

"A very bad man hurt her really bad some years ago. He cut them off," she whispered to him.

"That's awful! Well, I hope they let me fly and tinker with my flying ships. It is so hard you know. I want to spend all my time building my flying ships and inventing things, but dad hardly ever lets me, and I can't afford the things I need. He only gives me a tiny allowance. I wish we lived in a world where we could just be and do what we wanted. Then, I could spend all my time with my flying ships."

Celestina looked at him strangely. Until this moment, she thought all men were completely free to do and be whatever they desired, that it was only the women who were bound. "I didn't know you couldn't just do what you wanted to do. Me, well, I've had it drilled into me all my life that I have to do what the men tell me to do, that I can't have a life of my own."

"Why? Because you don't have arms?"

"Not really that. I am supposed to marry whoever they choose so they don't lose the *mentales* gifts I and my five sisters who are like me have. Tower women are like cattle, bred for their gifts. The only way out is to become a tower technician and work the networks all the time or renounce everything like my aunt did and join the Sisterhood. I can't join 'cause I've no arms, and they wouldn't take me because of that, and I don't want to be a technician either. So I snuck away with Fel to see the world a little and have an adventure before I get caged again. At least I can say I was free one time. But I think you will be allowed to work on your flying machines all the time you want. I bet they provide all the things you need to make more and invent things."

"That's awful, but I know dad arranged marriages for my older brothers and sisters. They didn't have any choices either, except they want to inherit the sheep ranch one day. I sure don't. It sounds like I am really going to like this, but I think it is terrible the way they are treating you, Celestina. I am really glad you snuck away so I could meet you. I thought you were going to say you were not free because of your arms."

"No silly, we six have all sorts of clever ways to do things, though not everything as I've discovered on this trip. But around the manor house and castle, we are pretty independent, just like other women. Now, I am seeing that is because they have arranged things so we can get by, like low tables and such things. You'll see what I mean when we get there. Hey, it's snowing." He helped her get her oil skin cloak over her and then put his own on. It wasn't cold and the large flakes were quite moist. The two amused themselves by trying to catch them on their tongues.

Fel, Simon here. Got some disturbing and bad news for you. We've had a traitor here at Brom Tower. We've caught him and have handled the security guard, but the damage is done and it severely affects your mission. It seems the other towers know we are after Gabe and his inventions and that you have a katalyein with you. Haverhills and Oakham have sent out riders to intercept you and capture both of them. Bedwurth is keeping an eye out for you as well, anticipating intercepting you when you get closer to them. What's your status and location?

Got Gabe and are on our way down his valley. Damn, this is really bad. How close are the enemy units?

Don't know. They've had several weeks to travel according to our traitor.

Okay, give me some time to think this through. I'll get back to you.

"Gang, we have really big problems! Simon just told me Haverhills and Oakham know about us and have sent out soldiers to capture Gabe and kidnap Celestina," Fel spoke up, startling everyone. Sally cursed vehemently.

"Why do they want me?" Gabe asked. "I won't let them get Celestina here, not without a fight."

"I think they are also interested in your flying machines, Gabe. The question is how close are those soldiers and what do we do about it?" Fel replied. "The nearest Sisterhood help is in Wycombe, Haverhills, and Oakham. We are way out in the foothills, many hundreds of miles from the Sisterhood safe houses. Shit."

Gabe looked up in the skies all around, before he said, "I can help you with how close the soldiers are, Fel."

"How son? I could use that information, it's pivotal."

"See that eagle way up there? I can use him and look for them. Give me a while," Gabe said, uncovering his crystal. Celestina watched him eager with curiosity. Before he focused, he whispered to her, "I love eagles and join with them and ask them for help. Watch." He concentrated and touched the big bird's mind. As she watched, the eagle soared in a circle over them and flew off to the south.

"Big trouble is putting it mildly," Sally said softly to Fel. "We can't out run them; horses are faster than the reindeer and this wagon. If we had a lot of snow cover and a sleigh, then we might be able to keep ahead of them, but we can't go north, we'd run right into them. East toward Wycombe?"

"No, they would expect us to make a dash for it, and out there on the rolling hills they'd catch us long before we made Wycombe," Fel replied. "We simply cannot hide our wagon tracks. If we were on horses, we'd have a chance of losing them, but with all the gear and supplies that we have, we'd need far too many packhorses. Besides, there's no place to pick up the horses, and the soldiers would soon find out we did that. We have to do the unexpected."

"Well, the reindeer love the snow," Sally grinned. "See how more contented they are now they have snow under hooves?"

"Snow. Let me think, Sally. You know, we are not too far from Cougar's Pass."

"Cougar's Pass? Doesn't that lead over the Goza Mountains into Almendia, Westerlings?" Sally asked.

"Right. It's the only southern pass over them, without going way to the south below Oakham, close to the ocean. I've been over it once on horseback, but that was in the summer."

"What's Cougar's Pass, Aunt Fel?" Celestina asked.

"Many years ago, John Cougar discovered a route across the southern Goza Mountains. Down here, they are not as tall and foreboding as they are further north. They will not expect us to go that way."

"But then we will be in the Westerlings. How will we get home?" she asked.

"We travel up their foothills and take the Valen-Exchange City roadway over to our side, but that's risky. Valen is in league with the aliens now. Lord knows what things the aliens have traded to Augusto Valen. Maybe even some of their flying machines. Yet, if we stay on this side, we are going to be trapped between the two groups of soldiers with no way to really avoid them, unless they are far from here, then we might have a chance to make a run for Wycombe."

"The eagle's back from up down south, and it's going north now," Celestina whispered, trying not to break Gabe's concentration. Fel handed the reins to Sally and had her continue on down the valley, while she got out her map to study it. What she critically needed to know was where was Cougar's Pass from where they were now. Pick the wrong valley to head up and they'd reach a dead end and lose valuable time, if not finding themselves boxed in by one or more groups of soldiers.

Fel decided to hold off making any decision to see what

information the lad had, if anything. Shortly, Gabe blinked and took a deep breath. "There, I'm back. Gosh, you are right. There are two large groups of soldiers heading towards us."

She leaned over the backboard and showed Gabe her crude map. "On this map, can you verify we are about here? Is this your valley?" She asked.

"Er, no, this next one. One bunch of probably fifty soldiers are up here, about a hundred miles from us. The other bunch has maybe forty riders coming up from the south, about eighty miles or so. What do we do?" Gabe asked, thinking rightly she needed to know where the soldiers were.

"Do you know where Cougar's Pass is at?" Gabe shook his head no. "What's that?"

"There is a pass that leads over the Goza Mountains. It is somewhere around here, but I'm not sure where. There is a dog breeder who lives near the mountains proper at the head of that valley system. I remember he trains them too."

"Oh, you must be talking about old Rafe Sikes. He has a large dog breeding and training ranch one valley down or south of here," Gabe replied. "We got some sheep herding dogs from him four years back. Don't know if there is any pass there, though."

Fel had to make the hard decision, but that came with her job. "Okay, Gabe, direct us to the Sikes dog ranch. Sally, can you nurse this snowstorm? I need a whole lot of snow dumped within a hundred mile radius of us; it will slow the horses and soldiers down. We're going to try our luck with Cougar's Pass. They will not be expecting us to go that way. Hopefully, before they figure where we've gone, we'll be at Exchange City."

"Interesting move, Fel. I would not have predicted this one, but rather that we would have made a dash for Wycombe. Maybe the soldiers will think like me," she grinned. "I'll work on the storm. Take the reins, please."

"I'll get you covered up, Ama Celestina," Gave volunteered, "and me too. It's snowing pretty well now." He wrapped them both in a couple of wool blankets and then pulled the oiled tarp over them, leaving their parka caps peering out of the back of the wagon. He called out directions as they rode along. Sally remained wholly focused on her work for over four hours, breaking off only when Fel gently called her attention to the fact they were pulling up to a snow blanketed ranch.

Chapter 12 Diversions

"You must be really desperate," the forty-five year old Rafe Sikes, commented. It was dark and snowing heavily outside his high foothills ranch. They'd pulled up by the stone complex complete with dozens of dogs announcing their arrival. Already six inches of snow covered the ground, turning the high valley into a soft, white collection of mounds with gray rock showing here and there. The branches of the pines that grew here and there around the valley were sagging under the wet new snow, the first heavy snowfall of the season.

Rafe had brown hair and a short beard. Kindly eyes denoted his friendly disposition. A widower, he had recognized Fel at once. "Ah, my flat chested Sisterhood fighter — good to see you again." Sally and Celestina held their breaths! No one dared tease her about her massive disfigurement. To their surprise, Fel laughed good-naturedly and shook his hand firmly. Evidently, Sally thought, there must have been some relationship between them some years before.

The dog breeder welcomed them and bade them spend the night, sending his three sons to help them get the snow covered wagon into their stable and reindeer fed. Meanwhile, he insisted Sally, Gabe, and Celestina come inside and warm up. "These are my older son's wives, Jill and Judy. I lost my wife during childbirth of my youngest son," he explained as the two young women barely eighteen, hustled to fix them something hot and prepare spare bedrooms. After Gabe took Celestina's heavy parka off her, he reacted as expected, full of sympathy for her and wondering what awful accident she must have had. Of course, she explained she was born this way. He replied, "Ah, I sometimes think this *mentales* gift is a two-edged sword. While it has brought us great success with our dogs, I lost my wife in childbirth because of it. Out here in the wilderness, we could not get the care she needed and we paid the price. Still, Jake has survived and has the Sikes' gift with our dogs."

Once Fel and his boys came inside, Judy and Jill had

251

tea laced with honey ready and had heated up the leftover stew from their supper. Sally added some additional bits from their supplies and the four ate their late supper. Over supper, Fel asked Rafe about Cougar's Pass and if it was traversable in the snow and in a wagon. That's when he had made his comment about Fel bring really desperate.

"Yes, desperate. You see, we have two large groups of soldiers from Haverhills and Oakham coming after us, trying to kidnap Ama Celestina here and Gabe. I am charged with getting them safely to Brom in the far north. We can't outrun them and they'd overtake us long before I could get us to Wycombe and into Sisterhood hands. I figured to do the unexpected and go over the mountains at Cougar's Pass, go up the Westerlings foothills, and cross back at Exchange City. Is it possible?" Fel asked, figuring, if anyone knew, it would be Rafe.

"Possible? Only with an expert guide, Fel. I know you've crossed it once, but that was five years ago and in the summer. In winter and with the snow that's coming, you need someone who knows the pass like the back of their hand. On horseback, you'd have an easier chance of making it. I'd recommend dog sleds as the safest way, but then you can't take a dog sled thousands of miles." He pulled at his stubby beard a little, as if making a decision that was going to be risky.

"Fel, Jake here is just sixteen, and he ought to have been sent to a tower years ago to get trained and get his power crystal. We've just not been able to do that yet. We are in kind of a no-man's land here at this ranch. Do we owe allegiance to Oakham or Haverhills? Personally, I don't care for either tower's attitudes. They've already come here and stolen away my two older boys into their armies without so much as a please. I've sent their wives and babies back to their parents because I don't know when or if ever the two older boys will ever return here."

"Nasty business, soldiering," Fel commented dryly. She didn't want to add to his worries by telling him the horrors of the battles she'd seen earlier this year. Were his boys some of those who had suffered horribly around Brownsville? She hoped not for Rafe's sake.

"Aye, my Jake needs to be tower trained and get his crystal, so I'll make you a deal. I'll lead you safely over Cougar's Pass if you will take Jake to Brom with you and see he gets trained and his crystal."

"Dad? Brom? That's way up north. You'll need me here if the soldiers come back," Jake protested.

"Look son, it is critical you get trained soon. I am already very lucky you've survived this long without the training. Fel's from that area, son, and has always had good things to say about Brom Tower. I sure as hell don't want you to go to Haverhills or Oakham; they will likely abduct you into their armies to go off fighting lord knows where like your two older brothers. No, you'll go to Brom and get trained. *Mentales* is nothing to take lightly. Your mother gave her life bringing you into this world. You owe it to her to get yourself trained before anything ill happens to you. There is a sickness that often strikes teens, and it is deadly, son. No, you go to Brom and that's that."

Turning to Fel, he asked, "So will you accept my offer?"

"How about a qualified one, Rafe? I cannot guarantee Jake would be accepted by the tower folk. I am an outcast to them, but I will plead his case to them," Fel replied.

Celestina spoke up, "Rafe, I will give you that guarantee on behalf of Brom Tower, since I am part of them." Fel knew she was taking a big gamble by speaking for Simon, but she was acting like an adult and decided to back her up.

"Good. Then this is settled. We will leave first thing in the morning. I will pack up my dog sled tonight yet. Boys, you can lend me a hand with it. Jake, pack your things; you can ride in their wagon and help them with whatever Fel asks," Rafe replied. "Judy, Jill, you show these kind folks to the guest rooms. They must be tired from their long ride today."

A while later, Rafe knocked on the room the three women were sharing. "Fel, a word with you," he called out. Fel slipped on her shirt and pants and stepped outside the room. They were just about to climb into the chilly bed.

"I've been thinking, Fel. You would fare a whole lot better if your reindeer were pulling a sleigh instead of a wagon, what with all this snow and winter coming on. If you like, I can

253

swap you one of my large sleighs for your wagon. What do you think?"

"I don't know how much snow will be on the alien's made roadway from Valen to Exchange City. Beyond that stretch, this time of year, there should be heavy snow everywhere so a sleigh would be ideal. Is yours large enough to hold all our stuff?"

"I measured it before I decided to suggest it to you, Fel. Yes, everything ought to fit nicely."

"Then, I accept your kindness once more, Rafe. Thank you," Fel gave him a smile he appreciated.

"Good. We'll swap your gear in the morning then. By the way, you know you'd always have a place to stay here." Rafe gave her a large hinting grin.

"I know that Rafe, and I really appreciate it. I've recently taken a free-mate. If things get bad for us, I may well come back here and take you up on that offer." He smiled, but sensed his disappointment that she was now married. If she were ever to marry a man, Rafe would be at the top of her list of candidates. Yet, she knew she would not. Always in the back of her mind was the fear her children would be like her brother and sister's, armless. She would not be a party to propagating that! Not ever.

"Sometime, bring your free-mate here. You are always welcome, Fel, you know that." He turned and she slipped back into the darkened room.

"What'd he want?" whispered Celestina. She was very curious. Was something happening?

"He is trading one of his large sleighs for our wagon. That will make our travel lots easier for us in the deep snows we are going to encounter. Let's get some sleep. This might be the last warm bed we have for months." She purposely didn't mention what else he'd said and certainly not why she wouldn't marry a man, not with Celestina present!

Taking a sleigh turned out to be a very wise decision. By morning, Sally's tinkering with the snowstorm was paying dividends. Over a foot of new snow covered the ground, completely hiding all traces that their wagon had come up the valley yesterday afternoon. The heavy snow continued to fall as they bundled up and headed outside to move their gear into the sleigh. Again, Celestina felt awful as she could do nothing to help them and really did appreciate Gabe's arm around her helping her keep her balance trudging through the deep snow that came up the sides of her tall boots. She also now understood why folks wore these tall boots, which came nearly up to their knees.

The temperature was not bitterly cold and much of this snow would begin to melt once the storm had passed. Sally's tinkering, however, guaranteed this would not happen for another couple of days. Fel wanted the trailing soldiers to be slowed down and Sally made sure of that detail. Before the storm ended, the region received nearly two feet of the white stuff, greatly hindering the soldiers, but at the time, Fel didn't know the magnitude of the delay Sally had caused. Now, her full attention was getting them safely up the valley and over Cougar's Pass into the Westerlings foothills.

Rafe and his dog sled with a dozen dogs led the way on up the valley behind his ranch. Fel and her team of reindeer and sleigh followed him. Celestina, Gabe, and Jake sat bundled up from the cold in the sleigh bed, the heavy oiled tarp covering them, leaving only their faces visible. Celestina was sitting between the two boys for warmth. As they began moving silently over the sea of white, she marveled at the sight and then began chatting with the boys. For the first time, really, she had the chance just to chat with boys her own age who were not tower folk. She was learning a lot.

Jake told her how his two older brothers were abducted into the armies and had no choice in the matter at all. He described how their wives had cried when they left, while they stood there watching and holding their infants. "Sad, really, sad," Jake explained. "Dad says soldiers usually get killed or badly wounded and none of us should ever expect to see them return. That's why he sent their wives and babies back to their parents in the next valley south of here."

All that day, they climbed steadily higher, and the craggy ridge lines began looking more like some giant's teeth embedded within pure white gums — spectacularly beautiful, but deadly. Visibility was still good, despite the constant snowfall. Late afternoon, they left the valley of the foothills behind, entering the actual Goza Mountains proper, dark, brooding, foreboding, and treeless. First, Rafe issued everyone thin, pod-silk scarves to wrap around their eyes to dim down the bright sunlight reflecting off the high altitude snow fields. Then, Rafe led them on a winding route that rose steadily up the side of a mountain. Late afternoon, he halted to make camp in a gorge on the north side of this first mountain, where there was shelter from the winds and blowing snow that continued to fall.

Bundled up heavily from the cold and snow, Celestina had little choice but to depend upon Gabe, who helped her with everything. Even trying to walk in the deep snow over the rough ground with its hidden stones was challenging for everyone, her even more so. That left Fel to help set up their tent, which was an oiled hide with internal poles, and deal with the necessities. Everyone had to struggle with the cold, snow, and heavy clothes, but managed.

Three long days later, they paused at Cougar's Pass, a curved dome shaped section between two taller peaks. Far above the timberline, their entire world was pure white. Without a guide, Fel knew they would have been in dire trouble. All her landmarks were buried beneath feet of snow. As the reddened sun sank in the west, all stood and took in the breath-taking view of the tall peaks thrusting high above them, jagged grey teeth. The air was thin and all found breathing difficult, especially the dry, frigid air. Even their charcoal in their small stove struggled to burn properly.

Billowing frost from his breath, Rafe pointed out their downward path. It curved between the peaks and then sloped gently on down to the upper Westerlings foothills some fifty miles ahead. From this pass, their route on the western side was quite clear, unlike that of the eastern side. Nevertheless, Rafe promised to guide them down to the foothills just to make very sure they did not get into difficulties. If they did, there was no one to lend them a hand. Few even knew of this pass through the Goza Mountains.

Three days later, Rafe brought them safely to the other side and the foothills. After giving his son a parting hug as well as Fel, he waved goodbye and headed his dogs back the way they'd just come. At least now the snowstorm had gone, and the weather pattern was now back to normal for this time of year. That meant much of the snow began to melt under late morning's warmth from the orange-red sun, only to stall in the late afternoon as the heavy clouds came drifting in from the far distant ocean. Evenings brought drizzle, rain, and more snow, but sometimes sleet and ice. Still, Fel knew soon, it would cease melting, and the rain would always be snow as the winter months arrived.

Her task now was to pick out a passage for them heading northward, but avoiding impassible ridge lines and all villages. She spoke the Westerlings dialect a little and Celestina was fluent in it, but the others could not. Besides, the fewer who knew of their passage, the better. This close to the Goza Mountains, there were few villages, mostly isolated pioneering farmsteads or ranches. Avoiding inhabitation sites was far easier than picking out their path across the tall ridges that were often impassible in stretches. Gabe helped her tremendously by scouting ahead using the various hawks and eagles, which were sometimes soaring above looking for small rodents or rabbits.

While their living conditions were harsh and cold, they soon settled into a routine and had little difficulties during their nearly eight hundred mile northward trip. All that changed in late November as they approached the paved roadway that led from Valen far to the northwest across the Goza Mountains just south of Plateau Grado and the spaceport to Exchange City on the eastern slopes of the mountains.

"Well, here comes the dicey part," Fel commented to Sally. "We have to follow the road over the mountain plateau pass the aliens and into Exchange City. At least the road is snow packed, but it looks as though there has been some traffic. Stay alert for trouble. We are really exposed for the next hundred miles with no options but to continue down the road. If the Haverhills or Oakham soldiers have figured out where we went and are, they could be waiting at the other end for us. Our gooses will be cooked in that case, so stay alert and hope we don't meet any travelers along the way." She pulled the sleigh up and onto the roadway, heading east. Secretly, she kept her fingers crossed.

Karolina enjoyed herself immensely now that Carmen was staying with them. Together, they had their plans for their new women's clothing and heels company organized. Although Carmen was pumping her full of the psi dust, here in November, she had not yet altered and received her *mentales* gifts, though Jarek had just recovered from his Verge Sickness. However, she continued her self-appointed role of tracking the various weather anomalies on Ashford-5.

She'd spotted a very large one down south in late October. The snowstorm, the first big one of the season down in the southern Goza Mountains, ought to have tracked on northeastwards out into the central Midlands. Yet it did not, stalling completely over the southern mountains and the eastern foothills adjacent to it. How strange she thought, since the anomaly lasted until the storm lost all its moisture. Why would anyone want to have all that snow dumped on them? She could easily see why people living in the central Midlands would want the storm diverted. Hence, she decided to monitor the geosat images of the area of the storm and the areas surrounding it. Call it a hunch, she explained to Carmen as the two women made love to each other.

Just after the storm ended, she noted a small group of travelers heading north from the western edge of the storm. *How strange, no others are this close to the mountains,* she thought. The strangeness grew as she realized somehow this group had crossed the impassible Goza Mountains down there. *Most interesting. Why? Why not go on down south and around?* She decided to continue to monitor them from the daily images of the satellite. Lech was wholly uninterested in this, but Carmen encouraged her to pursue it. She too was curious about these travelers.

As the days progressed, the travelers moved mostly northwards, though their path was a zig-zag one. From looking at her flat overhead images, Karolina had no idea why that would be so. And there were a good many other travelers coming and going she could see on the images, but this original group continued to hold her attention, though she couldn't say why. Perhaps it was because they crossed the mountains out of the huge anomalous snowstorm. *If I could talk to them, perhaps they might be able to give me some ideas about why the anomaly developed,* she thought. Carmen was amused with Karolina's fascination with the weather, but to her, it was obvious someone had tinkered with the storm, simple, though she herself could not do such a thing.

Carmen had other ideas, though. These fabulous clothes and heels they were going to begin marketing would make them a fortune, if only there was some way to get some prototypes scattered among the other towers. Create a demand for your product, she remembered her mother's lessons, but of course, she was selling herself as Augusto's Royal Consort. Still, Carmen felt the principle applied to their new business, Elegant Fashions Inc. She herself was constrained only to live at her Valen Tower or now the spaceport. How could she get their designs spread to other towers and castles? An idea formed and she began to feed Karolina's fascination with these travelers who were heading their way, albeit at a snail's pace. Well, that wasn't entirely true; they traveled as well as anyone in the heavy snows.

Of course, these travelers could be merely merchants or traders themselves. As time went on and as the travelers had avoided all major towns according to the geosat maps, Carmen began to think differently. They were not likely traders or merchants. Could they be more significant people? If even one or two were tower folk, then they could give them sample fashions to take back to their tower. Orders would likely follow. The main problem was the aliens were not allowed to mix with the Tierra inhabitants save at Exchange City, though obviously her father and Karolina's husband Lech were secretly violating the agreement. Could she and Karolina also do so? She broached the subject with Karolina.

"Dear, do you suppose if these travelers you've been monitoring come this way, we could intercept them? You could question them about the weather anomaly of yours, and then we could give them some samples of our new line of fashions, allowing them to take them to their cities and send us orders. The more widespread we can get our fashions known, the more orders we will have, until at last, Elegant Fashions Inc will be the largest and first global company on Tierra."

"Hum, I like that. How do we get around the Directive #5, I wonder? Plus, there is all that infernal snow out there. I know, we have our HQ there in Exchange City. Your people are allowed in there. Suppose that we take over one floor for our company. We could then waylay the travelers and bring them there. Of course, we'd need to have full bathing facilities. Lord knows how filthy they must be by now. Still, we'd have a controlled environment for them to try out our fashions."

Carmen backed her up. "Great idea, dear. I love it. Even if these travelers continue on north to Valen, we will be all set for other important people who frequent Exchange City. We should focus our best efforts on those with the *mentales* gifts. They are the most influential people on Tierra."

"Excellent my love, let's make it so! I can see it now, all the prim — native women," she hastily corrected herself, "will be elegantly and fashionably dressed. That alone will help turn this planet into a civilized one. Come on! We have work to do!" The two moved slowly across her room towards the door, their heels clicking in unison on the metallic floor.

Within two weeks, they had one floor, the fourth, all set up for their business and their initial supply of heels, dresses, and undergarments lined up. Additionally, they had four local seamstresses hired to make alternations and to make copies of the dresses and undergarments. Karolina took a different approach to the construction of the heels. She ordered an expensive heel making machine. One loaded a bin with supple, high quality leather and a second bin with steel and the machine would then turn out finished heels. Of course, there were dials to adjust, not only for the shoe size, but also style and finished colors. Carmen thought this might put local cobblers out of work, but they could not make these fine quality heels Karolina imported for herself and Carmen to wear. The machine could and Carmen accepted that. Her only wish was the psi dust would hurry up and work its magic on her lover, Karolina.

As December came, the snow depth on the roadway gradually increased. However, as Fel and her group continued along it, they were forced to stop. An alien machine came towards them. "What the devil is that thing?" asked Sally. Gabe, Jake, and Celestina peered from beneath their piles of blankets and oiled covering.

"I don't know, but we've got to get off this road," Fel gently pulled the team to the right shoulder, dangerously close to its edge and halted. Perhaps the machine would stop when it drew closer. It didn't. An enormous blade pushed the build-up of snow off of the roadway and down into the slopes below the road. Quickly, Fel got her team going again and moved the sleigh off to the left side, up tight against the mountain stone, just as the aliens and their machine drove past them. "Well, that's certainly clever," Fel turned to tell the others and watched it from the rear. "Clears the buildup of snow, making the roadway travelable despite the amount of snow accumulation. Clever." She got the team going again. The roadway was covered with an inch of very hard packed snow, almost ice, and perfect for their sleigh.

Next, they endured the roaring of mighty engines as several giant silver ships blasted off from the spaceport as they drove by the launching area. Others were landing, all oblivious to the natives of Tierra. Two days later, Fel began to relax, ahead lay Exchange City. Once clear of that, they would be nearly in their own Kingdom of the Angels. Likely, she would need to bypass Bedwurth and Wyth Towers, just to be perfectly safe.

Around noon, the tall alien buildings in Exchange City appeared and then shortly after that, the low, single story stone buildings of the humans came into view. Just as Fel began to relax completely, she tensed up. "Sally, what do you make of that?"

"So close and yet so utterly far!" she whispered. Six alien security men armed with blasters stood blocking the roadway just ahead of them. "Maybe they will move as we draw close," she added hopefully, but instinctively clutching her short sword at her side. Of course, a sword was wholly useless against blasters. Of this, Fel was acutely aware.

They didn't. One raised his hand and a mechanical box attached to his belt spoke up in crude Midlands dialect. "Halt. You are ordered to come with us to the HQ. Please do not try to resist us."

"What is this about? We are travelers trying to get to the city ahead. We are tired and hungry," Fel replied, doubting her words would have any effect on the aliens.

What do we do? Celestina sent her and Fel sensed her growing fears.

"Are we under arrest? What law have we broken? I assure you we did not intend to break any," Fel asked.

"No, the Sector ID Minister's wife wishes to speak with your party. Come with us now, please," the tall, thin man replied. He was shivering in his overly thin synthetic cat suit, ill-suited to the harsh winters of the Plateau Grado area.

"Lead on," Fel said and followed them. Quickly, four of them flanked her sleigh, two on each side. None seemed threatening and Fel's mind tried to absorb the impact of what the alien man had said. *Sector ID Minister? His wife?* She knew this was the most important alien man here on Tierra, the one who tried to kill Cassia, but what of his wife? Did she have equal importance? Fel had many questions and sent to the others: *Play along with them. Let's see what they want. Let me do the talking.*

They halted before the five story glass and metal building. The alien leader then said, "If you will disembark your carriage, one of my men will take it into the stable and guard your possessions. You are to follow me now."

"Where are you taking us?" Fel asked, as Gabe helped Celestina down and Jake moved to her other side. The teens intended to protect her, Fel noted. "I will hold you responsible if any of our possessions are stolen," she added.

"I give you my word as a Security Guard, no one will touch your sleigh, but we will feed those animals of course. Filthy beasts. Now then, we are going to the fourth floor. This way please." As they walked into the HQ building, many aliens in their non-descript, synthetic, grey cat suits stared at them. Well, they were a sight, bundled up in heavy parkas and cloaks, with thick fur caps and tall, leather boots. They followed the guard and entered a tiny metal room, barely large enough to hold them. Fel worried; she hated confined spaces where she could not fight, if the need arose. A series of buttons were on a panel, and the man who towered over all of them pushed the fourth one up.

"Oh!" Celestina exclaimed. Suddenly all felt motion and realized that by alien magic, they were rising in the air. Then, it stopped and just ahead of them an entrance sign in several languages read, Elegant Fashions Inc.

More surprising still, two women stood before them. One had yellow eyes and was obviously a Westerlings woman. She had long black hair and was perhaps the most beautiful young woman Fel had yet encountered. She wore a fancy, long black silk dress, accentuating her many curves and large bust. Her legs were covered with some kind of very thin stockings, black, and which they soon learned were called nylons. Her shoes matched her dress and her heels were extremely thin and pointed, rising to six inches. Standing next to her was an alien woman, at least six inches taller. She wore a light brown dress, similar in style, and the same black thin hose. Her heels were nearly identical to the Westerlings woman, but their color matched her dress.

"Welcome travelers to Elegant Fashions Inc. This is Carmen and I am Karolina, co-owners. Our goal is to establish truly elegant fashions for men and women across this world. First, you must be positively melting in those heavy clothes. We keep our office suite here at a comfortable temperature year round. If you will place your outer garments over there, please, we will take you into our appointment office." She looked at their winter coats with utter distaste, though she did try to conceal it a little. Carmen merely noted they wore typical winter apparel. She also noticed all five had yellow eyes, a very good sign she thought.

They did so and both women gasped when they saw Celestina's form and an equal gasp when they saw Fel was a woman. They followed the slow moving women, whose heels clicked on the metal floor. Fel sensed both lads were growing uncomfortably aroused by the two women's dress. Even she found herself attracted, especially to Carmen. After taking a seat before the metal table on plastic covered metal chairs, Karolina began.

"First, we need to obtain some background information about your group to better help us prepare a complimentary set of our elegant fashions for each of you. Now, I am a weather expert and as the Sector ID Minister's wife, I have full access to all our weather records. I am something of an expert weather forecaster, you see. Been interested in the path of storms on many worlds, all of which I can predict with total accuracy. Until I came here, that is," she added.

Fel began wondering where this was leading as Karolina continued. "On your world, I've discovered storm tracking anomalies. That is, storms that disobey all known laws of nature. Carmen here has told me there are some of you with the gift to control the weather. I've been keenly interested in that, you see. Anyway, back in October, I noticed a huge weather anomaly down in the southern foothills and Goza Mountains. I believe Carmen said it was somewhere between a place called Haverhills and Oakham. Anyway, I was watching the storm and following it, or rather where it didn't move, for days and then I discovered your party coming out of that area. I found that curious and have been monitoring your progress until now."

Fel suppressed rising anger. What did she really want? Sally had been the cause of the anomaly. Worse, how could the aliens be tracking them? Carmen felt the tensions of the two Sisterhood women rising and stepped in, "Karolina, these two here are members of the Sisterhood and often hire out as guides."

"Oh, I see. Pleased to meet them at long last. Now am forgetting my manners. Please, could you introduce yourselves?"

Fel didn't know Carmen and didn't know whether or not she could detect if they were lying. Hence, she replied truthfully. "Carmen is right. We are these people's guides. I am Fel, and this is Sally. We are escorting Ama Celestina del Fuego back from her visit to her homeland back to Brom Tower where she is an important young leader there. We are also taking these two young lads there as well for their needed tower training. All young *mentales* gifted must receive their tower training, as Carmen can explain to you. My heritage is also Westerlings and I know the land well. This is Jake and Gabe."

"Ah, I see. Yes, this makes sense. Very good. Ama Celestina, you are then the *very* person whom we wish to extend our complimentary offer," Carmen smiled. "But what awful accident happened to you?"

Celestina knew both women wanted to ask her that ever since Gabe removed her parka, revealing her form. "I was born this way. No accident. However, Fel has suffered horribly at the hands of some evil men. I do represent Brom Tower at the moment. What is this offer you refer to, if I may ask?"

Fel was greatly relieved Celestina took charge. Carmen obviously knew she and Sally were Sisterhood women and thus of no importance in the tower society. The lads were on their way there, so it fell to the teen to represent her tower.

"Simple, we want to outfit you all with samples of our elegant fashions at no cost to you. Take them to your tower and wear them. As you can see from our appearance, we do look very elegant, not like those awful synthetics the Rigel-3 personnel here wear or those bulky, unflattering garments that are so often seen at the towers, as Carmen has explained to me. Even you Sisterhood women could use a dash of real elegance in your lives. And we have equally fashionable, fine suits for these young men with you. All that we ask is when you arrive at your tower, wear them. You may accept orders for us, and we will give you a commission on those that you sell. Our goal is to help women and men of this world look their very best."

Karolina went on, "In your case, Ama Celestina, even our advanced medical technology will be of no use in replacing your missing arms. I am truly sorry about that. A hand, a foot, an eye, these are easily remediable. Now then, we really ought to see if there isn't something that can be done for your guide; breast reconstructive surgery is possible. If you will permit me, I will send for our medical doctor and get her opinion. If it is feasible, then in a gesture of goodwill among our races, I will see your guide gets it done at no cost, of course. Honestly, our fashions are designed for women with, well, you know what I mean."

Fel flushed; this was getting way too personal for her tastes, but Karolina continued. "Now then, first order of business. Let's get you all properly bathed, and then we'll get you measured and dressed in one of our most elegant fashions. If you will follow Carmen, she will see you are bathed." She motioned to Carmen who, with seductively swaying hips and dainty steps, led the way down a short hall to a pair of bathrooms. Meanwhile, Karolina summoned the base medical doctor and her portable medical lab, "No, it is not an emergency, just the possibility of breast reconstructive surgery," Fel heard her say into some kind of device as she left the room.

Fel was more and more self-conscious. She always bathed alone, utterly ashamed for others to see her massively scarred chest. Now she was going to have to endure it with her niece and Sally, since there was only one woman's shower room. True, Carmen gave Ama Celestina explicit instructions before she flushed and realized Fel or Sally would have to carry them out. *How horrid her life must be! Well, doll her up in our fashions and she'll look the best she can be.* Carmen left to instruct the two lads and then wait on them to appear wrapped in their large towels.

Celestina gasped quietly as she again saw her aunt's chest, but wisely said nothing. Sally avoided looking, focusing on figuring out how this alien bath shower worked. A pressure spray hit their bodies, washing the accumulated month of sweat and dirt from their bodies, though all three would have preferred a nice barrel of hot water and a long soak to this highly efficient alien shower device. However, the air dryer impressed them. In just a couple of minutes, Celestina's very long hair was dry — rather amazing the three thought. Further, the conditioner liquid Carmen suggested made their hair soft, silky, easy to manage, and with a noticeable fuller body. Celestina was pleased with it and asked Carmen if they also marketed that product.

"Now that is a good idea, Ama Celestina. I will look into it and send you word. Now then, let's get you looking just fabulously elegant, dear. Oh, Fel, wait here, the doctor will see you directly." Fel kept the towel wrapped around her chest, unwilling to reveal herself to this Westerlings woman, whoever she was. She kept focusing on just who this Carmen was, distracting her from the coming doctor, who she prayed would be a woman. If it was a man, she'd flatly refuse to let him see her.

Thankfully, the doctor was a female and the examination went better than Fel had anticipated. She had Fel unwrap herself behind the machine that appeared to block the woman's view of her. Then the machine moved up close to her body, pressing against her skin. She flinched a little from the shock of the cold plastic and metal touching her chest. The doctor didn't look at her, but intently studied the dials on the other side of the machine, which suited Fel enormously. At last, she looked up, "Yes, there is still sufficient mammary gland tissue for me to work our Imperium medical magic, young woman. I suppose you wish them to appear as large as the normal native women's breasts?"

"What about all the scarring? Will it hurt?" Fel asked wondering whether or not she should do this and whether the result would only make her look even more freakish.

"Yes, well, I will remove most all that in the process. No pain at all. I am going to have you sit down and allow me to readjust the machine. It won't take more than twenty minutes, and we'll have your womanhood restored. Honestly, if a man did this to you, he ought to have been killed or castrated," she said rather indignantly.

"I killed him," Fel answered her quietly, thinking perhaps the alien women were not so different from herself.

"Good for you! Men, honestly. Now then, please hold absolutely still. You won't feel a thing, I promise you, except for a couple of pinpricks. There, that's got you numb. Here we go. Just relax. I'll have you fixed up in no time. The stem cells are doing their thing. Honestly, I am so glad to get a chance to practice my medicine. So little ever happens on this base that I am bored out of my mind." The doctor chatted away while she worked her dials. Fel suspected the woman really had no practical medical knowledge, save which button to press, as

267

Cassia had done with the ancient machine of Doctor Zosia.

"There you go. All finished. Have a look and see if they meet with your approval. If not, we can make some minor adjustments," the doctor said rather proud of her work.

Fel gasped and felt them. They seemed real and much like the ones she'd lost. Far better, all that ghastly scarring was wholly gone! In fact, stare as she might, she could not see any visible signs of scarring around her new bosom. "Thank you, doctor. It is a miracle," Fel was speechless.

After the doctor left, Karolina entered, moving slowly on her high heels. "Wow! You look wonderful, Fel. What an improvement. Now then, follow me and I'll help get you into an elegant outfit as well."

A bit later, Karolina explained, "Nothing but the finest silk to adorn our skin. Panties first. This is a garter belt designed to hold up your black nylons." She explained and chatted as she dressed Fel, eventually sliding a white silk slip over her undergarments and thin hose. Then, she helped her into a form fitting, black silk dress that displayed more of her new cleavage than Fel thought modest, but the dress did fall to just below her knees, revealing her hose, which Karolina said made her legs look very sexy to others. At last, she slipped her feet into a pair of matching heels. "Now be careful wearing these for the first time. Take tiny steps like me. I'll show you. Let's join the others, shall we?"

"How can you walk in these?" Fel complained, but did her best to emulate the sleek alien woman. *After all, if she can manage, I can too!*

"Wow Fel! You look incredible!" Celestina gushed when she glimpsed Fel walking slowly to join Sally and her. She, too, was being very careful while walking, and with the stockings on, she couldn't use her feet as she normally would. Keeping her balance was extremely challenging for her, and she was very pleased when Gabe and Jake appeared in their new suits and Gabe moved to her side, slipping an arm around her for support. She was impressed he carefully slipped it beneath her long hair and not over it as many often did, which pulled annoyingly on her hair. Gabe was extremely thoughtful, she concluded, growing even more impressed with him. All three women wore similar black dresses, while the two lads wore fancy wool tweed suits with a matching vest and a narrow black tie. Their shoes were also made from the finest quality leather and held as good a shine as the women's heels.

All five felt the sexual arousals of each other and so did Karolina and Carmen. "Yes," Carmen explained, "these bring out the very best in both men and women as you can sense. Just look at how delightful Ama Celestina appears. The black silk lays so well over her empty shoulders, accentuating her form even more than before. Perfect, if I do say so myself!"

"Yes utterly perfect. Now if we could only get all men and women on Ashford-5, I mean Tierra, to wear such elegant fashions, I know the world would be such a far better place," Karolina exclaimed.

"Well, there is no doubt these are the most elegant fashions we've ever encountered," Fel replied, "but they are not too practical for daily wear."

"Yes, but for dances and other times, these are just fabulous, Fel," Celestina broke in, barely able to keep from saying Aunt Fel before these strangers. "We will be delighted to show them off to everyone at Brom Tower! I have five sisters like me who would just love to have an outfit like mine. Oh, will they ever be envious of me when I show them how I look!"

"Ama Celestina, nothing would give us more pleasure than to send another five back with you just for them!" Karolina replied, and Fel felt she was being genuinely sincere. "If you gentlemen will escort the lovely women to our desks, we will show you our first catalog of designs and work out how you may have others order their own sets."

After looking over their line of men's and women's fashions, Carmen summoned another native woman. "This is Mary Winters; she is in charge of customer orders. As you can see, she is also a telepath. So when you have an order, contact her and your outfits will be sewn and sent to you upon receipt of payment. We so look forward to your future orders, Ama Celestina. And if you have some design ideas, please don't hesitate to send them along as well."

"Oh dear, how time has flown. It is near suppertime,"

Karolina broke in. "Would you five please honor us by joining us for dinner? Our dining hall is on the floor below us and we do have a small choice of native dishes, though I do not know how good they are. Then, if you would like to spend the night with us, we have some bedrooms down on the first floor you may use. If you'd rather be on your way, then we will have our staff prepare the extra outfits to send along with you right away."

Celestina was very curious about the food and really was stimulated by her clothes and the impression she was making on Gabe. "Yes, that is most generous, Karolina. We'd love to dine with you. I don't want to take off my new outfit so soon."

Karolina laughed, "My dear Ama, neither do we nor do our husbands, I might add. They just love our new looks as well. A well-dressed person inspires other's confidence in them and their own self-confidence rises as well. Please, follow us. Gentlemen, escort your women." She said that last, because she knew the women would be teetering precariously on their heels until they got used to walking in them. Carmen took to them readily and expected the others would too. On the way to the elevator, she added, "Oh, our husbands will be joining us, I do hope that is acceptable to you."

Fel felt more ill at ease. In this outfit, she could barely walk, let alone fight. Still she sensed nothing ill coming from either woman and accepted the invitation. Besides, she was still amazed at how she looked and the incredible miracle their doctor had worked. For the first time in years, Fel felt like a woman again. She was no longer a *castinto*.

They met Jarek and Lech, who were patiently waiting for their wives. "I see now why we cannot dine in the port," Lech commented to his wife as she entered and introduced her guests. He stared long at Ama Celestina, admiring her and also studied the two Sisterhood women. In his mind, he saw two charming, good looking women, not the reputed fighters he'd read about in the secret documents.

Likewise, Fel kept Lech in sight from the corner of her eyes. Here was the vicious man who'd ordered her free-mate, Cassia's death! Here was the man who allowed his men to kidnap *mentales* gifted women and send them off-world into hell! Part of her wanted to slit his throat, but she could see no way to pull that off just now.

The meal was only passable, however. Fel suspected they had hired a second-rate native cook and they seldom had native cuisine. Tonight, it was stewed rabbit laced with deer bits, rice, and an assortment of overcooked vegetables. Carmen and Jarek ate the native food but Lech and Karolina ate their Rigel-3 dishes, which looked unappealing to the others, more like a blue glob of glue.

The conversation was generally light and insignificant, though Lech did ask where Brom Tower was located. Jarek asked a number of key questions until he was satisfied Ama Celestina really was from Brom Tower. After that, neither man said anything out of the ordinary, but did offer many compliments to the three women.

After the meal was finished, both men excused themselves, citing other duties. Lech did say, "Well, if all you women on Tierra wore such fine gowns and you lads, such fine suits, why, the world would indeed be wholly civilized! My compliments on your looks, ladies. Now, if you will excuse me, work calls."

Fel was in turmoil. Karolina was obviously trying to instil better relations between the two cultures, even to the extent of violating the lease agreement by healing Fel's breasts. On the surface, the two women were treating them exceptionally well. The free outfits probably cost a considerable amount, though Fel had no way of knowing for sure. Yet, her husband wanted Cassia dead for having stumbled into their routine kidnaping of young telepaths and sending the women off-world. Here was the man who was illegally having close dealings with Valen Tower, even going so far as to allow one of his own agents to marry Carmen from Valen and giving them the dangerous blasters.

Fel found herself trying to see what evil subterfuge Karolina and Carmen were trying to hide so well with their many gifts and plans. However, she could detect none at the moment. Had they installed something diabolical in her new breasts? A listening device of some kind? A tracking device?

How foolish I was to let them do this to me! She realized they'd picked on her single greatest weakness and used it to their advantage or had they? Could there be two sides to the aliens? Was it only their men who were evil while their women were good of heart? Fel could not resolve the conflicts at all. Somehow, Karolina had been tracking them all the way to Exchange City and that too frightened her. The aliens were too powerful, their technology too enormous in scope. Now they wanted the group to spend the night before continuing on their way. Why? Were they planning to eavesdrop on their private conversations? Of course, Fel knew if she were in their position, she certainly would do so. Yet, it was too late to get back on the trail; it was night and snowing again. She had no doubts Karolina would continue to track them and see if they did indeed go to Brom Tower. She certainly would do so.

Worse, she had to decide whether to stay or not and in short order. "Your hospitality has been superb. It is getting late for us and we need to get on the trail early. You mentioned we could stay here tonight?" Fel politely asked.

"Yes, it is getting late, and our husbands are anxiously awaiting us to join them. I assumed you would be staying. Rooms 1a and 1b have been prepared for you. I've taken the liberty of sending your original apparel there, as well as our gifts for you. We look forward to getting lots of orders from you and your friends. Again, we thank you for allowing us to interrupt your journey and for trying our new, exclusive elegant fashions for women and men. If you are ever here in Exchange City, do drop by here. Just tell the Security Guards at the main doors that you wish to visit Elegant Fashions Inc. They will bring you up to our suite. Thanks again," Karolina explained. Fel thought she sounded more like a saleswoman than the minister's wife.

"Thank you as well for everything," Fel replied in kind. Hastily, the others added their thanks to hers. Karolina and Carmen led the group slowly to the elevator and down to the first floor. Fel noticed all eyes glanced at them and some lingered as they walked down the hall to their rooms. After pointing them out, the two bid them good night and left. Fel heard Karolina order a guard, "Our electric car, please." She wondered what that device was but had no way to find out.

She sent to the others, *They likely have ways to eavesdrop on what we say, so talk only about how nice the clothes are, that sort of thing. We'll leave at dawn.*

"I'll loan you some of my tops, Fel. Your men's shirts aren't going to fit you now," Sally whispered as the three women finally finished storing their new outfits and prepared for bed.

Can we have a private talk when we get back? Celestina sent her aunt.

Sure dear. After we get back.

Although they anticipated more trouble along the way, the last nine hundred miles was routine. True, the snows continued and the accumulated depths continued to rise, but the reindeer and sleigh managed with little difficulties. The five were now well grooved in on what needed to be done, and Fel found the boys remarkably helpful and considerate. Still, she took precautions to bypass the tower towns of Bedwurth and Wyth, going around them, though it added a few more miles to their trip. On the twentieth of January 1132, they finally arrived back at Brom Tower.

Chapter 13 Inventions and Decisions

Gabe was wholly accepted almost at once. He gave a demonstration of his flying machines and Simon instantly gave him a job designing and inventing more. With unlimited resources, from Gabe's point of view, he no longer was limited to his crude attempts of thin, light weigh frames covered with shellacked canvas. One of the circles began using a network of crystals to fabricate very thin metal sheets that replaced the flimsier construction of his machines. Now he set to work building a glider that could carry at least four people, though he didn't know it then that it would be one person plus the weight of three others in bombs to be dropped on the enemy.

In talking with Simon, he mentioned there were other ways to rise into the air. He'd experimented a little with balloons, but keeping the air hot was problematical. Cassia stepped in and told them all about helium gas. Again, the circle set to work on constructing a network to extract the gas from the air, concentrating it into huge containers. Before this new year was out, the Jeffery Glider and the Gabe-mobile, the adopted name for his dirigible, took to the skies. Brom had finally gotten the means to defend themselves from attacks.

Jake Sikes received his germanium crystal and basic training as well. However, he decided to stay on at Brom, raising and training dogs to pull sleds. Simon was so impressed with how his father had used one to cross the mountains in the snow that he hired Jake to initially get a half dozen sleds and dogs ready for the coming winter.

Of course, everyone immediately discovered what the aliens had done for Feliciana Evita e Kaylee. After the lengthy explanations, Fel finally had the chance to speak privately with Cassia. "My you are looking big! Baby doing all right?" Fel asked.

Holding her large belly, Cassia grinned, "She's a strong one. Yes, she's fine. And you, I can't believe how good you look. I've missed you so, you know."

After a passionate embrace, Fel said, "Can you check me

over and see if they secretly implanted me with their devices or whatevers. I don't trust them at all. I hope you don't mind my having it done."

"No, I love the new look, dear. Let me make a thorough check. I don't trust them either. So you met my ex-boss who tried his best to kill us?" she asked, while beginning a very careful examination of Fel's new massive bosom.

"Yes, he seemed polite enough and definitely his wife Karolina has him wrapped around her fingers. It was hard seeing him as a killer though, yet he is, and a kidnapper as well. Then, there are all these fancy outfits they gave us. I can't imagine how they are using them for evil, though."

"The doctor regenerated your breast tissues, Fel. Nothing foreign is in them, but you were right to be concerned. I am surprised the doctor didn't implant a homing or id device, but she probably didn't because she considers you to be a primitive. If she were doing it to me, I am sure she would have inserted an id marker. You are A-Okay, my love. What a relief. Now you are a woman again, Fel."

Fel grinned, "I know, but it took me by surprise, and I was in a quandary about whether or not to allow them to do it. It happened so fast I never did really get to think about it. I hope you like them." A passionate hug answered that one. "I brought back one of their elegant fashion outfits for you too, but I think it'll have to wait until after our child is born, padrona."

"Okay, let's see the outfits."

As soon as Celestina returned and was debriefed by Simon, the five hovered around her, dying to hear all about her great adventure. She was only too eager to tell them and did so very proudly. Then, she had her gifts of the fancy fashions brought in for her five sisters. First, she had Sally help her into hers. As soon as she paraded around their suite, her sisters just had to try on theirs as well. All six were positively enchanted with the exotic outfits. They felt very sexy while wearing them, but were wholly dependent on others since they lost the use of their feet.

Before long, all the women of the tower got to see the incredible outfits and wanted some of their own. It was at this point that Cassia finally figured out the down side to these "gifts" from the aliens. With Fel at her side, Cassia brought it to Simon's attention, but he had already seen the effect.

"Look, while there is absolutely no overt danger with these elegant fashions, one can view this as a diabolical or insidious trap for the tower people," Cassia began.

"How so?" Simon asked. *Will she see what I'm seeing?*

"The women are so elegant and attractive in them that everywhere they go they create significant arousals in men. Likewise, when the men wear their fancy suits, the women who see them also get aroused sexually. In a telepathic society, such as we have here, that is going to cause some problems, since the nerve channels that our psi energies use also drive the sexual lines. Plus, each of us knows acutely when we have aroused another, and it pains us to feel their arousal and frustrations in their inability to express it and their actions to suppress those feelings. As I understand my training, a telepath should never arouse another unless he or she is prepared to satisfy that need in the other person, right?"

Simon grinned, "My, for an alien, you learn quickly, Cassia. Yes, this is precisely the effect I am now seeing. The question is what do we do about it? My wife will have my head if I don't permit her to obtain at least one of these outfits, and she's ordered me to get one of those suits as well. Yet, if we all start wearing these, sexual arousals will occur everywhere and frustrations will result. Our overall efficiency will plummet, to say nothing of more sexual encounters."

"I have an idea, Venerado. Why not allow those who want them to acquire them, but restrict the wearing of these elegant outfits to parties, dances, and festival times?" Cassia suggested. Simon bought that idea as it handled the situation completely. He allowed the orders to be sent off to the Elegant Fashions Inc. However, he also issued strict orders on when the outfits could be worn, especially by the women, much to the disappointment of Celestina and her sisters, who now wanted to wear them all the time.

A few days after they returned, Celestina got her requested private time with her Aunt Fel. "First, I want to thank you for allowing me to have my adventure. You don't know how much that has opened my eyes to the world."

Fel smiled, "Oh yes, I do. You've gone from being a seventeen year old girl to a young woman who knows how to handle herself and others in tight situations. I was very proud of the way you handled yourself, Celestina, very proud." The teen beamed.

"But. Oh where do I begin? Aunt Fel, I feel horrible and I can't talk about this to mom, only to you 'cause you understand me." She was near tears and Fel had not a clue or did she?

"Is this about Gabe?" she prodded.

"Yes. No. I mean you know I am utterly terrified I will have armless babies just like me! Everyone looks at us as if we are freaks or else helpless cripples. And now I know we really are horribly handicapped. Around here, our tower, the adults, Simon, they have made it seem like we can do anything — you know, door slats instead of knobs, low tables so we can more readily use our feet to eat, low kitchens, that sort of thing. But Aunt Fel, in the real world out there, we are helpless invalids. All the way back from way down south, I was totally dependent on Gabe and you for everything. I couldn't even go to the bathroom without one of you helping me out of the heavy clothes. We really are helpless cripples and I hate it. I can't have my children being like us; it's too horrible to wish on anyone, let alone my own babies, Aunt Fel."

Shit! I knew this was coming. She's facing what I went through! My answer: join the Sisterhood and never bed a man, not ever! Damn, what do I tell her? Truth, Fel, truth. You of all people owe her that much. She sighed and began, "Celestina, I had to face this very thing you are facing when I was about your age. Simon and my folks wanted to marry me off like my brother and sister to have more like you and my other nieces. I felt the same way as you do. Remember, I looked after all six of you for years and my heart went out to all of you. I swore I would never, ever have children like you six. I don't mean to make less of you or my nieces, Celestina, but I saw the horrible lives you were facing and just could not be a part of bringing more like you into the world. That's one reason why I abandoned the towers and everyone, joining the

Sisterhood. I swore I would never, ever bed a man, that I would never, ever bear a child from my womb. That was my solution, and I am praying Cassia's and my child will be normal. Cassia believes that will be the case since she is of alien blood. God, I hope she's right."

"But I can't join the Sisterhood, can I or my sisters? I mean we are so dependent."

"No, probably not, but if you asked them, they would likely consider admitting you." Fel at least didn't want to close that door. She was fairly certain the Sisterhood would make allowances if needed. "But honey, this isn't the whole problem, is it?"

Celestina slumped, her long hair falling over her shoulders. She tossed her head back, as she usually did. "No," she sighed deeply. "No, it isn't Aunt Fel. It's Gabe. I am madly in love with him and I know he is crazy about me. I can't tell you how hard I had to suppress my urges to kiss him and force him into bed with me. I want him to hold me and make love to me so badly I can hardly sleep at night without dreaming of doing that with him. I have to use my crystal's energies nearly all the time now to help me keep from broadcasting it to everyone around here. It's driving me nuts. Yet, how can I do this? They will certainly want to tell me whom I can bed and bear their child. I don't want to bear more children like me. Yet, I want to marry Gabe and give him our children, but I don't dare do that 'cause I don't want to make more like me. Oh, Aunt Fel, I am going totally insane, completely mad. What do I do? Is there no hope for me? My sexual urges are overwhelming me. Should I try to only express them to another woman because that's safe at least, like you and Cassia?"

As close as her nieces were to each other, Fel knew instinctively she was not just answering Celestina, the oldest, but all six of them. Evita was already hanging around Jake at every opportunity, even flirting with him a little, and he, her. Carmela was sixteen and Doncia and Gracia were fifteen now and all three looking at every boy in the tower, plainly envious of Celestina and Evita. Even Elena was thirteen and had become a woman while she was gone. How should she answer her niece?

"I'll be damned if I give you Simon's reply or your parent's answer or even the tower's notions, Celestina. I love you and your sisters too much to echo those answers. My life has been a very hard one I wouldn't wish on anyone. Everywhere I go, most hate and despise the Sisterhood and thus me. I don't think abandoning everything and joining the Sisterhood is the right answer for you and your sisters, Celestina. It may have been for me, but not for you six. Look, you six simply have to stop thinking of yourselves as freaks, as handicapped victims. That's self-defeating and will destroy any chance you have of ever being satisfied and happy. Yes, there can be no denying you have handicaps and that you need help from others when situations arise, as you did while we were traveling, but just accept them. Look, every one of us needs some kind of help and assistance at times too. No one is wholly independent; we are all dependent upon the help from others."

"My best advice is be true to your own self. Never, ever compromise with your own beliefs. That will destroy you faster than anything else. You love Gabe and Gabe loves you. That is what is; that is your reality. For heaven's sake don't deny it or ignore it or pretend it isn't that way. Don't withhold your feelings about him from him. Express them fully and see if he really loves you in turn. He might not and then again, he might."

"But what if he does? Then what? Oh, I think I get it. He's not of any of our so-called bloodlines, so we might have normal children, like you and Cassia?"

"I cannot promise you won't, but I can say you will love them all the same, just as I love you nieces."

"Your love for us is ten times that of our parents, you know that, don't you Aunt Fel? But wait! Simon and our parents will never allow us to marry someone not of their choosing. We're doomed! Wait! We can run away!"

"Think about that a second, Celestina. Running away might not be the best thing for you to do. Look at how dependent you are on having things around you set up for your special needs and how awkward it was for you on the trip. Before you think about running away, let me talk to Simon about Gabe and you. Let me try first, but you two had better see if this is what you both want."

"Okay Aunt Fel! I'll talk to him tonight after supper when we usually spend time together. They are keeping him really busy during the day working on his flying machines. Thank you, thank you." She jumped up and down, having no other way to express her happiness with what Fel suggested. Fel put her arms around her and pulled her close to her.

"Simon, yes, I know Gabe Jeffery is a total nobody in terms of your bloodlines here at Brom Tower," Fel pointed out. The two had met and Celestina told her Gabe was madly in love with her too and but could see no way they'd be allowed to marry. As she had promised, she met with Simon, explaining the young lovers to him. He reacted much as she'd anticipated, though he was containing his initial outrage response. She went on, "Look, do you truly know how these six really feel about themselves and their lives? All of them are absolutely terrified about bringing others as handicapped as themselves into this world. If you are not careful with them, you could well force them over the edge into insanity. I would not discount the possibility they would rather commit suicide than be *forced* to bear more children like themselves, Simon. That does them and you and everyone else no good at all."

"You think that is likely? That they would rather die?" Simon asked, rather startled. Fel realized he'd not thought about that possibility seriously, though she had the sense he'd perhaps considered it.

"More and more likely, especially if you breed them to men who are highly likely to continue those gene lines. Yes, I do, sir. On the other hand, if you allow them to marry someone who they love and who loves them in turn, they will willingly bear children, especially so if their husband is not of the known gene pool that gave rise to them. Besides, sir, look at where all your intensive inbreeding has gotten you. Mom has had four miscarriages and one who died shortly after birth. So many feeble children result now. Look at my own mom and dad. I'm twice as strong as dad, and I have had to work out hard all my life to be this fit. I am no longer one of your tower personnel, but I can see the results as clearly as anyone can.

You need to introduce outside bloodlines with my nieces. I don't know this alone will prevent their children from inheriting the katalyein gift or not nor do I know if their children will be like them physically. But I do know my nieces will at least take a gamble their children will be born with arms and have them willingly."

"So I am given a choice by an outsider," Simon pulled on his chin, but grinned at Fel. "I have long known our inbreeding is producing less than desirable side-effects, and you are right, we must inject a new bloodline or face an even worse situation. But are you sure they will consent to bearing children? Are all six of the same mind?"

"As to that second question, Simon, have someone bind your arms behind your back and then see how you manage life for a couple days like that. You'll soon have your own answer to that one. As for the first one, I can only say by allowing them to marry solely for love you stand the best chance they will agree to bear children. Force a marriage on them and you will risk them going insane or committing suicide or running away, though just between you and me, I doubt the Sisterhood would accept them. They need too much individual assistance with daily living. Still, they could abandon the tower or even go mad."

"Well, this Gabe fellow, he seems an okay fellow, quite the inventor, and his flying machines show great promise. She could do far worse. I will give my consent to them myself, Fel. If I have learned one thing this past fall and winter, it's I have been far too overly protective of the six. I've kept them like birds in a cage. Celestina's adventure with you has taught me that they are not utterly dependent, helpless women. I do hope she was not a heavy burden for you."

"No, she saved our butts several times. Yes, she has her own difficulties and likewise, she has her own gifts and abilities and skills. Allow her and her sisters to flourish and prosper and time will tell. Besides, do you really need six katalyein gifts at one time?"

Simon chuckled at her jest. "No, indeed we don't, but remember, Fel, we went for nearly a century without even one. I would hate to lose all of them when these six grow old and die, as we all must."

"True, Simon, true. Yet, perhaps their gifts will not die out, perhaps one of their children will have it. Children born out of love may well have such gifts." She didn't know if there was any basis for such an idea, but it sounded like a good, constructive thing to say to him.

The next afternoon, Gabe and Celestina came to Fel's room. Both were radiant. "Aunt Fel, you did it! Simon has agreed to let us marry! It will be in the spring, and I am going to order a white elegant gown from Elegant Fashions Inc. I want you to be my maid of honor. Please say yes, but of course, you will have to wear your fancy new dress as well. I'll get you a white one too. Aunt Fel, you have saved me and the rest of us. I and Gabe — we owe you our lives!" She chatted on excitedly and finally Fel was able to get in a word, agreeing to be her maid of honor.

Celestina added, "Plus, Evita is quite smitten with Jake. So maybe there is something with them too. Oh, I am so happy I could cry and I owe it all to you!"

Before long, they dashed off to work out their orders for Elegant Fashions Inc. Fel looked at Cassia and asked, "I wonder if I did the right thing? Will she curse me if she has armless children after all?"

"You did what is right, my love. That is why I married you. You always do what is right, no matter what others think or say or do. Come here; let's snuggle and you can feel her moving about again. What are we going to name her anyway? We can't use Rigel-3 names," Cassia replied.

"How about Angelica? Coming from us, she can only be an angel," Fel teased her padrona. When Cassia had their baby girl in late July, that became her name, Angelica Evita e Kaylee. As expected, the six nieces rejoiced, and Celestina held out great hope her children would be similar to Fel's. Their inherited genes didn't have to produce more armless children after all.

Part II Mass Destruction

Chapter 14 Countermoves

Venerado Augusto paced his private study. Things had changed, changed for the worst. Just as he made his big breakthrough with the aliens, all the other towers were ganging up against him and the aliens. *How dare they dictate to us, to me? We are stronger and more powerful than any one of them. I'll be damned if I'll let them stop me! May old Brom rot in his grave! It's all his insane division of land that's behind this. Once I have the combined strength of Portillo and Duero Towers behind me, I'll have enough power to stop the others. They'll see. I'll show them how it's done! The fools. This is our big breakthrough, a chance to get our hands on alien technology. I'm not going to let this golden opportunity slip away because of some frightened Amo's!*

A voice appeared in his mind. *It doesn't have to. Have your Círculo de mentes search here. Build a tower in Exchange City to protect the alien spaceport from the other towers.*

Who are you? Why are you telling me this? Yes, I like that tower idea, that's brilliant.

The voice was gone. Augusto found no trace of it. Rapidly, he checked over the crystal networks in the walls of his study. All were operational; no way could anyone have reached him telepathically though his barrier network. Yet, what other explanation could account for that voice in his head? He discretely opened his door. No one was outside. He glanced out of his window. Nothing there either. How utterly strange, he thought. Still the two ideas seemed positively brilliant. *I'll do it.*

A half hour later, his eldest son, Capo Armando entered his study. He was annoyed with the untimely interruption of his work. "I hope this is really important. You stopped my entire circle's work, you realize that? Couldn't this wait until our shift was over?"

"Sit down, son. Sit down! This is vastly more important than stone quarrying, vastly. I have a very special and critical assignment for your circle, son. I want you to take your circle on a little field trip to a precise spot about fifty miles north of here. Once in position, use your skills to open up a small tunnel to this precise cavern some five hundred feet into the bedrock. I'll show you the spot and what you will find there." He slipped into rapport with Armando and showed him the image of the cavern and precisely what he would find when he entered it.

"My god, dad! Are those what I think they are?" gasped a shocked Armando.

"Yes, eight new germanium crystals for our new network. Each is six inches around. The power of that new network will exceed three of our *Círculo de mentes* working in consort with each other! Take a hundred soldiers with you and whatever support personnel you will need, but get us those crystals! And get them soon! I know it's the dead of winter and the snows will be heavy, but there is no time to lose on this one, son. Make it happen," Augusto ordered sternly, overcoming his son's next unspoken objection. It was winter and travel in the high foothills was more than challenging, it was downright dangerous.

"Aye sir. Can I ask, how did you discover this, dad? This is the find of the century, right here in our own backyard!" an enthusiastic Armando asked and said.

Augusto smiled. *I'm not about to answer that one. Hell, I don't know how I discovered it.* "Consider it the skill of your Venerado, son. Now get going. We need that new network of crystals up and operational as soon as possible. Lord knows how soon the other towers might strike against us."

His son frowned, "Surely not in the winter, dad. Surely they will wait until spring. You can't march an army forth in this kind of weather."

"True, but they could well strike at the spring thaw, and we need to be ready for that strike. Make it happen son, I'm counting on you. Now leave me and make your plans. I need to talk with the alien leader." Armando bowed and left, his mind swimming with the potentials those giant crystals would have, immense power, mind boggling.

Augusto picked up the alien Communicator, but put it

285

down. He sensed his daughter Carmen was reaching out for him. *Dad. Carmen here. It's finally worked. Karolina has just come down with Verge Sickness and I have her under my care now. This spring, both Jarek and Karolina will need to come to Valen for training. I think the Lech will be contacting you about his wife's miraculous change soon. I've been monitoring him and he doesn't quite know what to make about the threat that you and he received from Venerado Simon Bolivar of Brom Tower. He is in fear of the unknown and doesn't quite know what to believe. Can he do what he threatened or not? Lech just doesn't know.*

Excellent, dear Carmen, excellent work. Actually, positively brilliant, my daughter. And how is your fashions company project working out?

She smiled, thinking, *My daughter? Dad has never called me that yet. He must really be pleased with my work!* She replied, *Excellent, we've made the initial out thrust into Brom Tower personnel to their six katalyein women no less!*

Good, impressive, my daughter. Keep up the good work. Oh, Lech is trying to get a hold of me now. More later. He broke their telepathic link and fiddled with the alien Communicator. "Hello. Augusto Valen here."

"Hello Augusto. I have some incredible news. You'll never guess what has just happened to my beautiful wife, Karolina! She's developed your *mentales* gift! Yes, thank god your daughter Carmen is here with us! Karolina has what your people call the Verge Sickness, something our medical staff knows nothing about. Carmen says Karolina will be fine in a few days, thank heavens! Once more, Augusto, I am deeply in your debt," Lech said rather excited. Augusto also picked up his unspoken thought: *Now I have to ask him to train her too, but how? That threat we received scares me. Does she really need to be trained?*

Augusto decided to address the alien's unspoken fears; it would gain him even more of an edge with the alien. "Oh, that is indeed incredibly good news! Wonderful, Lech. Wait until you take her to bed. Now then, that also means she should be trained along with Jarek this spring. An untrained telepath is both a danger to others around her and also to herself. Imagine, Lech, you are in a crowd of a hundred people and you are hearing simultaneously the one hundred people's thoughts — maddening to say the very least. So you just send her along this spring, and we'll see she gets the best training and also her own amplifying crystal, which will magnify her abilities and skills a hundredfold. I'm sure you will want her to have that power, right?"

"Oh yes, very much so! Augusto, that would be fantastic. I never imagined how considerate, kind, and wise you and your people actually are. I am deeply in your debt! Yet, that warning from the Brom fellow, frankly, that has me rather frightened. Can he really do things like that? Destroy our spaceships? You realized if they do that, the Imperium will make deadly counterstrikes, perhaps wiping all of them out? I'm sure they would use Nuclears on them." He realized Augusto had no idea of just how devastating Nuclears could be.

"I am taking positive steps to safeguard both Valen and your spaceport even as we speak, Lech. Now another key step would be for us to build one of our tower-castles there in Exchange City, where we would be close enough to provide quality protection for your installation, should these renegade towers try something. Plus, you always have that Ace up your sleeve: the magnitude of the Imperium counterstrike."

Of course, he had the counterstrike threat, but if he had to use that, he'd be in for far more "explaining" than he cared even to imagine. The idea of one of their towers close at hand where he could monitor their actions and capabilities would be a fantastic and unexpected godsend. Yet, the sheer magnitude of its construction held him back. "What? Build one of your towers there? Can it be done? Won't the other towers object? Won't it take decades to build? You have none of our massive construction machines," Lech asked. The idea of having a tower of telepaths close at hand to protect the base sounded like a terrific move, but in his mind, these primitives would need a decade to build one of those enormous stone complexes with its tall tower.

"Our circles can build it rapidly, but we'll need to get those personnel to Exchange City rapidly. The real problem is

Haverhills owns the land there. We'll never be able to get them to hand over some land on which to build it," Augusto pointed out the major stumbling block to the new idea that had appeared magically in his mind from the unknown voice.

Lech thought for a moment, Augusto had raised a very serious point. "Augusto, I think I have an idea of how we can get around that barrier. Give me a day or so to check out my idea and I'll get back to you. Having a tower in Exchange City is too good an idea to not implement." After a chatting for a few minutes, Lech ended the call and turned to his computer once more.

He brought up the plans for the square spaceport here on Plateau Grado, each side was precisely twenty-five miles long. He focused in on the extreme southeastern corner where their concrete roadway lay as it entered the outer edges of Exchange City, whose western outskirts now abutted the port-side barrier walls themselves. Nothing was there save a small building that housed some of their snow removal machinery. Well that can be moved easily, he thought, and checked the plans for underground utilities. None, save the security barrier that also could easily be moved. Lech smiled, "Perfect. It is adjacent to our HQ building in Exchange City as well, doubly ideal! Now to draw up an unbreakable lease."

The final lease agreement ceded a tiny square of land at the extreme southeastern corner of the alien's square to Valen Tower, three hundred feet on a side, sufficient for a small castle outer wall, a tower, and a manor house with stables. The lease expired on the same date as the alien lease for the spaceport. Based upon the unexpected changes in Jarek and Karolina, the lease required the tower train and provide crystals for any new *mentales* gifted that the aliens had, but only as a result of their being on Ashford-5. Augusto insisted on that reservation; he refused to train aliens who had telepathy and were from other planets in the first place. Of course, Lech quickly agreed to this minor stipulation, figuring that if two suddenly developed it, why, more were sure to follow. As per the usual agreements, the tower would be responsible for its own security within its walls and not subject to Imperium laws. Augusto had to agree to an additional provision requested by both Carmen and Karolina, namely that the dress code for all personnel who stayed in this new tower must be wearing elegant fashions approved by Elegant Fashions Inc. Augusto saw this as a way for his foster daughter's new business to expand, but Lech had an entirely different idea in mind.

To speed things along, Lech ordered the land be prepared for the initial construction, which amounted to snow removal and some minor grading of the bedrock there, making it perfectly flat. It was ready to for Augusto on the first of February 1132.

By April, Armando's group had recovered the huge crystals, brought them back to Valen, and had them fully operational. His circle and an architect arrived in Exchange City and began their work on the construction of the new tower. Four hundred soldiers and support personnel were with them. Augusto took no chances with them.

April also saw Luisa Mundo and her circle finally succeed in air car construction. She was now nineteen and a qualified network technician in her own right. Her twin brother Diego was similarly employed in the armaments fabrications circle, the AFC group as they were called. The evening of the fourth, Augusto held a large celebration for the air car construction circle, honoring them for their great achievement, brought about by Luisa's invention of the thin-shell skin, which so drastically lowered the car's weight that one man aided by the internal crystal network of the car could fly it easily for several hours and carry the equivalent of four passengers.

The night before, Carmen, Karolina, and Jarek had been brought to Valen Tower around midnight using one of these new air cars, much to the three's delight in being part of the first official use of the new invention. Naturally, the two women and Jarek wore their finest fashions to the celebration, attracting the attention of nearly everyone who saw them.

Jarek escorting Carmen and Venerado Augusto escorting Karolina entered the Great Hall where all the various circle members had gathered for the celebration, along with other key *mentales* gifted personnel. The trumpet fanfare ended the numerous conversations, and all eyes turned to the four as they entered the spacious room. Augusto made a brief speech. "Tonight, we celebrate the incredible achievements of our air car circle, whose dedication and labors have at long last given us our own means of air travel. One was used to bring my daughter and her husband here this evening, our first public use of this fantastic invention. As a reward for their stellar achievements, my daughter wishes me to tell you that her Elegant Fashions Inc will be providing all members of that circle with a complimentary set of their elegant fashions, similar to the ones they are wearing tonight." He chuckled, "I'm told I too will get one of these fine suits on the morrow." He seemed pleased with this and went on.

"This achievement means at long last Valen Tower is finally ready to take over its rightful role as ruler of all the Westerlings just as Adelmira Tower controls all the Easterlings. Tomorrow, we set foot on that path, but tonight, let us rejoice, celebrate, and extol the virtues of our air car circle. Let the festivities begin!" Cheers and clapping wrapped up his short speech, though many wondered what he meant by the tower being ready — ready for what exactly? Many would find out in the morning.

Diego took his sister onto the dance floor for the first dance. "Well, sis, this sure beats herding sheep at dad's ranch! You have done incredibly well, sis. I can't believe Augusto is giving you and your circle such a party."

"Well, we earned it, Diego. I got burned several times before I got it all worked out. Now we can fly to Benito at nearly a hundred miles an hour, two days travel for the three thousand miles. Think of the benefits that will have! If we can make them bigger and stronger, why, even dad could use one to take our sheep to Benito and sell them for twice the amount he gets for them. Plus, the people who get injured on our coast can be brought here to be healed in two days or we could send a healer there as fast. Think of all the good this will bring to our people."

"Yes, that's true, sis, but it can also be very helpful if we have to fight a battle. Say, you will look really good in one of those fancy dresses like Augusto's foster daughter is wearing. She looks really hot." Luisa sensed his arousal and soon sensed many men were getting rather aroused over the two elegantly dressed women, who were upstaging her circle members. The dance ended and she walked over to her fellow circle member, Macarena, who was stuffing her mouth with the sweet pastries at the refreshments table. Network work burned up calories like mad, but Macarena loved to eat anyway. She had already actually gained some twenty pounds since Luisa first met her last year.

"These are good," she said, mumbling slightly with her mouth full. "Have one or two or three, Luisa."

She mechanically picked up one and bit into it, sweetness flooded her taste buds. "Have you seen how the men are reacting to Carmen's dress? Karolina's too, and she's an alien!"

"How can I not? Well, we are supposed to get some like theirs, but I don't know if I want to be rousing all the men that are near me. Aren't we supposed then to satisfy their urges and needs we bring on? Are they trying to make us a pack of whores? No thanks. I'll stand here and eat these fine pastries. Have another, Luisa, they are really good. We sure don't get these very often, so make the best of them."

Luisa laughed and bit into a second one, when Carmen and Jarek slithered over to her. Well, that was her description for the slinky way Carmen walked in her heels. "Luisa, we just wanted to express our thanks for all your invaluable invention and work on these new air cars. We rode here tonight in one and it is absolutely amazing. Tomorrow, someone will drop by and get your measurements, and I'll see you get a fabulous outfit soon. The men sure do appreciate us looking our very best."

"Thanks, Ama Carmen, Amo Jarek," she replied, unable to think of much else to actually say. The two moved off heading towards another key member of their group, rather ignoring Macarena, who didn't mind that at all. Both teens preferred their plain tartan skirts. At least they didn't rouse the men they encountered.

Two days later, both the armaments fabrications circle

and the air car construction circle received new orders. "Pack you your things; we are off to join the army that is assaulting Puerto Tower," Luisa's Capo, Alberto addressed his circle of ten other members.

"But we aren't fighters; we're inventors," Macarena protested.

"We are to provide *mentales* support for our brave troops. We won't be actually fighting, I think. Come on. It's an order. Pack up what can fit into a pair of saddlebags. We leave in an hour," insisted the tall, thin lad who was only a year older than Luisa.

Although they grumbled, they obeyed. Macarena and Luisa returned to their room and began stuffing clothes into their bags. Luisa unfolded her mother's Sisterhood horse head earrings once more and gazed lovingly at them, the only thing she had of her mother's. She folded them back up and stuck them into the pack, along with the small knife her father had given her. "I never signed on to fight a stupid war," Macarena complained.

"Me either, but we can't back out right now I don't think. Bet you are glad you devoured all those pastries. We aren't likely to see more of them for a long time," Luisa teased her friend. Macarena laughed and the two headed outside to the staging area.

They were pleased to see Amo Enrico Valen, Augusto's younger son, would be leading them and controlling the army. When the several dozen finally filed out into the courtyard, Enrico addressed them all. "The army has been sent on ahead of us and we'll be riding hard to catch up with them. They number five thousand strong, but of course, they will need our aid handling the enemy lines, fortress, and their tower personnel. Now let's ride!" He finished his pep talk and neck reined his horse towards the western gate. Luisa mounted up, straightening out her tartan skirt she wore over her leather pants and soft leather boots. She pulled her horse in beside that of Macarena and they were off.

She glanced over at her brother. Diego rode tall in his saddle, pleased and proud to be riding out to take part in the conquest of Portillo Tower. Men, she thought.

292

Thirty days passed. Spring had come to these highlands. New life sprang up all around them, making the long days thoroughly enjoyable for Luisa, though the passing of such a large army trampled much of the new growth, turning it into mud. Still she enjoyed the fresh air, the smell of the grass she'd missed so much since being taken from her father's ranch and cooped up in the tower at Valen. She longed to be free to ride the hills, free from the cursed *mentales* gifts she had. Macarena also began to break free of her doldrums as well. In spite of the rough living conditions, she was more cheerful than usual.

At night, they pitched a small tent, handed to them from their supply wagon. Each circle had their own wagon that carried their bedding and food supplies. Before long, Luisa saw they were eating far better than the soldiers and asked her Capo about that. "Look, they are mere soldiers, used to tough conditions. They are depending upon you with your gifts to help them win the battle, and we need our calories to offset the drain that our psi powers take on our bodies. You know that." Well, she did, but still she thought it was unfair that she ate well while the thousands of young men didn't.

Always at night, the circle members camped behind the hundreds of soldier's tents. A dozen Sisterhood fighters, who had been requested to partake of this battle by Augusto, camped next to them. Her Capo explained it would be best if these women fighters were separated from the men. Fewer troubles and fights. Luisa could not help but covertly keep a curious eye on them whenever she could. After all, her mother had been one of them. She longed to go over there and chat with the women, but protocols had to be obeyed. Her Capo had issued strict orders for the circle members to stay clear of "those women," as he put it rather sarcastically. Again, she wondered why he had such an ill opinion of the women. After all, they were here to fight just as much as the thousands of men. To their credit, the Sisterhood fighters also kept to themselves as well, but several did notice Luisa watching them from time to time. Once, one even waved at her, causing her to flush.

The 5ᵗʰ of May 1132, the assault on Portillo Tower began just after dawn. Five thousand soldiers of Valen faced off against around three thousand from these northern realms. An impoverished zone, the town of Portillo held barely five thousand, cradled in the high foothills, rocky terrain at best. The tower sat on the highest point rising a hundred feet into the slightly cloudy morning sky. The connected manor house was secure within the ten foot tall stone wall around the tower complex. A smaller secondary wall some seven feet tall surrounded the town. Portillo's thousands were distributed equally within the tower walls, the town walls, and on the ridge line just south of the town, from where they could see the advancing lines of Valen's troops. All two of Portillo's circles were now standing on the roof and balconies of the tower, ready to cast their psi energies against the invaders. They reasonably expected to be able to withstand the siege, since Valen's army would have to smash their way through the town's walls first and after that, the tower's defensive walls.

As Valen's lines formed up, Enrico dropped back to issue orders to the two circles. "All right! Now you're talking," exclaimed an excited Diego. He'd just been ordered to take his circle up in the four air cars that were loaded with both fire bombs and acid bombs. The order: soften them up and punch a hole in the two gates and drop a load on the tower proper.

Luisa's circle was ordered to do what damage they could to the front ranks of the enemy soldiers and to be prepared to re-load the air cars when they returned from dropping their loads. "The Sisterhood fighters are ordered to stay close to you and provide protection for the two circles," Enrico explained. "You can depend upon them for your safety."

As Diego took off in his air car, the one Luisa had built herself, he sent, *Join with me and watch the action. Bird's eye view, sis.*

Luisa was emotionally shocked. Her precious invention, her laboring work was not being used as she had assumed or planned or desired, but was being used as a tool of war! *Can't, got to follow Enrico's orders,* she sent. *Damn them for perverting my invention!*

The air cars swooped and began dropping fire bombs

on the town along with some acid bombs. However, the acid bombs were being concentrated on four main targets: the front line of troops, the town's gates, the tower's gates, and the roof and balconies of the tower proper. Hideous screams filled the air, so much so that Luisa simply could not focus to use her own gifts. Suddenly from great catapults within both the town and the tower courtyard, acid bombs and fire bombs flew out at the attackers, detonating in loud explosions. Now the screams of Valen's men added to the hideous noise.

Before long, the entire town was ablaze and the surviving troops charged into the town, while the air cars landed to reload. Luisa mechanically went through the motions of carrying bombs from the large wagons to the flying machines she'd made or helped make. Smoke was thick now, her face, blackened from the soot. Breathing was difficult; acid fumes cut into her lungs. At last, the enemy artillery finally found their range. Bombs landed near her, knocking Luisa to the ground, momentarily stunning her.

That cost her dearly as in that instant, her mental barriers fell, and Luisa became suddenly open to and aware of all the others who still lived. The pain, the anguish, the terror, swamped her senses utterly until she thought she'd gone utterly mad. She covered her ears with both hands, trying to shut out the deafening horrors of the war going on around her. She could not. Her friend Macarena tried to pull her up and finally got Luisa back on her feet, just as a pudgy Sisterhood woman came running up to them intent on helping the two.

Just then, another artillery shell found its mark. An acid bomb exploded near the three. Suddenly, Luisa's hearing failed. Utter silence from her ears, but the terror, screams, and excruciating pain of others' minds still swamped her. That plus something new — she felt a hideous, sharp burning pain flowing down her right arm and the side of her face, a pain that escalated, and she herself let out a blood curling scream, though she heard it not. Hands rolled her over, only adding to the unbearable pain. The Sisterhood woman was trying to get her up again, pulling hard on her left arm. As she rose, she saw the face of Macarena dissolving from the acid, her flesh flowing down both sides of what had been her face, revealing only the bones of the front of her skull. Dimly she realized her sole real friend at the tower was dead.

The Sisterhood woman kept pulling her and for a brief moment, she stumbled blindly after her. The smoke and acrid fumes were too much and she collapsed again, her face and right arm throbbing in excruciating pain, her mind flooded with the horrors of so many others who were injured or dying. At last, beyond overwhelmed, Luisa lost all consciousness.

The Sisterhood cook, who was dragging Luisa away from the acid bath, which was eating into the very stone beneath the bodies that it was easily dissolving, looked over at her fellow sisters, but saw none. They'd taken part of that last hit as well. The acid was eating through her own boots and she knew she had to do something. Luisa's flesh was slowly bubbling and dissolving right before her eyes. Marla bent over and picked up the light-weight teen and began running through the chaos, smoke, and acrid fumes.

She knew the headwaters of the great Brozas River began here in Portillo and she wisely headed for the stream. It took her some time to get around the rear of the army, but at last, she saw the filthy waters and made for them, her own feet now raw and burning; the bottoms of her boots had vanished. She dove into the waters, bringing Luisa with her. The still bitterly cold waters stung her feet, but she held onto the unconscious woman, held her in a vice grip. Then she too lost consciousness.

It was dark when Marla regained consciousness. She was stuck up against some deadwood that had fallen into the creek. Her left hand was severely cramped and slowly she looked at it only to see somehow she still held onto the unconscious Luisa. Shivering like mad, she struggled mightily to get herself out of the freezing waters, dragging Luisa out as well. Sitting, she felt for a pulse and found Luisa still lived. Her right arm looked horrid, as did the side of the woman's face, but she lived. Marla also knew she had to get them both warm and dried off soon or neither would see the dawn of another day.

Where was she? Marla looked around for help and saw none. They had drifted several miles downstream from the battlefield. It was late afternoon and she estimated they had not been in the waters for more than a few minutes at most. She tried to stand, but her feet throbbed and she gave that up. Crawling, she moved up the bank in search of anything useful. At last, she found a small grove of thick, resinous pines and smiled. She'd lived in a remote part of the foothills most of her life and knew how to survive. Quickly, she found some sticks and began rubbing them together. Soon, it smoldered. Now she added some of the highly flammable resin and presto, her fire began. She added what dead wood she could find and then crawled back to where Luisa lay. With a great effort she dragged the small woman back to the shelter of her small fire.

Inside the crumbling tower, someone raised a white flag and Enrico called a halt to the battle. Valen Tower had won the day, Portillo Tower was theirs, but with a cost. Diego hovered his air car over their staging base, and used what little psi energies he had remaining to help the others in his circle push the still acrid fumes and smoke out of their zone and then landed. Everywhere he looked, he saw unrecognizable bodies, faces eaten away from the acid or burned by the hot fires. Their entire supporting circle was gone. Stunned, Diego went from corpse to corpse looking for Luisa. He no longer had any psi energies left even to send her a telepathic message. How long he looked, he could not afterwards say.

Late afternoon, Enrico came up to his stunned and exhausted circle and said, "Head over to that wagon, get some food and sleep. We have lost the entire circle here and all the Sisterhood contingent, but we won the battle. Well done, we could not have done it without your fine aerial support, now go eat and sleep." Mechanically, Diego complied, along with his other ten circle members, all too exhausted to do otherwise. Luisa is gone, his mind said, but he was too numb to register it just now.

Later, Enrico reported back to Augusto. *We captured a dozen tower members and have their pledge to work for us now. Their tower is destroyed; the acid is eating it away and parts have collapsed. The town really is nothing but a shell of buildings. We've captured about five hundred of their soldiers* who are not hurt, but there are well over a thousand of their soldiers who have taken grievous wounds. The acid and fires have eaten through flesh and bones. What should we do with them, dad?

Show me what they look like, son, Augusto sent. Dutifully, Enrico's eyes made another pass over the rows of soldiers lying on the ground, a few who were still conscious moaning in pain. Kill them mercifully. They can't live like men any longer. How about our casualties, son? How did the air cars work out?

Saved us. Air cars turned the tide and greatly minimized our losses. We've lost five hundred men with almost that many wounded by acid and fires from Portillo's catapults. Put ours out of their suffering too, dad?

Yes, that's best. We can't have limbless men clogging up out towns and villages. Bad public relations. Mercy killings for all those who cannot be expected to reasonably recover.

Okay. We lost the entire Sisterhood group and one whole circle. The enemy scored a direct hit on them with some acid bombs.

Dear god! Which circle?

The inventors group, not the skilled flyers. They are all uninjured, dad.

Good. Clean up the mess and get the army back here as soon as possible. Duero Tower is next. We must strike them soon before other towers make any attempts to stop us. We'll have the surviving Portillo members replace the lost inventor's circle. Good job, son.

You got it.

Augusto broke the connection. "Well, we've won. Portillo Tower is gone; we control the north now," he announced to the gathered crowd. "Someone spread the word to all the others. Now then, Jarek, tell me about this word I've heard but don't know what it means."

"Congratulations on your victory sir. What word?" Jarek asked, looking pleased. He certainly had picked the winning side this time.

"Nuclear. What does that mean? Really big bomb?"

Jarek grinned, "Well sir, that's one way of looking at it." He knew there were no heavy metals on this entire plant, so there was no danger in his revealing thermal nuclear reactions to the native leader.

Enrico gave the orders to one of his platoons of uninjured soldiers and they set about their mercy killings with some gusto. Already the many wounded had been lined up alongside the fast flowing creek bank, where some had been using the waters to wash off some of the lingering and still active acid. Hernando Polito had been a corporal in the Portillo army. Now he lay moaning on the bank of the creek. His right leg throbbed and ached, what little was left of it. Already he'd seen his lower leg's skeletal bones drop away from his knee when someone dragged him up to the bank where he now lay, quite uncomfortably with his full pack still fastened to his back.

He rolled his head to the right; he heard voices. Was someone coming to provide medical attention? His dulled mind saw enemy soldiers thrusting their swords into the fallen men's chests and then dragging their bodies away, tossing them like sacks of potatoes or flower into waiting wagons! He gagged. He was not dead, not yet. Carefully, he looked around. So many were already missing limbs or had some that barely looked like arms or legs. Hernando made a decision. *Live, damn it!*

He slowly eased his body down into the freezing creek waters, ignoring the sudden shock of the icy waters. He felt his body floating and then begin drifting down the creek. Pain flooded over him from his right upper leg and he passed out.

Downstream, Marla had gotten Luisa propped up against a tree where her body was being heated from her small fire. She heard a thud, looked back at the debris, and saw a man caught in it, just as they had been. "Ah well, best at least try," she murmured to herself and crawled over to the man.

Feeling a pulse, she began to drag him out too, but noticed his right leg was missing. For a moment, she thought about giving him a push back into the waters where he would surely die a merciful death. He was an enemy soldier. He moaned and her conscience kicked in. She dragged him out of the creek and up to the fire, propping him up beside another tree, but only after removing his pack. Then she added more wood to the fire and sat against a third pine, shivering like mad. Then she too fell unconscious.

Chapter 15 Survival

Marla awoke shivering again. The fire had died down to a few glowing coals. Darkness had fallen and a thick fog had set in, dampening her now dried clothes. The other two were still alive, but either unconscious or sleeping. Which? Marla had no way of knowing, she was not a doctor nor had she any gifts; she was just a cook. The bottoms of her feet still ached so she crawled around, and dragged a bit more wood to the coals and got the life-giving fire going again.

She was now quite hungry and decided to see if there was anything in the soldier's pack that she could eat. Marla tore into some jerky and found a small waterskin with a little water in it. Slowly her strength returned and she headed to the creek to refill the waterskin. On her way back, she decided she'd best spend her efforts finding enough wood to keep the fire going all night. Though it was May, the nights were still not much above freezing this far north.

While she sat back enjoying the warmth of her little bonfire, she noticed a rabbit nosing around and an idea formed. Using a bit of torn cloth from the soldier's pant leg, she fashioned a snare, much as she had done as a child. An hour later, she smiled as she began preparing roast rabbit. It was not much food, but a little something for the three of them, she thought.

The grease crackling roused Luisa, who moaned a little as she tried to get her bearings and sit up. "Am I dead?" she whispered.

"No, I've saved you, somehow. Got a rabbit cooking, crudely mind you. I've not got my pots nor spices. Here, can you eat this yourself?"

Luisa instinctively tried to reach for it with her right hand only to sink back, crying out in pain. She looked down at what remained of her arm and gagged. "Here, take a bit of water," Marla suggested, holding the lip to her mouth and draining a little out. That seemed to help and then she placed the piece of rabbit in her left hand. Luisa raised it slowly to her

301

mouth and began chewing.

The soldier now began stirring and Marla crawled over to him, repeating what she'd done for Luisa. He drank greedily and then ate ravenously, but doped off to sleep when he'd finished. "Who are you? Where am I? Who is he? God, I hurt so badly! My arm, my face. I'm starving," Luisa whispered, trying to find her voice. Her hearing sounded strange to her, like there was water in her ears somehow. She tilted her head from side to side, but stopped at once as moving it caused her face to burn once more.

"I'm Marla, Marla Blackwater, the Sisterhood cook. They are all dead and us very nearly, but I got us out of there. Don't know who 'e is, though, saved him too. Fished him out of the creek where we were. Can I borrow your boots? Acid ate through mine and I can't walk. I'll see if I can find us stuff."

"Stuff? Water in my ears. Am I dead? Boots? Sure, take them. I don't think I need them if I am dead," Luisa replied, half unconscious again. Her arm and face throbbed in pain and she felt rather dizzy too.

"Thank you ma'am," Marla said and pulled off her boots. "Bit big for me, but at least I don't have to crawl now. Going to find stuff; you rest up, ma'am," she said softly, but saw Luisa was also no longer aware of her. After checking on the fire and adding a few more branches, she got to her feet. They ached, but at least she could walk now. The fog had lightened a little and the two moons peeked out from behind dense clouds. "Got a break there, no rain or snow this night," she said to the fire.

She walked around the pine grove and found more dead wood, dragging it back to their fire. On her last trip back, she noticed other things had gotten caught by the blockage where they had and went to check if there were more who needed rescuing. Instead, she found several soldier's back packs had floated downstream and gotten hooked on the debris, just as she had. These she lugged back to the fire and began looking through them. She found a heavy pair of socks and stretched them on a pair of sticks to dry. She needed those. Between the three packs, she found more dried food and carefully laid those aside. A shovel, an axe, a knife, and several handfuls of silver coins were added to her growing pile of stuff. The bulk was men's clothing that she laid out to dry also. "No blankets or cloaks which would be useful and no cooking pots," she murmured. "Ah well, at least we have a bit of food. Probably I can make a couple good meals for the three of us out of it, if only I had at least one pot." She hadn't and after piling more wood on the fire, she laid back against a pine and dozed off herself.

The soldier moaning in pain roused Luisa. Her face felt the heat of the orange-red sun. She opened her eyes and saw men's clothes lying all around what had been a fire. Small wisps of smoke curled upwards, twisting this way and that in the ever so gentle morning wind. Across from her was a slightly pudgy woman covered in black soot and an equally filthy soldier, from Portillo from his uniform, but his lower right leg was absent. For a minute, her mind didn't register why that should be. Then her burning lungs caused her to cough up volumes of black mucus and the noise roused the pudgy woman, who also broke into a coughing fit. Their coughing woke the soldier who opened his eyes, looked around himself wholly disoriented, and began coughing himself.

Marla finally got to the water skin and helped each wash out their mouths, noses, and then take a long drink. "There now, that's better. I'll rustle up something for us to eat."

"Who are you? Where are we?" Luisa asked again, far more coherently this time.

"Marla Blackwater, Sisterhood cook. We were supposed to keep you Ama women safe, but that failed utterly. I think they are all dead excepting us. I dragged us into the water to help wash off that horrible acid stuff, which was burning through your face and arm." Luisa flinched, images of her dear friend Macarena came back to haunt her. She relived watching the woman's face melting away, leaving only exposed bone where her smiling face had been. The voice of the soldier brought her back to the present.

"I'm Hernando Polito, soldier of Portillo or was. Not anymore. My leg is gone! Hurts like hell. Acid I think. I saw it fall off once there was nothing left but bones. They were going around stabbing us to death — us wounded men. Had us dragged to the bank of the creek all in a line. Thought they were sending a doctor, but they were killing us instead. I didn't want to die, not that way, but maybe I should have. How can I live like this? The tower folks were supposed to protect us."

Luisa saw horrible ooze trickling from his right leg and moved over to him. "I have some healing skills. Let me have a look at what's left of your leg."

"You are one of those Ama women — you're from Valen. Please don't kill me, I want to live somehow."

"I don't want to kill anyone. Now be quiet and don't move." She focused and her crystal energized. She noticed her own right arm looked sickly and in desperate need of attention as well. As she began to home in on Hernando's leg, she realized he would die unless she acted, and she did so as much as she dared, saving some of her psi energies for herself and for Marla, who she'd forgotten to see if she was hurt. After an hour's work on what remained of his leg, she had the remaining rancid cells removed, the blood seepage stopped, and the barest beginning of a scab forming. She sighed and broke the connection. "There, please be extra careful of your leg until I can get back to it. I've gotten the particles out of it that could cause gangrene and the blood loss has stopped. Marla, how about you? I am sorry I forgot to check on you."

"My feet got burned. Acid ate through my boots and devoured my socks. You can have a look at them, if you are up to it, but you ought to look after yourself too, Ama," Marla replied.

"I will after I look at your feet. Thank you for saving us." The pudgy cook nodded and removed Luisa's boots, allowing the Ama to examine her burned feet. Again, Luisa activated her crystal and probed the woman's feet. Her wounds were not bad at all and within a few minutes, she had pink healing skin formed over them, much to the relief of the cook.

"Thank you, Ama. I've got food fixed, not much, I am afraid, only what I could scrounge from some soldiers' packs. Eat up. Now that my feet are better and I've got the Ama's boots, I'll see what else I can scrounge up for us." Luisa ate ravenously, having used up all her psi energies during the battle. That alone meant she was starving. Now she'd used even more, and knew she had to have calories quickly or her own body would start digesting itself. Fortunately, Marla also knew this from having been around her Sisterhood group and made sure Luisa had her portion as well. *I can do to lose a little weight,* she thought.

Once fed, Luisa then used her remaining potential of psi energies to work on her own body, mostly her right arm that had exposed bones in her forearm where the acid had eaten through skin and muscle tissue. When she finally sat back wholly exhausted, she had pink skin growing on her arm. She also knew she'd never really be able to use it properly again. Tomorrow, she'd worry about the side of her face, as she fell into a deep sleep.

Marla, her stomach growling, stood up, stretched, and tested her feet. With two pairs of socks and Luisa's boots, she could now walk almost normally. She set out to see what she could scrounge up. Having spent several years in the Sisterhood, scrounging was something she was exceptionally good at doing, for they never seemed to have enough whatevers, be that blankets, clothes, things to cook, sometimes even cookware. While many others took up fighting and such, she had no knack for that sort of thing. Really if the truth be known, she had only one real goal in her life: to find her missing younger sister who had been abducted, kidnaped, or somehow taken from their ranch home many years ago.

In the distance to the east, she saw black plumes drifting idly on the cool morning air. Portillo was destroyed, and she had no desire to go back to that nightmare hell hole from which she'd run. Looking in the other directions, she saw mostly the steep ridge lines and pine covered angular hills that led to sparse grasslands in their basins. Early spring offered her little wild berries or tubers. The grasses had only just begun to green up again. She spotted a well-traveled dirt track. Probably it led to Portillo from locations to the west, she concluded. Hiking to a ridge line, she got a better view and noticed a farmstead cradled against the ridge not two miles to the west. She wasn't into stealing and headed back to the pine grove. There, she gathered up all the silver coins and then headed off on the long hike to the farmstead.

Around noon, she returned, loaded with three blankets, two cloaks, and a large sack of food, including one copper pot. Now Marla was in business once more. Luisa was still sleeping but Hernando had awakened and was tending the fire. "Hello. Can I help some?" he asked as she dumped her load of scrounged things.

"Found us some food. Not the best, but I can make it taste halfway okay. Yes, need the fire going. I'll scrounge up some more deadwood and you can chop it up and tend the fire while I cook, Hernando. Careful with your leg, though. I haven't the faintest notions about nursing or healing. I'm just a cook." He grinned and agreed.

Around one, Marla had her pot brimming with a stew concoction and allowed Luisa to help herself first, having decided to wake her. "Thanks, I was starving, Marla. Here, Hernando, your turn. I'm afraid I ate quite a bit."

"Well dearie, you need it; you got to feed your gift if we are to survive. My feet are healing up fine, but your face, arm, and his leg need lots more tending, if you ask me," Marla replied. Hernando didn't understand and she added, "The Ama uses up a lot of energy when she works her magic, so she has to eat volumes. Of course, she doesn't get fat, unlike me. I love to eat, but then my body shows that!" She chuckled good naturedly.

"Well, I do feel better, Marla. Thank you. I'll check on your feet first and then his leg," Luisa suggested. An hour later, her feet were wholly healed and Hernando's stump looked a lot better, no longer in danger of either infection or bleeding again. She had a good layer of pink skin growing over it now. The right side of her face was a mess, but healing now too, as well as what remained of her right arm. She could barely move her fingers and, other than using her shoulder muscles to raise and lower it, she could do little else with it. Far too much muscle tissue had been dissolved by the acid. Still, what remained was also healing, a thin layer of pink skin now covered the bones in her lower arm.

"So what do we do now?" asked Marla. "You realize as far as the world out there is concerned, we three are all dead.

The bombs wiped out your entire circle, dearie, and my group of Sisterhood companions. I am sure they think we have perished too. After that nightmare, I don't want to go back."

"Dead? Yes, they probably think so. Honestly, Macarena's face — it was gone, the acid." Luisa couldn't go on — the images were too horrid to face again.

"I know dearie, I know. We're dead as far as they are concerned," Marla consoled her.

"Well, so am I, dead," Hernando added. "Now what do we do? I can't walk or fight. I wanted to live, but now how am I going to do that?"

"Well, you got your hands," Marla answered. "Have you always been a soldier?"

"No, I used to help dad run a spread with sheep. Can't do that anymore. Really, I liked to carve things out of wood. Did a lot of that before they drafted me into the blasted army. Lot of good that did me."

"Well, why not keep on carving things and selling them?" Marla suggested. "What about you, Ama Luisa?"

"Just Luisa now, I think. I won't have anything more to do with those towers! They perverted my inventions that were supposed to help everyone. They turned them into horrible weapons. No, if they think I'm dead, then they won't come looking for me or try to marry me off like some brood lamb. Maybe I should join the Sisterhood like you, Marla."

"No, dearie, don't. They'll just use you like the towers did. By law, the Sisterhood is required to help the towers in their wars when asked. If the towers think you are dead and your folks think that too, then you are free of them, as long as you stay away from them," Marla explained.

"What are you going to do, Marla?" Luisa asked, hoping to get some ideas from the slightly older woman. She had the typical black hair, though hers was curly and cut relatively short, not touching her shoulders. Her face was quite roundish with a round nose and pudgy cheeks. Marla was short and somewhat overweight. The soldier was perhaps half a foot taller than Luisa, thin and muscled. He had a small black moustache and oily black hair and eyes, so typical of the Westerlings lineages.

"Well, I am going to continue what I set out to do five years ago — trying to find out what happened to my little sister, Amy. She just disappeared from our small ranch one night, vanished. She had the gift too, and she sent me thoughts saying some men had taken her away, and I promised her that I would find her and rescue her somehow. She said she was being taken to the west. We lived in the Midlands foothills between Haverhills and Oakham. I joined the Sisterhood and began moving around, looking for signs of her. Took a while, but I know she is not anywhere around Valen now. So I got to look elsewhere for her."

Luisa made a snap decision. "Look, I've got nothing else to do, why don't I help you with your search, Marla? I know the aliens have abducted young women and taken them off-world, but if it wasn't them, maybe I can help you."

"Hey, I'll lend a hand too. I've got nothing else to do now," Hernando added, "that is, if you don't mind a cripple hobbling along somehow. Maybe I can crawl this way."

"Well, okay, I could use some fresh ideas, but we got to get out of here. There's a road about a half mile that way. Somewhere down it has to be a village where we can somehow get provisions," Marla suggested.

A short while later, she had their few scavenged possessions stuffed into three bags. With Marla on one side of Hernando and Luisa on the other and the sacks over their shoulders, the three began to figure out how to walk him over the rough terrain to the road. Eventually, the three got the hang of it and made it. Once on the dirt track, they headed west away from Portillo. While Luisa wondered how far the next village might be, Marla wondered how long their strength would hold up. She soon found out. A couple of miles later, Hernando and Luisa were exhausted, and rather than have him take a spill, Marla called a halt to their walk. All around them lay nothing but the wilderness. Complicating matters, the dark clouds soon promised rain and later at night, possibly light snow.

Just when Marla had about given up hope, she heard the sounds of an approaching vehicle. "This could be good or bad," she whispered. Luisa was too tired to care. Besides as drained as she was, she could do little about any trouble. Certainly Hernando couldn't either. The three waited nervously as the rickety sounds drew closer. At last they spotted an old worn-out wagon slowly coming down the track from the direction of Portillo. They blinked. It carried a half dozen well-armed soldiers towards them, one of whom was driving. From their uniforms, Marla and Luisa presumed they were from Portillo and had somehow escaped the slaughter.

Luisa spotted a curious detail, the driver had a crystal around his neck, and it was glowing softly. Her mind registered, *Why?* She was too tired to grasp at reasons. The soldiers either would help them or harm them. Just now, she was too tired to really care which.

"Could we possibly have a ride with you to the nearest town? I've got two badly injured with me," Marla spoke up as the wagon came close to where her companions were sitting directly in the path of the wagon.

The driver pulled back on the reins, halting the wagon just before Marla. For a moment, he looked over the three. Suddenly the soldiers vanished. All but one disappeared. The driver remained and the three saw immediately he was in very bad shape. His left arm was dripping blood from a crude bandage; he'd lost all but about six inches of the arm. Luisa could sense the intense pain the man was suffering and rose to her feet slowly, knowing she could help him a little.

"I will trade a ride for some help. I'm about done for. Name's Valerio Urbano," the bass voice of the soldier struggled to speak. Obviously, he was suffering and barely able to keep from passing out.

"I can heal a little bit more tonight. Tomorrow, I will do more, Valerio," Luisa explained. "Hernando, can you drive the wagon?"

"Sure, don't need my legs for that, not much anyhow, if'en I can get up there somehow," he replied. "You don't know how grateful we are for the ride, Valerio."

Using the last of his strength, the wounded man climbed over the back and into the bed. With assistance from the two women, Hernando manage to get himself up and into the driver's seat. The wagon had indeed seen far better days. It was old and rickety, barely holding together. Not much more could be said of the poor horse that was pulling it.

As the wagon began to move again, Luisa focused, activating her crystal and began to examine his wound. Someone had only done the barest minimal healing on the poor young man, slapping a tight bandage over his raw stump. He'd lost quite a lot of blood as a result. A full healing was beyond her psi energies at the moment. Thus, she set her goal of stopping the blood loss and removing bits of the infection that had already set in. Marla knew when Luisa was done, she'd need to eat again, so she rummaged through her bag to find what they had left she could eat without cooking. There wasn't much of that and she sighed. Worse luck, it began to snow.

Hernando spotted chimney smoke, and before long, he noticed a side track leading south. Suspecting they would expect a significant amount of snow during the night, he turned left down it, calling out, "I'm going to see if we can get shelter for the night."

A group of barking shepherding dogs announced their arrival and an older man stepped out of his wood frame home. Marla spoke for the group, "Excuse us, sir. We seek shelter for the night in your barn. I have three wounded from the great battle at Portillo who are in desperate need of shelter for the night. We can pay you a few silvers, sir"

"What news? We have two sons in their army. Please, what news can you tell us?" his face tensed, expecting the worst, yet daring to hope still.

Marla broke the ill and hideous news as gently as she could. The rancher left them, scarcely containing his grief. Meantime, Luisa finished what little healing she could muster, having exhausted her energies for the day. She accepted what little Marla gave her to eat and watched as Marla helped the two men down and into the hay pile. She'd been successful; his bleeding had ceased, but she knew his bandage ought to be changed. Lacking clean water and clean bandages, it was pointless. Tomorrow they might have better luck and some light. For now, her patient had fallen unconscious and she decided was the best thing for the man. Conscious, he'd be in an awful lot of pain.

They slept ill, though. In a semi-conscious, semi-sleep daze, off and on throughout the night, Valerio often moaned, waking the others. Luisa, however, slept soundly; she was completely drained. In the morning, the rancher did bring them a pot of steaming stew and Marla gave him a silver for it. One by one, she fed the others, lacking any plates of silverware. She did insist Luisa have a much larger portion, for which the teen was grateful. After that, Marla hitched up their horse and Hernando, waving goodbye, headed back out into the snow-covered world.

Refreshed, Luisa again set to work on Valerio's arm. When she finally stopped two hours later, she had the wound healing nicely. Pink skin now covered the end of his stump, and she'd helped his body get the stored up, pain energy flowing and thus vanishing. Now he only felt a throbbing in his stump, which Luisa had opened up to the air. "I got hit by a bomb at the start of the battle," Valerio began to explain. "Blew it clean off! I was screaming wildly and they hauled me down into the infirmary in the basement level of the tower. Someone there wrapped me up and told me they'd be back to heal me properly later. Later never came, just more and more wounded men, far worse than I. Some of their bodies were literally melting right before our eyes. Hideous, I've never seen anything like it. Our tower people were supposed to protect us against such wicked, evil magic, but they didn't. Then the ceiling began falling down on us."

"Well, I knew of a back door and made for it, just barely. I'm scared of closed spaces, and no way in hell was I going to get trapped down there! I just got out when it began crumbling — the whole tower! I was knocked out for a time. When I came too, I found this abandoned wagon and old plug horse and somehow managed to get her harnessed up. I snuck out the new back entrance where a whole section of the outer wall was gone. For a time there, I didn't think the wagon would make it in one piece going over that rubble, but somehow it did. Then, I found you. Thank you, Ama for healing my arm. Do you have any news?"

Marla related what she'd seen and Hernando told his

311

own story. "My god, they just murdered us survivors?" Valerio gasped.

"Yes, I guess I can see their point. With hundreds upon hundreds of us lying there mutilated and dying, how could anyone possibly have healed so many? Especially those whose bodies were being eaten away by the acid bombs. But I wanted to live, Valerio, though just now, I wonder if I made the right decision. How are we going to survive like this?"

"Oh, you are managing, Hernando. It could be worse," Marla pointed out encouragingly. "Besides, at this point, Valerio, you are now considered dead. No one will be looking for you."

"Dead? Oh! I see," he suddenly realized what she was implying. "I am free of being in their damnable army. Well, I can't play soldier anymore anyway," he added. "Thank you, Ama Luisa. I am deeply indebted to you for my arm. It is throbbing a little and itchy, but I'm alive thanks to you."

"You're welcome. It's the least I can do for you, since it was my people who gave you those awful wounds. We are all now just a bunch of broken pieces. None of us can play the game any longer. You two can't play soldier man, and I can't play tower technician and invent things to help our people. I can't believe they perverted my best invention of the flying car, turning it into a weapon of war. It was supposed to help us all get around faster and better."

"You can't trust them tower people. That's what I've got to say," Valerio cursed. Hernando agreed with him. "So what are we to do now? I can't go home. There's nothing there for me, a one armed cripple."

"None of us are going home, Valerio. We can't, we are considered dead by everyone. So I am going to continue to search for my sister who was abducted," Marla explained, going into what few details she had of her lost younger sister.

Luisa added, "I am going to help her search for her sister, but more than likely, she was taken by the aliens to some other world. I also thought of going around to the various towns and cities and condemning the towers, telling others just what they are doing. You know, look what they are doing to us, your young men and women — foment a rebellion against the towers or something. Alas, they'd only come after us and kill us if we did that. Besides, we are supposed to be dead. I've got no future. Look at me, my arm is useless and my face— well it's so hideous to look at, no one would even want me around them."

"Oh you look fine to me, Luisa," Valerio countered. He was also nineteen. "Of course, you can say that about me and Hernando too. How are we even going to live? Make a living? Go on the streets begging? I have just enough of the cursed gift to create illusions and such, but not much more. You are right, Luisa, we are broken pieces."

Marla sighed, "Yes, you and I, we are all broken pieces, except I'm broken mentally not physically, but, you know, I myself, I am not broken, not yet, and neither are you three. You, Hernando, you have skill with wood carving. Make yourself a wooden peg leg so you can walk again. I don't think there's much you can do about your arms, so let it be. Your bodies might be broken, but not yourselves."

She went on, becoming rather persuasive, "We four have luck on our side. Look, how many of your fallen comrades escaped the mercy killings? One, you. Valerio, how many of your wounded soldiers escaped the collapsing tower? One, you. Luisa, how many of your circle members escaped the acid bombs? One, you. How many of my fellow Sisters escaped them? One, me. The three of us were just about dead last night, what with the hard freeze and snow coming and us exhausted on the track and then Valerio here appeared. No, I think somehow we four have got a huge pile of *luck* on our side."

"I can see we must have, Marla, but we should use our luck to help others," Luisa thought aloud. "I have a gift and unlike the towers, it should be used to help the ordinary folks of our land, real help."

"I'll second you on that one," Valerio quickly jumped in. "We should use it to really make a difference, but what good are my illusions going to be? In the army, they wanted me to make our squad appear as if we had ten squads to the enemy. Say, the village of Los Gatos is coming up soon. Maybe we can get some help there."

313

An hour later, they rolled into Los Gatos, a rural village of nearly a thousand. In the center of the village on the south side of the square with its water well was an inn, El Mesón de la Casa de Gallina. "What's the sign say? My Westerlings isn't so good," Marla asked.

"The Hen House Inn," Luisa replied. "How much silver do we still have left? Perhaps we can get a room and board for a few days. I need to work on our healing still. Besides, we all are filthy and in dire need of some new clothes too."

"We got enough for the inn, but not much more," Marla replied, counting out the remaining silver coins. "Let's give it a try, shall we?" All agreed and they stopped before the inn. With some difficulty, they managed to get Hernando down from the driver's seat. With an arm over Marla and Luisa, he slowly walked to the front doors, followed by Valerio, after he tied the horse to the hitching post outside.

The main dining room and barroom was small and dimly illuminated. An older man stood behind the combination bar and reception desk. "We'd like two rooms and a bath, with meals of course. How much for two days?" Marla asked.

"Four silvers, but the food is going to be really poor. My wife — she's taken ill and is our cook. I'm afraid my cooking is — well let's say it is awful. I won't charge you for the food," he replied courteously.

"Say, I am a good cook. What say I give it a try, cooking for you until your wife recovers?" Marla asked, sensing their luck was still holding.

"That will be excellent, though I will sample your first meal and take it from there," he replied conservatively. Honestly, the four looked utterly filthy, their clothes, mere tattered rags.

Luisa spoke up, "I am a healer, sir. If you will permit me, I could see what I might be able to do for her."

"Would you? Oh my, yes, yes. She's got a fever and is in bed. After you get cleaned up, I'll take you to her room, Ama. You look like you've been in a battle. We heard there was a great battle at the tower up the road in Portillo." Marla told him the awful news and a very sober man took them to their rooms. They had a very difficult time getting Hernando up the stairs to their two rooms, but they succeeded.

Breathing heavily, Hernando opened the door to the room the two men would be sharing. He turned and said, "After we take our bath, what are we going to put on? These dirty clothes?"

"Wash them and let them dry. What else can we do? There's not enough silvers left to buy all of us new clothes," Marla pointed out. He nodded.

Two hours later, Marla and Luisa finally finished up. Marla had helped Luisa with her long hair and she'd washed their tattered clothes. Their bedroom looked like a laundry room. While they sat wrapped in towels waiting on them to dry, the innkeeper knocked and entered.

"Ama, I have brought you my wife's robe. I beg you to come now, she is having a seizure I think. Here, Marla, see if these will fit you. If so, the kitchen is behind the bar. We need lunch for ten people in an hour if you can manage." Both women thanked him and Luisa, covered only by the robe, followed him to the very end of the hallway where their private room was located.

She set to work immediately. The woman was having convulsions and was deadly ill. She shooed the innkeeper out and activated her crystal, setting to work. First, she focused on the blocked nerve channels that were now acting independently of her involuntary nervous system, stopping the convulsions. Next, she tediously began removing the infection germs that were ravaging her body and the fever broke. The woman was recovering but weak when Luisa finally ended and rose. Just outside the door, the innkeeper had been pacing all this time.

"She's recovering now, sir. Her fever is broken, the convulsions have ended, and I've removed the infection in her blood stream. It came from a cut on her finger originally. She is weak but will be fine in a few days. If I had not gotten to her when I did, she'd have died I'm afraid."

"Gracias! Gracias! Gracias, Ama Luisa!" he heaped thanks and praise on her. Marla had left her a large bowl of chicken stew in her room and she hastily downed the whole

315

bowl, quite greedily. Using so much of her psi energies burned up her body's calories at an alarming rate, as they always did. While in the tower, she didn't give it a second thought. That was the duty of the tower's servants. She sent a mental thank you to Marla for her thoughtfulness.

A short while later, the innkeeper came by to tell her that soon a dressmaker and a tailor would be coming by to give them a set of new clothing. "It is the very least I can do to thank you for saving my wife," he explained. "Oh yes, Marla will be cooking for me until my wife has recovered. You are all to stay here at no charge until she is able to resume cooking for me." Luisa grinned and thanked him. We continue to be incredibly lucky, she thought.

Their luck continued. While Luisa spent the early afternoon working on further healing of Valerio's arm, Marla had some time to spare before starting in on their supper. She did a little shopping, returning with some leather, a small sewing kit, a carving knife, and a chunk of wood. "Okay, Hernando, use these to make yourself a pegleg." He chuckled and thanked her.

By suppertime, Hernando was able to walk some on his own, though he still had to have help with the stairs. Later on, he modified his pegleg until he had it working well for himself. All four now wore new clothes, pants, loose fitting tops, and new leather boots. Marla looked quite pleased with their day's work, commenting on their continued good luck.

The next day, it continued. Several others had heard of Ama Luisa's healing of the ill innkeeper's wife and came to the inn asking for her help with other sick or injured village folks. While she took care of them, the two men worked on repairing the wooden banister railing for the innkeeper. A week later, they left the village with coins in their pockets, warm cloaks, a change of clothes, a new wagon, and a new horse. Their spirits were high as they headed on down the track towards the heart of the old Kingdom of Abvera.

In each hamlet, village or town they came to, they stopped and asked if there were sick or injured folks who needed help. Always there were and by the time they pulled into the great city of Malaca, word had spread of the coming of

Los Cuatro Santos. Their luck continued to manifest itself as they continued helping the average person, accepting in return what assistance the person could afford to donate in payment.

For the next forty years, Los Cuatro Santos roamed the entire Westerlings, healing the sick, the injured, and helping others in any way they could. Over time, others with the *mentales* gift joined them, especially as their fame rose. Always, the group's luck held, never abandoning them, until in 1180, Marla decided it was time for her to return to the ranch where she was born in the high foothills between Oakham and Haverhills. Her three companions went with her.

Chapter 16 Escalation and Expansion

"Well, we won; we control Portillo now, but such a cost!" Augusto exclaimed in the sternest voice Jarek had yet heard from the Venerado of Valen. "An entire circle — that is ten times too costly. The thousand soldiers lost can easily be replaced, but not a trained circle. We are going to have to come up with far, far better weapons before we tackle Duero Tower." He was addressing his Capo leaders, Jarek, his generals, and his immediate family members, going over the losses suffered in the taking of Portillo Tower.

Jarek spoke up, "Venerado, I have some ideas how that might be accomplished. I've done as you asked: researched major battles in history via the Imperium computer system. If I may offer an idea?"

Augusto looked at his alien foster son and nodded. *Perhaps this alien marriage will pan out after all.*

"The massive casualties we endured at Portillo came from their own soldiers firing their defensive catapults lobbing fire and acid bombs at our troops and circle members. What if there was a way to totally eliminate the enemy troops, leaving only the tower's circle members to defend their castle and tower? Sans all support troops, would not they capitulate at once?"

Venerado Augusto pulled on his chin in thought. He looked up at his eldest son, Capo Amo Armando. "Well, son, supposing it was just your circle defending all Valen with perhaps the other two circles with you?"

Capo Armando replied, "We'd have to sue for peace, dad. The tower cannot function with circle members alone, not for any length of time. There would be no way to defend the walls; they would be easily breached. With thousands of soldiers piling into Valen Castle, we would have few options. Yes, we could hold out for a while, but not long." Capo Basilio and Capo Camilo both agreed with him.

Augusto smiled and looked over at Jarek. "There's your answer. How do you propose to eliminate thousands of soldiers?"

Jarek's face broke into a snide grin. "With a toxic chlorine gas, sir. One whiff of it and your lungs burn up; huge blisters disfigure any skin that the gas contacts. Then, there is a nerve gas that totally paralyzes bodies and another nerve gas that quickly kills bodies with just a couple of minutes' exposure. However, if we issue suitable masks for our troops, they will be unaffected by the release of the gas. Of course, we cannot import it from the Imperium for many reasons; one being the use of such weapons is wholly against Imperium laws throughout the galaxy. Still, in time, I believe we can manufacture it in sufficient quantities to do what we need."

"The downside would be the winds that could disperse the gas," Augusto speculated and Jarek agreed that was true. "Once we use it, the other towers will soon develop their own versions of it as well. Still, if we can capture Duero Tower and their circles without losing troops or our own *mentales* gifted, then that would accomplish our immediate objectives. Camilo, make your entire circle available to assist Jarek with whatever he needs to get this new weapon ready for our assault on Duero Tower."

Time passed. Jarek's new weapon and defensive masks would not be ready until next spring, 1133. In response to the many protests over his building a tower in Exchange City, Augusto continued to tell the other Venerados they ought to build their own towers elsewhere and that he had no ideas of conquest beyond the Westerlings.

In actual fact, as much as Venerado Simon wanted to counter this huge threat, he had no real means. Why? Oakham and Haverhills were battling it out for control over some of the more valuable lands around the Wyndl River. Bettingham and Bedwurth were in open conflict over similar lands around the junction of the Wyndl and Wal rivers, near Wye. None of these four towers had any available means to counter Valen. Worse, Rusden and Oakham had just begun a new battle near Leedsburough, further complicating matters.

Venerado Simon made what eventually became the wisest decision made during the middle years of this century. He chose to build up his own forces and not engage in any armed conflicts, doing what he needed to do to preserve peace in the cold northern realms of the Midlands. Thus, in the end, he eventually held the largest force when the time came, but that would not be for many years.

On a lighter note, Elegant Fashions Inc. mushroomed into one of the largest businesses, planet-wide. Augusto promoted their fashions to his *mentales* gifted as well as other noblemen and women throughout his vast territory. Why? He realized the coming battles would likely cost him some of these extremely valuable telepaths. It became obvious that both men and women became highly aroused when so elegantly dressed, yielding pregnancies at nearly double their previous rates. That meant in some twenty years, there would be a much larger number of *mentales* gifted personnel for Valen.

Within a few years, the other towers also realized this along with what Augusto's future plans held. Thus, they encouraged their own men and women to begin dressing in these elegant fashions as well, in spite of the fact that tower work efficiencies dropped as a result. All the Venerados began planning for the future. Of course, Carmen and Karolina greatly benefitted financially from all this, much to their pleasure.

Wyth Tower decided to build an extension tower and castle at Welsham, which was located in the far east of their territory, some two thousand miles distant. Bettingham Tower took note of this and hastily laid claim to a new castle and tower in Wye, raising the stakes for supremacy over that disputed zone. Not to be outdone, Haverhills Tower began construction on a complex at the extreme eastern portion of their territory at Northend, nearly three thousand miles from their main tower. The idea was to put their presence securely in these most distant portions of their allotted territories.

Oakham Tower, fighting two opposing towers, had not the resources to construct an additional tower. Adelmira had no reason to do so and neither did Rusden. Duero concentrated on building up its armed forces, expecting Valen to invade their lands at any time. Brom Tower simply continued on its own path, constructing helium dirigibles and gliders in quantity.

However, all towers began to send out spies to the other towers in an attempt to keep tabs on their opponents. Most were ordinary men who were well paid to infiltrate the other tower's main cities and gather intelligence. These men were exceedingly hard to detect by the towers who mostly ignored these spying attempts, though they sometimes let slip false data designed to confuse the other towers. Only those with the gift were allowed into the towers proper, and their service staff was heavily tested for honesty.

In the spring of 1133, Duero Tower and castle fell without Augusto losing a single soldier, let alone any of his precious *mentales* gifted personnel. Jarek's various gas attacks launched from their air cars were incredibly deadly. Over five thousand soldiers defending Duero died horribly painful and disfiguring deaths. As predicted, Duero Tower surrendered at once. Much to Augusto's benevolence, he absorbed their three circles into his own, after informing them that any sabotage or treason on their part would be met with a painful death by the new gases.

As the years rolled by, the death toll continued to grow at a staggering rate. All the towers who were fighting had little choice but to adopt the methods pioneered by Augusto. Seriously wounded soldiers were given a merciful death. They simply could not afford to drain their towns and villages of care takers for men who had lost one or more limbs in these conflicts. It was cost effective to eliminate these "broken soldiers."

In 1150, the stakes were raised by Valen Tower. Armando took over as Venerado when Augusto died. His mighty forces swept around the southern edge of the Goza Mountains and into Oakham, where a two year long battle for the tower was fought. Naturally, by this time, Oakham had provided mask protections for its soldiers and had their own supply of the deadly gases. When the tower finally fell in the summer of 1152, nothing remained but rubble. Not even the stones were reusable, most had suffered acid melting or *mentales* gifted disruptions of their internal composition.

Embolden by his victory, Venerado Armando laid plans to assault Haverhills from both the south and from their northern tower in Exchange City. In 1158, Haverhills Tower and castle fell, but not before their key circle personnel evacuated and headed for their new tower at Northend.

Of note, the lands around these two cities, Haverhills and Oakham, became uninhabitable for nearly fifty years. The volume of poisonous chemicals spread over the land killed off the vegetation and animals. Only around 1210 did hardy plants begin to appear in these kill zones.

From Haverhills Tower, Armando headed for Bedwurth Tower. With its capture, Valen would control all the lands surrounding Plateau Grado and the aliens. Hence, he would receive all the yearly lease payment, the iron ore and gold, which he coveted. The alien ore made superior swords.

Bedwurth Tower fought long and hard. With plenty of years to prepare, they fielded a large number of flying vehicles, far more than those of Valen. For several years, it seemed that Bedwurth would prevail. The death toll was staggering, particularly so for Valen, who lost three men to every one that Bedwurth lost. The Valen forces began to rely on the alien blasters to shoot down the aerial vehicles, but often that caused even more problems. When they exploded or crashed, they released their cargo of fire bombs, acid bombs, or gas bombs, with a heavy death toll on Valen's ground forces.

When Bedwurth Tower fell in the summer of 1178, their surviving members had already fled to the safety of their new tower in Wye. There, they began preparing their counterattack. The loss of life during this conflict was staggering. However, the god Wystan loved it, but he too was soon to be overwhelmed by the coming battle.

Venerado Armando was appalled at the cost of taking out Bedwurth. Hence, he begged Jarek, "Please, foster brother, we simply must have a new super-weapon. If we don't, it is only a matter of time before Haverhills and Bedwurth counterstrike us. We are now terribly weak and incredibly vulnerable. Our forces are so spread out that we can barely maintain order in our new territories. Please, I beg you, come up with something we can use to take out Bettingham. Once they are gone and perhaps Wyth Tower too, we will own the vast majority of the Midlands. Only Rusden will stand in our way of controlling most all of it. We will be the superpower of Tierra."

Jarek rose to the occasion. "There is one thing that will guarantee total victory without our loss of life. Nuclears. However, Tierra does not have any of the heavier atoms that are needed to make these massive bombs. Other planets, of course, do have them, but obviously we cannot import them. Not directly," he smiled snidely once again. "For a price, they can be obtained on the black market, but it will take time, especially since Tierra is a closed planet. They cannot be shipped here directly."

Armando's face fell. Here was just what he needed, but with no way to acquire them. Jarek continued his wicked smile. "Give me time, brother, and I will get one for you. Perhaps, I can obtain two. We'll see."

"If you can, you will become the savior of Valen. I will see you are rewarded greatly, foster brother," Armando replied eagerly. "Time we have. I don't foresee anyone launching a counterstrike against us for a number of years. It will take them time to regroup, rebuild, and retrain. Time we have, Jarek. Get us the Nuclears." Jarek nodded, the grin still on his face.

Neither of the two had the faintest notion this very action would bring an unforeseen disaster to them all. As far as Jarek was concerned, the right credits in the right hands would eventually yield a clandestine delivery of one or two Nuclears.

The middle years of this century are filled with tale upon tale of horror, pain, and suffering. Not only were circle members impacted, but even more importantly the average man and woman bore the brunt. Sadly, those *mentales* gifted in power seldom paid the slightest attention to those, only to their own *mentales* gifted.

Part III The Blackwater Ultimatum

Chapter 17 Amy Blackwater

One night in 1128, just after her sixteenth birthday, Amy Blackwater was abducted from her home somewhere during the wee hours of the morning. She owed everything that happened after that to the simple fact she wore her new germanium crystal around her neck at all times. In fact, she'd just returned from Haverhills Tower, where she had received their standard basic training and her crystal. Thus, when she regained consciousness and found herself tied and gagged, being flown somewhere in an alien flying machine, she was able to telepathically contact her sister, Marla. While her sister did not have the gift, at least she wanted her to know what was happening to her and that she was terrified out of her wits. Amy, wholly confused, focused on where her body was at. *If I know where I am at, then I might be able to find my way back.*

Soon, strong arms carried her aboard a darkened ship. Her heart sank as she was thrown into a dark closet-like room. Soon, she heard the vibrations of the ship's engines and felt herself in motion. It didn't take her long to realize she was being not only kidnaped, but being taken to some other world. Depression set in on the young teen, whose whole life was ending in that dark, oil-smelling closet. She lost track of time, having no way to reckon it any longer. Eventually, an alien smelling of alcohol came to her and untied her. He spoke through a metal box attached to his utility belt.

"You are being taken to Etinne-3. Once there, you are the property of Elder Sims, who has purchased you for your telepathic abilities. Come with me. I have a room for you. It's a long flight." Mechanically, her body followed his, but her mind did not. For days, she considered ending her own life. Her metallic room held numerous items by which she envisioned that she could do so. Yet, something held her back. Something her abductor had told her: telepaths were exceedingly rare throughout the galaxy and that she'd be well treated and rewarded for her services. If she could get enough rewards, perhaps she could purchase a return flight to her home world.

Days later and after transferring ships three times, Amy finally arrived on the blue-green world of Etinne-3. Elder Sims was humanoid, but very obese and short. Nevertheless, he controlled a vast gemstone cutting empire that spanned three planets. "You will be attending my purchasing meetings where you will let me know if the sellers are trying to cheat me by passing off stolen diamonds, commercially manufactured stones, and such. I have two of these meetings each month. Other than those days, the rest of the time will be your own, though you are not permitted beyond my walled and heavily guarded estate. You will want for nothing, elegant clothes, the finest foods, whatever. Now then, we must make up your Imperium ID card. My secretary will assist you with this. My next meeting is in three days. Jasper, tend to our latest acquisition's needs. That will be all." Again, his actual voice sounded more like a child's babble, but the monotone ULAT box attached to his belt had spoken his words in her language.

Amy had not said a single word to her new owner! Further, he didn't think of her as anything beyond a truth teller, just another one of his tools of the trade! Confused, Amy didn't know what to think, but a tall, skinny man wearing a very fancy, silk suit rushed up to her and said, "If you will follow me, miss." Amy did so, once more noting his own language was unintelligible to her, but the strange box on his belt did speak in her Midlands dialect, although somewhat crudely.

Inside a room whose walls appeared to be a seacoast with rolling waves ebbing and flowing, Amy found herself staring at them. "Oh, it's just a 3-d hologram. Surely you've seen them before."

"No. So real." She reached out to touch the water only to meet with the actual wall itself.

"Sorry. Can't understand you. Here, I need to adjust my ULAT. I've got one for you to wear on your person at all times so we can understand you too." He fiddled with his ULAT and asked her to repeat what she had said. "Ah, that's better. Now I am understanding you. We'll get you into some proper dress and then give you your ULAT." She asked what it was and he launched into a long explanation that boiled down to the device translating one spoken language into another. Amy soon learned just how vital this communications device was.

"Now then, you know about ID cards?" he asked politely.

At least he is being kind. "Er no. I was kidnaped from my world and brought here. I don't know anything at all."

"Oh dear, totally ignorant! And I was so hoping to get time to play a round of squirrel golf yet today. Ah well. The Imperium ID card contains all there is to know about you, your name, your age, your health status, and so on. Most importantly, it contains your credit account number so you can access your credits from anywhere in the vast Imperium. Plus, here on the estate of Elder Sims, it will allow you access to those areas in which you are permitted to move freely. Here, I'll show you." He slid his card through a device beside a door. Amy heard a click and the door opened.

"Now then, let's get your card registered with the Imperium. Elder Sims is depositing one hundred thousand credits into your account the moment we have it established."

"What's a credit? Is it like our copper and silver coins?" Amy asked, having just seen some concepts in Jasper's mind.

"Ah yes. Some primitives refer to it as money. It is the universal means of exchange among all worlds in the vast Imperium."

"Is a hundred thousand a lot, then?"

"Oh my, I should say so. I work for Elder Sims and he deposits nearly that amount in my account each year. It's as much as a spaceship captain makes or so I'm told, a princely sum. Our many gardeners who work on the estate here only make twenty thousand credits a year. Now then, your name for your ID card?"

"Amy Blackwater."

He typed it into the computer terminal and frowned as the screen displayed three dozen identical names in the Imperium registry. "Well, that is a common name. We must add some more to make it unique. Might I suggest adding your planet of origin? Such as Amy Blackwater of Etinne-3?"

"But I don't come from here, wherever here is. Amy

Blackwater of Tierra."

After typing that in, he smiled. "Well now, that is indeed unique. There does not seem to be anyone else with that name. Further, there doesn't seem to be any planet with that name either. How strange. No mind. Your age in years and months?" He had to explain that a little further. The Imperium had its own calendar and the computer merely translated her years and months into the date that she was born, well approximately that is. The length of a year varied widely, but since everyone entered in the same manner, all dates were at least on the same scale, while often wholly inaccurate. He typed in sixteen years, one month. After entering a bit more data, he had the computer take a quick snapshot of her face and then the machine shot out her ID card with her picture on it along with other data, though she could not read the Imperium script.

She was then given her own private room, strange new clothing, and shown where the dining facilities were located along with how to operate the food dispensary machine. As the days passed, Amy found she had the run of the huge estate with its many strange sights, sounds, smells, plants, and animals. After a month of exploring, Amy became utterly bored with her new lifestyle and began to take advantage of the many learning computer programs that were available in her room.

Several months later, she was able to read the Imperium Standard (IS), the language in universal usage throughout the vast Imperium. While each planet had their own sets of languages, interplanetary business was always conducted in the IS language. Now she could read the writing on her own ID card and noted the addendum that had been added recently. She'd undergone some telepathic testing a month ago. She'd thought the testing had been unbelievably crude, but Elder Sims and the tester man seemed highly pleased with the results. Her ID card pronounced her to be a Class V telepath. Now she researched that designation and found it meant the person could both send and receive thoughts, nothing more. *Well, I can do a whole lot more than that! Even a child with mentales can do that!*

328

As the months progressed, Amy grew even more bored. Still, she knew she needed to learn all she could and spent hours at her computer terminal studying all it offered up to her. Additionally, she began working on her other *mentales* gifts, strengthening them. After that, she began to dabble and see what else she could do.

Having no idea at all what was or was not possible and with no one to teach her, she doggedly continued to experiment and dabble. Soon, she figured out how to levitate small objects and push them around. Emboldened by this, she continued to work at it to see if there were upper limits to what she could lift or move. Gradually, she was able to handle objects that were larger and larger as well as heavier.

Two years passed and her list of "gifts" had quintupled. Whatever she set her mind to doing, she eventually succeeded in accomplishing. She took enormous pleasure at planting thoughts into another's mind and getting them to act upon them. At first, the notions she planted were harmless, mere childish pranks. Soon, she came to realize just how powerful this gift actually could be. Further, she had two hundred thousand credits in her account and no real way to spend her funds.

The next big break came a month later when a high ranking Imperium consulate came to visit Elder Sims. She couldn't pronounce his name, though he looked more like a real person to her than Elder Sims and Jasper did. He kindly suggested she call him simply Ben, which she did. The two chatted at length. She learned Ben was a powerful Imperium employee, quite influential. He in turn became fascinated with her. That she had the largest bosom he'd ever seen and the longest hair, also played a role. She knew Ben was highly aroused with her body and took a gamble.

She planted the idea in Ben's mind that he should take her away from this boring job and planted the idea in Elder Sims' mind that he should take this opportunity to get rid of her, that she was costing him far more credits than she was saving him in his business dealings. To her amazement, both men reacted as if they had these very thoughts themselves. This became a turning point in Amy's life in more ways than one. That she could so easily control men's minds, making them do as she desired, made a long lasting impression on her. That evening, she boarded Ben's private spaceship and left Etinne-3 never to return.

She took up residence on Hatfield-4 near the central bulge of the galaxy that formed the heart of the vast Imperium. Here, she found vastly more information available to her. While she helped Ben by becoming a spy for him, she gained access to sensitive information. Ideas began to form in her mind. Some she put into play. Before long, Amy had created thirty new ID cards for herself, using various names and occupations. Some Ben had her use in her spying career for him.

Five years later, Amy had visited dozens of worlds on her own, made many key contacts, and had finally decided upon her own path outside of the Imperium. True, she now had millions of credits doled cleverly out to all her thirty identities. More importantly, she had the knowledge and skills to succeed. She lacked only one more skill, which she then set about remedying. She needed to learn to program the Imperium computer systems and hack into them. A bit of top secret searching using Ben's login and password, which she cleverly read from his mind, she discovered the name and location of the most wanted hacker in the Imperium. *I should learn from the best,* she thought.

It was not hard for her to arrange a visit to Centauri-2. Ben insisted she take a month's vacation, echoing the idea she implanted into his mind. After thanking him, she did just that, arriving on that blue world. Seventy percent of the planet was water and it had a bright yellow sun. This was a slum world, she soon discovered and was forced to use her mental skills to kill five lecherous men who tried to abduct and rape her before she was able to establish an Internet chat with the Sly Fox, the avatar of the hacker.

She typed in, "I want to learn to hack into the Imperium computers, to learn to program them to do what I want them to do. I can pay you for your services."

"How do I know you are not the Imperium cops out to get me? I am watching you now." Amy smiled. This guy was good. She resisted the urge to look all around the decrepit coffee house in reaction.

"If you are, then you can see my boobs. Have you ever seen any like them, eh?" Amy decided to play the sex game. After all, it worked beautifully with Ben. She had full control now over her body and simply pushed any fertilized eggs out of her womb, aborting any possible chance of pregnancy. Further, she had worked out how to heal her own body both of injuries and illnesses. Even poisons. She'd ingested small quantities and then trained her gifts to expel them as well. Amy was good, that she knew. If he was looking at her right now, she'd play the sex card.

"Silicone?" came the typed words on the screen.

"Real," she typed back. "Don't believe in artificial anything. What you see is what you get. Interested?"

The screen action paused a minute. Then Sly Fox's reply came. "If you are serious about this, go to Belt's Hotel. Ask for room 42 and take no substitutes. It'll cost you. Once in the room, take off all your clothes, stand in the center of the room, and await further instructions. Bye." The connection session terminated. Amy didn't hesitate, but asked the waitress for directions and headed there straight away. She had to dodge three other men who came after her, killing one who was overly persistent with his knife.

The hotel was a very sleazy one. Amy thought it had not been cleaned in years! A burly man with several days' stubble on his face looked up as she walked in. "What'd ya want here?"

"Room 42 only. Cost?" Amy replied sternly.

"Hundred credits up front, lady of the mammoth knockers," he replied with a snide grin. She inserted her ID card and punched in the amount, which was instantly transferred to the hotel's account. *It never ceases to amaze me how easily financial transactions take place within the Imperium. That has to be a double-edged sword, if only I can find a way.* She accepted the card key and noticed it said Room 43. She handed it back to the grubby man, who growled and handed her another key, this time the right one.

She climbed up the stairs whose walls were covered in graffiti and then walked down the long hall, illuminated in a dim red light. Amy had no misconceptions about the true nature of this hotel. She paused at the entrance, verifying the room number. She inserted the key card and entered. The place was dusty and could use a good cleaning. There was a distinct odor about the room, not a pleasant one, and Amy made the connection at once. Many sexual trysts had taken place here.

After glancing around the room seeing two chairs, the bed, and one mirror on the wall and one over the bed, she did as ordered, removing her Imperium cat suit and unpinning her long brown hair, letting it fall to her calves before shaking it out a little. Amy put her hands on her hips and then slowly pivoted around in a circle, figuring the Sly Fox had some cameras secretly spying on her. If so, she would give him her best view. She waited.

Before long the door opened, and a woman holding a blaster stepped inside. This was not what Amy had been anticipating! "So you are serious, Amy of the many names. Just who are you and where do you come from? Planet of origin?" The woman had an alto voice and also had the *mentales* gifts, of that Amy sensed immediately. She could tell little else from the form, Sly Fox wore completely non-descript robes, hiding her body from view. The cowl completely hid her face from view. "Don't try to lie, I can tell lies instantly."

"So can I. I am from Tierra, though I know that planet is not in the Imperium catalogues. Still, it is where I am from. Now answer me, are you Sly Fox?"

The woman threw back her cowl and Amy spotted the familiar yellow eyes with brown spots. "Yes, you are looking at her. Incredible! Tierra. Damn! I am from Tierra too. Up by Haverhills. And you?"

"A small ranch between Haverhills and Oakham. I got abducted by the aliens from Rigel-3. And you?"

"Jan Bellweather. Same here. They took me about eight years ago, but I managed to escape the idiots who bought me. I've been on the lookout for others from our world, but so far, you are the first I've found." She slipped off her own robe and revealed her own body, which was very similar to Amy's. She had the identical massive bosom and equally long brown hair, so typical of Midlands women. She laid her weapon down and walked over to Amy, then gave her a welcoming hug, slipping into rapport with Amy.

Oh how I have longed for the touch and feel of one of our own, one who can appreciate what our touch can mean and bring!

I know what you mean. The men merely use our bodies and discard the real emotions and feelings.

Pleasure me, Amy, please, I beg you. I've longed for this for years and years. Amy complied and Jan reciprocated. Later, Jan said, "Thank you that meant the world to me. Get dressed. I'll take you to my place and then we can talk in private."

In a secret basement room beneath an abandoned factory, Jan had set up her extensive operations. She'd had the good fortune to have been purchased originally by the ID division, looking for a good spy. Jan had quickly discovered she had a knack for their computer systems, though the ID division never had the faintest notions she did. Slowly but surely, she'd acquire all her equipment on the side and then had staged her death in the field. Using one of her new identities, she'd gone underground. From her headquarters here, she had hacked into all the vast Imperium computer networks, amassing a small fortune in credits along the way. Naturally, she had them dispersed among her various identities as well, so as not to draw undo attention to the size of her fortune.

Jan explained, "I have got enough credits to pay for a space flight home, but no one knows where Tierra is located."

"Yes, that's what I've found too. I've a mind to create some havoc in the Imperium, revenge for stealing our lives from us," Amy admitted. "That's why I want to learn to do what you can do."

Jan grinned. "Like minded. We make a pair, Amy. Let's!" Thus was born the nefarious "company" known throughout the underground within the Imperium as the Black Security.

For over fifty-five years, Black Security took revenge on the Imperium. Riots began here, a diplomat died there, a revolt was squashed here, a revolt started there. Blasters and Nuclears were delivered or intercepted. Assassinations occurred. Anything was possible, but for a price. The two women slowly setup a vast secret organization spread throughout the entire known galaxy. In 1183, Sly Fox and Eager Beaver, as Amy was known, had amassed billions of credits, all spread out uniformly among their various "identities." Their organization was based on cells. Each cell contained six members, only their leader knew of the contact in the higher cell, though the higher cell knew the identities of those in the lower cells for which they were responsible.

There was no question of a cell member's loyalty. It was common knowledge that anyone who betrayed Black Security would be killed painfully. Eager Beaver saw to that detail herself. She only had to be located on the same planet as the traitor for her to reach out with her gifts and exterminate the guilty party. True, her "gifts" continued to grow. Amy had no idea her power vastly exceeded even that of a combined *Círculo de mentes* and then some!

Of course, in 1185, Amy's body was really seventy-three years old, Jan's was seventy-four. However, they had long ago purchased their own Rejuvenation Machine for twenty million credits. When they reached fifty years old, they took their first treatment, which took thirty years off their appearance, with all the great benefits of regained, youthful bodies. The procedure took off thirty years the first time it was used on a body. The second use on the same body only took off twenty years. The third usage, only fifteen. The fourth, only ten, and so on. When they reached a real age of seventy, both used the machine a second time, again appearing as twenty-year old women again, much to their immense pleasure. In 1185, their bodies appeared to be about thirty-five years old, but their next treatment would only knock off fifteen years, again making them appear as twenty year old beauties. However, they resisted the temptation just yet, knowing only fifteen years would be given back to them this time.

Chapter 18 The Discovery

One evening as Jan prepared to bed Amy, her longtime lover, her computer console began blinking. "Oh darn, how inopportune," Jan teased the waiting Amy, who grinned.

"Best look at it," Amy called out from beneath the satin sheets of their bed. They still resided in the secret basement beneath the decrepit ancient factory.

"My god, someone else is trying to purchase two Nuclears. How strange. I'd best look into this some, my love," Jan replied, suddenly very interested in the anomaly. Amy, too, became curious and rose, donning a satin robe and sliding in beside her lover, putting her arm gently around Jan's waist.

Jan's fingers flew over the keyboard. While most searches were voice activated within the Imperium computer systems, Jan continued to use the keyboard for two reasons. One, it was vastly more difficult to trace her searches, and, two, she could obtain far more accurate results in much less time. "God, this is strange. Look at all the steps they are taking to keep this on the QT! Who the hell is the buyer and where the hell are they to be delivered?" she said in her alto voice, tinged with annoyance. "They are trying to get them from Black Security! What the hell is going on?"

"Don't know. We've not had any such requests for ages. Nuclears are outlawed," Amy replied. "We have to trace this back to the origin point. Who wants them, where, and why?"

"Wow, this is one of the most devious routing coverups I've seen, love," Jan pointed out. "But they haven't faced the Sly Fox!" An hour later she looked up with a most satisfied grin on her face, the one Amy loved to see.

"Yes, dear?" Amy teased Jan, coyly.

"Well, they were ordered by a field agent named Jarek Lajda who works for the Sector ID Minister, one Lech Kuba, that's Rim Sector 15, a fairly recent operation dedicated to the expansion of the Imperium's reach into the outer realms of the galaxy. It's based on a planet called Ashford-5, which is a closed world where the Imperial Directive #5 has been in force

335

for centuries. How strange. Why would they want two Nuclears?"

"Don't know. This is getting stranger by the minute. What do we know about this Ashford-5? I've never heard of this one," Amy answered, growing more curious by the moment.

"Damn, it required level ten security clearance to find out more. Damn," Jan swore angrily, but calmed almost at once. "Dear, our pleasure must wait a little longer. Sly Fox wants to know more." She giggled and Amy did too, looking over her lover's shoulders, admiring the speed with which Jan typed and cracked through levels of security barriers.

In a half hour, both women stared at the screen, stunned. At last, Amy found her voice, "Jan! That's Tierra! Home! My god, we've finally found our home world!"

Jan's face swelled with tears. "I never thought I'd ever find it, not ever. Amy, I want to go home somehow. I know probably everyone I knew there has grown old and died, but I'd like to go there, smell the air, see the snow, feel the pod-silk again."

"Me too, me too." Amy's mind was flooded with childhood images. Her dear older sister's face appeared; she was the last person from home she'd talked to as that spaceship left her world behind so many years ago.

"Ah, the getting there is damn near impossible," Jan finally got her wild emotions under control. "It's a closed world. No alien intervention is possible. It is a transfer base only. If we could get a ship there, we'd be forced to leave Tierra after refueling. They have top security protocols to prevent unauthorized arrivals to the station. Damn, damn, damn."

"Well, there has to be a way, love. We've always found a backdoor to get what we want. Let's do our usual research on it. Now come to bed. I thirst for your body," she teased Jan who willingly complied.

The next day, both agreed they would have to allow the sale to go through. If not, the forces on Ashford-5 would be alerted to them at the least and likely would try other sources. Black Security was not the only company from which Nuclears could be obtained. Of course, these bombs would have to be stolen from archival storage facilities, which only added to the cost to the buyers. "We must delay the sale as long as possible to give us time to work out how the devil we can get there and get off that base," Amy concluded.

They carefully reviewed all the security protocols in place on Ashford-5. Of course, this data was classified at security level ten, but Jan had already cracked that bit. By noon, both women realized there was no way they could get themselves there and off the base without bringing down a massive woman hunt on their heads. Sector ID Minister Lech was fully following all the required protocols as demanded by Directive #5, though he was obviously violating that directive in various nefarious ways. They needed a fool proof way to not only get there but be allowed off base, legally.

"We must make use of the Exchange City somehow," Amy declared, reviewing more documents.

"Yes, but they only allow registered traders off the base. It will take us several years to get ourselves established there in that category. Even then, we will be closely monitored, especially with what we can bring along with us," Jan pointed out. "They undergo top level searching of every item they bring with them to Ashford-5. No contraband is the idea, though Lech violates that on his whim."

For two days, the women were quite depressed. There seemed no way they could get there without triggering a massive manhunt, let alone bring their accumulated possessions with them. They were so close and yet so very far.

Amy didn't stop her searching. Ignoring all other Black Security business, she plowed into all avenues used in interplanetary travel. Then she came upon the ancient diplomatic immunity clause that was still rigidly enforced throughout the galaxy. High level diplomats were never subject to either weight limitations or to any screening or searching, not ever. They could travel to any planet in the Imperium, untouched by any and all security measures, as befitting a diplomatic emissary. Slowly, she got the idea they could get to Ashford-5 under the cloak of diplomatic immunity. But whose diplomats? This was one area neither had much experience in playing a role. Normally, they countered against diplomats, not joining them or being one of them.

After more research, she found virtually no diplomats ever went to Ashford-5. The records showed none had gone there for over a hundred-fifty years! Her hopes sank once more. Still, Amy was thorough, if anything. She setup a search to check on the possibility some diplomat somewhere had booked a diplomatic passage to Ashford-5 for some future date. She held out little hope whatsoever any would turn up.

Suddenly, Amy let out a war hoop! "Jan! Look at this, Emperor Chieng Sango of the Ataro Empire of the Twelve Sacred Planets of the Wasp has scheduled a full diplomatic meeting and tour of Ashford-5 to take place nineteen months from now. Jan, this is a perfect cover for us to get there."

Jan frowned, "I've heard of the Ataro Empire. Let me do some research before we get our hopes up to much, love." She typed away and sat back scrolling the pages her computer program had returned. "Well, the Imperium is going way out of its way to keep this emperor happy and satisfied. Actually, he controls thirty-six planets in the Ataro System, wealthy ones too, I might add. I can see why the Imperium wants to keep their emperor happy. They are a peaceful lot, by all reports. Their emperor runs a just system of planets, by all accounts. No wars for many centuries. Ah, from time to time, they send their children, who are called queens, off to the member planets to help in keeping the peace and settling disputes."

"There must be a catch somewhere," Amy broke in, now looking over Jan's shoulders.

"Oh! I guess there is!" Some images of Emperor Chieng Sango and Empress Amaka appeared on her large flat screen. Both women stared in disbelief, before Jan scrolled to the accompanying text. The two older people had yellowish skin, but their waists were incredibly tiny, perhaps a foot in circumference, if that! Combined with the fact neither appeared to have any arms, the two looked amazingly like wasps! Then they noticed their feet. Both appeared at first glance to have no feet at all, but then they saw that was mere illusion. Both were standing on their toes with their heels arched high in their very tiny shoes. Then they read the accompanying documentation.

> The emperor and empress of the wasp cult have kept the peace in the Ataro System for nearly two millennia. Chosen to fill these posts at birth, their bodies are modified shortly after birth. Internal organs are moved, and the characteristic waist binding is done at that time. In the adults, waists are extremely tiny, giving rise to the illusion of wasps, which these worlds hold sacred and worship. Additionally, the chosen one's feet are also modified at birth so their feet have a super high arch, the front of their heels aligning with the rear of their toes. Wearing their special shoes, they appear to have wasp-like feet. Additionally, the arms of the chosen ones are also removed at birth.

> The reason for these drastic body modifications, seen as barbaric on most worlds, lies in the absolute power the emperor and empress wield over their system of planets. Their word is law and binding. To offset this immense power, the high priests of the Holy Wasps remove their rulers' arms and hobble their feet so the emperor and empress cannot abuse the mighty powers entrusted to them.
> Their children are similarly handled at birth and, when they reach adulthood, are sent off as their representatives to various planets within the Ataro System. Called kings and queens, they have total power and adjudicate disputes, subject only to the emperor and empress.

> While seen as brutal treatment on many other worlds, within the Ataro System this practice has produced over two millennia of peace. There has not been an open conflict for over two thousand years,

quite unlike the Imperium, in this reporter's opinion.

"Incredible," Jan murmured. "Does this help us, love?"

"Don't know. What's that next one say?" Amy asked. Jan scrolled down to an advertisement that appeared last week. They read it together.

Help wanted. Ataro System. Emperor Chieng is looking for a young woman to become their next queen. The successful woman will be between eighteen and twenty-one. Must be willing to have her body transformed into that of a Holy Wasp. Also wanted: a domestique whose duties are to look after the new queen's needs, including feeding her and dressing her. Send bio to...

"How convenient," Amy mused, as a plan formed in her mind. "We ought to apply and take this position, subject to making darn sure we are on that diplomatic visit to Ashford-5."

"But love, isn't this a bit drastic? I need my hands to run my computers."

"I know, love. I'll apply for the queen position, and you apply for the domestique position. We can stall the actual delivery of the Nuclears until just around the time of that proposed diplomatic visit. We can take all our stuff with us and arrange for its shipment to wherever we want, after it gets moved from the port into Exchange City. We are going to need to establish some contacts there in Exchange City as well. What do you think? We can be home at long last in some eighteen months!" Amy said, growing more excited by the minute.

"But look what they will be doing to your body, love," Jan hesitated.

Amy countered, "With you looking after me, I'll do fine. Besides, I really don't use my hands much anyway. My *mentales* powers don't need them. Look, I don't see any other way of getting there, do you?"

Jan admitted, "Well, no. Besides, I am really getting tired of running Black Security. It's the same thing year after year. Assassinate this person, start a riot there. I just want to go home and live and breathe the fresh air of the foothills once more before I die."

"You aren't dying anytime soon on me, Jan, but I know what you mean. So do I. Come on. Let's hit the rejuvenation machine and get our applications sent in fast."

During the next week, the two made their preparations, crating up their valued possessions and moving them into the spaceport storage rooms. From there, they could order them shipped nearly anywhere in the galaxy. All they needed was computer access to send the shipping orders. At the end of the week, they received two tickets on the next spaceship bound for the Ataro System.

When they boarded Galaxy Ten, Amy realized they were flying first class and on a very fast ship, one of the newer models that cut travel time in half. Jan always traveled first class. Two boring days later, they stepped off onto the tarmac on Ataro Prime, home of the emperor and empress. This system's sun was bright yellow and warm and the air was clean and fresh, quite the opposite of the stale, recycled air of the spaceship. A man wearing a business suit with twin tails met them as they disembarked. "Are you the applicants?"

"Yes, I'm Amy Whitewater. This is my dear friend Jan Willow. We are from Ceti-6."

He smiled pleasantly. "Ah, excellent. If you will follow me, I will take you to Emperor Chieng and Empress Amaka. They of course will want to interview you, but if I do say so myself, you two have the highest qualifications of all the applicants to date." Jan returned his smile, *We ought to have. I prepared the apps myself!*

As they followed him walking across the concrete tarmac to a waiting air car, Amy probed the man's mind a little. Finding what she desired, she asked, "Excuse me sir. One thing that I was a little hesitant in putting down on the application, though it did not specifically ask for such, is telepathic ability. Will that be a hindrance or a benefit?"

He stopped abruptly and turned to face her. "Oh my yes! That would be a great benefit. We didn't put that in the ad primarily because a real telepath is so very rare. If you have your credentials, please *do* show them to the emperor." He turned and led them towards his waiting air car. Jan gave Amy a brief grin.

As they drove through the huge city, they noticed many life-sized statues of the emperor and empress. Even more interesting, they spotted many buildings designed to look like wasps as well. The ground floor of these looked more like a giant sphere or bulb with a tiny cylindrical connecting section that joined the second floor, which was also shaped like a bulb. Some were three stories tall, remarkably resembling wasps. Noticing the two staring at them, the man explained, "Oh, those are our Holy Temples."

Shortly, he stopped at an enormous complex where dozens of wasp-shaped buildings rose from the ground. Green grass actually grew in the intervening spaces between the buildings. Neither woman had seen real grass for many decades and admired it. Seeing their visible reactions, he proudly chatted some, "Oh yes, we cherish nature, and the gardens are just lovely, attracting many wasps who come for the pollen. If you will follow me, the emperor and empress await you. Your bags will be brought here shortly and taken to your quarters."

They followed him inside, past several security men. It felt strange walking into the bottom of a bulb shaped room, but once inside, it was even more curious. Well decorated, it felt comfortable and somehow homey. Having curved walls with curved windows seemed strange at first glance, but all the usual things were inside: reception desk, chairs, a picture gallery. They walked to the center where the elevator was located. Now they realized the elevator was housed within the small cylinders that connected the bulb shaped portions. They went up to the third floor.

When the doors opened, the unmistakable fragrance of fresh flowers greeted them. The huge room was filled with them, many lining a red carpet leading up to two thrones. On either side, a number of smaller thrones were unoccupied, presumably for the queens or children, all whom were currently on other planets. Ahead, a well-dressed man stood beside the emperor, while a woman wearing an elegant satin gown stood beside the empress. Both rulers looked exactly like their photos in their ad and closely resembled the statues the two had seen on their way here.

As in any court, there were a fair number of courtiers present standing off to the far right and left. Many of the women also had been modified into wasps as well as some of the men. Each of those also had a servant at their sides.

Amy tried to avoid staring at the emperor but could not. His waist was so tiny she thought she could put her hands around it. His white satin shirt was tailored to fit his unique shape. His white satin pants also were fitted to his form, with a contrasting black belt around his tiny waist, adding to the tiny wasp waist illusion. She noted the ULAT attached to it and relaxed. Language would not be a barrier here. Her eyes turned to the queen, who also wore a form fitting white satin dress, accentuating her form greatly adding to the wasp illusion. She too wore a black belt with attached ULAT box. Both of their feet were incredibly tiny and only with care did they both rise as the Amy and Jan finally approached their thrones.

"Welcome to Ataro Prime. I am Emperor Chieng Sango, my charming wife, Empress Amaka. Welcome indeed. We have reviewed your applications and are so thankful you have accepted our invitation to be interviewed for this position. First, I ought to add we are in need of another queen. Much is happening on one of our planets that needs a firm hand guiding them down the path of peace. Hence, we've had to accept the simple fact we must hire another queen. Of course, had we known years ago six children would not be enough, why, we could have tried for more." Empress Amaka chuckled slightly and gave him a wry grin.

"Now then, I must be wholly up front with the both of you, before we get down to the actual interview. Amy, you realize if you are chosen to become our next queen, then you will have to undergo irrevocable body modifications? Your arms will have to be removed; it's painless, of course, but permanent. Not even the Imperium out there with all their marvelous machines can restore them." Amy nodded and he continued. "Also, while the empress and I have ten inch waists, as is right and proper, since you both are grown women, we cannot approach that tiny of a waist line for you both. We will be able to remove a couple of your ribs and adjust the location of some of your internal organs, but the resulting waistline will be twelve inches at the very best, perhaps fourteen inches. We'll see. Again, rib removal cannot be undone. Finally, your feet will have to be modified into a high arch, such as ours. This is easily done and painless too, I might add. As I understand it, this process can be partially reversed by Imperium medical machines. So I ask you, Amy, are you willing to undergo this irrevocable transformation into our Holy Wasp form?"

"I am sir," she replied, wondering how she ought to address an emperor. We ought to have looked that up. Are we getting too cocky?

"Excellent. Now Jan, as her proposed servant, you will keep your arms so you can become hers. However, you will have your waist shrunk as well as your feet altered to match Amy's. In addition, all our domestique have their voice boxes altered so they cannot speak. Only the emperor, empress, and queens are allowed to speak, never their domestique helpers. Of course, this alteration is remedial by Imperium medical procedures. So I ask you, Jan, are you willing to undergo this transformation so you may serve Amy her with her needs? Oh, I forgot, you will both be taught sign language so the domestique staff can communicate with us, as needed."

"I am sir," Jan replied without hesitation. They had several of these medical machines packed away in their many shipping crates.

"Oh excellent, both of you, most excellent." He seemed exceptionally pleased, admitting, "So many of the applicants in the past never get beyond this point, you see, though quite why they failed to read the entirety of the ads eludes me. Now then, let's go over your qualifications. If you don't mind my saying this so directly, your extremely large busts really caught our attention. Such will greatly add to your overall wasp appearances. Might I ask if they are real?"

Both women smiled. How many times had they heard this asked? "Yes, your medical staff can verify they are indeed real," Amy replied, grinning broadly.

They chatted a bit about the requirements of the job, how much the two women would need to learn about their culture and ways and especially the various methods Amy would use in her adjudication of conflicts. Amy then asked, "I hope this is not a problem, but I am also a telepath."

Emperor Chieng looked up. Slowly a big smile appeared on his face. "Oh my! Yes, that is not a problem, rather the opposite! You are even more qualified to be a queen." Several hushed voices echoed from both sides of the room, all expressing surprise and pleasure. After a few more questions, he said. "Okay then, we accept you, Amy, to become our next queen and you, Jan, to become her domestique. If you will follow Anyang, she will take you to your new quarters and then to our medical facilities. Your training will commence soon."

Amy added, "One more thing, sir. We both would love to travel and see some of the other worlds, if that is possible."

"Oh my yes. In fact, we have heard of a strange planet, Ashford-5, that has an orange-red sun. We have our hearts set on visiting that world next year. The trip is already arranged. Your training should be finished by then, and we would love to have you both accompany us on that little trip. Amazing idea, an orange-red sun. I simply cannot picture that. Ours is bright yellow, you see."

"Oh thank you, thank you so much. We would love to see that amazing sight as well. It would be something to remember always. Thank you so much," Amy poured it on thick, but was really implanting firmly in both of their minds that the two rulers simply *had* to take these two along with them on their trip, no matter what else they did.

They followed the middle aged woman. Anyang was a domestique and as such she couldn't speak and they couldn't decipher her sign language yet. They did get a good look at her feet and shoes along with her quite minuscule waist. Only the flat of her toes made contact with the ground. Her shoes were extremely tiny, unlike anything the two had ever seen before. A thin, spiked heel touched the backside of the toe portion of the shoe and was built into the arch up to the heel, giving her barely a few inches of surface area on the ground, thus creating the illusion of a wasp's appendage. She walked both very slowly and very carefully.

They left this building and passed through a formal garden alive with wasps and gorgeous flowers. The odors were fantastic, such smells the two had never encountered before, delightful to their senses. They entered another similar building and were taken to the third floor where they found their bags had been brought. Amy said to Anyang, "This is our shared room?" Anyang nodded and motioned for them to follow her.

She led them to an adjacent building that had the universal red cross emblazoned above its entrance, signifying the medial department or hospital. Here, a woman doctor met them and dismissed Anyang. Once more, she went over the procedures with the two women and then gave them some juice to drink. Within minutes, both women were unconscious, and the medical staff set to work on the required modifications.

They were awakened a few hours later. Neither felt any pain but both felt a tight, unrelenting pressure around their waists and chests. "The pressure comes from the corset binding around your waists. You will need to wear them at all times, except when bathing. In time, you will get used to them, everyone does. Both were sitting in a reclining recovery chair and Amy tried to sit up but her arms weren't there.

"Oh!" she exclaimed. Jan tried to sit up and found her waist didn't bend in the slightest. She tried to say something but had no voice. "How do we breathe?" Amy asked.

"Take short, shallow breaths. You'll get used to it. You can only bend at your hips now. Also, you will find you need to eat more frequently but in much smaller quantities. We've pushed some of your organs up and others, down. It takes some getting used to. Now then, the next step is to get you both up and dressed properly. Anyang here will assist you both, though in the future, it will be Jan's duties to get you properly dressed. If I so say so myself, Amy and Jan, you will make a very spectacular queen and domestique. Your new shapes are just incredible, so wasp like. I am very pleased with the results, very. I am sure our esteemed emperor and empress will likewise be highly impressed with your wasp appearance.

Anyang, will you dress them now? Then show them to the dining area of their hive? I will check on your health tomorrow, but in all my years doing this, there has never been a complication afterwards."

Anyang began helping the two dress. Their binding corsets were made of steel re-enforced satin, white. Black nylons were then attached and a strapless satin slip covered their shapely forms. Each was then helped into a white satin dress, which again only served to outline their new wasp forms. A black belt with a ULAT box finished them off. Jan made sure they still were wearing their germanium crystals and kept Amy's out of its pod-silk covering, resting the gem on her chest. Finally, Anyang produced matching white satin shoes, perfectly fitting their strangely shaped feet. Amy suspected while they were unconscious, others had measured them for a such a fit. Their dresses were tight around their hips, but fell like a pencil from there on down, hemmed just below their knees. Anyang then helped them brush out their hair, removing their bluebird clasps, signing they were to allow their hair to flow freely.

Next, Anyang moved between them, putting an arm around each woman. Soon the two figured out Anyang wanted to help them learn to walk. As they tried their first steps, Jan's free left arm flew wildly about as she tried to keep her balance. Amy, just as precarious on her feet, couldn't and depended wholly on Anyang. Jan sent, *God! We won't be moving fast. No running for us ever again. How are you doing?*

Not good. If it weren't for Anyang, I'd be on the floor ten times now. I think I am going to really need you, love!

Anyang led them slowly out of the medical building and back to their new quarters. She did her best to keep Amy from falling down, but by the time they made it to the entrance, Amy had finally gotten her panic under control and saw the images in Anyang's mind. *Take tiny, tiny steps and slowly,* she sent to Jan.

Once inside, she led them to a door on their right. After opening it, she pointed to a buffet line where they could get something to eat. Another domestique pointed to a sign that showed the times food was available. Amy couldn't read the script, instead read the woman's mind. Meals were available six times each day, but the amounts were positively tiny by the standards Amy and Jan had always consumed. Still, Amy was stuffed when Jan finished feeding her. *Wow, she's right, we can't hold much at one time now,* Amy sent to Jan.

Next, Anyang took them to the elevator and showed them how to get to their bedroom on the third floor. After that, she led them to the room on the left, opposite the dining room. Here was where the two would be receiving their education, and such began right away with learning sign language. Both women quickly realized the only people allowed to care for them were other domestique women who could not speak and a very limited number of male advisors who could speak. However, all had the usual wasp appearance. Thus began long days of training for both women.

Within a month, Jan's training had come to an end. She and Amy could communicate using their special sign language, as well as with the other domestique staff. Jan now knew what all she had to do for Amy, most of which both women had anticipated long before coming to Ataro Prime. Nothing new there. From this point onward, Jan had merely to be quietly at Amy's side while Amy worked on learning all she needed to know. Hence, Jan had many hours where she was not needed, and she began checking on their computer systems. Once she verified the precise date of the trip to Ashford-5, she then sent out orders for their many crates to be shipped to the same spaceport where the spaceship they would be taking was stationed. Finally, she sent shipping orders to have their crates loaded onto the very ship they'd be using to make the vacation trip to Ashford-5. After that, Jan became terribly bored.

One evening while Jan was brushing out Amy's hair before bed, Amy said, "You know these people may actually have something of importance here in settling disputes. Today, I learned they believe if two people are fighting or are in conflict with each other, then there must be a third person behind the scenes fomenting or egging them both on to fight. They claim no two people will come to blows unless there is someone in the background actively working to get them to fight each other. Tomorrow, I am supposed to practice discovering who that third person is in conflict situations. It's part of what I am to do as their queen."

Can that really be true?

"I don't know, but they say so, and I am supposed to get trained in how to find this third person. We'll see," Amy replied.

The next day, with Jan at her side, Amy entered the room opposite their dining hall where two advisors now sat waiting patiently for them to arrive. On either side of them, two other men sat — their domestique helpers. Amy found it hard to believe the men when they began acting out their roles; they weren't good actors.

"Asida here is a low down cheat. He's no good and has been robbing us blind, my queen. I demand he be arrested and tried for his crimes against me! If not, I will kill him myself with my bare hands, if necessary!" Amy suppressed a giggle; the man had no hands or arms.

"He lies, my queen. Bapoto here has been stealing from his own company! He is the thief, not me. He is a low down, good for nothing drug addict, stealing from his own company to support his addiction! I should have killed him last night, and I swear to you I will stab him with my dagger today! The world will be a better place once I kill the drug addict!" Again, Amy fought to keep from laughing hysterically; he had no arms either. Their proposed threats seemed so incongruent to their physical bodies.

"Okay," Amy began trying to put what she had been taught yesterday to work for her. "Bapoto, can you think of anyone who may have told you Asida is a cheat? That he is robbing your company? Or that is he is no good? Come on, surely someone has mentioned this to you, right?" Amy had to probe him a little and nudge him, but soon he responded. "Jan, take what he says down for me please."

"Well, Chidi told me he saw Asida robbing my money bag. He said Bapoto was nothing but a cheat and I should get rid of him," he replied.

"Hey, wait a minute, Chidi told me you were a drug addict and were stealing from the company to pay for your next high," the other man interrupted.

"I've never touched the stuff in my life, Asida. How can I possible wield my butcher's knife while high on dope? Can't be done!" the first replied.

"Well, I'm no thief, Bapoto. I run the mill and make more than enough money. Surely you already know that. Chidi has been lying to us both!" the second man added.

"My queen," the first broke in, "we should get Chidi in here and find out what has really been going on. I did count my funds last night and have come up a hundred credits short. Someone has been stealing from me. I've the paperwork to prove it."

Amy smiled. "Okay, Jan, we need to find this Chidi fellow and interrogate him. I suspect we will find the missing credits in his possession." Jan wrote as fast as she could, not for the first time wishing she had her computer instead of the paper and pen.

Bapoto nodded, "Well done, my queen. You handled that perfectly. Indeed, Chidi was the truly guilty party, having stolen the credits and placing the blame elsewhere than on himself." Amy smiled, this was actually working out. "Now then, here comes the next one for you to solve."

The two men ran through a number of other scenarios. Amy had to figure out the real culprit each time. The going got tougher, though, and soon Jan had written down five names on each side of the argument as having said something against the other. Amy then looked over what Jan had down and spotted one name that was on both lists. She picked that one and soon saw the relief on both men; she'd found the guilty party once more. So it went that afternoon.

Several months later, the two were summoned before the emperor and empress once again. Slowly the two made their way to his building, sharing thoughts about what this summons was about. Neither had any notion. Jan had gotten very adept at anticipating Amy's needs and was handling them almost automatically without Amy even mentioning she needed some assistance. Still, Amy had Jan keep her arm around her waist while they walked. With so little of her feet on the ground, walking only on her toes was treacherous for her as she had almost no way to keep her balance, aside from wobbling her whole body, which looked anything but queen-like. None of the others seemed to wobble like she did.

After what seemed an eternity, the two entered the throne room and made their way up to the smiling pair. Carefully, both rose as the pair drew close to them. "Amy, Jan, you have both surpassed our wildest expectations in your education. Amy, you have completed all we would ever expect our queen to learn and in record time! The only area that remains a problem is your walking."

"I can't seem to do it without Jan's support, sir," Amy replied, inwardly smiling at her apparent success in the other areas.

"Well, Queen Amy, that is to be expected. We, my darling empress and I, as well as many others here, had our feet fixed when we were babies and have been walking since then. If I were to be fully honest with you, Amy, I would have to say you are making remarkable progress with your walking. I had anticipated you would have had major problems dealing with your loss of arms as well. Yet with that you have coped amazingly well. In time you will master the art of walking gracefully once more."

"Thank you, sir." Also, Jan signed her thank you as well.

"The reason I've summoned you both is the situation on Daros has worsened faster than we anticipated. I must send a queen there at once. As you are my only unassigned queen, I want to send you to Daros and let you handle the situation."

"But sir," Amy protested. All of a sudden, their long range plans to return to home to Ashford-5 were in dire jeopardy. "We don't want to miss the trip to the other worlds, the planet with the orange-red sun!"

"And neither do we, Amy. We've grown fond of your company and progress. We believe you will become one of our very best queens ever. No, if you are half as good in the field as you have been here in your studies, you ought to have that situation cleared up months before our departure date. If you do, then we *insist* you come with us to see this unusual planet."

Amy and Jan had little choice but to accept his word in the matter. That night, Jan packed their things into two trunks, adding several more of their special satin gowns and apparel, along with three pairs of their shoes. Not knowing if they would return here before leaving for Ashford-5, Jan also packed their other few belongings as well.

Chapter 19 The Arrival

On July 10th 1185, the luxury liner Star Blazer set down on Ashford-5 bringing Emperor Chieng Sango, Empress Amaka, Queen Amy, and their domestique staff with them, Tafair, Ayira, and Jan. An assortment of their advisors and related domestique accompanied them. As they began disembarking the liner, Sector ID Minister Lech and his wife, Karolina, were there to meet these important diplomats from the Ataro Empire. Of course, both wore their finest elegant fashions, and, for once Karolina was very pleased she had worn her best dress and tallest heels. The stunning white satin suits and dresses blended with their own fine quality silk dress, though Karolina was a little annoyed their heels were far higher than her own and began wondering if she could do something about that in the future. She *hated* to be out-done in fashions!

Emperor Chieng's advisors had sent advance messages to Lech so they would not be taken by surprise by their strange wasp-shaped bodies accompanied by their domestique staff. Still, Lech and Karolina could not help staring at their arriving guests. *They really don't have arms! My god, look at their tiny waists! And their heels. I am undone,* Karolina thought. *Well, I will be a gracious host anyway, even if they outdo me.* At least Lech had been briefed as to expected protocols. He bowed graciously to the emperor first, then the empress, and finally to the queen, ignoring their equally impressive domestique staff and the line of aides with their domestique staff bringing up the rear.

"Welcome to Ashford-5, Emperor Chieng. I do hope your stay will be most pleasant. If there is anything you desire, please just ask," Lech said formally.

Emperor Chieng bowed in return. "Ah, just being here is inspiring. Such sky color and the sun — it really *is* an orange-red. Bit chilly though. We would like a grand tour and we've heard there is a place called Exchange City where we can see the local inhabitants and how they live. We would like very much to visit that place, if it can be arranged, of course."

"Why yes, that can easily be arranged, Emperor Chieng. I will have my assistant, Jarek, and his charming wife, take you there tomorrow, though I can't imagine what you can see in this rather primitive, backwards planet."

Amy sensed that was precisely how he felt about her home world. It was all Amy and Jan could do to keep from jumping for joy. The smells, the dim illumination, the chill on the wind — all brought back a sea of early memories for the two women. Yet both were plunged back into the present time at the mention of the man who had ordered the two Nuclears, scheduled to be delivered in another month or so. Why did Jarek want them? What was going on here? Neither dared ask anything for fear of giving themselves away. Already Karolina noticed their massive bosoms, comparing theirs to hers. Besides, their yellow eyes with brown spots also tended to give them away.

"Oh mere curiosity, my good man," Emperor Chieng replied. "You see on Ataro Prime, our sun is a brilliant yellow, and we were all curious what it would be like to have a dull orange-red sun. I must say I am most impressed, Minister Lech, most. So quaint, so unusual. At least every couple of years, we believe our emperor ought to get out and visit another world, just to broaden horizons and not get so focused on our own world that we lose touch with reality. I must admit Empress Amaka and I were intrigued about a world with such a dim sun and so far from our system. We have planned this short vacation for several years now. I do hope we are not interrupting your important business, Minister Lech."

"Oh no, not at all. I am most honored that you and Empress Amaka have chosen Ashford-5 for a visit. As you know, it is a closed world, save for some minor trading in the Exchange City, so there is very little for you to actually see of this world," he tossed out, wondering if the emperor realized fully what the designation meant.

"Yes and that was another reason for our choice. There are so few closed worlds in the vast Imperium, and none of our previous emperors has ever visited one. I felt it would be wise for us to visit one. This way we will have a better notion of what that designation actually means and can rule our system

354

far better. *Knowledge*, minister, is highly valued in the Ataro System."

"Excellent then. I have instructed the groundsmen to transport your baggage to your quarters. As you can see, that tall building is the headquarters, while the smaller one is our barracks where I have set aside the Royal Suite for you and your aides. I do hope you will find the accommodations satisfactory. Nothing here is opulent, I am afraid. This is a working spaceport and little else."

"Oh I am sure we can rough it for the few days we will be here, minister."

Empress Amaka asked, "Say, I cannot help noticing you and your lovely wife are wearing very nice apparel, while all the workers we see scurrying about are wearing those awful looking Imperium cat suits. We on Ataro Prime believe in wearing very elegant dress. I do like your dress and heels, Karolina. They do you justice."

"Why thank you, Empress Amaka. We always try to look our very best, set a good example as they say. In fact, working through Exchange City, we have been trying our best to get the men and women of this world to dress better. Of course, they do not have satin here, only silk, so we are somewhat limited in the choice of materials. Ah, here we are. Your quarters. Your bags have already arrived. If you would like some time to freshen up, that's fine or we could take you to our private dining quarters if you are hungry." Karolina played hostess.

"Actually, we are rather hungry. Could we impose on you for a light lunch? You see, we are accustomed to eating rather small amounts rather frequently. Our waists, you see," Empress Amaka answered.

They took the group to a room that had been converted into a private dining room capable of handling the entire party. After their domestique staff helped each get seated, they took their positions to the left of each. As the meal was served, Karolina asked, "I've been meaning to ask you, how do you manage to have such tiny waists?"

Empress Amaka chuckled a little. Reading the woman's thoughts, Amy knew she often was asked this question. "When we were born and selected to become the emperor and empress, they modified our bodies some. Lower ribs were removed, especially in the men, and our internal organs were shifted up and down some. We always wear a satin corset that keeps our wasp-like form. You see, all of us in the Ataro System worship wasps, and we leaders attempt to fashion our forms after them. Even our feet have been altered to look more wasp-like."

"But your lack of arms?" Karolina asked what had been troubling her from the instant she first saw them disembarking the luxury liner.

"Oh, that has nothing to do with wasp shapes. No, that has to do with us personally," the empress continued, accepting a bite from Ayira. "You see, the Ataro System now has thirty-six planets in it. The word of the emperor, the empress, and our queens is law. What we say must be obeyed, no questions asked. We have what you might call 'supreme power.' Yet, this ultimate power must be tempered, for what is to keep one of us from abusing such authority? Hence, two millennia ago, the practice of removing our arms began along with our feet modifications. Even though we three here wield vast powers, we cannot become tyrants and abuse our positions, because we are utterly dependent upon our domestique to assist us with most everything. Of course, the domestique cannot speak; they've had modifications too. As you've seen, they communicate with us via sign language. So we have in place a perfect set of checks and balances against the abuse of our powers in our system. It has been one hundred percent effective for over two millennia now, during which time, there has not been a single battle or war or armed conflict. Our word is law, but we are helpless to abuse the trust placed on us by our people. Works perfectly. My, this dish is delicious, Karolina."

Karolina smiled, for she had chosen this delicacy with the empress in mind. She too could use a computer to her advantage. "Might I ask another question, empress?" Amaka nodded, taking a sip from the cup held up by Ayira. "I could not help noticing Queen Amy's bosom and that of her domestique are nearly the same as we women on Ashford-5 and their eyes are yellow, like mine. Yet, you and your husband's are not."

"Oh, well Queen Amy and her domestique came to us from Ceti-5, I believe. We all much admire both of these young women; their forms do *so* emulate our Holy Wasps, don't you think, Karolina?" The minister's wife smiled and nodded. She didn't dare come right out and ask if either had telepathic ability. She could sense they both did. It would be an affront to ask such a deeply personal question of total strangers. Nothing of further importance was discussed and shortly the visitors retired to their new quarters. Amy and Jan had their own room and found that their bags had been brought here.

We must be overly cautious and say as little as possible, Amy sent. *Karolina has the mentales gift, though I don't know how the aliens managed that. Keep your eyes open for more of the Rigel-3 people who do have it. That could complicate things for us.*

Right. I felt her touching my mind, but I kept my barriers up. Still, she is overly curious, I do think. We must be cagy. I am checking on the unloading of our many crates now. Pretend you are dozing or something so you don't need me for a few minutes.

That's easy. I am a little tired and overly stuffed. I ate too much.

A half hour later, Jan looked up and signed to Amy, who allowed Jan to help her into a sitting position which was extremely difficult for her to do alone because of the steel encased corset. *Okay, our crates are on their way to one Jonah's Warehouse in Exchange City where they await our next instructions. Now how are we going to commandeer a shuttle to fly to your old ranch home?*

After thinking a bit, Amy sent, *What about our asking Lech for a short fly about to get an aerial view of the port and the neighboring city? Say we want to get ourselves oriented spatially before we make the sightseeing trip to the city. Would that work?*

Possibly. But what about the crewman flying us?

Leave him to me. Can you fly it? I need my arms, which I now don't have.

Sure, there isn't a shuttle made that the Sly Fox can't fly. I can get us off the radar really fast. Get us to your old home and then crash the ship into the side of a ridge. I hate to kill the pilot, but what choice do we have?

None. That's regrettable, but after all, it was these very same Rigel-3 people who abducted us from our homes and sent us off-world so many years ago. Payback time.

Jan grinned and sent, *What about our bags here? I don't want to lose them. When do we make our escape?*

Can you re-tag them and have them forwarded to the warehouse too? We can pretend our bags somehow got mixed up at the spaceport back home.

Jan grinned; she loved how her lover's devious mind worked so rapidly in a crisis. A few minutes later, she'd altered their bag tags. Shortly after that, the automated machinery activated and she placed their bags on the conveyor. Promptly, they vanished from their room. *I do love these idiotic mechanized systems, dear. Plug in the new commands and presto, the machines take it from there. No human intervention is required. Our bags are now on their way to the warehouse and will not be opened. I flagged them as having already passed through customs inspections. So much for Lech's security around here. I wonder if he is in on this Nuclears deal?*

Don't know. I've been thinking about whether or not we should meet this Jarek fellow. Could be tricky for us, especially if he also has the mentales gift. Besides, we are supposed to get that trip tomorrow. Should we try to get the fly over yet today? It's only around noon, local time. Let's make our break now, but should we tell Chieng and Amaka we are taking a fly over? Amy asked.

Jan bit her lip and signed yes. *We should, after all that they have done for us. Then they can properly grieve for us when they learn the shuttle crashed in the mountains.*

A half hour later, the two women made their painfully slow way out across the concrete tarmac following an impatient Rigel-3 man. Chieng and Amaka thought this was a great idea to get their queen oriented, and Lech was more than willing to oblige them. Jan had some difficulty lifting Amy into the craft and the man kindly offered to help them both aboard, taking the opportunity to feel their bosoms. Both women knew they had greatly aroused the man, who tried to hide it from them. Soon they were airborne and making their fly over, covering the twenty-five mile width of the port rapidly. Then, he flew over Exchange City as requested.

During this time, Jan familiarized herself with the auxiliary controls, in preparation for taking over the flight from their pilot. Amy's crystal began glowing bright blue. She took over the motor controls of the pilot. At once, Jan began flying the shuttle, making the craft do wild, crazy motions, as if something had gone very wrong with the craft. Then she ducked well below radar range and pushed the throttle to maximum thrust, heading due south at close to six hundred miles an hour. She set the navigation controls to the head of the valley Amy had carefully designated long before they left their basement headquarters. They arrived in less than an hour. Meanwhile, Amy forced the pilot's voice to radio in an emergency distress call, citing massive engine failure coupled with a complete navigational breakdown.

"There it is! My old home! That's the ranch house! Put us down there. I am getting really excited. Will my family still be there? Is anyone still alive?"

Hold your horses, love. Here we go. Jan landed the shuttle craft and got herself out and then struggled to get Amy out. Meanwhile, Amy simply sent the right thought into the pilot's body and he died instantly. If no one was here, Amy planned to return to the spaceport or possibly check on Jan's old home. Only if they found Amy's relatives here would they then destroy the ship, but they had to act fast. Lech was sure to send out a rescue ship at any moment. It might already be tracking them.

Neither woman had yet attempted to walk on the rocky, rough ground that was Tierra, and they suddenly discovered walking was incredibly difficult. However, the front door opened and several people filed out. Amy recognized her older sister at once, in spite of the woman's advanced age. Marla was now seventy-eight years old.

"Oh my god! Amy? Amy Blackwater? Is that really you?

It's Marla!" the old woman called out, leaning heavily on an old man who walked with a stiff right leg, which the two soon saw was a wooden pegleg. Behind them another older woman, Luisa, now seventy-one, followed, leaning on another man who was missing his right arm.

"Marla! My god, it is you! It's me, Amy! I've finally found my way home!"

Marla was crying tears of joy, but asked, "Oh my god, what's happened to you?" She meant her lack of arms, Amy picked up. "You look just like I remembered you. How can this be? You should be in your seventies, an old woman like myself!"

"It's me. Alien rejuvenation machine, sis. We've used it twice just to get back here. Sorry, I can't hug you, though I would give anything to do so."

"Never mind that dear. So many men and women are now missing limbs." Marla hugged her sister tightly, sobbing all the while. Even Jan found herself crying too. Then Jan realized they needed to destroy the ship.

I will destroy the ship now. Okay?

Yes, do it. I can't keep from crying, Jan.

"What's happening to your ship? Are the aliens bringing you back?" Marla asked. All four watched the ship take off, seemingly on its own. Jan was piloting it remotely, having triggered her pre-planned flight path. Jan and Amy turned slowly to watch too. The ship took off at a high rate of speed, maximum thrust and slammed into the distant side of the south ridge. A fireball explosion resulted.

"There, we are now all considered dead. We've escaped. Can we get inside? We can barely walk in these heels. Oh, Jan here cannot speak any longer. I'll explain inside. Mom and dad?"

"Oh sis, they are long dead. All our family are. Only I am left now. We just returned a month ago and found the old ranch had been abandoned. Most of it is totally rotten and run down. But we all knew we just had to be here for some reason. We four are always immensely lucky. I've been looking, searching for you, Amy, ever since that night you were taken from us. All these years, we four have been looking for you.

And here you are at long last!"

"Dear, why don't you help your sister navigate. I can manage myself," Hernando suggested, noticing how precarious Jan and Amy actually were, as they tried to keep their balance while only their toes touched the uneven ground.

Inside, Amy found her old home a complete mess. Marla and her friends had managed to make a small portion livable again, but only barely. Still, they had a warm fire going and the teapot waiting. After sitting Amy down carefully on a chair that had seen better days, Jan took a seat to her left as Marla and Luisa poured out the tea. "Sis, this is my life-long lover and best friend, Jan Bellweather, who was also abducted from her ranch further north of here. We finally found a way to get back here, but it demanded we make sacrifices. I lost my arms; we both got our waists shrunk and feet modified, as you can see. Also, Jan lost her voice, but we made it back here."

Marla introduced her lucky friends. "My husband, Hernando Polito, he comes from the Westerlings as do the others. Our children are all grown up now and have married and scattered to the four winds. This is my dear friend Luisa and her husband Valerio Urbano. We were all involved in the first huge war of the towers, back in 1132." Marla spent an hour relating a fast synopsis of their four lives and the incredible luck that always followed the four.

"She's right. We were minding our own business, when all of a sudden, Marla here says we just have to return here to her old abandoned Midlands home. So we did just that. Now we see why," Hernando added proudly. "Your sister has been the kindest woman I've ever met."

Amy, in contrast, knew she had vastly more to tell her sister. Yet, so much of it all would be far beyond anything Marla or the others could possibly imagine. "Jan and I have been on many, many planets, and done many, many strange things. We have been what most would call underground rebels, fighting the Imperium all these years, trying to find our way home. Until very recently, we had no idea where in the entire universe Tierra was located. At last, we discovered the aliens call it Ashford-5. In monetary terms, we have both amassed a huge fortune by even the Imperium standards, to say nothing of having brought some of their technology back with us. One device is their rejuvenation machine, which we've each used to take fifty years off our bodies. Once we have retrieved it from storage in Exchange City, we can use it on you four, if you like."

Marla smiled, "Sis, I have no doubt that you could. But considering the horrid state that our world is now in, frankly, I don't want to live another fifty years. It has become a hell hole, but more of that later. I want to hear more about yourselves."

"Okay, sis. Maybe Jan and I can do something about that state, once we know all about it. Anyway, since this is a closed world, we found it nearly impossible to get back here. Finally, we found a way. We came under diplomatic immunity as part of Emperor Chieng Sango's group. However, to do so, I had to become one of his queens." She began to relate what they had done for the past many months. This, the four could rather follow, especially since they saw the visual connection to wasp shapes as soon as Amy mentioned it.

Marla began crying when Amy finished, "You had your arms cut off just so you could return to me. Oh sis, you shouldn't have done that! Not for me."

Amy cried too; she was home but so helpless now. She wanted to reach out to the old woman, but had no way to do so. All were sobered instantly as the drone of another shuttle craft broke the stillness of the room. "Shit, they are coming to search for the wreckage already. Okay, can you hide us? If the aliens come, say nothing about us, only that you heard a loud noise outside." Amy pleaded. Marla rose and led the two into her makeshift bedroom. She helped them onto the bed and covered them up with an old, worn out quilt. She joined the other three who were looking out of a glass-less window towards the south, where another shuttle was hovering over the still smoldering remains of the shuttle Jan had destroyed. As they watched, a disintegrate beam destroyed what little remained of the ship so none of the alien materials could fall into the hands of the locals. Luck was again with Marla as the craft then left the area. All on board were marked as lost in the unfortunate crash of the shuttle. Amy hoped Chieng and Amaka did not take their loss too badly, but had no way of knowing, save using telepathy, which would give everything away.

After the aliens left, they again returned to the makeshift table in the living room. Again, they chatted until Marla had to prepare their supper. After that, Amy said, "We need to head north to see if we can find any of Jan's relatives alive. From there, we need to get into Exchange City and retrieve our many crates. If we can recover our medical machine, we hope to be able to undo the damage done to our feet at least and we hope to fix it so Jan can talk again."

Marla laughed. "Sis, you are looking at Los Cuatro Santos, the four saints. We are the luckiest four people on Tierra — have been for over fifty-three years now. It all started because we four decided in spite of all that we endured, we wanted to live and to help others, especially Luisa, who can heal, and Valerio too. Everywhere we go, we help others as we can and they in turn help us. Out back, we have a fine wagon and team. We've plenty of food on hand, and clothes too, fitting for this climate, though your fancy dresses are the prettiest I've ever laid eyes on, sis. If anyone can find Jan's folks, it is us. We are lucky. You will see."

"Aye, phenomenally lucky," Hernando added. "Besides, your sis is the world's greatest cook!" Amy grinned.

Luisa spoke up, "Jan, let me have a look at you and see if there is anything I can do for your speech. I can't use my right arm, but I manage without it fairly well." Jan nodded yes vigorously. Only now did she hate terribly not being able to utter a sound.

After activating her crystal, Luisa set to work, examining Jan's throat. Soon, she opened her eyes. "Well, they have inserted some kind of object that is keeping your vocal cords from vibrating. If given enough power, I can lift it out of your body, but to do so would require a full circle's power. If we can get you to one of the remaining towers, they might do this for you. I am so sorry I am unable to help you, Jan."

Jan signed a thank you, but she slumped, and Amy knew she felt really badly that she was now unable to speak. Well, they had paid the price needed to return to their home land. Marla then insisted on getting some sleep. "When you get as old as we, you need much more sleep." Amy smiled and wished her sister would change her mind and let her use the rejuvenation machine on her and the other three.

There were not enough workable beds and Hernando insisted Jan and Amy sleep with Marla. He crawled in with Valerio and Luisa. For the first time in fifty plus years, Amy rested her shoulder on her older sister. Both women realized this and sobbed for some time. Jan, however, began to think of her own relatives. Were they alive?

The next morning, the two discovered that although they moved extremely slowly, as they had been doing so for the last many months, Marla and her three companions were even slower. Old age was taking a terrible toll on the four, although outside, they were severely hobbled, unlike Marla and the others.

While Marla whipped up a nourishing breakfast, Luisa rummaged through their spare clothing to find something for the two to wear. While their white satin dresses were elegant, they were wholly unsuitable for this land and its weather. Besides, their white dresses would set them apart instantly. By the time Marla called out for them to come and get it, Luisa had the two dressed reasonably well. While there was nothing she could do for their shoes and feet, she did have them in leather pants and a heavy linen blouse that mostly fit, as long as one ignored their waists. She'd lent them each a bluebird clasp and Jan and Amy felt human once more, their hair tied back the way they had always worn it.

As Jan fed Amy, Marla suggested a plan of action. They'd pack up everything and head north to see if they could find Jan's relatives. Based on Jan's telepathically sent data, Marla guessed her home ranch was around a hundred miles further north, well into what used to be Haverhills territory, before its annihilation by Valen Tower. She estimated they would be there in four days.

Riding in the wagon bed, Amy and Jan breathed in the heady fragrances of summertime in the high foothills of the Goza Mountains, odors they'd only know in childhood. Both were supremely happy to have made it this far. Also, they began to admire Marla and her group. At every ranch they came to, Marla insisted on stopping and asking if they needed any healing or other services the four could provide. During those four days, Luisa healed three sick men and one broken arm. After that, Jan and Amy joined her, helping as they could as well, though Amy had a more difficult time of it.

When they arrived at Jan's childhood home, her heart sank. The entire ranch had been destroyed by Valen soldiers as they passed through years ago. Only a burned out shell remained and there was no trace of her relatives. Although they continued to ask others they met, no one remembered any of the Bellweather clan.

Two days after that, they halted before a large warning sign. "We have to go around here. The battle for Haverhills Tower has poisoned the very soil for miles around the old city. Nothing grows or lives out there. It is a dead land, thanks to the tower's circles!" Marla spat on the ground and the men swore silent curses. Luisa merely grimaced and glanced at her useless right arm. They carefully detoured around the destroyed land, thankful at least someone had placed markers periodically around the dead zone, warning travelers. The detour added another two days to their travels, but allowed them to heal another three men, who in return added to their supplies. On the twenty-first of July, they finally arrived at the outskirts of Exchange City.

Amy and Jan now had to make some decisions. Having spent the past days with Amy's aging group, lucky though they may be, their bodies were old and certainly not up to handling the heavy crates that needed to be recovered. At least three more wagons would be needed to haul them to wherever they might go. Staying in Exchange City would be perilous for the two, since they could be recognized. Amy took a chance and explained this to her sister.

Again, Marla and her luck rose to the occasion. "Say, we ought to use the Sisterhood. I was once a member before that battle. They think I'm dead. So I want it to remain, as do we four. However, I think we could hire the Sisterhood to take us wherever you want to go, sis. Let me go ahead and see what I can work out with them." Amy smiled and agreed.

Hernando drove the wagon through the crowded

streets, arriving before the Sisterhood house. "How on Tierra did you find this place, Hernando?" Amy asked, very much impressed.

"Oh, just luck. We go by what feels right. You tell her, Marla," the old man suggested.

Marla smiled, "I think you said it right, dear. Now let me make some inquiries." She slowly climbed down, helped by the one armed Valerio. She made her slow way to the door, knocked, and then entered when a young woman opened the door. Marla was gone for a half hour, during which Amy worried continuously some alien would come along and recognize her and Jan. None did however.

Then Marla came out accompanied by a middle-aged woman. "Hello. I am Angelica Evita e Kaylee." She was fifty-three and a veteran fighter, well-muscled, yet very much feminine. "Marla here has been telling me a very unusual story. Could you all come inside? Our guild mother and I have many questions to ask of you before we can accept your mission. Do you need help getting down?"

"Jan can't speak. Yes, I do, please, we are a mess."

Angelica grinned, and Amy felt her strong arms lifting her as if she weighed little. "You don't have any arms, do you? What happened to your feet? I can see a story coming now."

A few minutes later, the six sat around a wooden table with Angelica and her house guild mother, Rebecca, who was perhaps sixty. "We have heard of Los Cuatro Santos, and we thank you for all your kind deeds to our people," Angelica began, bringing a smile to Marla's face and that of Amy's too. She was suddenly very proud of her older sister.

"I guess Jan and I have a lot of explaining to do, though she can't speak at the moment." Amy began to relate their tale, at least as much as she dared. Some of it would be far beyond their capacity to understand. She said mostly what she'd already told her sister.

When she finished, Angelica replied, "Most interesting. I can tell you are telling the truth. My mothers were Fel, one of the most famous Sisterhood fighters, and Cassia, an alien from the port. She was at one time a field agent for them. Long story, but I am their child, don't ask me how two women can manage to begat a child, but Cassia bore me. I can tell you about that later on. What is important is I understand much of what you are saying. I still have access to mom's alien machines, including her healing machine."

"But Amy and Jan, no longer is Tierra the way you left it. Back then, as I understand history, it was a time of relative peace. Since then, it has been nothing but escalating wars between the towers, well most of them. It began with Valen Tower taking out Portillo Tower, which Marla and her group were part of. I'll let them describe the horrors there. Since then, the horrors have only grown by leaps and bounds. You've seen the dead zones around what used to be Haverhills. Oakham is also a dead zone for miles around it. Bedwurth Tower fell as well, but most of their people evacuated to their new tower in Wye. Wyth Tower is planning to evacuate too but as yet, they've not decided on the location. Bettingham is preparing for the long anticipated assault by Valen Tower, whose armies are staging south of there across the Southfork River. I am afraid you've returned in time to witness the destruction of everything."

Jan made some signs to Amy. Oh how she wanted to tell her about the Nuclears and what they'd discovered, although she now deeply regretted having shipped the Nuclears here. Amy talked for her. "Angelica, it's far worse than that. We know Jarek, the field agent of Lech's, has purchased two Nuclears. These are humongous bombs that will wipe out whole cities, vaporing everything within miles of the city. They will be delivered to him in about six more weeks. It's all hush, hush, secret and all that. Nuclears are outlawed on all planets in the Imperium, for obvious reasons. If we can get to our gear we have stored in that warehouse, Jan and I might be able to stop them from igniting."

"Shit! This is even worse news. God damn all men everywhere!" Angelica cursed. Hernando and Valerio grimaced, but only agreed with her, despite the fact they were men. After all, they began as soldiers making war. Her anger dissipated rapidly as her fighter training kicked in. "Okay, then there is only one option left to us. The only sane tower left in the Midlands and the Westerlings is Brom Tower in the far

north. That's where I am stationed. I led my group here to
trade our furs for swords. In July, the aliens make their official
lease payments of iron ore and gold. That's when we can get
the best deals for our furs. My group will retrieve your crates
and take them and you back to Brom, where you can plead
your case to the Venerado there. This is way beyond anything I
want to handle — a bomb that can vaporize an entire city.
Good god! God damn men anyway! If only women could get
control." Amy smiled, but wondered if that would be any
better.

"I think Jan ought to come with us, not you, Amy. You
are too much of a liability. No offense, but with no arms, we
can't be looking after you too. Jan will be enough of one with
her feet so hobbled. Marla, bring your wagon into the stables
here and wait for us. Oh," she looked at Rebecca, who smiled.
She didn't mind her authority being overlooked.

The guild mother merely said, "You are right, Angelica.
I'll look after these. You do what you must to get their things.
May Lysandra watch over us all."

"Who's Lysandra?" Amy asked. While Jan disappeared
with Angelica, Rebecca began a rather lengthy tale. Marla and
her group listened in as well. Amy, of course, really didn't
believe there was such a thing as a goddess.

Angelica, Jan, and some fifty Sisterhood fighters pulled
up at the warehouse. Jan produced the corresponding
shipping tags and the burly foreman led the women to the
many crates. "Gosh, these are heavy," Angelica grunted. Jan
smiled and activated her crystal, focused, and used some psi
energies to help the women lift the crates. As anticipated, five
wagons were fully loaded with their things. While the foreman
was intensely curious about just what the crates contained, he
knew better than to mess with Sisterhood fighters, especially
fifty of them. Besides, he'd heard of Angelica, a fierce fighter.
Rumors suggested she'd once emasculated a man.

Two hours later, the wagons returned to the large
stables of the guild house, accompanied by a cold, late
afternoon rain. At least, it would not turn to snow, Angelica
muttered to herself. Inside the packed house filled to capacity,
she and Jan joined Amy and Marla, as Rebecca finished up her

lengthy discussion of all the news. Since Jan couldn't speak, Angelica did. "Okay, that's done. Five wagons fully loaded. We are going to need at least one more wagon to carry our supplies."

"Jan can give you some funds to purchase one," Amy volunteered. "Thank you for doing this for us." Jan made some gestures, and Angelica grasped she wanted to know how much silver.

"You can pay after I get them. Now then, we best work out just where we are going and the route. As I said, Brom Tower is about the safest one around, but the climate there is darn cold. The winters are awful."

"Let's go with safe. I trust your guidance, Angelica," Amy stated, glancing at Jan who nodded as well.

"Okay. Then, here are the problems we face getting there. We have to detour around what used to be Bedwurth and its castle and tower. There is a huge dead zone that covers a radius of fifteen miles around the tower there. Nothing lives within that zone. What's bad is we cannot return the way we came. Loaded with bundles of furs, the wagons were not heavy. So we opted to take some really rough tracks to the west of Bedwurth, little more than deer trails, meaning we were in some very impassable terrain, right up against the mountains. Often, we physically had to push the wagons over some of the barriers. With your heavy load, we cannot hope to return that way. Hence, we face going eastwards around the Bedwurth dead zone."

"Why is that a problem?" Amy asked.

Tracing a route on her map, Angelica pointed out, "Valen's army and support personnel are always traveling from here in the city, up north and veering east along the Southfork River towards their staging area south of Bettingham. It is highly likely we will run into one or more groups of soldiers, quite dangerous."

"Is there any safe route?" Amy asked.

Angelica sighed, "Well, if it is safety you desire, we could head due east from here, making for Wye and then cross the Wyndl and head up its northern bank to Brom."

Jan sent, *Good god! That is five times longer! We'll be*

til fall getting there, Amy.

Amy countered, "That's no good at all. We need to get there much sooner. I have a feeling we have maybe six weeks to get ready for the attacks. The number of lives that are at stake here are enormous. Get us there the fastest way possible. Leave the handling of any hostile soldiers to me. Trust me and leave the soldiers to me and Jan."

Is she some kind of utter fool? Leave the soldiers to an armless woman who can barely walk? Is she mad? Hell, this is turning out to be death run. "Okay, we go north and then eastward around the dead zone. We'll stay east of Wyth as well, coming into Brom from the east, that will be the easiest for heavily loaded wagons. Get some sleep; we leave at the crack of dawn."

"Good. One more thing, Jan and I ought to ride in the lead wagon so we can have a clear view of fire against hostile soldiers," Amy added. Angelica shrugged and agreed, but shook her head in dismay, figuring these women would be the first to die if the soldiers attacked them, which in all likelihood they would.

The air is so cold and crisp, Jan sent Amy as they sat on the driver's bench of the lead wagon, waiting for their Sisterhood driver to mount. Angelica was busting about, issuing her orders to the assembled group of fighters.

Refreshing. Lord, how I've missed this. Fifty plus years, Jan. Now we are back. If we get stopped, don't hold back. A few dead soldiers cannot compare to a Nuclear, Amy sent back. Soon the group began rolling down the streets of Exchange City. Already many were on the streets, going about their business. More than a few wagons were also heading north out of the city. As they topped one rise, they could see an group of army supply wagons a mile ahead of themselves. A group of mounted soldiers accompanied the dozen wagons. Amy sensed Angelica's unspoken curse.

The orange-red sun angled down from the east, their right side, casting long shadows that steadily shrank as the ruddy orb climbed higher in the sky. Rough boulders lay everywhere and their trail wound its way around them. Here and there, hardy, wind-blown pines sparkled the reddish light in their drying needles. Steadily, the air warmed and the smell of fresh resin began to dominate all other odors. Amy and Jan had tears of happiness dripping down their faces; they'd missed this so much and for so long that neither had any words to describe their intense feelings that first morning on the trail. Not even the slow buildup of clouds from the southwest that began shortly before noon could dampen their mood.

Angelica had quite a different mood. She was sizing up the soldiers ahead of them. *They nearly match our force. Bet they are carrying more acid bombs and fire bombs in those wagons. I don't see any air cars or catapults so they can't use them against us, I don't think. Could we take them, one on one? Too many casualties on our side. No, best adjust our speed to keep them a mile ahead of us. If they turn off, we'll keep on going north, if possible. Yet, if they are carrying more bombs to the front lines, wouldn't it be wise to destroy them here before they were able to use them against Bettingham? No, then we'd just make another dead zone right here on the main route north. Hell fires! What would my moms do?* She had no instant answer and let that notion pass.

Ahead, the army convoy halted to rest their horses and grab some lunch. Angelica duplicated them, keeping a mile separation between them. Nevertheless, she posted six guards to keep a sharp watch on them, alerting her if they made any attempt to backtrack to her group. The soldiers were doing the same thing, keeping a sharp watch on the Sisterhood wagons and fighters.

"If they stop for the night before we do, then we can pass them," Angelica explained to her assembled women who were grabbing a light lunch. "Then put some distance between us before camping. On the other hand, maybe they will push on late into the night and leave us behind."

"What if they turn around and accost us?" asked her second in command, a woman named Beth.

Angelica looked over at Amy who was being fed by Jan and sighed. "We are supposed to leave them to Amy and Jan." Beth gave her a questioning look as if Angelica had just lost her wits. All she could do was shrug her shoulders.

Late afternoon brought a light, cold rain, as usual this high in the foothills so close to the mountains. Ahead of them, the army convoy pulled off into a small glen that offered some hardy grasses for their horses along with a batch of resinous pines. Angelica instructed her group to continue onwards, even though the light dimmed with the orange-red sun now behind the western mountains. "I know the trail. We go on for another five miles. There is a good spot with grass and water too." Beth smiled, she too knew that spot.

When Angelica finally felt she'd put enough distance between the army convoy and themselves and reached her camping spot, full dark accompanied by a steady drizzle made setting up camp rather miserable. Still, Amy and Jan marveled at the utter efficiency of these amazon women who went about their tasks of setting up camp, collecting firewood, and cooking supper — all without anyone issuing any orders, except to the six newcomers. Amy felt really frustrated; she missed her arms now more than ever before. She and Jan had great difficulty even walking the short distance to their latrine. Neither complained vocally, though.

The next morning, Angelica explained to everyone, "Today we should reach the Bedwurth dead zone and have to head east. We are likely to encounter Valen solders. So stay alert everyone."

Around noon, Angelica told Amy her outriders had spotted some Valen scouts who had spotted their wagons. "Somewhere up ahead, you will get your soldiers. Are you sure we are to leave them to you two?" she asked, giving the helpless women a last chance to change their minds.

"Absolutely. Leave them to us, Sly Fox and Eager Beaver. She's Sly Fox and I'm Eager Beaver," Amy replied very seriously. Angelica merely shrugged and nudged her horse on ahead of the lead wagon.

Late afternoon, they veered right towards the east. Ahead lay a blackened area devoid of all plant life. Dead pine trees stood in some unreal matchstick forest. They had reached the Bedwurth Dead Zone. "My god!" Amy whispered.

The bastards! Jan sent angrily.

They had not gone two miles to the east when a band of

seventy Valen soldiers rode up to them. Their leader had an outlawed blaster drawn, while his men had crossbows and swords at the ready. As he rode up pointing the deadly weapon at them, he called out, "Halt and be searched."

Angelica stared at the weapon and knew it spelled instant death. Amy and Jan acted, and their crystals glowed brightly. To Angelica's and everyone else's total shock and surprise, the man with the blaster died instantly and his blaster floated over and into Jan's outstretched hand. Amy barked out loudly, "Leave us instantly or die!"

Three men fired their crossbows at the leaders. Mid-flight, the quarrels stopped as if they had hit an invisible wall, dropping harmlessly onto the ground. The three shooters fell off their horses, quite dead. Then pandemonium broke out among the remaining soldiers, as one after another fell off their horse, dead before they hit the ground. Amy and Jan vented their pent up anger. The sight of the dead zone roused a vicious anger in both women and they withheld nothing.

When there were no more soldiers, the two blue glows finally subsided. Nearly speechless, Angelica muttered, "Holy shit! My god! They are all dead! How?" Fifty Sisterhood women began whispering similar words among themselves.

"Amy, are you all right?" Marla called out from their wagon far to the rear.

"Fine, no one is hurt, the bastards," Amy yelled back to her older sister.

"What the devil happened to them?" Angelica finally found a coherent thought.

"A thought can kill," Amy said calmly. "We best get going. There could be more where these came from."

"You, you did that? A thought?" Angelica asked, still dumbfounded. She'd never seen anything like this. Bombs, yes. A rain of arrows, yes. A circle working together, yes. But two women seemingly doing nothing at all? Never!

"Yes. Jan and I have lived a lifetime combating the Imperium and whatevers. Of course, the Imperium considers us, Sly Fox and Eager Beaver, to be the most feared and hunted assassins in the entire galaxy. From their point of view, we are just that, but then again, they made us what we are.

Come on, it isn't wise to linger here, though I would relish taking out another bunch. That was enjoyable, a tiny bit of revenge for those lost at Bedwurth," Amy replied.

Angelica resisted the temptation to round up the horses, confiscate their swords, and such. They hastily drove on eastward until Angelica thought it was safe to veer back northwards once more. It was full dark and drizzling before she found a safe ford across the Southfork River, some thirty miles east of Bedwurth and ten beyond its dead zone. They camped just outside a small village that night.

The next ten days were more idyllic. Here within the borders of the Kingdom of the Angels, life continued as if nothing had ever disturbed it. Nut tree farms dotted the landscape along with green pastures filled with sheep. Fields were bordered with low stone fences made from the stones dug from the fields they enclosed. Occasional farmers and shepherds waved as they passed by. Several nights, Angelica sent some of her fighters into the villages to bring back a keg of ale for her group. For these ten days, time seemed to slip back into the way of life that Amy and Jan had known in their childhood and early teens, quiet, peaceful, laid back, the era of peace the Brom Compact had brought to Tierra.

The last day of their trip, the land rose continually, as they approached the town of Brom, cradled up against the base of the Goza Mountains. Here the air was chilly even at noon in August. Then they saw Brom Tower and the castle up ahead, towering over the walled town proper. Now would come many explanations and many decisions and actions.

Chapter 20 The Blackwater Ultimatum

They arrived on the first of August. Angelica chatted away. "Here in Brom Tower, you will find quite a lot of women like yourself, Amy. They have a very rare and unique *mentales* gift called katalyein. My moms helped the tower men to realize that their five generations of inbreeding led to disaster. While they finally did recover that lost gift, the price they paid was steep. Now these women are encouraged to marry outside their direct lineage. Strange as it is, only the women have the gift, the men do not. The women and girls who look like you, Amy, are all my nieces and cousins, in one form or another. Anyway, if anyone has any kind of blockage of their *mentales* gift, they come here and one of the katalyein rapidly removes that block."

"Brom Tower now has six complete working circles, more than any other tower. The others have suffered attrition from all the wars, you see. The reason for so many goes back to the former Venerado Simon Bolivar, who allowed the tower men and women to begin wearing the Elegant Fashions Inc wear — rather similar to the fancy white dresses you two wore along with heels sort of like the ones you are wearing. Men wore handsome suits and women, elegant dresses and impossible heels. Well, you can imagine the arousals that resulted. They have had a huge baby boom here at Brom," Angelica chuckled. "They even tried numerous times to marry me off to some man or join one of their circles. No way, not this woman! I take after my moms. At least they still accept me in their councils; I'll give them that, even though I am a sworn member of the Sisterhood, like one of my moms."

"One piece of advice, you will do well to wear your fancy white dresses. Most all of them wear fancy outfits, unless they have to leave the complex or do some other work. Of course, those who are like you, Amy, always wear their fancy outfits and heels. It gives them a feeling of self-respect they often lack, though that is not so much the case these days as it was back when I was a child. According to my Rigel-3 mom, there is a recessive gene that is responsible for their lack of arms, but then I have no idea what a gene is, way beyond me."

"Now what you should know is the Venerado is Simon's youngest son, Pete Bolivar. He's sixty-three and is calling the shots at Brom now that Simon's gone. For a time, his older brother Rolf had the position, but he's sixty-seven and in failing health. Of course, the stewards actually run the domestic side of the place. Ben and Misty Waters, brother and sister, handle these things, which in my opinion is the tougher challenge. There are over five hundred eighty now living in the tower-castle complex. They are in their fifties, so it'll be Ben and Misty who will be arranging your quarters."

Amy sensed how deeply Angelica felt about the town and tower; this was the woman's home. The closer Angelica got to Brom, the faster she chatted away. Amy also sensed a deep fear that before long, Brom too would be destroyed — another dead zone joining the other three. *I am not going to let that happen here. This place is like home to me. It's my world and I'll be damned if I am going to let the corrupt Imperium destroy the best of our world.*

"How many people live in this quaint town?" Amy asked Angelica when she could squeeze in a word.

"Well over seven thousand. I know, it is not as large as Haverhills or Oakham or Bedwurth used to be. Honestly, these are hardy souls — have to be to put up with our long winters. Oh, I've sent word ahead to Venerado Pete Bolivar and tried to sort of tell him about you two. He wants to meet with you first and then see about getting you two settled in. I think he wants to know something about you before he lets you talk to the whole group. Of course, I think everyone ought to hear your story," Angelica pronounced.

They approached the massive gate house that led into the huge courtyard of Brom Castle. The two spotted the largest manor house that either had ever seen and beside it rose the tall tower proper. The town, castle, and tower were incredibly picturesque nestled against the grey mountain proper. The gate keeper waved to Angelica and motioned for her to pull up at the large entrance to the manor house with its ornate double doors. As they did so, an old man stepped out. His hair was grey, but his eyes were sharp. He wore a fine, brown, pod-silk suit with tall soft leather matching boots. Angelica whispered, "That's Venerado Pete Bolivar."

His bass voice called out, "Welcome again, Angelica Evita e Kaylee. Welcome visitors. If you two and Angelica will follow me please? Our hands will see to the others." Amy sensed he meant her sister and her three friends. Jan helped Amy down, while Angelica tied the team to the hitching rail. She led the way after shaking Pete's hand. Both slowed their pace when Pete saw the two women moving even slower than the women here did in their fancy heels. He took them into his private study Venerado Simon had used before him.

Once they were seated, he asked, "First, quickly Angelica, how went the mission?"

"The aliens gave all the iron ore and gold to Valen's people, just as we suspected, sir."

He frowned. "Okay then. Who is who?" He looked at Amy and then Jan.

"I am Amy Blackwater. This is Jan Bellweather, who is unable to speak, sir."

"Welcome Amy, Jan. I've heard some strange things about you two from Angelica here. You both were abducted by the aliens long ago?"

"Yes, we both were. They took me when I was a teen. I am now eighty-five and Jan is eighty-six."

"Now come now, you don't look a day over twenty-one!" Pete growled, obviously not believing her.

"Alien rejuvenation machine. We've used it twice. Had to in order to survive. My sister, Marla, came with us, and she looks her eighty-seven years. If you don't believe me, ask her."

"Damn, so then there is such a machine as that."

"Yes, we brought one of them with us, along with a number of other Imperium machines that we need. Long story, sir. We both have spent nearly fifty plus years covertly fighting against the corrupt Imperium across many planets. Honestly, we are on their most-wanted list. She's number one and I'm number two, but we think they have their priorities backwards." Jan chuckled.

"I see. It looks like your battles have taken quite a toll

on you both."

Amy picked up his intention and replied. "No, we never got a scratch from that. Our grossly altered bodies were done so we could actually return here to Tierra and bring along our many things. That's a long story. However, time is of the essence here. We know field agent Jarek Lajda is about to receive a shipment of two Nuclears. These are outlawed bombs that are so terrible just one of them, when detonated, will utterly vaporize an entire city and make the land around there uninhabitable for nearly a century. We know he is getting them because we shipped them to him, making sure they arrived after we got here first. We aim to put an end to these wars and Imperium meddling in our affairs."

"You gave them the bombs?" Pete's ire rose. "How could you?"

"If we did not, then he would have gone elsewhere to get them. This way, we are controlling when he gets them and hope to prevent their usage. We need to act fairly quickly though."

"What do you need from us?" Pete asked.

"A big room where we can set up our things and see about getting Jan's voice back. Then, we need to be given a fast history lesson on what's been happening on our world since we were abducted. I have some ideas about how we can stop them. Venerado, you must understand, this is our home too, and Jan and I simply will not let the aliens and the ignorant Valens destroy it, not ever. If necessary, I can kill every damn alien on the planet and all those in Valen Tower too."

He gave her a queer look of disbelief. He was staring at a fairly helpless woman — no arms, tiny, constricted waist, and feet distorted and effectively hobbled. While she no doubt had good intentions, her statement seemed fanciful.

Angelica saw his disbelief rise and interrupted. "Sir, as we approached the Southfork River, we were stopped by seventy soldiers from Valen, and one pointed a blaster at us. Amy and Jan killed every one of them and captured the blaster as well. They used their *mentales* gifts, that I am certain. You can ask any one of my fifty Sisterhood companions, they all witnessed it. Ungodly, only took a minute. They even fired some crossbows at them, but their quarrels met something like a magical, invisible force barrier, dropping harmlessly onto the ground."

Pete's eyes opened wider. "Hey, a thought can kill," Amy added, as if everyone knew that fact. Evidently Pete did.

"Okay, I've seen that done, but only rarely. I will get Misty and Ben to get your rooms prepared. Angelica, I am giving them the large room next to yours. It is probably best if we keep all the alien machines close together. I will send Ama Luisa Wycombe to assist you with anything else you may need. I can call an emergency meeting of the entire tower at, say, just after supper. Will that be acceptable?"

"Yes, I am afraid our story is going to be a rather long one, but everyone should know the details," Amy answered. Jan nodded. "Please have someone assist and look after my aging sister and her group. They are in their eighties and this trip has been overly hard on them."

Misty was fifty-nine with light brown hair, draped down her back, as was the custom. Her face was round with a dimple on her chin. Her attitude was more than friendly, but very businesslike. She ran the domestic activities for the entire complex, while her older brother, Ben, sixty-four, handled the security for the complex. He was a fighter by nature, but was planning to retire soon, passing his post along to his son. While he wore a really nice suit similar to Pete's, Misty wore a silk gown, quite sexy, Amy thought, and very high heels. Both would soon see that the women all wore the sleek pod-silk gowns and heels around the complex, unless they had to do physical work or go into the town proper.

As she led the two down a long corridor and up a flight of stairs, she commented, "Well, I do believe your heels exceed any we have here. They are intriguing. Say, are you two really in your eighties? You look barely twenty."

"Yes, we are. We've used the rejuvenation machine twice now. Had to in order to be able to get back here to our home world. We'll tell you about it at the meeting tonight," Amy answered.

"Well, here is your room. If you will note the low bar, it's so our women and girls can open them. You won't find any door in this entire complex you can't open with your feet, Amy. We've done everything possible to make our children's lives as livable as possible. You'll fit right in. Perhaps some can teach you how to do some things you don't think possible. Anyway, your crates are being man-handled up here now. Ben's seeing to it. Angelica's room is that one next to yours, that is, when she is actually here in the manor house. She's gone a lot of the time. Ah, here comes Luisa now. She will show you what is where and can help you with anything you might need. I must see to the emergency meeting details now. You will have quite an audience tonight, over five hundred, I expect, excepting the smaller children, of course. Luisa Wycombe, this is Amy Blackwater and Jan Bellweather."

Luisa was as armless as Amy was and had rich black hair that fell nearly to her ankles, tied in the back with a bluebird clasp. Her bushy eyebrows and roundish face gave her a somewhat of a pixie look. She wore a light blue silk gown, the ruffles at her shoulders accentuating the fact her arms were missing. She also wore very high heels, but no hose. "Hi, pleased to meet you. In case you don't know, this is how we open the doors around here." She carefully balanced herself on one foot and used the other to slide the bar back. She pushed gently on the door, opening it, and stepping inside. "Bed, desk, table, and a whole lot of space. Ben is bringing up your crates. I hope they all fit in here. Oh, yes, the bath. If you will follow me, I'll show you where we bathe on this floor."

A half hour later, all their bags and crates were in their room, and Amy felt awful that she could do nothing to help Jan begin to unpack them. She and Luisa stood back and watched. Jan sensed her lover's feelings and sent, *First thing is to get our medical machine going and see what we can repair on our bodies, love.* She found the right crate. *Can you pry it open for me?* Amy grinned, for this was something she could do. Her crystal began glowing and the sides of the crate were wrenched off with a squeaking noise. *Thanks. Give me a couple of minutes.*

"Say, that looks like Angelica's machine she has in her room, the one that her alien mother got working again," Luisa pointed out. The two chatted while Jan began assembling the machine and got it ready for operations.

Shit! How the hell am I going to operate it if I am the patient? You haven't your hands anymore.

Let me see what I can do anyway, love, Amy replied, stepping up to the doctor's side of the machine. Using her gifts, she moved one assembly over to Jan's neck and positioned it properly. Then, she turned it on and began working it. She found it slow going without her hands and fingers. Amy took it slowly and carefully, not daring to make any mistakes with Jan.

"I think we can get your voice back. I want you to take a deep breath and hold it when I tell you to and try not to choke as this plastic thing comes out of your neck or voice box, it says here on the dial."

Ten minutes later and Jan exclaimed, "Hooray! I can talk again. God that was awful! Okay, I can take it from here. You slip in there and let's see if there is anything that can be done for our waists next. It has been so damnably hard to breathe, and I am sick of eating minuscule meals all the time." A bit later, Jan announced, "Well, they did remove some ribs and have moved organs around. According to the readings, if we take off the corsets, over time, our organs will shift back to where they belong, but the machine suggests our waists will remain fairly small even then. Now let's see about our feet. We need a chair."

"I got it," Luisa said and began pushing a chair over for Amy. Jan thanked her and then spent nearly an hour examining and re-examining Amy's feet.

"Damn, Amy, we can only undo part of the damage to our feet. Come around here and see for yourself." She did so and Luisa stuck her head in between them as well. Her curiosity was also roused.

Amy said, "So this is saying that part of the warping can be undone, but that our feet will never be able to go flat on the floor again — that we'll still have to always wear around six inch heels?"

"That's how I read the output, but we don't have such heels, love."

"Oh, we do! Let me help you out. Go ahead and fix them

as you can and then you can tip toe to our supply room. There, we can find the perfect fit for you both," Luisa said very proud of the fact she would really be able to help them.

Another half hour later, the two tip toeing women stared in disbelief at the wall rack filled with various heels in all sizes and heights, including boots. Quickly, Jan began trying on pair after pair. At last, she announced, "Size eight for me works best. Now to get you fixed, love. Luisa, this is a life saver. It's so much easier to walk in these than what we were forced to wear." Shortly, Amy had her new ones as well, size nine. Plus, Jan found them each a pair of tall boots, suitable for outdoor wear, especially in the deep snow. As they walked back to their room, Amy only echoed Jan's comments. Walking was now vastly easier for her. That was something, at least. She knew there was nothing at all that could be done about her arms, but she knew that from the moment the emperor had described what she would have to have done to become a wasp queen.

Next, the two took a long bath and again Luisa came to their rescue, bringing them each a new fancy dress, light blue. "While your waists look baggy, as Jan said, maybe in time they will fill out. If not, we can have a seamstress take them in to fit you better. Now that's the dinner gong. Come on; we don't want to be late to your huge welcoming dinner." Heels clicking on the stone floor, the trio headed off to the Great Hall, where nearly six hundred had gathered.

Amy and Jan were rather shocked to see the sheer number of armless women present, ranging in ages from their sixties to barely able to walk. Amy tried to count them, but gave up after two dozen. Amy kept her eye on Luisa, who sat next to her and her husband and children next to him. She deftly used her feet, but Amy decided against trying that here in public. Instead, she activated her crystal and used her psi energies, allowing Jan finally to be free of the task of feeding her. Of course, nearly everyone cast numerous glances their way and even some at Marla and her group, but they were old folks and were quickly forgotten by all the younger ones here.

With the filling dinner done, Venerado Pete introduced Amy and Jan and turned the discussion over to the two. Amy did most of the talking; Jan always preferred her to do so, since she felt more at home with her computers. She described how she and Jan had been kidnaped and taken off-world, sold into slavery as telepaths. She rather glossed over their fifty years of subversion work, summarizing it rapidly and succinctly. She did dwell more on how they had finally discovered their home world, thanks to Jarek's clandestine ordering of two Nuclears from their secret organization. Amy described in some detail what they had done to get back here and why, though she cast the wasp culture in a good light. At least now, they would understand why she'd given up her arms — to get home.

As the hour was getting late, Venerado Pete told Amy that in the morning, he'd send their best historian to her to help bring the two up to date. Then he requested a planning meeting by tomorrow evening. As the folks began to file out of the Great Hall, Amy found herself being mobbed by the armless contingent, especially the younger women her apparent age or less. She received all manner of promises to show her how to do things in their special ways. Luisa finally had to intervene so Amy could finally get out of the room, laughing all the way. She called out, "Later, once I get things handled. Since I won't ever have them again, I will take you all up on your offers." She received a number of cheers and "Okays."

"Maybe it won't be so terrible, my love. They seem very happy and able here," Jan commented when they were back in their room. "I'm going to check on things before bed. I want to know precisely where the Nuclears are at now."

Amy stood before their full-length mirror and took a good look at herself and her new dress. "I do look good in this style dress. She's right; it really does accentuate my look."

"Of course, love, you are damnably sexy," Jan teased her. "Say, the Nuclears have arrived, today in fact. They are not scheduled to be picked up for two days yet, only *now* they will have to wait a week."

"Why?"

Jan laughed, "I just flagged them as quarantined for a week. The crates were exposed to a virulent plague." Both women laughed. Jarek would be a bit frustrated to find out about the unexpected delay.

The next day, Ama Blanca Brom, their forty-five year old historian arrived just after breakfast. She too had long black hair, as did most of those with Westerlings blood. Using her foot, she slid a chair over and sat down. "I'm supposed to fill you in. Where should I start? I've been keeping a lengthy journal of all the goings on since I was five and learned to write with my toes."

Amy laughed. "I guess you are going to have to teach me to do that too." Blanca grinned and began answering their questions. After two hours, Amy and Jan began to realize the extent of damage that had been done to their world.

Just then, they were interrupted by a loud noise coming from one of Jan's devices. She quickly flipped a switch and fiddle with a dial. Voices were heard.

"I'm sorry, Jarek. It can't be helped. The Imperium slapped a quarantine on the package for you. You can have it in seven days. How's everything out there in the field?"

"That's the ID Minister," Angelica's voice interrupted them. She'd heard the noise and came to investigate. "That's Jarek talking now."

"Okay then, seven days. Valen is about ready to launch an attack on Bettingham Tower. I think it is going to occur on the fifteenth of August."

"My god. Do you think these Valen people will actually succeed? Lord, how everything is coming unhinged on this world. Who had any idea they could have such violent political upheavals? Certainly not I, but then, we are not to become involved. Imperial Directive #5, of course."

"Right boss, no interference. I will merely be there as an observer."

"Okay, keep me posted. By the way, Carmen and Diego send you their best wishes. I think she wishes you would return soon. Over and out." Jan's device went silent again.

"It scans all frequencies and locks on to any broadcast on any wavelength that is in use anywhere in the Imperium. My own invention," Jan explained rather pleased with her cleverness. "I'll keep on monitoring. We might learn something else."

"It sounded like the minister doesn't know Jarek's role in all this," Amy mused. "Come on; it is time we talked seriously to Venerado Pete about all this. We need to get folks out of Bettingham pronto."

An hour later, the two women stood alongside of Pete in the tower next to the Communications Network of crystals. All three were furious with the Venerado of Bettingham Tower. He refused to abandon the tower and complex wholly. He did agree to evacuate the town and some of his *mentales* gifted who wished to leave and go to their new tower far to the east. "Now what?" Pete grumbled, very much annoyed with his counterpart.

"Jan and I need to know about these networks. They didn't have them when we were last in a tower half a century ago or more," Amy replied. "How do you make these awful weapons, these murderous bombs that create the dead zones? How do you fly the air cars? Exactly what is a crystal network?"

Pete laughed, "Which one do you want answered first? Just teasing. Okay, I'll take it from the beginning." For an hour he, talked and showed them firsthand the many different crystal networks in operation here at Brom Tower. Slowly, both women began to see just how these networks had been severely abused by all the towers, Brom included. After all, Pete pointed out their own stock of devastating bombs to be used if they were attacked.

Later that night after supper, Pete asked, "So what are we to do? In a few more days, Valen is going to unleash a nightmare on us all."

Amy bit her lip. "We are going to teach them all a lesson they will never, ever forget. I am afraid I'm going to allow Valen to destroy Bettingham, but in doing so, they will also be destroying themselves and setting the stage to put things right all over Tierra, once and for all time! Come on, Jan. I need you to write for me. Blanca hasn't yet taught me to write with my toes, so I need your fingers again." Jan chuckled.

Pete added, "She does have very pretty letters. Does a really good job of writing." Amy smiled. Perhaps one day she

could learn, but not today. She was mad. No one was going to
do anything effective about the situation on Tierra, but she
and Jan were.

Back in their room and paper in hand, Jan was ready.
"Take this down, love."

The Blackwater Ultimatum

Men have controlled our towers and caused untold
pain, suffering, wars, and strife for over a half
century. Starting today, this ends. They have
forfeited all their rights to rule. From this point in
time onwards, no man will ever be allowed to be the
tower's Venerado. Only a woman may hold this post.
No man will ever be allowed to be a circle's Capo.
Only a woman can now be the circle's Capo. Anyone
who violates this will die by my hand at once.

Beginning today, all stock of weapons of mass
destruction, the fire bombs, the acid bombs, and so
on, shall be permanently disposed of in a safe
manner that will not harm our planet any further.
Failure to do so will result in the deaths of the top
leaders of the tower until this order is complied with
fully. Later, an emissary of mine will visit your
location and verify compliance has been fully met.
Anyone making weapons of mass destruction in the
future will be summarily executed by me, no
questions asked, no mercy shown, period. There will
never, ever be another dead zone on this world.

As the circles of all towers have been routinely
ignoring the needs of the people within their lands,
every other week, all circle members will spend an
entire week out among the various towns and
villages of their territory tending to the needs of the
common man, whatever that need may be from
healing to constructions. Failure to carry out this will

result in the death of every member of that circle. Again, no mercy will be shown, as the circles have not shown the slightest mercy to the average person who lives in their territory and who has been paying yearly tithes to support the circle and whose young men, by the thousands, have been brutally sacrificed in their ill-advised wars.

From this point in time onward, the only combat weapon that is allowed is one's own body such as a fist or a weapon that is handheld, swords and knives, for example. Even arrows and quarrels cannot be used as a weapon to harm another human. If you wish to fight, then you must be willing to face your opponent head on, face to face, and he must have an equal chance to slay you as well with what he has in his hands. Anyone violating this order will be slain at once, no mercy shown. If you doubt me, ask the Valen army about what happened to seventy of their soldiers around Bedwurth dead zone two weeks ago. As the towers have sucked up the life blood of the young men of their lands, nearly destroying a whole generation of young men, they have proved themselves unworthy to rule that territory. From this day forward, the rulership of their territories is hereby removed from the towers. Instead, each territory shall elect their own civilian leadership. Call them kings and queens, if you so desire, but they cannot ever be tower members. A person can choose to belong to a tower or to lead their people, but not both. Anyone caught doing both will be executed. Again, no mercy.

As Tierra needs overall leadership, from this day forward, there shall be an emperor and empress who preside over all the other leaders. They will be housed in the tower in Exchange City. At least twice a year, the leaders or their delegates will attend a meeting with the emperor and empress, whose word is law, period. Down the road, the leaders shall be allowed to elect their emperor and empress, but not until we are satisfied that all laws and my ultimatum have been fully and completely implemented. The emperor and empress shall rule using the principles of ethics, not morals, basing their decisions on actions that create the best or optimum survival of all concerned.

Valen has violated our lease agreement with the aliens and acquired a cache of alien weaponry. These must be turned over to your emperor within a month. Failure to do so will result in all personnel who are located around said contraband being killed and the illegal items confiscated. If I have to come and confiscate said contraband, the penalties that I will inflict will be both harsh and severe and I will show no mercy.

Finally, all this strife and disaster has its root cause the powerful crystal networks in use at all the towers. Beginning today, all crystal networks will be destroyed, with a few exceptions. The Communications Networks, the Healing Networks, and the Security Networks may continue operation and new ones of these types created in the future as needed. All others must be destroyed. Again, we will be closely monitoring this. Failure to comply will be swiftly and harshly dealt with, of that I assure you. There will be no more opportunities allowed for towers to create networks that bring such devastation to our world, not ever again, I so swear.

Precise dividing of the territories among the towers
will be forthcoming soon. At that time, it will be the
responsibility of the new female Venerada to inform
the cities, towns, and villages of their ability to elect
their own political leaders and to send them to the
biannual meetings with the emperor and empress.
However, the former Brom Compact rules regarding
the yearly tithes will remain in effect, since now half
of each month, the towers will be directly aiding
their people with their very real needs.

Unlike the Brom Compact with which you had to
agree and sign, the Blackwater Ultimatum does not
have to be signed. I will rigidly enforce it. Violation of
this ultimatum brings dead and I show no mercy.

"Wow, love, you used pretty strong language. Who is
going to be the new emperor and empress?" Jan asked looking
at Amy. "Oh no, not us?" Then she giggled. "Okay do we fight
over who is who?"

"You will be the emperor, love. I don't have arms and
hands to do the writing and I doubt I'll be able to learn to use
my toes in time," Amy teased her.

"You won't be making me wear one of the men's suits
will you?"

"Your luscious boobs wouldn't fit them," Amy replied,
grinning broadly. Both chuckled.

"Seriously though, Venerado Pete isn't going to like this.
Nor are all the Capos here," Jan pointed out the obvious.

"I'm not going to tell them about this ultimatum ahead
of time. Keep it between you and me for now. What I still need
to be certain about is whether or not Minister Lech is involved
in all this in anyway. Certainly, his incompetence has allowed
it to happen; plus he probably thinks he has an inside track
into the workings of Valen Tower now, since Jarek is married
to Carmen. What bothers me is that according to Blanca,
Carmen ought to be eighty-five years old, but she appears to be
thirty or so. I can understand Karolina appearing to be thirty
something; she's undoubtedly had several rejuvenation

treatments, just as we have. Carmen must also have been given it, probably because she's Jarek's wife."

"Violations right and left," Jan replied. "You know, what bothers me the most is here we are, finally home, and all that we knew before is gone. All my family, all my friends, everything. I know I'm seventy-three, but crap, we've outlived everyone that meant anything to me, excepting you, of course."

"I know. I cringe every time I see my sister. She looks so aged. I know her days are really numbered now. She is my only remaining tie to my past. I hate the thought soon I will lose even that last thread. This rejuvenation process has a very nasty side effect. We outlive nearly all those around us. Kind of grim. I don't think I will ever use the regeneration machine again, not now that I'm home. What would our new friends think or say?"

"My thoughts exactly. Yet, we still have each other; plus, there are all these new folks here at Brom. I rather like them, as a group. Very much like a large family. Say, do you regret we've not had any children in our seventy plus years?" Jan asked.

Amy sighed. "Only the other night when all the young ones surrounded me. Suddenly, I knew what I'd missed out on, not having children. Yet, Jan, the life we were forced to live just to survive — we couldn't have done it if we had children with us. Now, yes, I am really sad we haven't been mothers. I guess we will have to be mothers to our whole world instead."

"Yes, me too. Seeing all these bright, cheery kids running around — I suddenly realized what I'd missed. Still, I can't stand a man touching me that way, not after all the rapes I've endured," Jan added.

"Same with me. I've lost count of them. Killed some of my rapists though over the years. So here we are in a place and time where we really could become mothers and neither of us can tolerate a man long enough to get the job done," Amy sighed.

"We'll just have to be satisfied with being mothers to our world, my love. I guess I can live with that," Jan concluded.

The night before the fifteenth, Amy left strict orders they were not to be disturbed in any way for any reason the following day. Everyone in Brom knew this was the day the alien weapon would be used against those remaining in Bettingham Tower. The mood around the entire tower was a quiet anxiety, an anxiousness filled with dark foreboding.

"Okay, we are all set. The recorder will record any conversations that appear on any frequency of the aliens. My monitors are in place. Are we ready?" Jan asked.

"I am as ready as I'll ever be. I will be drawing upon your strength today my love."

"I will not fail you. Let's teach them a lesson they will never forget. After all, we are the Sly Fox and Eager Beaver. No one in the vast Imperium has ever touched us," Jan said, sitting down on their floor across from Amy. Both women crossed their legs and activated their crystals, filling the room with a pale blue glow. The ruddy sun's orb creased the eastern horizon.

Amy's awareness expanded outward across the entire continent. One by one, she picked up the consciousness of the many *mentales* gifted. Multitasking, she zeroed in on Jarek, who alone knew actually how to operate the Nuclears he'd purchased. She found him climbing into one of the Valen air cars. She mused a moment on the fact that a whole network of crystals powered the car. She could reach out and disable the crystals, preventing the craft from lifting off the ground or even doing that while it was airborne and en route to the target. While that would prevent the destruction of the tower, it would not provide the means by which she could deliver her ultimatum and have it universally accepted by the living *mentales* gifted individuals. The sole damper she installed was on the young children. Only they would not bear the full brunt of what was about to happen.

Amy waited patiently, like a tiger on the prowl on Centauri-3, where she'd once been on a jungle hunt, gotten raped, and killed her rapist. Now she began to see from Jarek's eyes and it was at this point she opened up her channel of communication into every *mentales* gifted mind on Tierra. Everyone now saw Jarek in the air car hovering over

Bettingham. They saw him release the bomb and dart away at a tremendous rate of speed. Everyone felt the explosion of the nuclear warhead as it detonated, the intense, searing heat, the concussion blast. More importantly, they all were overwhelmed by the incredible volume of the victims' pain, fright, shock, and terror. At last, each and every *mentales* gifted experienced just what their victims did as they died a horrid, painful, terrified death.

Amy and Jan's combined gifts allowed them to slice through all personal defenses, all mind blocks everywhere. For a moment, Amy had considered amplifying the emotions and sensations and pains of the victims, but decided to leave it be utterly and starkly real. All would have firsthand knowledge of just what they had done to others with their acid bombs, their fire bombs, their chemical bombs, and now their Nuclears.

Jarek held his hands over his head trying desperately to block it all out, he couldn't and everyone saw the giant mushroom cloud develop over what had been Bettingham. The entire city and all who had failed to flee were simply vaporized. Worse, the radiation fallout created a dead zone five times the size of the other dead zones and one that would last for a century. Any living thing entering this zone got radiation sickness and died painfully.

Amy and Jan allowed the many connected minds to absorb the horrors they'd just experienced before Amy took the next step. When she felt the timing was right, she spoke directly into all those minds. Jan held up her ultimatum and Amy read it into all the *mentales* gifted minds on Tierra. Then Amy deactivated the network and watched as Jarek and his air car plummeted into the mushroom cloud, ending his extended lifetime. Radiation fried him before his disabled air car smashed into the remnants of the explosion.

Unknown to either woman, another being floated high above Bettingham, thoroughly intent upon watching this, the greatest of the battles ever fought on Tierra. Wystan was taken by complete surprise with the intensity and violent energy flows of the explosion. Like water being sucked up in a straw, Wystan was pulled from his location and smashed far below the surface, back into the hot lava near the core of the planet.

He went wholly unconscious, overwhelmed by the unexpected violent energies. There Wystan would remain oblivious to the world for a very long time.

Ultimatum delivered, the two broke their connections and disconnected from their crystals. Jan looked at Amy. "We did it. If that doesn't work, then these people are not human beings after all, but mere robot machines. God, I'm hungry. Oh, I don't suppose anyone here is in any shape to fix us some food."

"I over did it again, Jan. I am very weak. I need calories and fast."

"On it." Jan jumped up and tried to move swiftly to the door. In the heels, she lost her balance and hit the floor hard. "Oops. Forgot. Can't go fast anymore. That hurt." Amy listened to the click-click of Jan's heels trailing off down the hall. Then, she slumped over, totally exhausted, trusting her lover to bring her lifesaving calories soon.

As Jan moved through the corridors to the kitchen, she found stunned men and women. Most could not even utter anything coherent as she passed, hardly noticing her. They had made an impact, she observed, but perhaps a bit too strong of an impression. Jan shrugged it off, recalling the dead zones. At least by the time she carried a tray back to their room, some were pulling out of it. That was a good sign.

She found Amy slumped over and proceeded to feed her. As the sweet honey hit Amy's system, she began to pull out of her exhaustion. "I rather overdid it, love. Thanks," she whispered. Jan nodded, but didn't say anything. Time enough for that when Amy was back to battery.

Recovering from the wild and emotional experience, Venerado Pete made his way to their room and knocked before entering. "That was quite an effect, Amy and Jan. Now that tower and city is wiped out. Yet, the huge army of Valen is still there and occupying half of the Midlands. If we get rid of our stockpile, get rid of we leaders, get rid of our networks, you are dooming us to being puppets of Valen. There is nothing to keep Valen from expanding even more. You can't be serious are you?"

"I will see to it Valen retreats immediately back to the

Westerlings," Amy answered him. "I need to recover a little. I used a lot of psi energy breaking every *mentales* gifted adult on Tierra to make sure they all got a taste of what they were actually doing to human beings. The next action, I assure you, is to get Valen's army out of the Midlands and quickly. Trust me. Meanwhile, don't destroy your stockpile of bombs or your offensive networks, but do start working out some transitional women leaders here. I will need to meet with both your current leaders and your new women leaders to help work out reasonable territorial boundaries."

"Whew, that's better. For a minute there, I thought we would have to do this instantly. I'll get to work on it, but nothing will be of any use unless you can by some miracle stop Valen and its army," he replied extremely seriously. She picked up he'd been worried about them all his adult life and that he'd been preparing Brom Tower to be able somehow to hold out against them.

"Say, could I make use of one of your circles for a short while? I need to retrieve that second Nuclear and then make contact with Valen Tower," Amy asked him.

A half hour later, Jan and Amy joined with an entire circle, which flowed them their psi energies. Based on Jan's data, Amy knew where that second Nuclear was being stored and suddenly it was no longer there, but appeared beside them. "Yep, that's it," Jan commented in a matter of fact manner, though she recognized from its labels where the Black Security personnel had stolen it.

Next, Amy intended to make an illusion of her body appear in Valen Tower, their most secure room, but to do so, she first had to destroy their Protection Network of crystals. *What a huge tower! This has got to be the largest tower around, Jan.* The protection network of crystals glowed brightly as they attempted to keep her out. She opted for a flare of the dramatic. Amy poured so much energy into the crystals that they exploded and shattered into dust. Free of that barrier, she delivered her message. She had the undivided attention of the circle members who were there plus the other capos and their venerado. Her message was simple. "Get all your soldiers out of the Midlands immediately and evacuate your new tower on the edge of the alien's base or I will drop the second Nuclear on Valen Tower and Castle, though it will also vaporize this entire city. You will not get a second warning before I drop it on Valen. I expect to see fleeing army soldiers later today and that tower emptied within a week."

"You wouldn't dare do that! We've just won the war," shrieked their venerado. Amy merely sent the proper thought into the man's mind and his body died instantly.

"Do it now or I will return and eliminate more of you. Do I make myself clear?" Amy's projected image declared loudly and sternly. Several circle members nodded and she withdrew her image.

"Thanks, gang. That did it. I would appreciate it if some of your circles, who have the ability to do so, will begin observing the large Valen armies and see that they are retreating," Amy suggested. Ama Luisa grinned, "You got it Empress Amy." She and her circle members left their room. Because of their psychic link, they'd all seen and heard what Amy had just done at Valen Tower. They couldn't wait to tell the others about it.

"Now then, Lech has to go," Jan said and I know just the way. Amy gave her a quizzical look and she explained. "He has just allowed a Nuclear to be brought to an Imperial Directive #5 protected planet, given to the 'locals,' and detonated — to say nothing of all the other minor breakages of that directive. I am sending notice of this to his boss, along with documentation of said blast taken by their own sensors at the spaceport. I do so love mindless machines, so easily controlled by Sly Dog," she laughed and hit the Send button. "There, Lech will soon be arrested and taken off-world. I suspect his wife will also go with him. She's the only one besides Carmen who can identify us as the wasp diplomat queens, once we take our positions as Emperor and Empress of Tierra. What do we do about her?"

"I think we can convince her to keep quiet about us. She will be the sole owner of the Elegant Fashions Inc now, and we'll let her run her business as long as she says nothing about us. I think with all we've done, she'll have the message loud and clear," Amy replied. "Now we have to divide up the territories in an equitable manner with readily identifiable borders. That was one of the major flaws in the Brom Compact."

She and Jan headed off to find ex-Venerado Pete; they needed a detailed map and knowledge of what towers were where exactly. He felt more relaxed as Amy was at least consulting him still in these matters. "Would you be content to continue to control all the lands from here north of the North River?" Amy asked.

"Absolutely," he replied. Now the real work began. Obviously, Adelmira would still continue to control all the Easterlings, while Valen would do likewise for all the Westerlings, since there were no other towers left in the Westerlings. Bettingham's remnants now at their new tower in Welsham would control a rectangular area south of the North River, over to the mighty Wyndl River down to the Wal River. Northend Tower, that now held the Haverhills survivors, would control a similar rectangular area south of the Wal River, east of the Wyndl River, down to the Brown River. Wyth Tower could continue to control all the Kingdom of the Angles, save the Brom area in the far north with the Southfork River marking the historical southern boundary of the kingdom, as always. Wye Tower, that now held the Bedwurth survivors, would control a rectangular area south of the Southfork down to the Salt Creek and from the Goza Mountains over to the Wyndl River, lands once owned by Haverhills Tower, that was a currently an uninhabitable dead zone. Rusden Tower would continue to control everything south of the Salt Creek as they had been doing, save for the disputes they'd had with the now defunct Oakham Tower. Thus, there were now only eight towers, not counting the new ultimate seat of power at the tower for the Emperor and Empress in Exchange City.

Later that day, one by one, Amy contacted these towers and dictated their new territories, now very clearly delineated. Unlike the Brom Compact, her land divisions were very clearly marked so there could be no further land disputes. That handled, the two now began recruiting personnel to form up a single *Círculo de mentes* for their tower in Exchange City, along with support personnel and much needed guards. She decided to form up what she called the Imperial Guards, who would provide security for their new complex in Exchange City. To help alleviate anticipated bickering, Jan decided they'd recruit from all the other towers and lands. Each soldier would have a three year term of service, during which time they would receive the best training possible, with swords, of course. Thus began the planet-wide honor guards, the Imperial Guards, whose members slowly gained the highest respect.

Within five years, being selected to spend a term with the guards meant excellent pay, terrific training, and if accomplished successfully, a great deal of respect from everyone when they returned to their homelands. For a long time, these were the best trained swordsmen on Tierra, greatly envied by all the other leaders.

However, the battle scars did not evaporate overnight. Far too many held onto old grudges. Minor conflicts did erupt here and there, particularly in the Haverhills-Oakham areas where so much bloodshed had occurred. Still, as the new century dawned, Amy and Jan, the Empress and Emperor of Tierra, ushered in a new era of peace.

Part of their success came from Amy's training as a wasp queen. She proved her skills first at Brom. Venerado Pete was still reluctant to give up his post and control over Brom Tower. With Jan doing the writing, she asked him why he felt so strongly against Valen Tower and their army. Of course, he rattled off all the destruction they had done, but she persisted and asked him who had told him about these atrocities. She called in some of his personnel who he named and quizzed them similarly. After three long days of questioning, one name continued to appear on nearly all his advisor's lists. When she brought him before them and Venerado Pete accosted him about all the alarming and distressing news he'd related to others, the man attempted to flee. Shortly after that, under intense interrogation, he turned out to be a Valen spy sent to Brom Tower to instill fear and terror of Valen, preparatory to a planned future attack by Valen's army. Once he was rooted out, the situation at Brom Tower calmed down considerably.

Amy and Jan decided to hang on to Brom Tower's

arsenal for a while longer, taking it with them to their new tower in Exchange City. They wanted samples to study so when they visited the other towers they knew precisely what they were looking for, especially since Valen Tower attempted to hide or disguise much of their stockpile of weapons of mass destruction.

Three days after the Nuclears attack, the Goddess of Life and of Death, Lysandra, appeared to Amy and Jan, while they were preparing for bed. Her shimmering form got their instant attention. "Who are you? What do you want?" Amy asked, taken by surprise. She and Jan were seldom surprised, had not been for many years. Neither could afford to be, not in their line of previous work.

"I am Lysandra, Goddess of Life and of Death. I came to thank you both for ending the infernal wars of Wystan. In fact, you have actually put him back to sleep. He was fomenting much of Valen's lust to conquer our world. May he sleep for centuries!" Amy detected a little animosity in her tone. "As a reward, I give you your heart's desires. I'm sure you will know what to do with it," she added with a coy grin and flash of her eyes, if eyes they actually were. She then vanished as if she'd not been there.

"Did you see her too?" Amy asked, rather in disbelief.

"Yep, so that is a goddess. I guess we need to take their tales of gods and goddesses seriously, my love," Jan replied.

"Well, if I hadn't seen it with my own eyes, I wouldn't have believed it," Amy pronounced. "I've seen many strange things in our many years out there among the planets, but nothing like Lysandra. Interesting. I think she was pure being and pure energy."

"I don't know what else you can call her, unless that was a projection like we sometimes use," Jan replied. Suddenly, she grasped herself. "Oh my god! Amy, something is happening to me!" Quickly, Jan finished undressing and both women stared at Jan, gaping.

"Well, I sure know what that's for," Jan finally exclaimed as her passions began growing. "To bed, my love," she teased. The next night, Amy's body altered. Nine months later, each bore a daughter, their first and only children. Love's

rewards finally blessed these two women.
The End.

Other Books by Vic Broquard

Without Warning (fantasy)

The Trident Series: (fantasy)
      Volume 1 The Trident and the Book
      Volume 3 The Trident and the Scepter
      Volume3 The Trident and the Resurrection

The Adventures of Elizabeth Stanton Series: (science fiction)
      Volume 1 The Evolution of the Path
      Volume 2 The Great Messiah
      Volume 3 Of Kings and Queens and Troubadours
      Volume 4 Chaos in the Aftermath
      Volume 5 Power Plays
      Volume 6 Age of Exploration
      Volume 7 Abducted
      Volume 8 The Emperor and Empress
      Volume 9 A Job Worth Doing
      Volume 10 Degradation
      Volume 11 The Second Crusade
      Volume 12 When Worlds Collide
      Volume 13 Dark Ages

The Lindsey Barron Series: (fantasy)
      Volume 1 The Rod of the Apocalypse
      Volume 2 The Board of Governors
      Volume 3 The Crown of Moses
      Volume 4 Dominus for President
      Volume 5 The National Health Care Program
      Volume 6 States Justice
      Volume 7 Cross and Double-cross

Zoran Chronicles Series: (fantasy)
      Volume 1 A Dragon in Our Town
      Volume 2 Dragons, Power, Courts, and War

Planet of the Orange-red Sun Series: (science fiction)
        Volume 1 When Kingdoms Fall
        Volume 2 Dark Ages
        Volume 3 Age of the Towers
        Volume 4 Difficillis Exitus
        Volume 5 Age of the Lords
        Volume 6 The Renegade Tower
        Volume 7 Rebellions
        Volume 8 The Aliens Return
        Volume 9 Power Struggles
        Volume 10 Guilds, Genetics, and Gods
        Volume 11 Magi, Witches, Swords, and Superstitions
        Volume 12 The Voyage of the Eagle's Seed
        Volume 13 Justifications
        Volume 14 Responsibilities

The Return of the Wizards: Twelve Companions – The Making of Wizards (fantasy)

www.ingramcontent.com/pod-product-compliance
Lightning Source LLC
Chambersburg PA
CBHW051953060726
47506CB00012B/917